BENEATH THE WILD BLUE

THE STORY OF AN AIR FORCE FAMILY

MARIAN MCCARTHY

THE AIR FORCE SONG

Off we go into the wild blue yonder,
Climbing high into the sun;
Here they come zooming to meet our thunder,
At 'em boys, give'em the gun!
Down we dive, spouting our flame from under
Off with one helluva roar
We live in fame or go down in flames
Nothing'll stop the U.S. Air Force!

—Words and music by Robert Crawford

BENEATH THE WILD BLUE

A Novel

By Marian McCarthy

Created with Vellum

To Mom, Dad, Susan and Barney

PART I

Blastoff

PROLOGUE

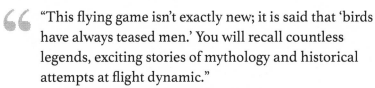 "This flying game isn't exactly new; it is said that 'birds have always teased men.' You will recall countless legends, exciting stories of mythology and historical attempts at flight dynamic."
—Nancy Shea, *The Air Force Wife*

APPLE VALLEY, *California*
January 28, 1986

DURING HER YEARS as an Air Force wife, Fritzi Stoddard knew her husband would always fly, would always go to war, would always bear the responsibility of giving orders or obeying them. Now that he was retired, he would always tune in to watch a NASA launch on live television.

The hospice nurse had just gone home, having seen Fritzi through a long night of pain. Now, settled in her recliner, Fritzi opened her eyes and took a breath through the oxygen tube in her nose. The hit of fresh air settled her stomach and focused her mind on her husband, sitting there on the edge of his chair, excited as a Little Leaguer at the World Series.

"The Challenger is going back up today," he said, eyes bright as a boy's. He tucked a blanket around her feet. "I thought we could catch the liftoff together."

Fritzi sat back in her recliner and laughed. Her Colonel Joe Stoddard (USAF, Retired) couldn't wait to watch the liftoff, imagining himself at the helm of the spacecraft. Joe was the quintessential aviator, always focused on the sky, his senses keen, his neck muscles tense, his temples pulsing with the tempo of the countdown.

The goddamned Space Race. Joe had nearly qualified to be an astronaut, but without an engineering degree, he hadn't made the grade. Instead, he'd dutifully put in his hours as a test pilot in the early years, risking his life and their livelihood to prove he had all the Right Stuff—only to play second fiddle to younger, better educated men who were destined for glory. But Joe wasn't in it for the glory. He just wanted to fly, higher and faster and farther. To experience zero gravity. To witness the instrument panel's soaring numbers.

Joe sat on the edge of his seat, keen on the play-by-play broadcast from Mission Control, as a calm, steady voice announced: "Liftoff of the twenty-fifth Space Shuttle Mission, and it has cleared the tower!" Excited faces in the crowd looked aloft at the Shuttle, propelled by two phallis-shaped rockets, piercing the impossibly blue sky. "Throttling up..."

LIKE AN AIRBORNE ULYSSES, Joe used to rely on Fritzi to mind the home fires, keep the children safe and clean and obedient. Most of the time, she managed. She'd forced herself to live without fear while her husband was at war, to stay busy with the four children, to be a leader among the other wives on all the bases they'd lived.

It turned out she was too fearless, too busy, too untested. Fate stalked even the most cheerful mother and the most dutiful wife. One child, buried. The other three, scattered to the far corners of the earth. They didn't see the kids often, but that was all right. Their children hadn't been raised to cling to any one place. They had been raised to make their own lives, to bloom where they were planted, or to uproot and find a better place.

Fritzi and Joe had settled in a golf course community in Southern California because it was near Vandenburg Air Force Base, where they could still go to the commissary and BX. Their entire subdivision was mostly Air Force retirees, now rootless and baseless, grounded pilots and flight engineers with enough hard-earned time to hit the golf course and play duplicate bridge. It was a tidy neighborhood, developed by a retired Air Force major who'd gone into real estate. There were five different house models, all named after Air Force bases: the Tinker, a low-slung ranch; the Dover, a two-story colonial; the Travis, a breezy California-style split level; the Andrews, with a white-pillared front porch; and, finally, the Hickam, which was like the Travis, only with a lanai room in the back. The Hickam was more expensive than the other models, but Fritzi told Joe she deserved to live in a home with a Hawaiian lanai room—even it was in the California desert.

Two years after they moved into the Hickam, Fritzi got sick. At least, sick enough to seek treatment. A pack and a half of Chesterfields each day for forty years had taken their toll on her lungs. She'd always coughed a lot, but lately there was blood. Exploratory surgery revealed both her lungs were full of tumors. Worse, she had a spot on her liver. The oncologist recommended cobalt treatments and chemo. Fritzi had dutifully tried them all. Each of the three kids visited at different times, but she sent them home cheerily and told them not to worry. She and Joe knew she was dying. They didn't need to share that misery with their children.

SUDDENLY, Joe was on his feet. In the TV screen's blue sky, the rockets and the Shuttle became a plume of smoke in the shape of a Y chromosome, swelling and billowing, then dissipating into plunging wisps that tumbled into the ocean.

"Turn it off!" Fritzi commanded. "For heaven's sake, Joe! I've seen enough!"

Joe's shoulders began to shake and he covered his face with his hands. A wave of nausea made Fritzi retch, but Joe took no notice. He did not turn off the television, not even after Mission Control announced that there was "obviously a major malfunction."

Fritzi yanked the oxygen tube out of her nose and hoisted herself out of the recliner. Stumbling over the blanket around her feet, she managed to grab the remote from her husband. Joe caught her before she could fall and held her close. Fritzi vomited on his shoes. They stood there on the soiled beige carpet, holding each other, crying.

Who decides who goes and who stays behind? For so long it had been Joe, leaving Fritzi to mind the home front. Soon, it would be Fritzi's turn to go, leaving Joe grounded, looking into the sky for answers in her contrails.

PART II

Wild Blue

1

> "In 1487, Leonardo da Vinci made a systematic study of the flight of birds. His manuscript entitled *Flight Versus Birds*, written in Florence in 1505, is illustrated with a sketch showing the aviator in a horizontal position flapping the wings of a plane by means of ropes."

—Nancy Shea, *The Air Force Wife*

JANUARY, 1948
   Lackland Air Force Base, Texas

YESTERDAY, he reported for Officer Candidate School and today, he lay on his bunk and opened his first letter from Fritzi. Some of the boys had given him a hard time when he'd gotten the baby-blue envelope at their first Mail Call, but Joe didn't let it bother him. It smelled of her rosy perfume, the fancy one called Shalimar. He slit it open with his pocket knife, laid back and looked at her swirling handwriting, imagining her dashing it off and putting it in the post a week ago so he would have it to open today. Fritzi Fontaine was as passionate as she was thoughtful.

DEAR JOE,

By now, you are probably settled in and doing lots of exercise and training. I hope you get to fly soon, because I know that is what the Air Force means to you. Write to me about your adventures; it's boring as hell here. When you are back, we can get married and move far away. I'm so proud of your career as an aviator. The skies above want you to explore them, just as I want to explore you when you return.

Today, I got to cut the ribbon on the new Ford dealership out near the highway. Ho hum! Being Miss Montrose is full of excitement! My picture will be in the paper tomorrow, and I'll send it to you. I hope you put it up on your wall.

Your pinup,
Fritzi

JOE STODDARD'S first love was flying. As a boy on his family's farm in Louisiana, he would climb into the hayloft and leap from rafter to rafter with his arms spread wide. Back then, it seemed that he could glide farther than the flying squirrels that nested in the red oak trees. But a squirrel was not an eagle, and Joseph Randall Stoddard aspired to be an eagle.

So, he planned his work and worked his plan. The backside of the barn overlooked a grove of loblolly pines that let the wind whistle through their branches and call to him. When the whistle was high and the pines swayed back and forth like the metronome on his mother's piano, Joe climbed to the barn roof and grabbed the umbrella he'd stashed under the eaves. He listened and waited for an upward gust, then leaped into it with the open umbrella. For a few sublime seconds, young Joe was airborne before he began his drift to the bed of pine straw he'd carefully raked to break his inevitable fall.

His landings were sometimes rough, resulting in skinned knees and once, a broken collarbone.

In his fourteenth year, Joe found work at Laroche Aviation, where he kept the hangar clean and learned to be a flagman for Marlon Laroche as he piloted the old Stearman on crop dusting missions. Marlon paid Joe in flying lessons. By the time he was eighteen, Joe was flying Marlon's routes, dropping so low over the sorghum fields that he could spot the caterpillars on the plants he sprayed.

Joe discovered his second love in the ninth grade. Fritzi Fontaine walked into history class, swinging her hips and laughing at the top of her lungs. She wore a dark green sweater that set her auburn hair ablaze in the autumn sunshine. She settled effortlessly into the desk in front of Joe, oblivious to the hangdog stares from the greasy boys on the back row, unaware that she had just caused his own heart to race like an engine. She crossed her long legs, ladylike but somehow seductive even in bobby sox and saddle shoes, and Joe's mouth went dry just seeing her foot bob up and down in front of him. Smitten didn't begin to describe what he felt. Joe Stoddard was downright sick with love when he first laid eyes on Judge Fontaine's titian-haired daughter.

But Joe was tongue-tied, so he couldn't compete with the gaggle of girls and smooth-talking older guys who made up Fritzi's entourage. He just gazed at her hair in history class, tried to catch her eye in the hallway, and swallowed his pride when older, more suave guys escorted Fritzi to the homecoming dance and the Winter Formal.

In January, Fritzi didn't come back to Montrose High because her parents had sent her to a fancy girls' boarding school in New Orleans. After that, Joe found it much easier to breathe. With Fritzi out of sight, he could concentrate on flying once again.

By the time he graduated from Montrose High in the class of 1943, the U.S. was at war in Europe and the Pacific. Joe enlisted right away in the Army Air Force. After basic training, he was shipped off to Dijon Field in France, where he served as an aircraft mechanic on the B-26. He longed to fly the big bombers, but as a kid fresh off the farm, the best he could do was earn the rank of sergeant and receive a Good Conduct Medal before he was honorably discharged.

At home, Fritzi Fontaine was back from boarding school and had just been named Miss Montrose. Joe mustered his courage and asked her out to dinner at the Chatterbox.

"Daddy is old-fashioned," she said over the phone. "If you want to go out with me, you have to speak with him first. Don't worry; I'll tell him you're a nice young man. Just make sure your shoes are shined. Wear a coat and tie."

The Fontaines lived in the old family home, an estate a few blocks from downtown Montrose. A fancy arch over the front driveway spelled out "Fontainebleu" in wrought iron letters. Joe followed the circular driveway and parked his truck just south of the front door so it would not be visible from the porch. When he rang the bell, a tall Negro man answered and showed him into Judge Fontaine's study.

Judge Fontaine sat behind a mahogany desk and rose when Joe entered.

"How do you do, sir?" Joe held his hat in his left hand and stretched out his right.

"Sergeant Stoddard, we welcome you home and honor your service." The Judge shook Joe's hand and motioned for him to take a seat in front of the desk. He poured bourbon from a crystal decanter into two highball glasses and offered one to Joe.

"Thank you, sir," he said, watching the older man for a cue. The Judge sipped and Joe followed suit.

"Let's get right to it, Sergeant. Many young men want to court my daughter, as you might imagine, so I've come up with a few criteria to guide her suitors. Fritzi tells me you have a dinner date tonight, and that's fine, considering you are a veteran and son of a local family. But I've set some guidelines I believe are in my daughter's best interest. Any serious contenders for Fritzi's hand must be one of the following: a doctor graduated from medical school, a lawyer with a respectable practice, a businessman with a good reputation and money in the bank, or an officer in one of the United States Armed Services. My daughter will not be marrying any students, preachers, oilfield work-ers, farmers, or enlisted men. Are we clear?"

"Yes, sir," Joe replied. "I'd also like to report, sir, that I received my acceptance today for Officer Candidate School in the new U.S. Air Force. When I complete my training in six months, I expect to receive a commission as a Second Lieutenant." He was already one step ahead of Judge Fontaine, and determined to keep it that way.

"Congratulations to you, Sergeant," the Judge replied. He downed his bourbon.

Joe nodded and swallowed the rest of his drink. "I haven't told Fritzi yet, but I will be training in Texas for several months."

"Good luck." The Judge rose and shook Joe's hand, then slapped him on the back.

After their first date, Fritzi Fontaine and Joe Stoddard were insep-arable. Joe had been through the war and Fritzi was sick of small-town life. It was as if they were thrown together in a whirlwind of ambition, hanging onto each other for dear life.

When he graduated with honors from Officer Candidate School, Joe returned to Montrose and secured the Judge's blessing to propose to Fritzi. She not only said "yes," but surprised Joe with her aggressive passion.

"Look, Lieutenant. We're getting married," Fritzi said one night when they were parked on a back road by the farm, under a starlit sky. "Why shouldn't we make love like adults?" She scooted into his lap and kissed him. "I have a diaphragm," she whispered. "There's nothing to worry about."

They set their wedding date for October, just before Joe was to report for duty as a test pilot in New Mexico.

2

 "When you became engaged, you, too, chose a career in the Air Force.

You should know that every officer in the Air Force has an 'effectiveness report'...
In time, his wife also has an 'unwritten efficiency report,' unfiled but known, labeled and catalogued throughout the Air Force."
—Nancy Shea, *The Air Force Wife*

Montrose, Louisiana
October, 1948

SHE HAD BEEN CHRISTENED Francine Isabelle Fontaine, the only child of two parents who adored everything about their precocious red-haired daughter. At the age of six, Francine decided to go by "Fritzi." It sounded crisp and energetic, like her. Years later, she insisted that even her children call her Fritzi, because "I will not be a stodgy old *mother*, or a cloying little *mommy*."

"If Lieutenant Stoddard could just see his bride now! Flaunting around in her underwear," Mother said, sniffing into a hankie and bustling around.

Fritzi would rather have been married in a smart suit, but Mother insisted on a custom-made satin and lace get-up like Princess Elizabeth's gown for her wedding to Prince Phillip. Fritzi hated the gown and postponed putting it on as long as possible. She stood on the upstairs veranda, laced into her corset, garter belt, and stockings.

"I'm just having a cigarette before I get all dolled up, that's all. I'll just be a minute."

Fritzi winked at Lieutenant Stoddard himself, who was standing in the yard, looking up and admiring his smoking bride-to-be. She laughed, stubbed out her cigarette in a flowerpot and blew him a kiss.

Fritzi looked at herself in the full-length mirror and smiled. She looked like a pin-up queen in her underwear, so it didn't much matter what she looked like in the dress. Let the honeymoon begin!

On Monday of the following week, the *Montrose News Star* ran the story of the Fontaine-Stoddard nuptials:

> *Miss Francine Isabelle Fontaine recently became the bride of 2nd Lt. Joseph Randolph Stoddard. The ceremony, officiated by the Rev. Stanley Bridges of the First Presbyterian Church in Montrose, took place in the gardens of Fontainebleu, the bride's ancestral home.*
> *The bride, daughter of Judge and Mrs. Stanton Fontaine III, wore a handmade lace and satin dress of the same design that England's Princess Elizabeth wore at her own nuptials last year. She carried a hand-embroidered handkerchief from her mother, along with a nosegay of white chrysanthemum and stephanotis.*
> *The mother of the bride wore an aubergine silk jersey dress by Hardy Amies with a corsage of white calla lilies. The mother of the groom wore a beige broadcloth suit accented by a red rose corsage. Maid of honor was Flora Fontaine, first cousin of the bride.*

*Best man was Bud Caraway, childhood friend of
the groom.*

*After a honeymoon in Hot Springs, Ark., the couple will be
at home on Sandia Air Force Base in Albuquerque,
N.M., where the groom is stationed as a test pilot.*

FRITZI NUZZLED next to Joe in the front seat. "Can't we go any faster?" she pleaded in a sweet-baby voice.

"Darlin,' you know I can't afford to get pulled over. I'm up for promotion to first lieutenant and I've got to keep my nose clean." Joe took his eyes off the road to kiss his bride on the mouth. "Hot Springs isn't far. We'll be at the Arlington before you know it, and then ..." He moaned because Fritzi had unzipped his pants and was messing around. "Let's not get carried away, now..."

"Oh, hush! It was bad enough we had to spend our first night in my old bedroom. I swear, having Montrose in the rearview mirror is the best thing that could ever happen to us. Mother and Daddy would expect us for dinner every Sunday night if we didn't move far away. And your mama! She would always want her beloved 'Son' to be at her beck and call. Step on it! Let's put as many miles between them and us as we can!" She uncapped a bottle of Schlitz and took a tug.

"I'll drink to that!" Joe said, grabbing the bottle out of her hand.

"ARE you sure you don't want to dine downstairs? You brought all those pretty dresses. I want people to ogle my bride and be envious." Joe nibbled at Fritzi's neck.

"I know. Mother had all those things made so I'd have a proper trousseau. But I'd rather save them for the Officers' Club in New Mexico. They'll look nice and fresh in the dust-blown desert." She rolled over to kiss him on the mouth. "Let's spend our honeymoon in our birthday suits."

"Just as God created us. Like Adam and Eve?" Joe lit a Chesterfield and passed it to Fritzi.

"Just like the sinners we are," she agreed, exhaling a stream of smoke. She reached for the Room Service menu in the bedside table. "But even a sinner like me knows her husband has to eat. Here," she said, "order us up a post-coitus feast. I'm starving!"

That week, they didn't stroll along the shady boulevard in front of the Arlington Hotel. Joe never wore his white dinner jacket to accompany his bride to the Vapors Club for cocktails and dancing. They never set foot into the sulphur-smelling old bath houses built over the natural hot springs, and they didn't take in a movie at the theater across the street from the hotel. They made love and ate and drank and made good use of the Honeymoon Suite, paid for by Judge Fontaine as a gift to the newlyweds. Fritzi, having promised to drop her parents a line before they headed out to New Mexico, dashed off a postcard on the last day, thanking Mother and Daddy for the "gorgeous wedding" and the "wonderful sightseeing" they were doing. She even lied about the "relaxing mineral bath" she'd enjoyed at the Buckstaff. She dropped it into the mailbox at the front desk just as Joe finished checking out.

They set out for Albuquerque in a driving rain with, as Joe said, "limited visibility." Near Texarkana, a deer bolted out of the woods, grazing the side of Joe's Ford as he swerved to avoid it. "Dad gummit!" Joe said, pulling over to the shoulder. They both got out to inspect the damage to the rear fender. The deer had left a small dent, smeared with blood and feces, before it had bounded back into the woods. Fritzi leaned over and threw up her breakfast. Joe handed her his handkerchief and rubbed her back. Concern for his wife trumped his anger at the deer for damaging the Ford.

They got back into the car, Fritzi having assured Joe that she was all right. She felt queasy until they reached the outskirts of Dallas. The sun finally came out and followed them all the way to Ft. Worth, where they spent the night at a motor court. They left before dawn the next day, Joe determined to reach Albuquerque well before dark. As they grew closer to the base, Fritzi saw Joe's hands clench the steering wheel, his eyes focused ahead like a hawk homing in on its prey. This man was no longer her bridegroom. He was Second Lieutenant Joseph Stoddard, about to report for duty. And, she was now Mrs. Stoddard, reporting for duty as the young officer's wife.

There was no base housing for married junior grade officers, so they rented a two-bedroom adobe house with an apricot tree in the walled back yard. Fritzi found that the dry air agreed with her sinuses; she did not miss the stifling humidity of Montrose. She did, however, grow out of those beautiful dresses from her trousseau, as a visit to the base hospital confirmed what she'd suspected for awhile: she was pregnant. The diaphragm had been more trouble than it was worth. She liked to think that her eggs and Joe's sperm were somehow destined for each other, and that no barrier could have kept them apart.

When she broke the news over the phone to Mother and Daddy, Mother sobbed and insisted that Fritzi spend the rest of her pregnancy "at home" in Montrose, where Dr. Pike could take proper care of her and the baby. "He delivered you, honey. He's a man we can trust," Daddy chimed in.

"My home is with Joe, now, and I couldn't possibly consider it," Fritzi snapped. "We have very good doctors here on the base. I'm an officer's wife now, and Joe needs me here."

A month later, Fritzi glowed with pride when she wrote her parents to tell them that Joe was promoted to first lieutenant and assigned to a B-29 squadron charged with testing the Superfortress bomber. They ran daily test flights from Sandia Base to a base in Utah. They were mostly day flights, so Joe was always home for supper, full of stories about the new airplane and how excited he was to be part of the team to test it on takeoffs and landings.

Fritzi had taught herself to cook plain, good food—the kind Joe was used to on the farm. He was happy most of the time with her simple preparations like braised pork chops, canned green beans, and dinner rolls. She bought the dinner rolls in a package at the commissary because she had never learned to bake or had any interest in learning now. (Mother had always warned her to be careful not to become proficient at menial tasks, lest she be expected to perform them on a daily basis. Baking, Fritzi believed, qualified as menial.)

APRIL 3, 1949

THEY NAMED him Joseph Randolph Stoddard, Junior, and called him Rand. Fritzi believed the baby had saved Joe's life. If she hadn't gone into labor on that April morning, her husband would be dead, along with the rest of the crew of the Superfortress. Joe had been scheduled to co-pilot the plane on a test flight, but Fritzi *had* gone into labor at two in the morning. Reluctantly, Joe called his duty officer to beg off the assignment and took Fritzi to the base hospital at three. At five a.m., the Superfortress exploded on the dawn horizon. Now, Joe not only had a son, he also had his life. Nine men dead. Nine men he'd worked with; flown with, trusted to make sure the plane was in fine shape. Six of those men were fathers. Now, Joe was a father, too, able to hold his son for the first time because he had not been aboard.

Joe argued that he could have saved the flight if he'd been there. With his astute eye, keen sense for detail, and strict adherence to checkpoint protocol, Joe would have alerted the crew about *something* gone wrong.

Time and again, Fritzi argued that the accident investigators from the Pentagon had searched, but were unable to find the technical or human fault that caused the crash. "It was fate," she said. "And your son's birth saved you from it. He's your savior!"

"For creep's sake, Fritzi, don't get sacrilegious."

The "savior" argument always got Joe's goat, and Fritzi delighted in goading her husband to worship their young son as much as she did.

Worship was the right word. Fritzi could gaze for hours into the boy's cornflower blue eyes. She insisted on keeping his bassinet in their bedroom, and she awakened at the slightest whimper from their son. It seemed to Joe that she craved holding the boy, comforting him with warm bottles, cooing into his ear. He longed to separate her from the baby as he would a calf from its mother, but his heart melted when he saw how tender she was with the child. He also knew that if he dared intervene, she'd turn on him like a mama bear, and there would be no reckoning. He had nothing to complain about, after all. Fritzi somehow still had energy to jump his bones on the living room couch after Rand was sound asleep in the bassinet.

Fritzi had not enjoyed pregnancy. She hated growing out of her clothes, the awkwardness of moving around in a larger body, the swollen breasts and nauseous mornings. But the moment she saw Rand's eyes look into hers, she recognized the best part of herself. A new life—a boy—created in her own image. The very act of childbirth had filled Fritzi with tremendous pride, a sense of physical and mental achievement of Olympic proportions. She was strong, capable, revered. She was a mother, a superwoman with boundless energy and a libido that kept Joe grinning from ear-to-ear.

Rand wasn't a fussy baby. She'd heard other young mothers in the Officers' Wives Club complain of colic and diaper rash, but Rand was a dream baby, content with his formula, easily comforted back to sleep after 3 a. m. feedings. He sat up at six weeks, began to crawl at four months, and by his first birthday he was walking and running like a born athlete. His milestones delighted Fritzi, thrilling her with pride and the expectation that she was raising a bona fide genius.

With her superior pride in her son, it was a wonder Fritzi had any friends at all among the young officers' wives. She made an effort to keep her pride to herself. She became a bright, funny friend to other young wives in the squadron. They knew they could rely on Fritzi to watch their children if they had an urgent appointment, whether it was at the doctor's office or the beauty parlor. Fritzi enjoyed the hustle-bustle of other children in the house, and secretly delighted in comparing Rand with the "average" sons and daughters of her peers. Her energy seemed boundless.

Her mother called long distance once a week, insisting that she visit to help her daughter and give her a rest.

"Mother, I honestly don't need the help. Rand is such an easy, wonderful child. I love doing my own cleaning and cooking. I've learned so much living out here," she'd say brightly each week. "I like being independent."

The last thing Fritzi wanted was for her mother to invade her New Mexican paradise. Mother would find the adobe architecture stark and confusing, and she wouldn't understand why the yard was landscaped with gravel instead of St. Augustine grass. Fritzi cringed to think of her mother's reaction to the many Indian and Mexican-American families who lived in the neighborhood. There would be nothing for her mother to do but fuss about the dry air and the dust storms. She wouldn't be interested in visiting the regular tourist haunts that delighted Fritzi: Old Town with its margaritas and spicy food; the Acoma Pueblo to see the weekly tribal dances performed for tourists; Sandia Crest, where they picnicked on cool Sunday afternoons. Plus, they had no spare bedroom, now that Rand had moved into his own room. A visit from Mother was just out of the question.

3

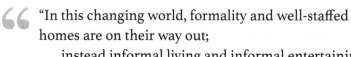 "In this changing world, formality and well-staffed homes are on their way out;
        instead informal living and informal entertaining are the new order."
        —Nancy Shea, *The Air Force Wife*

1950

Sandia Air Force Base, New Mexico

ON THE FIRST Friday evening of the month, Joe would join the other young officers at the Officers' Club for "Beer Call," a happy hour that extended long into the night. The men would smoke cigars, play pool, and eat hamburgers in the men-only Officers' Grill.

"That's fine if you want to go out with the boys," Fritzi said when Joe told her his plans. "I'll just make plans with the girls."

She had a dangerous tone in her voice. Joe deferred, knowing his night of camaraderie was at stake if he questioned what her "plans" were.

Fritzi borrowed Joe's duty roster, called every young officer's wife in the squadron, and invited each of them to join her on the patio for margaritas on Friday. The other women were to bring hors d'oeuvres and any children too young to stay home by themselves.

Only seven of the twenty-two wives showed. Fritzi greeted them in a Mexican fiesta dress she'd bought in Old Town, with little Rand at her side. The other women came in proper white gloves and prim dresses with petticoats, more suitable for an officers' wives' tea than margaritas on Fritzi's patio. They brought freshly groomed children: two babies not yet walking; a five-year-old boy with freckles and a yo-yo; a seven-year-old girl with long braids; and four toddlers, two boys and two girls.

After one of Fritzi's margaritas (or two), the young mothers removed their shoes and gloves. Sandra Ferguson borrowed her son's yo-yo and began entertaining the group with tricks. Wanda Fuller bounced a baby boy on her lap while eating most of the Fritos that Nancy Shulmeier brought. Wanda's seven-year-old daughter, Lucy, took charge of the toddlers and had them playing school in one corner of the yard. Out of the corner of her eye, Fritzi saw the five-year-old boy unzip his pants and pee behind the apricot tree. What the hell, she thought, knowing the kid's mother would swoop down and discipline him if she said anything. Let the kids have a little fun, too. She mixed another batch of margaritas. And another one after that.

By seven p.m., Fritzi was serving peanut butter sandwiches to the hungry kids, praying that she wouldn't run out of Wonder Bread. After the margaritas ran out, Millie Hodges from next door made a beer run and opened bottles of Falstaff to pass around. Sandra Ferguson bummed a cigarette from Helen Patterson, and Wanda Fuller ~~was~~ let her baby crawl in the sparse grass. Fritzi took it all in, knowing that her little get-together had secured her place as queen bee among these repressed women, freed by her invitation to laugh and let loose in her back yard.

By eight, most of the women were languidly gathering their whiny little ones and bustling around to pick up dishes and what was left of their hors d'oeuvres. Helen emptied two full ashtrays and

Nancy gathered the cast-aside shoes, matching them up in pairs for the women and children to pick up as they left. By 8:30, the whole party was cleaned up, kids bundled into cars, and plans made to gather at the Stoddard patio the next month.

Joe came home a little after ten, long after Fritzi had put Rand to bed. She was beginning to doze off when she heard Joe's key in the door. She could tell he'd sucked on a Sen-Sen to disguise the beer on his breath as he dove onto the bed next to her.

"Darlin'," he said, looking up at her with the rueful face of a child in trouble, "I've got orders for Korea."

Fritzi pushed him away and turned on the light. "*No.*"

"Baby, I don't have any say-so about it. They need pilots. I've got orders," Joe said in a drowsy voice.

"So, what about me? What about Rand, and the life we've made here? What do they expect us to do?"

Joe took a deep breath and sat up straight. "Honey, the Air Force expects me to go where they send me. You and Rand will have to go home, I guess, and just live your folks, if that's what you want to do. Or you could live with Mother."

"Are you out of your mind? For your information, *this* is my home —*our* home, not my parents' place, and certainly not your mother's. I'm not having this, not having to go and smother myself back in Montrose while you go off to maybe get killed! That's not what I signed up for!"

"Don't be silly, Fritz. Orders are orders, and I've got to report May 1. We can telegram your parents tomorrow and put our things in storage back in Montrose. It's only for eighteen months, two years, tops. I'm not going away forever."

"Well, what if you do? What if you get shot down, or blown up, or crash the goddamn plane you're flying? Where does that leave me? What about us?"

"Honey, I promise you, if I am killed in action, you and Rand will be well cared for. There's life insurance, and you'll be eligible for widow benefits. And, you know there will never be anyone else for me. When I come home, we'll get a good stateside assignment. Come on, you knew this was a possibility. You'll see. It will all work out." He put his arm around her, but she pushed him away.

"I'm not buying it. You'll just have to call the Pentagon on Monday and tell them the deal is off. You've got a wife and a young son now. You've served your time at war. Let someone with nothing to lose go to Korea in your place." She got out of bed, grabbed her chenille robe and stomped into Rand's room.

"Wait, don't wake the baby..."

"I have no intention of waking our son," she whispered as Rand stirred in the crib. "I'm getting an extra blanket for you to sleep on the couch tonight."

She tossed a blanket at him and retrieved his pillow from the bed. "Here," she said. "Good night."

She got into bed, pulled the covers over her head and began to sob.

AT FIVE IN THE MORNING, Fritzi gave up on sleep and went to the kitchen. Joe was sitting at the table, drinking coffee. His eyes were red and ringed with shadows. "You know I can't call the Pentagon," he said. "I have to go, you have to stay, and that's all there is to it. We can't afford for you to rent a place here or anyplace else while I'm gone. And I don't want you going to work. You've got to raise our son, be there for him, even if I can't."

"I know," she said, pouring coffee for herself. "I know it, and I don't like it." She sat, pouting, holding her face in her hands.

"Well, then let's do something you *do* like," he said, setting his cup on the table. He led the way to the bedroom.

Around nine o'clock, Rand called from his bedroom. "Mama!"

Automatically, Fritzi rose and reached for her robe. "Wait," Joe said, pulling her back into bed. "Let me get him. I'll feed him breakfast while you sleep in."

"I'm still mad as hell about Korea, you know," Fritzi said, easing down into the sheets.

"Yeah? Well, you'll just have to get used to it," said Joe. "And so will I." He pulled on his robe.

FRITZI SPENT the next month packing up the house and saying good-bye to Millie, Helen, Sandra, and all the other young wives she had befriended. Mrs. Quigley, the squadron commander's wife, hosted a farewell coffee in her home. The women had pitched in and bought Fritzi a turquoise address book. They had all entered their names in pen, but their addresses were in pencil.

"Keeping a neat address book is a big challenge in the Air Force," said Mrs. Quigley. "If I could start over again, I'd do it this way: the friends in ink, the addresses erasable. So much neater than making new entries and crossing out old ones. It would be so much easier to put together my Christmas card list every year."

Fritzi thanked them all, laughing and putting up a good front. "It'll be so great to be back in Montrose for a while," she lied. "I do miss Mother and Daddy. This way, Rand can get to know his grandparents."

"You're brave," said Sally Carroll, a pale newlywed with skinny arms. "Don't you worry about Joe? It's no picnic over there. He'll be away a whole year. Aren't you afraid he'll get...lonely? I hear those Korean girls are—well, *easy*."

Fritzi looked into Sally's blank eyes. She wanted to slap her. Instead, she said, loud enough for Mrs. Quigley to hear: "My husband did not join the Air Force so he could cheat on me with a Korean girl. He joined the Air Force to serve his country, and that's what I expect him to do."

The women closed ranks around Fritzi, and Mrs. Quigley asked, "Who wants more coffee?"

Sally, red as a beet, put down her cup and slipped out the front door.

THEIR HOUSEHOLD GOODS went into storage. At the end of April, Joe drove Fritzi and Rand to Montrose. They set out at six on a Friday morning, with a thermos of coffee and a makeshift bed in the back seat for Rand. As they left the driveway of the little adobe house on Navajo Street, Fritzi dared not look back. That happy, sunny, dry place, that house where she'd been a hostess and playful mother to her young son, was a thing of the past. Now, she was going back in time, moving in with Mother and Daddy, abiding by their rules and their schedule. The iced tea glasses at the dinner table, sweating in the humidity, the Melrose silver, polished by a maid every week, the bowl of magnolia blossoms. She let out a grand sigh.

"What's wrong, honey?" Joe put his hand on her knee.

"You know what's wrong." She swallowed hard. "I'm going from being a wife in charge of my own home and our own son, back to being the doted-on daughter of Fontaineblue. Mother has hired Viola back to take care of Rand. She's arranged for me to be accepted into the Junior League. Daddy had my old room repainted and converted the front bedroom to a nursery for Rand. If they don't smother me, I might just hang myself with Spanish moss!"

Joe gave her a stoic look. "You'd better take care of yourself so I have somebody to come home to. You're so much luckier than some of the wives, who have to rent cheap apartments and take jobs while their husbands go to Korea. I'm going to be out there, flying B-52 missions. I don't need to worry about you, because you'll be safe and cared for in Montrose. That's a load off of my mind. Think of somebody other than yourself, Fritzi. It's what an Air Force wife *does*."

She clamped her jaw shut and swallowed tears, turning to face Rand in the back seat. He was standing up, grasping the velvet cord strung along the back of the front seat and swaying to and fro with the car. Just then, a truck in front of them blew a tire. Joe swerved the Ford, just in time to avoid rear-ending the truck. Rand fell on his bottom, hit his lip on the back seat and began to cry.

"Now look what you've done!" Fritzi said, hiking her skirt and climbing over the bench seat to comfort her son. "Think about something other than the Air Force. That's what a good husband *does*."

She could see Joe's jaw tighten, his temples swell and ebb as he staunched his anger. He was a big man, strong, but she knew he would never hit her. Nevertheless, she rather enjoyed taking him to the boiling point and watching him slowly compose himself. An officer and a gentleman, her man. She sometimes wished she could control herself with the same cool determination, but it was not her gift.

"Pull over at that gas station," she said evenly. "Your son's lip is bleeding and he needs a clean diaper."

Joe obliged silently. He used the men's room and smoked a cigarette while Fritzi cleaned up Rand's lip and changed his diaper.

When they pulled away, Fritzi sat in the back seat and read a Golden Book to Rand. Joe drove in silence all the way to Tyler, Texas. "May as well eat now and fill up at the same stop."

Fritzi loved Joe for many reasons, but the main reason he'd won her heart was his decisiveness. Most of her suitors had coddled her and catered to her like simpering lap dogs. Not Joe. He didn't cajole her or argue over choices. If something was practical, if it made sense, it was right. There was no superstition, theology, or guessing allowed. She guessed this was why he was a good officer. And, by all indications, a good husband. A decent father. A good man. Her man. She loved him enough to get mad as hell at him sometimes. Right now, she was mad as hell at the Air Force for sending him into combat.

4

 "Wise young couples have their children in the early years of
their married life if that is at all possible."
—Nancy Shea, *The Air Force Wife*

Montrose, Louisiana

Joe had been in Korea two weeks when Fritzi realized her monthly Aunt Flow was late. In fact, two weeks late. Normally, the rich smell of fresh chicory coffee gave her a reason to get out of bed. Now, it made her want to heave up her empty stomach.

Mother fluttered and fussed over her. Why wasn't she eating her eggs? Josie had made her favorite quince jam—why didn't she want some on her biscuits? She poured a glass of freshly squeezed orange juice. "At least get your blood sugar up," she begged Fritzi.

Fritzi took a sip. The sweet-sour citrus sent her straight into the hall bathroom. Mother picked up the phone and made an afternoon appointment with Dr. Pike.

"YOU ARE EXPECTING A CHILD, MRS. STODDARD," Dr. Pike said after her examination.

Well, of course I am, you old coot, she wanted to say. Honest to God, why did men think they delivered all the answers when she knew her body's rhythms, her periods, her own lovemaking history? She'd ditched the diaphragm after the first few times. Why should she have to stick something inside her when she knew she wanted more babies? How could she not want to produce another Rand, another perfectly wonderful child, to populate their world? With a little Rand in the house, she and Joe hadn't had as much time together as before. But when they did make love, they went at it like rabbits. She didn't want to stop and stick in a diaphragm every time their urgency overcame them.

"Well, good," Fritzi said. "If I'm going to be in Montrose, I might as well be working on something!"

On the way home, Fritzi drove Daddy's Lincoln straight to the Western Union office. Mother, who had insisted on accompanying her to Dr. Pike's, sat in the passenger seat. "I can only guess that you are in the family way," Mother said, her powdered face flushed with excitement. "Is that what Dr. Pike said? Why won't you tell me?"

"I'll be back in a second," Fritzi said, parking the Lincoln. "The father should be the first to know."

Inside, she dictated the telegram:

BUN IN OVEN STOP EVERYTHING FINE STOP COMING IN
DEC STOP
DON'T GET KILLED STOP LOVE

BACK IN THE CAR, Fritzi punched in the cigarette lighter on the car's dashboard and fished a Chesterfield out of her purse. The lighter popped out, red and ready to light. She stuck it to her cigarette, breathed deeply, and exhaled a cloud of smoke toward her mother.

"Francine! Did you march in there and tell that telegraph agent

Marge Shipley about your personal condition? The news will be the talk of the town now."

"I can't help it if Marge has a job, and that job is running the telegraph," Fritzi said, backing out of the parking space and heading toward home. "Who's going to talk about it, anyway? It will be painfully obvious if people see me walking around in a couple of months. I really don't care. I just wanted Joe to know first."

"Propriety is something very important to our family, and you know that. With your father a judge and all..."

"Well, it's not his baby! It's mine and Joe's, and in my world, that's about as proper as it gets. After all, we are of the same race and we are married for almost three years, Mother." She blew more smoke.

"Why are you smoking, anyway? It's a cheap, nasty habit. Especially in public, driving a car. You probably shouldn't even be driving now, in your condition. When are you going to grow up and be a lady, Francine?"

"I am a grown woman, an Air Force officer's wife, and the mother of one and one on the way. Unlike you, I learned to drive and make decisions and send telegrams and endure my husband's absence while he serves his country. If I want a cigarette, I'm having one." She jerked the Lincoln to a stop at the light on Main and Cherry.

Mother pitched forward, angry. She opened the door, got out, and began walking on Cherry Street toward home.

Fritzi watched her mother mince along in her pumps, shirtdress, white gloves and purse. A proper lady, all right. Born in another era, stuck in a bell jar of expectations and duty, perceptions, and appearances. Doomed. In her daze of hormonal anger, Fritzi felt a heavy sadness for her mother. She threw out her cigarette and turned onto Cherry Street. She'd been right, but she had to apologize to poor Mother, who knew no better.

She pulled up beside her mother. "I'm sorry. Do you suppose Josie can make me a milkshake for lunch?"

Her mother stopped, turned toward the car. Fritzi felt a pang of guilt, seeing the tears in her mother's eyes. "Of course, honey. If it makes you feel better."

JOE'S MOTHER, a widow, needed to know about the pregnancy. One humid afternoon in mid-May, Fritzi drove out to the farm with Rand. Daddy had wanted to drive her, but she insisted he stay home while she took the Lincoln. "I'm a grown woman, Daddy. I have a mother-in-law who needs to visit with her grandson and learn about the new baby on the way."

She turned the big car off the paved asphalt of County Road 57 and onto the gravel that led to the Stoddard farm. Rand, standing on the floor of the back seat, squealed with delight as gravel pelted the underside of the car. Fritzi took a deep breath, preparing herself. She had dressed carefully in a simple navy skirt and blousy striped top. She wore her red Keds with ankle socks, eschewing a suit with heels. She knew that Mrs. Stoddard would meet her in her best housedress, worn, thin cotton crisply starched and ironed. She'd be wearing those black lace-up witch-looking shoes with stockings, no doubt. Her gray hair would be pulled into a tight bun at her neck. Her mother-in-law was as practical as she was predictable. Dowdy and boring. No sense of style.

Do not think unkindly of the woman who gave birth to your husband. Agnes Stoddard approached the car as Fritzi pulled into the dirt drive next to the unpainted, dun-colored house. She was dressed just as Fritzi had predicted and reached for the back door handle with a weathered hand. "*Junior!*" she exclaimed, reaching in to lift Rand out of the car.

Rand's face twisted into a pout and his eyes clouded with tears. He looked at Fritzi. "Mama!" he cried.

"Oh, now, none of that! Come give Grandmother some sugar!" Mrs. Stoddard said, her face tense and determined.

Fritzi got out of the car and grabbed Rand to shush him. "How are you, Mrs. Stoddard? Don't mind Rand. He's a little grumpy today because I cut his nap short. So nice to see you!" She rocked Rand on her hip and reached out one arm in a semi-hug toward the woman.

"He'll learn, I hope, to come to me properly someday," she

replied, nodding solemnly. She turned her back on Fritzi and mounted the porch steps. "I've made some iced tea. Come, tell me what you hear from Son. I haven't gotten a letter from him in a few days." She motioned to the old wooden chairs on the porch. A small table held an aluminum pitcher, two tumblers and a plate of what appeared to be last night's dinner biscuits.

Fritzi bristled. She was lucky to get a letter from Joe once a week. "Oh, I think his new assignment is challenging. But he's staying safe and counting the days until he can come back stateside," she managed to say cheerfully. She sat down, Rand clinging to her and ogling his grandmother.

"As am I. They're calling it a conflict, what's going on in Korea, but from all accounts it's a full-on war. Son is flying bombing missions, I know, although the Air Force won't let him write that in a letter. He could be killed any day, though I pray to Jesus to watch over him. Here, Francine, have some iced tea." She poured from a sweating aluminum pitcher into a blue aluminum tumbler.

Fritzi accepted the tea and sipped. No lemon, she knew, and pre-sweetened with a modicum of sugar. Lemons and sugar were too expensive to waste on flavoring beverages. She knew that her husband had grown up proud but poor. Thank God he didn't make a show of it like his mother did. *Do not think unkindly...*

Rand squirmed in her lap and made his way to the floor. He spotted the biscuits and reached for one. "Cookie!" he cried.

Mrs. Stoddard slapped the top of the toddler's hand. "No, Junior. You have to ask first."

Rand stopped and looked at the woman, incredulous. Then he glanced at Fritzi and burst into tears. Instinctively, Fritzi scooped him into her lap.

"Can you say 'Please,' honey? 'Please can I have the cookie?'" Fritzi's voice shook with tamped-down anger. *The hag.* Rand was just a three-year-old. A brilliant one. He had manners, but he was still just a child.

"Please?" Rand blinked away tears and looked pitifully into Fritzi's eyes. She reached for one and gave it to him.

"Thank you," Rand said.

"We do teach him manners, you know," Fritzi said. "Everything is just so unfamiliar to him here, that's all."

"No need to make excuses for the boy. He'll learn the proper rules with a little discipline." Mrs. Stoddard nodded at Rand and smiled. "Those are biscuits, Junior. They're not cookies. Say 'biscuit' for Grandmother. 'Biscuit, please.'"

Rand's face clouded in confusion. "Bikkit. Please." He tried to bite into the hard biscuit and stuck out his tongue. Unable to eat it, he threw it off the porch and into the dirt in the yard.

Mrs. Stoddard shook her head in disgust. "Wasting food is wrong, Junior. Now the ants will be all over that..."

Fritzi interrupted her. "Mrs. Stoddard, I'm very sorry that my three-year-old son tossed the biscuit on the ground. I promise you we will pick it up and throw it away as we leave. This visit isn't going so well so far, but I did want to tell you some happy news myself."

"Oh?" Mrs. Stoddard raised her eyebrows above her wire-rimmed glasses.

"Joe and I are expecting again. The new baby will come in December."

"My goodness. You two certainly aren't wasting any time with your family planning," she said. "I thought you looked a little heavy. I hope you have a girl!"

"We are thrilled, of course, although Joe won't be here for the birth."

"Poor Son. He is such a good father, he should be here to see this little one into the world." She shook her head as though the whole thing was a tragedy.

Fritzi stood up and took Rand by the hand. "We'll be on our way now. So nice visiting. Come on, Rand, we'll pick up that old hard biscuit."

Agnes Stoddard sat on the porch, stoic. "All right, then. Good-bye."

FRITZI SPED OFF, sending a spray of gravel from the Lincoln as she peeled out onto the road. When she could no longer see the farm-house in the rear view mirror, she tossed the goddamn biscuit out the window.

Fritzi wrote to Joe almost every day, glossing over the unfortunate visit with his mother. Joe was the older of the two Stoddard children. His father had died in a tractor accident when Joe was just ten. Joe's younger sister, Lila, suffered from polio and died a year later. Fritzi knew Agnes Stoddard had seen more than her fair share of hardship, and so had Joe. Still, Fritzi found it difficult to accept her mother-in-law's brusque treatment of Rand, but she wouldn't write to Joe about that. Instead, she wrote about Rand's growing curiosity and the adventures they had together, exploring the gardens and Fontainebleu.

> Today, we skipped rocks across the pond, then borrowed the
>   spaghetti strainer from Josie to catch tadpoles.
> Your son is a gentle, kind nature lover, careful not to hurt
>   any living thing. But, like you, he is brave as hell and is
>   sturdy and quick and strong. I have to watch him
>   closely, or he'll try to swim in the pond! He loves
>   climbing the old gnarled crepe myrtles along the stream.
>   Their branches are low, and he's learned to pull himself
>   up, balance, and climb almost out of my reach!

She knew these antics would delight Joe, who longed to share adventures with his young son. He'd be proud that she wasn't sissy-fying him, although she did let Mother parade him around in smocked rompers when she hosted her bridge club. Fritzi dressed Rand modestly, refusing to deck him out like Little Lord Fauntleroy on Sunday mornings for church. Daddy liked to hold Rand's hand and walk to a front-row pew at First Presbyterian. "For now, Daddy is showing our little man the ropes of manhood. But we can't wait for you to come home and finish the job," she wrote.

By July, Fritzi had gained nearly twenty pounds, a fact she never disclosed in her letters to Joe. Dr. Pike told her she was apt to become a "fat lady" if she did not slow down her weight gain. "Wouldn't it be a shame for our young lieutenant to come home to a plump little matron next year?" he asked her.

Fritzi was mortified, swearing to the doctor that she would go on a salt-free diet and watch what she ate. She gave strict orders to Josie: no more fried chicken for her, no cherry pie. She would have to ignore her cravings for strawberry shortcake and buttermilk. She restricted herself to fresh fruit and vegetables, which were plentiful in summer. She learned to eat ripe peaches raw, not in a cobbler, and green beans without salt pork. Damned if she was going to be a "plump little matron." She'd show that old sawbones Pike.

But by the end of August, Fritzi's fingers looked like sausages, and she could no longer wear her wedding ring. Her feet and legs had swollen to nearly twice their normal size, and sweat drenched her clothes as soon as she put them on. Mother insisted that she stay in bed with the fans blowing on her full blast, in her darkened bedroom. (Fritzi suspected that Mother was ashamed of her ballooning size, and didn't want her to be seen around town, a huge pregnant woman with no wedding ring.) Worse, Fritzi had no energy for little Rand, who whined for his mother to come outside and play. Viola became his new playmate, telling the boy that his mama was all "swolled up" and had to rest up for the new baby. Daddy took the boy for a daily ice cream cone at Dairy Freeze, which seemed to appease his need for Fritzi. But she missed her boy, her man, her energy, and her figure. She felt like a beached whale.

"Swolled up" she was, regardless of her salt intake. She tried the diuretic Dr. Pike prescribed, but that seemed to make the swelling worse. Mother applied cool compresses to her forehead, insisting that if she could just cool down, her body might release some of the excess fluid. (Mother, it seemed, got more giddy with stupidity every day. Didn't she know that *sweating* releases fluid? It would have made more sense to offer a hot compress and turn off the fans, Fritzi thought.) Dr. Pike came every few days to take her blood pressure. He seemed more and more concerned as Labor Day came and went. On the first of October, he ordered her to be admitted to the hospital for the rest of her pregnancy.

"No, goddammit!" Fritzi cried, tears streaming down her puffy cheeks. "It's bad enough I'm cooped up here like a caged hippo! I'll be damned if I'm going to lie in a metal bed and have nurses poking at me at all hours!" She hardly thought of the baby growing inside her. All she could feel was her own expanding flesh, stretched so far she wondered if it could ever spring back into place once this ordeal was over.

She wept as she was loaded into the ambulance. Mother and Daddy saw that she had a private room, overlooking the courthouse square. The worst part was, only children twelve and up could visit. That meant Rand could only wave at her from the courtyard below her window.

There were flowers from the Ladies' Circle at First Presbyterian and from Mother's bridge club. The Junior League sent her its latest cookbook, *Morsels from Montrose*, which made Fritzi want to throw up because her stomach had started hurting. One day, she got a dozen yellow roses from Joe, which sent her into a deep depression. She demanded to know who had told him she was in the hospital, but Mother and Daddy pleaded innocent. It was embarrassing, all this attention to her swollen self, and she didn't want her husband worrying when there was nothing he could do.

She existed on tapioca pudding and bananas, but still swelled. On the day after Halloween, Mrs. Stoddard visited her. Fritzi turned her face toward the wall and pretended to be asleep.

"My dear, you have nothing to be ashamed of," said her mother-in-law softly. Slowly, Fritzi turned toward her, pretending to wake up. Mrs. Stoddard looked pale and tired, standing there in a faded cotton dress. "God has blessed you with a baby, and sometimes, bringing that little one into this world is a cross you have to bear. Your first child came easily, I know. This one is making it hard on you, yes. But it's still just a little baby." Mrs. Stoddard touched her hand gently. "Just a little baby."

The words made Fritzi cry fresh tears. "I'm a mess! Joe wouldn't be proud of me at all. I don't deserve those flowers he sent. And I'll bet you're the one who told him about this…"

"I sent Son a telegram, because he ought to know you're having a time. It's his child too, partly his making. It's not just your burden to bear."

Fritzi couldn't believe her ears. She'd never heard such kind words from her mother-in-law.

"Thank you," Fritzi said, squeezing her hand. "Thank you, Mrs. Stoddard."

"Please, dear. You've earned the right to call me Agnes."

THE WEEK BEFORE THANKSGIVING, Dr. Pike ordered a Caesarian section. "You've got pre-eclampsia, Mrs. Stoddard. You are swelling and your blood pressure is dangerously high."

"You mean I could die?"

"Yes, you could, and so could the baby. Be brave, now. Your baby will be born a month too soon, but it's plenty big. We have to deliver. Today."

FRITZI AWOKE in the recovery room, thirsty and sore and confused. This birth was far from the Olympian feat she'd accomplished with Rand. A nurse in a stiff white uniform stood over her. "Congratulations, Mrs. Stoddard," she said. "You are the mother of a strong, healthy little girl."

"Where is she?"

"In an incubator till tomorrow. We have her under observation, but she is doing fine. When you are able, I'll take you to the nursery in a wheelchair. You can see her through the viewing window."

"Can I have some water? And ice?" Fritzi coughed, her throat sore and her mouth dry. "Is she pretty?"

"Oh, yes, ma'am. She is beautiful."

The nurse lied, Fritzi thought later when she saw her baby in the incubator. She was round and fat, with skin the color of ripe radishes.

Unlike Rand, whose newborn head had been covered in peach-colored down, this baby had a head of swirling dark hair that looked matted and greasy. Her face was squinty and her lips made round, sucking motions.

A girl who looked like that would need a name that promised beauty, Fritzi knew. "We'll call her Linda. Linda Francine Stoddard," she told the nurse.

5

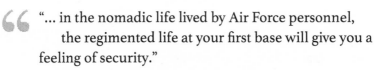 "... in the nomadic life lived by Air Force personnel,
the regimented life at your first base will give you a
feeling of security."
—Nancy Shea, *The Air Force Wife*

MCCHORD AIR FORCE BASE, WASHINGTON

AFTER KOREA, the sharpest young Air Force pilots had been assigned
to bases on the West Coast. Here at McChord, Fritzi's First Lieutenant
Joe Stoddard was working in the 567th All-Weather Wing, testing jet
interceptors and air defense radar. After more than two years in
Korea, Joe now worked on state-of-the art technology that could
detect and intercept enemy aircraft. He had earned a promotion after
flying more than 250 successful bombing missions in the B-52 in
Korea and had decided to make the Air Force his career.

Fritzi had been a big factor in that decision. After nearly two years
of living under her parents' roof in Montrose, giving birth to Linda
without Joe, and tolerating the suffocating provincialism of life in
their hometown, she was more eager to join the regular Air Force

than Joe was. Not long after Joe returned from Korea, his mother died suddenly of a heart attack.

"There's nothing to keep you in Montrose; no reason to go back to the farm," Fritzi said one night after his mother's funeral, holding him close in bed.

"You're right," he said, stifling a sob, "I don't have anyone to worry about here."

"Well, I do," Fritzi replied. "Mother and Daddy will worry me to death with all their nosiness if we don't get out of here."

"Give me a chance to think about it. I haven't been back long enough to breathe, and I just lost Mama. I don't know what to do about the farm. Awful lot going on right now, Fritzi. Don't start pestering me about big decisions just yet."

"I didn't mean to pester." Fritzi kissed him. "You've got time. Time to think, time to rest up for whatever's ahead." She propped herself on one elbow and looked into his eyes. He was exhausted. She stroked his forehead, watching him drift into a deep sleep. The Air Force had given him thirty days to decide if he wanted to rejoin as a regular officer. That gave her twenty-nine days to convince Joe to take her into the wild blue yonder.

A week later, they sat on the upstairs veranda, just off her old bedroom at Fontainebleu. Fritzi decided it was time to give it to him straight.

"I want out of Montrose," she said. "I don't want our kids growing up here, picking ticks off them out on the farm. "

"Come on, now, it hasn't been that bad, has it?" Joe lit two cigarettes and handed her one.

"It's been hell," Fritzi said, blowing smoke into the summer night. "I'm a grown woman, but all I'll ever be here is Judge Fontaine's daughter. An aging Miss Montrose. Mother is breathing down my neck all the time, telling me how to raise the kids. If we don't leave, they'll tear us to pieces."

"I wouldn't have to go into farming. I could always work for old Marlon Laroche, crop-dusting. Maybe even buy him out, add a couple of planes and operate out of the airstrip south of town," Joe said.

"Yes, you could. But that would mean borrowing money—of course, Daddy and Mama will want to give it to us—but either way, we're in debt to somebody. I just don't see it. Rand will be in first grade in the fall, and Linda, she is a quick learner. They'll outgrow all the kids here, and they'll be stuck. They're smart enough to go to college, do things kids around here aren't raised to do. We can't just stay here and let them stagnate."

"Montrose was good enough for me," Joe said proudly. "I didn't go to college, but I qualified as an officer and got into flight school. I'm a darned good navigator, pilot, and flight engineer, too, and I didn't need to go to MIT to learn that."

"Yeah, big shot," Fritzi said, pulling his ear. "You did that because you were in during the war. If you'd stayed here, you'd still be farming and crop-dusting."

"So what's wrong with that?"

"Come on, Ace." Fritzi laughed. "You love flying. It's in your blood. And you don't want to dust crops, inhaling fertilizer in a buzz-by plane, either. You like flying the bombers, the big planes. You love the power, the freedom. You can't deny that."

"I love *you*," he said, leaning closer for a kiss.

"Then prove it. Let's blow this town and take on the world together, Lt. Stoddard." Fritzi stood, stubbed out her cigarette in a flowerpot, and went inside.

So HERE SHE WAS, on a cool, gray September morning, seeing Rand off to his first day of school in Elementary School #2, just off McChord Air Force Base in Washington State. Back in Montrose, the kids would be sweating through their new clothes, swatting at mosquitoes as they walked to school.

"Bye, Rand! Be nice to the teacher!" Fritzi swallowed a lump of sentiment and waved at the big yellow school bus from the Clover Unified School District. Rand, carrying his Roy Rogers lunch pail and wearing a rain slicker, was on his way to his first day of first grade. Linda, now four, waved wistfully at the bus. She was going to be lonely now, without her brother.

The three other mothers at the bus stop turned to walk back toward base housing, along with Fritzi. Two of them had had young children, and one had a newborn in a pram.

"How old is your little girl?" asked a small dark-haired woman with a little boy.

"She's four," Fritzi said, reaching out to shake the woman's hand. "I'm Fritzi Stoddard. My daughter here is Linda."

"Oh, hi," said the other woman, nodding and smiling without offering her hand. "I'm Maude, and this is little Danny." She pointed to a boy dressed in pajama pants and a T-shirt, who held a piece of toast smeared with jam in one hand. "He's five." Danny licked his fingers.

"Say hello, Danny." He grasped his mother's skirt and hid behind her.

"Hello, Danny!" Linda, easily an inch taller and a few pounds heavier than the little boy, chased Danny out from behind his mother and began a game of hide-and-seek.

Fritzi noted the size difference, but also noted with pride that her daughter was immaculate, dressed in a smocked plaid dress with a navy blue sweater. Danny squealed and offered her the sticky piece of toast. Linda took a bite, then gave the toast back to Danny.

"Looks like they've made friends," Fritzi said. "We live over there, in the duplexes. Do you want to come by for a cup of coffee? We just moved here, and I don't know many families on base."

Maude looked across the street. "You live in officers' quarters—in *those* new duplexes?"

"Yes. We just moved in last week."

"You go to any of the Wives' Club meetings yet?"

"No. Like I said, I've been busy moving us in, getting my son ready for school. I'd love to put on some coffee. You and Danny come on. The place isn't fixed up yet, and I haven't unpacked everything..."

"No offense, but you don't seem like an officer's wife. You aren't acting stuck-up."

"Why would I?"

"Because it's sort of—*illegal*—for us to be friends," Maude said, looking at the sidewalk.

"What in the world are you talking about? I never heard of such a thing! Come on, I insist. We can visit and Linda can play with Danny." Fritzi began to walk toward the duplex.

Maude stopped in her tracks. "Look, lady. My husband is an airman first class. You could get in plenty of trouble for inviting me over. It's against the rules."

"Well, then, let's break the rules. It can't hurt anyone. And I'm dying for some company. We're just two girls, having a cup of coffee. It's not like we're plotting to overthrow the Air Force. We're still American citizens, and last I heard, we have the right to assemble."

"I'm sorry. Thanks for the invitation, but I just can't." Maude grabbed Danny's hand and headed across the street.

Linda ran after them. "No, honey. Go on with your mother," Maude said, shooing her back.

Linda stopped in her tracks and let out a loud wail. "But I wanted Danny as a friend," she cried.

Fritzi took her daughter's hand and headed home. "So did I, honey. I guess we don't know the rules about making friends here yet. Don't you cry. We'll find you another playmate over in our neck of the woods."

Back in Albuquerque, they hadn't lived on base. Fritzi's friends were the women whose husbands worked with hers—all officers. Fritzi had carefully organized her Friday night margarita party on the patio to include only the wives whose husbands were attending Beer Call at the Officer's Club with Joe. Now, she realized how naïve she'd been. It had never occurred to her that there were other members of the squadron, men who were not pilots or navigators, who wore stripes on their sleeves instead of insignia on their shoulders.

Clearly, she had a lot to learn about the Air Force and its hierarchy now that they lived on a base. Maude had just awakened her to

a fact of life: base housing was just as segregated as the neighborhoods back in Montrose. There, the "silk stocking district"—the
stately old mansions with the wide front porches and the white
columns like the one where her parents lived—occupied a discrete
section just north of the town square. West of the square were the
newer neighborhoods of small, neat shotgun houses, built for white
collar workers at the railroad and in the oil companies. Farther out to
the west were the newer suburban ranch houses on big lots, where
the new Ford dealer built his home. To the south were the poor white
neighborhoods, where blue collar railroad and oilfield workers lived.
To the east was colored town, small run-down houses where
domestic servants and small business owners for the Negro community lived. Outside the city limits to the east, there were shanties
inhabited by Negro sharecroppers and their families, while white
sharecroppers and cotton mill workers lived in trailers and shacks
outside the city limits to the west. The poorer the neighborhood, the
darker its residents. In Montrose, segregation was based on race. On
base, segregation was based on rank.

Back inside the red brick duplex, Fritzi surveyed the four brown
boxes that remained to be unpacked. They contained the most fragile
and least useful of their household goods: china, crystal, and silver
they'd received for wedding presents. To Fritzi, the fancy wedding
gifts were symbols of their domain away from Montrose, tangible
evidence that she was now Hera to Joe's Zeus. The only problem was,
there was no place to put them. They had a new Duncan Phyfe
dining table and chairs, but no breakfront or buffet to house the
china and silver she intended to use for elegant entertaining. She
spread a quilt for Linda on the linoleum floor in the living room.
"Here, honey, play awhile so I can get these things unpacked," she
said. Linda, always content with a pile of books, settled onto the quilt
and began turning pages in *The Poky Little Puppy*.

Fritzi opened the Venetian blinds in the dining space window and
looked at the tiny front yard, planted with thick green fescue. In the
Base Housing Handbook they'd received upon arrival, she'd learned
that it was their duty to keep the grass no longer than three inches.

Planting of shrubs, trees, and permanent landscape items was not allowed, but seasonal flower plantings were fine as long as no grass was removed. The rules also stated that the tacky blinds were "property of the U.S. Air Force" and had to stay in place. The blinds might look all right if they were framed with drapes. She had never learned to sew, but surely she could rig up something to make this place look less like a barracks and more like a home. There was so much about this generic space that needed the touch of a homemaker. For one thing, the walls were all freshly painted a peculiar shade of olive green, a color that darkened the rooms, making it necessary to read by lamplight during the day. The only good thing about the color was that it seemed to make handprints and scuffs disappear into its dull sheen. The rules were clear: "The Housing Officer maintains a strict schedule of painting and repairs to ensure that all quarters remain in good condition. Residents may not change the paint on any interior or exterior walls of Base Housing units."

Their duplex had two floors. Downstairs had a small kitchen, a living area and a dining area. Upstairs were two bedrooms and a small bathroom with green and brown tile. The kitchen was a small efficient place with an electric stove, a Frigidaire, and a sink. Three built-in wooden cabinets held their everyday dishes and glasses. A tiny window faced the back porch, a slab of concrete that the Base Housing Guide referred to as a "patio." Beyond the patio was a clothesline, which probably wouldn't get much use given the rainy climate. Beyond the clothesline was a large common lawn shared with another row of duplexes.

Upstairs, Fritzi had managed to fit their double four-poster bed into the master bedroom with just enough space to walk around on either side. Rand and Linda shared the second bedroom, furnished with two tiny twin beds, a bookshelf, and a chest of drawers.

In the basement of each building was a laundry room with a free washer and dryer. Back in Albuquerque, Fritzi had gotten used to going to the neighborhood Laundromat twice a week to wash their clothes. Having the laundry downstairs would be a new-found luxury, even if she had to share it with the family next door.

Forget it. There was absolutely no place to put the china and crystal. They could stay in boxes, and she could get a few things out for holidays when they gave parties. For now, she covered the boxes with the red-checkered tablecloth from the picnic basket they'd received as a wedding gift. With a sigh, she sat on the couch and lit a Chesterfield. She reached for a pencil and paper and began to make a list of items they'd need to spruce up the place: drapes for the front window and master bedroom, four area rugs, café curtains for the kitchen window. A pink bedspread for Linda's twin bed; a blue one for Rand's. They might have to share a room, but at least they could personalize their beds.

She had shopped at the commissary, but never at the Base Exchange. Would they carry things like curtains and area rugs? She doubted that. Joe had given her complete charge of the checkbook (he took care of the savings), and she knew they had only $27.98 to last until the end of the month. Buying anything other than food was out of the question. Besides, Joe took the car to the flight line and she had no transportation.

To hell with it. She stubbed out her cigarette in the ashtray. There was no way a bunch of store-bought drapes and rugs were going to turn this place into the kind of home she grew up in. It was up to her, now, to turn this place into the kind of home her kids would grow up in, and that wasn't going to happen sitting inside and contemplating the olive green walls.

"I have to potty," Linda said, tugging at her skirt.

"Well, hurry upstairs so you can do so," said Fritzi. "When you're all done, we're going out for a walk, to meet our new neighbors."

"Can I get a friend this time? Can I go to school like Rand?"

"Of course you can, Linda. But first, let's go introduce ourselves to the people next door."

FRITZI HELD Linda's hand and rang the doorbell on the neighboring duplex.

"Yes?" A chunky little woman with frizzy hair opened the door.

"Hello, I'm Fritzi Stoddard, and this is my daughter Linda. We're your next-door neighbors? I guess we'll be sharing the washer and dryer downstairs."

"Oh! I shoulda known, shoulda called on you like the Welcome Wagon when I saw the truck moving in your furniture," said the woman. "Come in, won't you? It's a mess, but I'll bet you recognize the floor plan."

"Thank you. We really can't stay. Just wanted to say hello."

The living area had a toy box plus a tired--looking sofa covered in chintz. In the dining area was a Danish Modern table with four chairs, covered with newspapers, magazines, and books.

"It's no problem, really." Her neighbor spoke in a brash, Yankee tone that was new to Fritzi's ears. Then she stuck out her hand for Fritzi's firm shake. "I'm Myrna, Myrna Shelton. I hail from Brooklyn, a long way from here. You sound like a real Southern belle. Are you?"

Fritzi laughed. "You might say that. I'm from Montrose, Louisiana. So is my husband, Joe. Lieutenant Joe Stoddard. We just transferred here last week. My older boy started school today, and Linda here is in need of a playmate. Do you have any children?"

"What? Doesn't the mess in the living room give it away?" She laughed and yelled toward the upstairs. "Levi! Babs! Get down here! We have company!"

Two dark-haired children with identical bowl haircuts appeared at the top of the stairs and raced each other down, tumbling, to the bottom.

"Hi! I'm Babs. This is Levi," said one of them. Levi held a toy airplane and zoomed it in front of Linda's face. Linda reached up for it, laughing, but Levi zoomed it out of her reach. The three children sped off into the living room and out the back door, onto the little patio.

"Be nice, don't go past the clothesline. Linda's mom and I are going to have a chat." Myrna told them. She cleared two places on the sofa, where they could keep an eye on the "Have a seat, Fritzi. I'm sorry, but I don't have any coffee—fresh out. I could give you a glass of water if you like."

"No, thanks. I don't mean to interrupt your morning, but I just wanted to introduce myself. In case we run into each other doing laundry or such. How old are Babs and Levi?"

"They're five. Twins, wouldn't you know? They're about to drive me nuts, but hey, that's what kids do. Linda?"

"She's four. Very active, curious. Looks like they are getting along fine out there. And we have a son, Rand. He just started first grade today."

"Oh, yeah. I hear the elementary school isn't too bad. It's not New York, mind you, but not too bad. Some of the teachers have masters' degrees, I'm told. Wish they had a kindergarten. The twins are dying to get out and do something other than go to the playground and run up and down the stairs. Oh, my husband is Leonard. Len. Lt. Len Shelton. He's from Brooklyn, too. Want one?" She offered Fritzi a Kool.

"Oh, thanks, I'm dying for a cigarette. I'll pay you back—just didn't bring my purse with me."

Myrna reached for a fancy lighter on the cluttered coffee table and they both sat there for a moment, smoking. "We moved here, let's see, it'll be three months ago next week. It's not a bad place. A lotta rain, cloudy. But at least there's a green space for the kids to play, and I can't complain about the free washing machines downstairs. It's a palace compared to the little apartment we had in Brooklyn. Len was serving in Korea, and I had to move in with his crazy mother. Me, the twins, two cats, and my mother-in-law, all in a fifth-floor walkup. It was the pits."

"I know what you mean. Joe was just in Korea as well. We'd been out in New Mexico, but when he went overseas, I went back to Montrose and lived with Mother and Daddy. They have a big old place, plenty of room, but I just about suffocated from the heat and humidity and, well, you know...I was used to being the head honcho of my own hacienda, so to speak, and to move back to Montrose was like going back in time."

Myrna laughed out loud, hearty as a donkey's bray. "Honcho of the hacienda. That's rich! I hear you, my friend. Base housing is the bee's knees if it gets us out from under the old homestead. Life in the Air Force sure beats Brooklyn. At least, so far."

"We've never lived on base before, and I've got to tell you, it's just as segregated as it is back home. I was at the bus stop this morning seeing my son off. I met another mother there, invited her by for coffee. She tells me, 'No, you live in officers' housing. We can't be friends.' That was quite the shock!"

"Yeah, well, you'd better get up to speed, sister. There are rules in this world, rules that apply to you and your kids. Believe me, there are lots of rules!" Myrna stood up, went to the table in the dining area and rummaged through magazines and piles of books. "Here! I knew I had it somewhere! Len's commanding officer's wife gave me this right before he left for Korea. If you don't have one, borrow mine." She handed Fritzi a book as thick as a dictionary, bound in blue with silver lettering: *The Air Force Wife.*

Fritzi thumbed through, amazed. "My lord! This looks like Mother's old Emily Post."

"You got it, but believe it or not, people in the Air Force really care about those rules. Of course, you being a Southern belle and all, you probably grew up proper, with doilies and cloth napkins. For me, it was a real eye-opener. What to wear to a Commander's Call. Calling cards. How to greet senior officers in a receiving line. It's all there!"

"What about being friends with enlisted families? It really hurt Linda's feelings when that woman and her little boy refused our invitation. Is that true, that enlisted wives and officers' wives can't be friends?"

"Sort of. Believe it or not, your husband, as an officer, could get in trouble for it. If that woman's husband was under your hubby's command and you were buddies with his wife and kid, your husband could get criticized for showing favoritism because you had befriended his family. Fraternizing with the underlings—that's a no-no. Rank has its privileges, but also its responsibilities. And in the Air Force, rank is everything."

"I can see I have a lot to learn. Are you sure you don't mind if I borrow this book?"

"Be my guest. I've got it imprinted on my brain. It's a real life-saver."

"Thank you so much, Myrna! I mean, *can* I call you Myrna, or is that against the rules?" Fritzi laughed.

"Yeah, you can call me Myrna. Our husbands are both lieutenants. If we outranked you, it would be Mrs. Shelton. I'm not kidding!"

Fritzi opened the back door and called to Linda, who was up to her elbows in mud under the Shelton's clothesline.

"We're making mud pies!" Linda said, grinning widely. Her plump face was streaked with the product. Fritzi laughed and went outside to take her daughter's hand.

"We'll take the short cut home, straight to our back door," she said to Myrna. "Thanks so much. Next time come and call on us!"

AFTER LUNCH, with Linda bathed and down for a quick nap, Fritzi dug deeper into *The Air Force Wife*.

When the mail came, there was a letter from Mother. She was worried about Fritzi's "accommodations" up there, in what Mother imagined to be the frozen North. Also, crime. Had she read about some murders in Seattle? Did they ever see bears? How far were they from the mountains, the ocean?

Honestly, Mother had no sense of geography because she'd never been anyplace. She loved Fontainebleu; that was her world, her pinnacle of ambition. She had married the Judge, whose family were wealthy cotton brokers, and he had inherited the home. A feudal situation, really. Complete with servants, who, like their slave ancestors, were Negro. Daddy had been a few places, back when he traveled the circuit. New Orleans, of course, even Houston. He'd gone to law school at Harvard, but that was the last time he'd seen Boston. "Who wants to visit a big, crime-crawling city, full of Yankees?" he used to say.

Yankees and Rebels. They still talked in Montrose like people in the northern United States were the enemy. As if we hadn't all sent sons to fight in Germany and France, to the Philippines and into the far reaches of the Pacific. In those distant places, all those young Americans fought the enemies, real enemies, but her parents' generation still talked of Yankees. Southern tradition. Southern values. Like they existed anymore. The war had changed everyone. But aside from sugar, bacon, dairy, and gas rations, her parents seemed to live the lives they were used to—lives insulated by privilege and circumscribed by the Montrose city limits. They had no son to send to war; Daddy had been too old to be drafted, and besides that, he was a judge and a member of the Civil Air Patrol. Mother hadn't gone to work in the factories, because it wasn't appropriate for a judge's wife to work anywhere. Not to mention, there weren't any factories to speak of in Montrose.

Fritzi's children would be different. She would be a different mother. A better mother. Her children were bright, inquisitive, and she and Joe would show them a new world, where America was the greatest country and a victor in a war fought with superior air power. And her Joe was one of the pilots that had made that possible.

Joe had told her he was worried that she'd get homesick this far from Montrose. But, as she had told him when he made plans to become regular Air Force, her home was with him. Montrose was a steamy, swampy place, where her parents would do their best to smother any chance they had of building a life on their own terms.

She went back to reading *The Air Force Wife*, determined to learn the rules, backward and forward. In her experience, Fritzi had found that rules were easily bent and broken if you knew how to play the game.

6

 "Air Force children on the whole are well disciplined,
orderly, and courteous,
    but always remember they reflect you and their
home training."
    —Nancy Shea, *The Air Force Wife*

McCHORD AIR FORCE BASE, *Washington*
    1957

RAND WAS ALMOST three when Linda came along, a sister who liked
games and models and the same comic books he did. He and Linda
shared a room in the duplex on McChord and they were inseparable
on the playground. Then, when Rand was eight and Linda was five,
there was suddenly another sister: Debby, a tiny squealing baby who
threw their world off balance.

Up until Debby's birth, Rand had been Pop's "buddy," Fritzi's
"handsome boy," and Linda's best friend. When Rand saw Debby's

tiny pink face peeking out from her flannel receiving blanket, he could see a formidable otherness, something very unlike the sister he already knew. He assumed Debby would be like Linda, sturdy and lively and up for the next adventure. But watching Debby in the old bassinet that had once been his, Rand saw someone fragile, a delicate fairy princess sleeping under glass, a baby rabbit huddling in a nest. He could see her pulse throb through the top of her head, where he knew the bones had not yet fused, and it bothered him. He had to bite his tongue to prevent himself from thinking about sticking a sharp pencil into that throbbing place, just to see what would happen.

He didn't like that Fritzi had to fuss over the baby, boiling bottles and changing her tiny diapers. He didn't like that Pop got up in the mornings to make breakfast for him and Linda, because Fritzi had been up all night with the baby. He didn't like the baby's faint cries and blubbers that interrupted his sleep deep into the night, the sounds of her spitting up and the frightening gurgles. Sometimes, Linda would awaken in her bed and they'd whisper to each other: "Why can't the baby go to sleep? Why can't Fritzi make her stop crying?"

Once, the crying got so bad that their neighbor Mrs. Shelton came over in the middle of the night while Pop and Fritzi took the baby to the hospital. Rand and Linda, wide awake, had listened through the thin walls, heard the throw-up sounds, the gurgle. They heard the front door open and close, and Pop's voice downstairs and Mrs. Shelton saying, "No problem, really, don't worry about a thing. Just go."

Rand and Linda pretended to be asleep, but in reality they sat up with flashlights under the covers. He read a Superman comic book, while Linda looked at the pictures in the illustrated *Alice in Wonderland*. They were still awake when Fritzi and Pop returned just before sunrise, and they heard them tell Mrs. Shelton that the baby had to stay in the hospital, in an oxygen tent, for her breathing.

"That lucky Debby, getting to sleep in a tent," Linda whispered to

Rand. He agreed, imagining that the tent his tiny sister inhabited must be a plastic bubble of air that could fly. Lucky, indeed.

The next morning, no one got them up for school. They woke at ten o'clock to Pop making pancakes in the kitchen and Fritzi in the shower. Rand thought his parents looked like themselves that day. They didn't look like the sad, sapped out people they'd become the day Debby came home from the hospital.

He knew this memory stemmed from his selfish, unsympathetic view toward his new baby sister, but he knew Linda shared the same viewpoint. Together, they were a united front against this alien, this invader, Debby.

In 1959, Pop got promoted to Captain and the Base Housing Office moved them to a three-bedroom house a few blocks away from the duplexes. They no longer shared a laundry room with the Sheltons, and Linda could no longer wander out the back door to visit Levi and Babs. The Stoddards now inhabited a one-story ranch house in a neighborhood with higher ranking officers.

For the first time since Linda was born, Rand had his own bedroom. It was tiny, but it had a window that overlooked the small back yard. The previous owners had planted (against Base Housing regulations) a spindly willow tree between the house and the cedar privacy fence. Rand kept his blinds open at night, just to watch its limber limbs sway in the wind. Sometimes, they'd whip against his window, and he imagined them to be the arms of aliens, scratching, prying to get in, to kidnap him and take him on a space journey.

He saved up his allowance and his birthday money from his Montrose grandparents. Soon, he had enough to buy an airplane model kit for the B-52 Stratofortress. He would rather have bought a rocket ship, but he knew Pop had flown the Stratofortress, and he wanted Pop to tell him about it, to help him put it together. They could be buddies again; Pop could sit down next to him with some airplane glue and the blueprints and make something happen. Fritzi let Rand borrow the card table to set up in his room so he could spread out all the pieces. Rand was good at organizing, under-standing the blueprints, and setting each piece out in a logical sequence so they could begin building together. He borrowed Fritzi's colander and carefully rinsed all the pieces in the bathroom sink. (Fritzi told him this was only possible during Debby's afternoon nap, because now that she was walking, she'd want to grab all the pieces and put them in her mouth). Of course, Linda wanted to be part of the process, but Fritzi shooed her out and gave her a Betsy McCall paper doll with four outfits to cut out. Linda fussed and threw the paper doll and scissors across the living room, waking up Debby.

Quietly, Rand finished rinsing the parts for the B-52 and laid them carefully on a hand towel to dry. He folded the towel around the parts and transported them to his room, where he carefully laid it on the table. When he was sure he'd left none of the parts in the sink, he quietly closed his bedroom door against the squealing Debby, the ranting Linda, the yelling Fritzi.

"By God, Linda, I ought to swat you silly! Pick up that mess and throw it in the trash. March, young lady!"

"I want to build the airplane with Rand. It's not *fair!*"

He heard Linda stomping down the hall toward his closed door. Instantly, he grabbed the handle so she couldn't open it. With all his might, he held onto that handle while Linda, screaming and pounding, threw a fit on the other side.

"Let me in! I want to build! I want to build with you, Rand! I don't want a stupid paper doll. I want to build an airplane!"

Rand gritted his teeth and opened the door an inch. She grew quiet and looked up at him with pleading brown eyes.

"You can come in on one condition," he said.

"Just let me in. I hate paper dolls!"

"OK, two conditions. One, you shut up. Two, you stop saying 'hate.'"

"All right."

Linda marched into his room, her dark eyebrows gathered like storm clouds.

"Sit over there on the bed," he said. "You can watch me, but you can't touch any of this. It's very important that it stays in order."

"But I want to help. I want to build."

"You can, you *can* help. But first you have to watch. Sit on your hands so I'll know you're watching."

She did.

Fritzi, holding a whiny Debby on her hip, pushed the door open.

"There you are, Missy! Get back into the living room and clean up that mess you made! I mean every single scrap of paper, too. And leave your brother alone. He's trying to build a model."

Linda marched toward the door. On the way, she kicked one leg of the card table and sent most of Rand's model pieces to the floor. "Hate, oh hate!" she muttered under her breath.

Fritzi grabbed a hank of Linda's hair and forced her to her knees. Rand had never seen his mother so mad. "Pick those up, young lady! I've a mind to tan your hide! Apologize to your brother!" She held her hand high, ready to slap Linda's face.

Linda squinted at Rand through tears as she picked up the pieces. "Sorry." Fritzi let go of her hair.

Rand had to tamp down his anger. "Now just get out before you ruin everything!"

Linda stomped into the living room and began gathering the pieces of Betsy McCall and her "new school wardrobe."

"Give me those scissors," he heard Fritzi yell. "That's the last time I ever, *ever* try to get you interested in paper dolls, you hear? You had your chance, and you just tossed it out the window, Missy. You quit snooping on your brother and start getting interested in something for *girls*. Now go to your room. Get out of my sight."

By then, Debby went into a full squall, and Rand heard Linda stomp into the girls' room and slam the door.

He couldn't blame Linda for liking the models. They were much more interesting than a doll made out of paper. Still, he figured the house was calm for a while. He'd have the peace he needed to put the card table in order, so Pop could come home and help him start gluing the first pieces. He decided to put the B-52 in flying mode, with no landing gear. And when it was time to paint it, he'd ask Pop how to make it look like it was flying in combat.

That night, Pop didn't come home for dinner. He phoned and told

Fritzi he had to go in for a briefing and he'd be home around ten.
Fritzi packed the kids into the Ford station wagon and drove to
Burger Chef.

He was already in bed when Pop got home. Rand listened
intently from his room, cupping his hand to the wall he shared with
his parents' bedroom. Pop's briefing turned out to involve his
temporary duty assignment (TDY) to Elmendorf Air Force Base in
Alaska.

"Why *Alaska*?" he heard Fritzi slam a drawer. He could hear the
tinkling of ice in her cocktail as she took a sip.

"I told you, honey. We're flying supply missions up there to build
the new radar system. After I made captain, they reassigned me to the
62nd Wing. They've upped my security clearance, and tapped me to
fly the C-124. I'll train here and get my clearance by the first of the
June. First of July, I'll head to Elmendorf, and I'll be home at the end
of September. The time will fly, you'll see."

"A whole summer, Joe? Rand and Linda will be out of school;
Debby is still in *diapers*, for God's sake." Her voice was shaky, like she
was going to cry. Rand had never seen his mother shed a tear. He
tiptoed into the hallway to listen through their closed door.

"Fritzi, you can do anything! You could build the radar system
yourself in half the time it will take us. You've done a great job with
the kids—I know I haven't been a big help lately, but I am moving up
and I've got to prove myself in the 62nd. This is where the Air Force is
sending me."

Rand thought he heard soft sobs, some muffled blubbers, and his
father whisper "Oh, baby, don't cry." Then there was kissing, and the
regular moaning and shuffling sounds he was heard from their
bedroom.

The next morning, Pop woke Linda and Rand up early. Debby
was already up, in her high chair, and Fritzi was frying bacon.
Outside, the sun was just beginning to peek through the low cloud
cover. The dining table was set, and Fritzi told Rand and Linda to
take their places. Rand felt his heart begin to pound against his ribs
so hard he feared he was having a heart attack. Fritzi handed Rand a

plate of toast and set a platter of scrambled eggs and bacon on the table.

"Pop's got some great news," she said brightly. She was in a brown chenille robe, her hair bright as fire.

"Yes." Pop cleared his throat and shot Fritzi an odd glance. "Well, Rand, you and Linda understand that I'm a captain now, and I'm flying a new plane. The C-124, with the 62nd Air Force." He served himself a couple of slices of bacon and took a sip of coffee.

Linda blinked. "Yeah? So what's wrong?"

"Nothing! Nothing's *wrong*," said Fritzi, frowning at Linda. "Listen."

"I'll be going to Alaska starting the first of July," Pop said. "I'll be there for three months, working on a new radar system. I'll be home at the end of September."

Rand thought of the card table in his bedroom, the Stratofortress model he'd hoped to build with Pop.

"So what will happen to us?" Rand asked.

"Yeah! Are we going to Alaska, too?" Linda chimed in.

"No, you'll be here, at McChord, at the same house, starting at your same school in the fall. Fritzi will be here, and your life will be just the same," said Pop. He began to stuff eggs into his mouth and he didn't look up for a long time.

Debby started fussing and kicking her spindly legs against the high chair. She reached toward Fritzi.

"Just a minute, Deb." Fritzi abandoned her breakfast and took Debby into the girls' room.

Rand looked at Pop. "What about the model we were going to build?"

"Son, I'll work on it when I can with you. I'll bet you can be a big boy and finish it yourself, so you can show me when I get back, right?"

"Right." Rand looked at his napkin.

"Are you going to see some bears, Pop? Can you bring us some presents?" Linda said brightly.

"You bet, Sugar! But I have to count on you two to help Fritzi here at home. Rand, you'll be the captain of the house, and Linda, you'll be your mother's first lieutenant. Your mother will need all the help you can give."

"I want to be captain, too," Linda said. She stomped into the bedroom.

Pop put his and on Rand's shoulder. "You can do this, Son. I'm counting on you."

Rand nodded and excused himself, hiding his tears until he got to his bedroom.

IN THE THIRD week of July, Fritzi's father, "Judge," drove up from Montrose in his big black Lincoln. Rand liked everything about Judge —his tallness, his big fedora, the way he always smelled like shoe polish and pipe tobacco. Rand's memories of staying at Fontainebleu when Pop was in Korea were blurry, but pleasurable—afternoons fishing in the stocked pond. Lemonade, delivered in a red wagon, by Josie, the cook. Throwing balls for Hap, the old bird dog, to retrieve. Fritzi had been sick for a long time in the hospital before Linda was born. Rand had spent endless hours with Judge, exploring the outdoors and also in Judge's office, which smelled musty like important books, and where there was a special bell that summoned Miss Euna, his secretary.

Seeing Judge at the base house on McChord was all out of context, Rand thought, as he watched the Lincoln pull into the driveway behind Fritzi's station wagon. When Judge stepped out, he was still tall, with a skinny face that always looked slightly solemn.

Fritzi had been up most of the night with Debby, who was sick with another ear infection. She peered wearily through the kitchen blinds. Rand and Linda ran out, arms open. "Judge! Judge!" they cried.

""Where's my girl?" Judge called, holding his hat in his hand. He was wearing khaki pants and a short-sleeved striped shirt. "Y'all go back in there and get your mother!" Judge said, giving them each a quick hug. "Tell her I want to see her walk on out with the new baby!"

Fritzi ran her fingers through her hair, hoisted Debby to her hip, and opened the front door. "Daddy! It's so good to see you!"

"Darlin', you're thinner than you were last time. And you are looking worn out. Give me that baby girl so I can hug on her!" He reached for Debby and picked her up.

Debby promptly burst into tears. Rand and Linda stood awkwardly aside. It seemed to Rand that Fritzi was crying when she hugged her father. Next to Judge, Fritzi looked very small; not like a mother at all.

"Now, then, we're all going out to Howard Johnson's to eat," Judge said, opening the car doors.

"But, Daddy, I'm not dressed..." Fritzi protested.

"You look good enough for Ho Jo's, Sister. Come on, you all, let's get your mother out of the kitchen and go eat us some fried clams."

Howard Johnson's was a big restaurant out on the interstate, a large modern building with an orange roof that reached far into the cloudy sky. Inside, the tables were turquoise and the seats were covered in orange Formica. The place seemed to Rand like it had landed from some other planet. And the food! Linda and Rand ate two plates of the all-you-can-eat fried clam dinner.

"Now, then," Judge said when dinner was over. "Let's go home so Rand and Linda can get packed. We've got to make an early start in the morning!"

"What? Where are we going?" Rand asked, excited.

Fritzi sighed and put down her fork. "Your grandpa wants you to go with him for a visit to Montrose," she said, pushing her hot turkey sandwich around on her plate. "You're invited to stay for a month, and then fly home on TWA!" She ended the sentence on an up note, then smiled a pale smile and sipped ice water.

Rand and Linda exchanged excited glances.

"But what about you, Fritzi? And Debby?" Linda asked.

"Oh, you know Debby has asthma," Fritzi said. "It would only be ten times worse in Montrose. She and I are going to stay here, on base, while you two go off and have fun! It will be just like going to camp!"

"We've never been to camp," Linda said, her eyes wide.

That summer sealed the bond that Rand and Linda shared as the first-born of the Stoddard children. They drove four long days with Judge in the Lincoln, stopping at Stuckey's and A & W Root Beer stands from Tacoma to Montrose. Judge loved to drive, and would start off well before dawn, allowing Rand and Linda to roll out of bed and travel in their pajamas, with pillows and blankets in the back seat. Around noon, Judge would stop to refill his coffee thermos and let the children stretch their legs at a gas station. They changed into clothes in the back of the car and washed up in the gas station bathrooms. They spent three nights in Holiday Inns along the way, in Iowa, Kansas, and Arkansas. For Rand, the trip was a long, dreamy ride in the comfort of the Lincoln's velour back seat, days drifting into darkness, nights into Holiday Inns, where he and Linda swam in pools until their fingers shriveled and their eyes turned red from the chlorine.

"You children need baths!" Grandmamma held a handkerchief to her nose when they tumbled out of the Lincoln in Montrose. "Viola will help you get cleaned up. Run upstairs now!"

Rand and Linda did as they were told. When they were bathed and clothed in their clean pajamas, they sat down at the big dining room table to a baked ham dinner prepared by Josie, complete with scalloped potatoes and the fresh green beans.

"And for dessert, we have caramel layer cake!" Josie announced when dinner was finished. She brought out the tall confection on a crystal cake platter and began to slice into it.

"Oh, Linda and I will pass, Josie," said Grandmamma. "We're watching our figures."

Rand saw Linda's bright round face go slack. He could tell she was biting back tears. He wanted to embrace her, share his cake with her, but he dared not be defy their stern Grandmamma.

Later that night, Linda was bundled off to bed in the room that used to be Fritzi's, and Judge took Rand to the guest room, which he dubbed "the bachelor quarters." Both bedrooms opened onto the upstairs veranda. As soon as they were left alone, Rand heard Linda knock on his veranda door. He went outside and they sat on the wrought iron porch furniture, watching fireflies dart below on the grass. Cicadas chirped as night gathered around them.

"I feel bad about the cake. It wasn't that good anyway," Rand said.

"I hate her. I don't want any of her stupid cake." Linda crossed her arms over her belly. Rand could tell she was fighting tears. "I hate it here."

"Well, you'd better buck up, because we've got another three weeks before we can go home. It's really not that bad. I had a lot of fun here with Judge when you were a baby and Pop was in Korea. We'll go fishing, explore the land. You know, our family goes back for generations here. The Fontaines were some of the original settlers. People here think of our family sort of like royalty."

Linda laughed. "That's a load of crap. Grandmamma is just a mean old witch. I like Judge, but *she* hates me. She made me step on her bathroom scale before dinner, and she said I weighed too much for my age. You never had to put up with *that*."

"Well, how much do you weigh? I'll bet it's not all that bad. I don't think you're fat."

"I'm not telling! Fritzi thinks I'm fat, too. Grandmamma says we're going shopping on the square tomorrow for some clothes that 'fit properly.'"

"What's wrong with the clothes you have?"

"I asked her. She said a young lady like me should never be 'seen on the street in a pair of shorts.' Those were her exact words."

"Well, what are you supposed to wear in summer?"

"She says dresses. I hate her. I hate dresses. At least Fritzi lets me wear what I want."

In the moonlight, Rand could see a tear run down his sister's cheek. Linda sniffled and ran her finger under her nose to catch the snot. Rand went inside, grabbed a tissue and handed it to her.

"Thanks," Linda said, blowing her nose. She went inside and turned out her light. Rand sat out for a long time, thanking his lucky stars that he'd been born a boy.

THE NEXT MORNING, Judge had already left for the courthouse when Rand and Linda went down for breakfast. Grandmamma was in the solarium, reading the newspaper in her flowered bathrobe.

"Oh, good morning, dears! Come have a seat. I hope you slept well."

They took their seats at a round glass table set with flowered placemats and napkins. Josie appeared from the kitchen with a tray of eggs in fancy china cups. She set one at each place. Rand and Linda exchanged confused glances. Rand picked up his egg and tapped it on the table.

Grandmamma reached across and grabbed the egg from his hand. "No, no, no, dear! Hasn't your mother ever shown you how to eat an egg properly?" She set the egg—which thankfully, had not been broken-- back in the cup and took her seat. "Watch carefully and do as I do." She tapped the top of her egg gently with a teaspoon and broke off a small piece of shell. Daintily, she maneuvered her spoon into the soft-boiled white of the egg and took a tiny bite. Then she sprinkled salt and pepper on the egg. The next bite she took revealed the bright yellow yolk. She managed to scoop the yellow liquid expertly into the spoon without spilling a drop.

"Now, you try it," Grandmamma said. "Go on. Tap tap with the spoon. That's right."

Rand managed to tap the top of his eggshell off and capture both the white and the yolk in one bite. Linda, however, grew impatient after the first tap and demolished her egg with a hearty tap on the second try. The yolk, littered with eggshell, ran onto her plate in a yellow heap. "Ew. I really don't care for eggs, Grandmamma," she said, her face red. "In fact, I am allergic to them." Her mouth formed a firm line and she folded her hands over her chest.

"Well, your mother never mentioned that to me!" Grandmamma said. "All right. Josie, bring her some toast, dry, please?"

"Yes, Grandmamma, it's true. Linda breaks out in a rash if she eats eggs of any kind," Rand chimed in, confirming the lie. He felt for his sister. She couldn't catch a break in this house.

Linda sat and munched the dry toast, then washed it down with orange juice. She excused herself from the table.

"Linda, don't forget, we have some shopping to do. I'll send Viola up to help you with your hair. Try to choose something presentable from the things you brought."

That's how the rest of the visit went for his sister. While Rand was free to roam Fontainebleu, fishing and catching tadpoles under the watchful eyes of either Judge or Leo, the gardener, Linda was whisked away by Grandmamma to get prissified. One day, Linda was subjected to a beauty shop appointment, where she received a haircut and a permanent wave that made her dark hair curl around her round face and "show off her gorgeous brown eyes," as Grandmamma said. Linda also came home with pale pink fingernails and toenails, as she was subjected to a manicure and pedicure at the beauty shop. She was fitted with fancy new dresses. She wore one the next day, to sit by Grandmamma's side and observe her finesse at duplicate bridge. Linda wore the others, complete with itchy, hot petticoats, to accompany Grandmamma to a Garden Club luncheon, a DAR meeting, and a piano recital by a girl her age who was studying under the "renowned" Virginia Walden, who, according to Grandmamma, had "trained all the best Montrose girls—including your own mother." In the evening, as Grandmamma and Judge were enjoying a before-dinner cocktail in the front parlor, Linda was made to parade around in one of her new dresses with Webster's Dictionary atop her head.

"You're so lucky to be a boy," Linda told him at night on the upstairs veranda. "This is the stupidest place in the world and when I get home I am going to burn all these dresses and chop off all my hair."

Still, Rand admired his sister for putting up with Grandmamma's attempts to make her into a "little lady." He could see that his sister possessed something that he did not: faith that this, too, would pass.

7

❝ "Wise young couples have their children in the early
years of their married life if that is at all possible.
Sometimes, however, families cannot be planned too
accurately,
since 'Man proposes, but God disposes.'"
—Nancy Shea, *The Air Force Wife*

SEATTLE INTERNATIONAL AIRPORT

"SEE, Debby? That's where the plane will land." Fritzi pointed with
her lighted cigarette while her other hand held fast to the hand of her
youngest child. "Then Rand and Linda will get off and go come down
the stairs."

"When? When they coming?" Debby jerked at Fritzi's arm and
jumped up and down.

"Stop it! You'll tear my arm out of socket!" Fritzi said, stubbing out

the cigarette in the communal ashtray near the window. "Settle down,
Little Sis. They'll be here when they get here."

Exhausted, Fritzi took a seat facing the window and let Debby
run free in front of her. The child had so much energy, you'd think
her battery would run down. But not Debby. She was always wound
tight as a top, poised to spin in every direction.

These three weeks without Rand and Linda had been difficult,
but also easy. Debby demanded so much attention, and without the
older siblings around, Fritzi could give it to her. She'd taken her to
the Officers' Club pool every day, and later to the park with swings in
the green space behind the officers' quarters. She let Debby play with
other young children, and met the other officers' wives who popu-
lated the lounge chairs at the pool every weekday in summer. They'd
all sat and watched while their children played in the wading pool,
smoking, drinking iced tea, bundling their shivering children in
towels if it was a characteristically cool Washington morning.

But this summer had been hot, one of the hottest on record, and
enough sun to bleach Debby's fine blonde hair nearly white. Fritzi's
shoulders were peppered with tiny brown freckles, and just last week,
Fritzi noticed a small brown area had begun to appear on her face,
just above her right cheekbone. About a quarter inch of darkened
skin in the shape of Africa. She could style her hair to cover it on days
when she took the time to apply makeup and fix herself up. No one
else could see it, she convinced herself. But she could. And she knew
exactly what it meant.

She and Joe had conceived another child on his last night at
home. It was too early for her stomach to start lurching in the mornings, but she recognized the familiar mask of pregnancy on her face
the moment it appeared. She'd seen the same map of Africa on her
upper right cheek back in Albuquerque before Rand, and in
Montrose the summer before Linda. It seemed to her that her fair
skin was translucent, betraying all her secrets before the rest of her
body could confirm it through missed periods, hormone-laden blood
samples, and urine laced with pregnancy chemicals. She was indeed
expecting.

She'd been right to send Rand and Linda to Montrose with Daddy. She hated to do it, but there was a strange rage building inside her from the moment Joe had left for Alaska. Anger at her own abandonment, deep, crazy anger that crept inside her like a parasite and grew each day she had to manage Debby's demands, the squabbles of Rand and Linda over paper dolls and the Stratofortress model. Linda's refusal to be a girl. Rand's refusal to make friends. Debby's constant dancing, demand for attention, grooming, fussy eating, ear infections, fragile health. Everything. It was too much without Joe. Each night, they gathered at the dinner table and it was the same: fuss fuss fuss. Who was eating their vegetables? Who wouldn't drink their milk? Debby barely picked at food, while Linda wolfed down man-sized portions of everything. Fritzi had quit cooking after a while. Burger Chef was just off base, with a drive-through window, and the kids loved every bite. She even let Linda have milkshakes, and the poor girl's girth was growing to show for it. Let them stay up late, let them be wild, let them sleep till noon, but just make them quiet. Just make them leave her alone. The anger lay coiled in her gut, ready to strike like a rattler at any given child who threatened her short moments of peace. She feared that anger, kept it tamped down, for fear that it would take everything and everyone she loved and strangle the life out of them.

Then Daddy had shown up. She couldn't remember talking with him or Mother about the way she felt, but somehow he knew. He knew he should take Linda and Rand away, give them what they needed for a while, so Fritzi could get some longer moments of peace. Without Linda and Rand, she could handle Debby. She got a breather. Felt the anger die down a bit. Then saw the reason for it all: the map of Africa on her face.

She wasn't crazy. Just pregnant. School would start for the older children, and Joe would be home from Alaska in 30 days. She could make it now. It would be all right.

"Fritzi! Here comes the plane!"

Debby jumped up and down as she watched the silver DC-10 slide into place in front of the window. Ground personnel slid the stairs up to the door. Fritzi held her breath until she saw Rand, tall as a beanpole, appear. He was wearing a coat and tie, looking like a miniature lawyer or political candidate with his tall, erect posture (thank you, Joe, for the military example) and solemn, sunburned face. Then came Linda, dressed in a Glen plaid shirtdress, with white socks and shiny Mary Jane shoes. God almighty, her hair was short and curly, but she looked a bit taller, too, and slimmer. And like a *girl*. Fritzi lifted Debby onto her hip and flew down the steps, into the terminal, and outside to the tarmac. Her heart beat against her chest so hard she feared it might fall out, but she didn't care. Her kids were home. Home where they belonged.

And she wasn't crazy. Just pregnant. Thirty days, and they would all be together again with Joe. A family again. With a new member on the way.

Late at night, Fritzi sat at the dining room table and thought about what to write to Joe. She wrote him every other day, sunny news about the children's activities and their "exciting" trip to Montrose, detailing their flight home aboard TWA. She knew she needed to let him know about the new baby, but somehow she couldn't find the words. What could she tell him about this strange journey of carrying a child and caring for it once it appeared in the world? She knew Joe loved his children, saw them as proof of his virility and also proof of his mark on the world.

But for Fritzi, motherhood was neither proof of her status as a human being nor an especially joyful experience. She loved each child fiercely, but she was first to admit that motherhood was damned hard work. Being a mother had never been a specific goal for her, but once she had children with Joe, she dutifully assumed the responsibility and the workload. The job meant walking a thin line between vigilance and nonchalance, with the goal of raising obedient but independent individuals. It was exhausting, and sometimes, Fritzi felt overwhelmed by the challenge.

She had plunged into marriage with Joe because she was in love with him and his body. She knew all about "family planning" and she had tried the diaphragm. She hated sticking something inside her before making love. The act was so calculated, so cold. So much like the prick-teasing prudes she'd grown up with in Montrose. She wasn't one of them. She was an authentic woman, someone her mother would never understand; someone who reveled in the fierce love of her husband because it simply felt good.

The other wives she'd met that summer at the Club spoke of their children as though they were prodigies. "Ralph Junior is going to be a great pitcher for the Reds someday. He's already throwing no-hitters in Little League." "Just watching my Ruthie dance brings such joy to my heart. She truly has talent, and I just know she will be a big star someday." "My Gina, she's a scholar. Made straight A's last year, even though we had to move here mid-year. She'll go to a Seven Sisters school. Maybe Radcliffe." "Frank is a real brain. Not much for sports or girls, but he's so good at math it's scary." Blah blah blah. Even: "Carla's not very smart, but she has a pretty face, and she will make a great wife for some lucky second lieutenant."

How could these women project all that on a mere child? Of course, Fritzi had been guilty of recognizing Rand's exceptional intellect as a young child—she had reveled in his milestones, far ahead of the children of her peers back in Albuquerque. But as Rand grew up, he got shy. He didn't want to stand out in the crowd; didn't seem to care if he had any new friends on the new base. So Fritzi had stopped bragging, stopped projecting. She simply decided that Rand would be who he was going to be: brainy, handsome, shy. Artistic in a way most boys didn't care about. Deeply connected to his sisters and his parents. Rand was becoming his own person, and it was no longer up to Fritzi to project who and what he was going to *be*. He already *was*.

Linda, on the other hand, was a conundrum. She had taken over Fritzi's body while she was inside, sending her blood pressure through the roof and bloating her until the only way out was to deliver Linda to the world. Ta da! Large and in charge, unruly and smart-mouthed, no matter what Fritzi did. Competing against her brother for attention and recognition, although there was no contest, because Linda was big and plain and just not as smart. Linda had come into the world with her own agenda, and she made that clear by the time she was old enough to walk. Fritzi wouldn't dare project the path for this moody, stubborn child. Linda was carving out her own destiny; not by looks, but by sheer determination and the resolve never to be regarded as "normal." Fritzi loved her all the more for it.

Little Debby, born in 1957, with a heart murmur. Delicate and demanding at the same time. Asthmatic, colicky, prissy, precise. She was little, but she, like Linda, was a fighter. Fighting for attention, for a place in a family with two older siblings already vying for first place. At least Debby was beautiful. Tiny and blonde, Joe called her "Tinkerbell" when she first began to walk in her dainty, tip-toe manner. Debby was always dancing, seeming to hear some strange music from another realm that gave her caramel eyes a dreamy, trance-like gaze. The other mothers at the Club would "ooh" and "aah" over her tiny feet, her delicate eyelashes, her perfect white-blonde braids. The club women would project that Debby would become a dancer or a movie star who would play the mysterious, vanishing blonde. Fritzi laughed at their predictions on the surface— she wasn't one to naysay the predictions of the other wives—but in a repeated nightmare, she would see adult Debby playing a frail, stran-gled corpse in an Alfred Hitchcock thriller.

Fritzi had grown into motherhood as her children had grown into human beings. With Rand, Fritzi had fallen purely in love with the boy who had her looks and Joe's intellect. But with Linda, child-bearing had threatened her life and had produced a large, plain, dark-haired daughter who seemed oddly disconnected from the sugar-and-spice of little girldom. Fritzi felt bad for thinking that, but she did have to face facts that Linda was not a pretty child, and showed no promise of growing into a graceful, beautiful young woman. No ugly duckling/swan here. Just Linda, plain as dirt, competitive, and keen, with Joe's thick brows and large ears and the gait of a plow mule. Then Debby: demanding, sickly, a tiny kitten of a child whose mewling and wheezing robbed Fritzi of sleep, sanity, and joy. The petite three-year-old who looked so sweet but could stir up a tempest with the slightest whimper.

What had fatherhood become for Joe? With Rand, Fritzi sensed

Joe's jealousy of the little boy. She tried fervently to make it up to Joe in the bedroom once Rand was asleep. She managed to don the black negligee and the passion she felt for her gorgeous and brilliant husband. But he was in Korea when Linda was born; he had no place in holding his new daughter, looking into her eyes, and perhaps seeing something beautiful that Fritzi had not. As if to make up for his absence, he championed Linda at the expense of Rand, and this was not helpful to the day-to-day management of their children. Joe could throw everything out of balance just by giving into one of Linda's requests to read her a book, or recognizing the nice work she had done in setting the table. Fritzi could see Rand take in his father's snubs, see his beautiful face sag with disappointment, see his shoulders slump when he gave up on completing the Stratofortress with Joe. Then there was Debby, who demanded so much early medical attention that Joe had become their in-house paramedic, running the child back and forth to the base hospital, picking up prescriptions at the dispensary, occasionally fixing breakfast for Linda and Rand when Fritzi had to catch up on sleep. In the darkest nights while Joe was in Alaska, Fritzi wondered if her husband sought out temporary duty away from home, raising his hand every time there was flight training for an exotic new aircraft that could fly him far, far away from the pressure cooker they had created by having three very different and very demanding children. Now they were expecting their fourth. There would be challenges with four—more challenges than she cared to think about.

It really did make sense when she thought about it. Fritzi, full of fire and passion, determined to put Montrose in the rear-view mirror, and Joe, the handsome dark pilot who couldn't resist her—of course they had created challenging children. They couldn't possibly create cookie-cutter kids who would play for the Reds or become the perfect homemaker for a dull second lieutenant. They were the Stoddards, inventing their lives as they lived them, far from the conventions of Montrose, in a new world that could welcome the challenging genetic mix that only they could concoct through their lovemaking.

Fritzi loved each of their children in a way that sometimes frightened her. She would kill *for* them, but sometimes she just wanted to kill *them*. This was the challenge of motherhood. She knew each of her children better that they knew themselves. In the end, there was truly nothing to worry about. They had been conceived and nourished in her body, and they were now present in a world where she and Joe could offer them travel, education, excitement in discovering each new base and each new adventure that lay ahead. Their children were poised for a future that Fritzi could never have imagined growing up in Montrose.

She recognized the irony in letting Daddy pack up Rand and Linda and take them to Montrose this summer, when she needed a break from the cacophony. She knew that Mother would try to girlify Linda, and she knew they would treat Rand like a prince and let him have the freedom he longed for. She knew Linda would likely grow to hate her grandmother for putting her on a diet and making her conform to the Montrose ideal. (Fritzi herself had been made to conform, and the result was spectacular in Mother's eyes, because she'd won a beauty pageant.) But these experiences, she reasoned, would be good for both Linda and for Rand. They were safe there, in the care of her parents, although there would be expectations for manners and appearance that weren't enforced all the time at home. It was, as Joe would say, "good training for young officers" to experience different challenges. Fritzi, after all, was worn out. She needed the time, and when it was all over, she knew Linda and Rand could turn their backs on Montrose with renewed appreciation for their three-bedroom ranch house on McChord Air Force Base.

A fourth child. How could she put that into words? Fritzi stubbed out a cigarette and closed her eyes. Perhaps a fourth would balance the fracas, provide a counterweight to three individual siblings vying for recognition. If there was another girl, perhaps Linda and Debby would bond in playing with her, dressing her up, teaching her how to hold her own. If, pray God, there was another boy, oh! How happy that would make her, and Joe would be crazy with joy! Rand could have a brother, someone to balance his hermit ways, someone to make him a more regular guy. A baby boy could have no better brother to look up to than Rand. Fritzi shook the thought from her head. Better not to tempt fate by wishing for a boy and being disappointed by a girl. Whoever and whatever Baby Stoddard #4 was, he or she would just *be*. Projecting a life on a mere fetus was only creating a delusion; a delusion that no real child could possibly live up to.

Fritzi was, after all, 39 years old. The doctors would tell her that she might have a mongoloid child. They might recommend a therapeutic abortion. Let them. She knew in her heart that whoever this child was, she and Joe had created it, and it would be born to take its place in their family.

SHE WROTE to Joe every other day. The APO in Alaska was unreliable. Sometimes he might get four or five letters at a time, all out of order. He wrote her back once a week, printing in his ALL CAPITALS block letters, that he appreciated the news from home, wished he could be there to share the summer, but was obviously enthralled by the new aircraft he was learning to fly and whatever else they were doing up there. He couldn't write much about his work; Fritzi knew that it had something to do with radar detection to protect them from the Russians. Joe wasn't much of a reflective guy; she was lucky to get anything in writing from him at all—especially the LOVE, JOE at the end. He wasn't big on mushiness.

This child, this tiny new one that announced itself with a map of Africa on her cheek, would be a blessing and the last pregnancy for her. Of course, Joe would be thrilled. He was overjoyed at the news of each child, and he looked forward to seeing "who would come out next." He told her that together, they made magic. He loved her so much, he saw each child as a miracle sprung from her womb. Fritzi often had to remind him that their children were people, with individual brains and complex wiring, a genetic hodgepodge created by crazy passion between two people. As a mother, she had come to understand this and respect it. In her dreams, she could never have imagined having a daughter like Linda. The only thing they had in common was boldness, and Fritzi was thankful for that. A girl with so many strikes against her in the looks department needed to be bold —what would Eleanor Roosevelt have been without boldness? Her husband certainly wouldn't have been elected president with a big, ugly *meek* woman at his side.

Fritzi was no meek woman, no simpering little wife who would politely write to her husband to inform him that their fourth child was on its way. She put away the stationery and went to bed. Tomorrow, she'd send a telegram:

FOURTH STODDARD CHILD IS WHEELS UP
AND ON COURSE stop ETA: FEB. OR MAR.

8

❝ "Air Force children are tough, resilient, and self-reliant.
Early in life they learn to solve their own problems, to
get along with all classes and all kinds of people,
and to make necessary social adjustments."
—Nancy Shea, *The Air Force Wife*

MCCHORD AIR FORCE BASE, WASHINGTON

WHEN LINDA and Rand arrived in Seattle, Fritzi rushed forward and hugged them so tightly Linda could barely breathe. There was something desperate and scary about the way her mother held them, as though they would vanish again and never come back if she let go. Tears streamed down Fritzi's cheeks while she was smiling. Linda thought she could have stayed there forever, smashed against her mother and brother at the same time, inhaling Fritzi's smell: Shalimar mixed with the familiar whisper of cigarette smoke. Finally, Linda was home.

Debby jumped up and down outside their hug circle. When Linda caught a glimpse of her little sister, she could see Debby's hair was so blonde it was almost white. Debby also had a few freckles, and she was less like a babbling toddler and more like a little girl. She had on a red polka-dot sunsuit, red ribbons at the end of her braids, and white sandals instead of baby shoes.

Linda knew she looked different, too. The first thing Fritzi said to her was "My God, Linda, you've lost weight!" She said it like it was a compliment, and Linda took it as one. Linda wore a dress with an itchy petticoat; she couldn't wait to get home and change into some shorts.

"The two of you look like a pair of grownups! What did Judge and Grandmamma do with my kids?" Fritzi said playfully, ruffling Linda's hair. "Let's go get some ice cream, and you can tell Debby and me all about your adventures in Montrose."

Fritzi drove them—oh, how Linda had missed riding in the way back of the station wagon—to Dairy Queen. Over a chocolate-dipped cone, Rand and Linda told Fritzi about their visit. Linda let Rand go first, because she didn't have anything to say but how miserable she'd been.

"I caught a catfish in the pond down by the old horse barn," Rand said, licking his cone. "Judge took me down to the courthouse a lot. That old building is full of history, you know. Tons of marble, imported from Italy through New Orleans. Big pillars, Corinthian, they're called. Judge introduced me to lots of people; I got to see the bailiff swear people in while he was on the bench. The bench, you know, isn't really a bench, it's where the judge sits, and it's a big chair, behind a high desk so he can see everyone in the whole courtroom. The perspective from up there is quite interesting. It helps create the illusion that you, if you are judge, are looking out at a world that depends on your verdict. Verdict, you know, is the opinion, what the judge says, and…"

Fritzi cut him off and wiped some melted ice cream off his suit jacket. "Oh, you've become such a little man, haven't you? And you, Linda, are a regular little lady!"

Linda felt a heated blush bloom on her face. She licked the last bit of ice cream until she could bite into the cone. She crunched away at the cone, relishing every morsel. It seemed like years since she'd had anything so good.

"I don't want to be a little lady," Linda said, wiping her lips. "Grandmamma dragged me around town the whole visit with her, to her bridge group and her garden club. Those ladies are nice, but they are all boring and they smell like toilet water."

Fritzi threw her head back and laughed loud and long. Linda hadn't seen her mother laugh like that all summer. Something had happened while she was gone. It was like their old mother was back, the one who liked to laugh and eat ice cream. It was so good to be home.

A couple of weeks later, Linda started school at Elementary School #2 in Tacoma. Despite her summer weight loss, she was the tallest and biggest girl in her class, and she was proud of that. Her hair had settled down from the permanent Grandmamma had insisted upon, and she wore the dresses Grandmamma had bought her for school, minus the scratchy petticoats. She had a pretty teacher named Mrs. Higbee, who wrote assignments on the board each morning and promptly left the room for a coffee break. It was shaping up to be a great year.

TOWARD THE END OF SEPTEMBER, Pop came home from Alaska, and it was like a birthday and Christmas and the best day of your life all rolled into one. Linda had almost forgotten how handsome he was, with his slick black hair parted on the side, combed neatly above his wide, intelligent forehead. His dark brown eyes matched Linda's, and she loved staring into them. She had been the odd one out all summer, with her red-haired mother and brother and her platinum blonde sister. When they'd go swim at the Officer's Club pool, the other mothers asked Fritzi if Linda was a distant cousin or perhaps an adopted child.

"What on earth makes you think you can ask a rude question like that?" she heard Fritzi say to the lady who asked if she were a "natural or adopted child." "Linda is indeed our daughter—conceived by

Joe and me and brought into this world through my own womb, I'll have you know. She looks exactly like her tall, handsome father. Dark hair and eyes, olive skin. She is all *ours*."

Linda wanted to run to Fritzi and hug her, but she didn't dare let on that she was eavesdropping while paddling around the wading pool, pretending to be a seal.

Pop brought them each a gift from Alaska. For Rand, a small replica of the C-124 aircraft he'd learned to fly. For Linda, a book about the Iditarod dog race, complete with color photographs of championship sled teams. (She was thrilled, imagining mushing dogs through the snow, caring for the dogs, fending off predators that threatened them on their trek.) For Debby, he brought an Eskimo doll, with real fur on its parka.

"She's not a baby doll," Debby complained, pouting.

"I know, Tinkerbell. She's an Alaskan Eskimo doll. Eskimos are people who live up in Alaska. You can play with her just the same, but don't take her clothes off. They're meant to be kept on, so she can stay an Eskimo. All right?"

"But I wanted a baby doll."

"Don't be silly, Debby," Fritzi said. "You already have a baby doll. You don't have an Eskimo doll. And besides, this isn't Christmas. This is September, and we are celebrating Pop's homecoming. Y'all run on back to your rooms for a while and play with your new things. Pop and I have some things to discuss."

Linda watched Rand go into his room and put the new C-124 on the shelf with his other models. Debby slammed the door in the room she shared with Linda. Linda took her Iditarod book and tiptoed into the hallway, then crouch behind the bookcase that held their Encyclopedia Britannica. It was a great listening spot to hear what Fritzi and Pop were discussing in the living room.

"When did you say you have to report for duty?" Fritzi asked him. Linda could hear the tinkling ice cubes as they mixed cocktails.

"Not until November 15," Pop said. He sounded upbeat, like that was a long way off. "Long before the baby will come. We'll be settled at Wright-Pat by the time he's born in February."

"I said February, or March," Fritzi said, "And it could be a girl. There's no way to tell this early, and you know it!" She laughed a strange laugh.

They were kissing, Linda knew, because there were murmurs and little lovey sounds for a while. She peeked around the bookcase and saw Fritzi was sitting on Pop's lap.

"Baby, I'm so proud of you!" she said. "A test pilot! And maybe one of our newest astronauts!"

"Yeah, well, let's not count our chickens before they hatch, but it could happen. I'll be assigned to the unit that's doing all the zero gravity studies, and I'll be flying different jets on touch-and-go missions. No more long TDYs! I can help with the kids. And, my God, honey, I'll be there for you this time. I won't leave you hanging with a bun in the oven and three kids underfoot. I had no idea you were having such a time this summer."

"Come on, Captain, I didn't 'have such a time.' I can handle our kids; I signed up for this duty. But it was great when Daddy came and got Linda and Rand. They were constantly at each other, and Debby —well, she's a handful. I didn't know at the time that I was pregnant. You can't blame me for being a little nutty with a new one on the way!"

Linda held back a gasp. *A new one?* Another child? Rand and Linda—*at* each other? They were just normal, like they always were. Linda would rather hang around with Rand than anyone else, and Fritzi knew that. But Linda couldn't help it that she didn't care about the stupid Betsy McCall paper doll. She wanted to work on the Stratofortress with Rand. Did Fritzi send her away so Grandmamma could somehow fix her, make her a better girl?

Linda sneaked across the hall and tapped on Rand's door.

He opened ~~and~~ it a little and glared at her. "What do you want? Go look at your book. I'm busy with my models."

Linda put a finger over her lips and pushed her way into the room, closing the door behind her. "I just heard Pop and Fritzi say we're moving, to a place called Wright-Pat. And Fritzi is expecting another baby!"

LINDA AND RAND were stuck taking Debby with them on their last
Halloween to trick-or-treat in base housing at McChord. Rand had
put tin foil over a big packing box and cut holes in it for his eyes and
went as a robot. Linda wore jeans and one of Rand's shirts and tied a
bandana on the end of a broomstick and went as a hobo. Debby was,
of course, a fairy princess, wearing a frilly dress with a tin-foil crown
on her head. It was cold, and they all wore raincoats over their
costumes. Fritzi gave strict orders not to trick-or-treat in enlisted
housing because some of those people may not have enough money
for candy. "Just stick to the officers," she said.

WRIGHT-PAT TURNED out to be Wright-Patterson Air Force Base
outside of Dayton, Ohio. When all the furniture was packed and
loaded into a moving van, Linda was thrilled that they all got to stay
in the Bachelor Officer Quarters, which Pop called the BOQ, for a
couple of nights. They ate take-out fried chicken and watched
Twilight Zone on the black-and-white TV. It was a comfort, Linda
thought, to have the whole family sleeping in one big room—Pop and
Fritzi in a double bed, she and Rand on twin beds, and Debby on a
rollaway cot. The *Twilight Zone* episode that night had been particularly scary. An old lady woke up in her country farmhouse one night
to see a little space man, no bigger than a toy robot, walking around
her house and telling her what to do. Linda thought of Pop and the
possibility of his becoming an astronaut, which she understood was a
space man. Soon there were a bunch of other little space men, and
then, she really didn't know what happened to the lady because she
was too scared to watch. She burrowed under the covers and went to
sleep with the soothing sounds of her whole family, including the
new one inside Fritzi, watching TV in the same room. Pop and Fritzi
were right there to protect them. No space men could get them
during the night.

Pop said there wasn't any base housing available for a captain's family of four children at Wright-Pat. He'd gone looking in a nearby town called Fairborn and found a two-story red brick house with four bedrooms and one bathroom, a real basement, and a closed-in garage. "There'll be snow in the winters there, and we'll need to keep the car in the garage. Plus, the owner left a swing set in the back yard," he told Linda as they loaded the car early one morning. "It's a great place, and I can't wait for you to see it."

They drove for three days in the station wagon. Linda couldn't sit in the way back because it was packed with their luggage and some boxes they'd need until their household goods arrived at the new house. One of the boxes was full of Rand's treasured plane models: the C-124 and the half-finished Stratofortress. "I don't trust the movers to pack them," he had told Fritzi. "They're valuable and if they're broken they can't be replaced."

Fritzi, of course, obliged. Linda thought her mother let Rand do just about whatever he asked.

"But I wanted to sit in the way back," Linda whined, "And now there's no room."

"It won't kill you to sit in the middle seat with Rand and Debby for three days," Fritzi said, "We all have to make sacrifices when we PCS."

"PCS" stood for "permanent change of station." It annoyed her that Fritzi called it that, like she was some sort of military official instead of their mother.

THE HOUSE in Ohio had wooden floors and a real fireplace in the living room. Outside, there was a huge expanse of lawn, and a big, spreading maple tree that had just shed all its orange leaves in the front yard. In back was a closed-in garage big enough for two cars, and best of all, a swing set. It all felt like paradise to Linda. The only homes she'd known had been on an Air Force bases. Now, they were living in a real town, with a supermarket a few blocks over, sidewalks, and neighbor kids whose dads wore regular suits and ties to work.

There was a basement, scary and dark unless you turned on the light at the top of the stairs. Fritzi had, at long last, a place to put a washer and dryer, set up an ironing board and an old table for folding clothes. There was also plenty of space to run and play in the basement if it was cold or wet outside. Linda could draw with chalk on the cement floors. She and Rand took some of the bigger packing boxes and cut doors and windows in them, creating a playhouse. Rand insisted on taping waxed paper on the inside of the windows. With a Marks-a-Lot, he drew panes and shades on the waxed paper, to make it look more like a real house. Linda used up an entire purple crayon to color the front door. Rand drew shutters and colored them brown.

On the first floor, there was a kitchen big enough for a table and chairs, and, Fritzi pronounced, plenty of space for a dishwasher. "It's high time we got one, Joe. With our fourth child on the way, we ought to have every modern convenience we can afford. And we can afford one. I found one on sale in the Rike's catalog."

Pop, of course, bought Fritzi the dishwasher, as well as a new, larger television for the big living room. The tube on their old set was getting dim. They seldom watched it because all they could see were ghosts where the people ought to be. Rand claimed the old one for his room.

Downstairs, Pop and Fritzi had a large bedroom next to the bathroom. Next to them was a room for Debby, but just until the baby came. Upstairs were two more bedrooms, one for Rand and, at long last, one for Linda. The ceiling in her room was low and slanted because it was built directly under the eaves. Rand had to duck when he came in to visit, but it was just right for Linda. She had a yellow chenille bedspread that left red dot imprints on her face if she lay on top of it.

Pop was home almost every night, no more TDY, because now he was a test pilot. He flew all kinds of secret and not-so-secret planes at Wright-Pat. Now that Linda's room wasn't next to her parents, she missed out on a lot of their late-night conversations. However, Linda had eavesdropped enough to know that Pop was sort of a second-runner-up to become an astronaut. He knew several astronauts already in the program: Ed White, Gus Grissom, and he'd met Chuck Yeager. (Linda had never heard of them at the time, but years later, when Grissom and White were killed in the Apollo 1 mission. Pop always said they were "murdered" by NASA.)

That fall, Rand and Pop built roaring fires in the red brick fireplace. Linda couldn't wait to load the dinner dishes into the dishwasher so she could get one last swing on the swing set before dark. Pop and Rand built a sandbox in the backyard. Rand liked to say he was way too old to play in it, but he often posed some of the plastic dinosaurs from his collection atop sand hills, with twigs as trees and a bucket of water dumped to make a stream. He had an old Brownie camera, and he took strange black-and-white photos of those dinosaurs. He saved up his allowance to develop them and he pasted them in a spiral notebook, labeled with the date and the place of each "sighting."

Tommy was born in March of 1960. When Fritzi and Pop brought him home, he smiled at Linda. Unlike Debby, who cried like a banshee every night for months, Tommy was a happy baby, able to hold enough formula to sleep nearly through the night. Linda saw the love in her parents' eyes when they looked at him. At long last, they had an easy child. A child made of their dreams, an answer to prayers. (If they ever prayed. They never said, and she never asked.)

Linda wasn't jealous this time, like she had been with Debby. Linda and Rand joined together as a junior set of parents, always available to watch Tommy, play with him, diaper him. Debby, on the other hand, acted out. She was used to being the baby, and she took an instant dislike to their pudgy, grinning new brother. She grabbed toys out of his playpen, imitated his cries in a whiny, bitchy timbre, took his bottle away before he was finished. One time, Linda saw her "accidentally" poke him with a diaper pin. Tommy let out a wail.

"Get away from him, *now!*" Linda shouted at Debby. She looked at Linda with startled brown eyes and began to cry in unison with Tommy. She backed away from the changing table, holding her hands in the air as if Linda were about to shoot her. Tommy rolled on his side. He would have fallen to the floor if Linda hadn't stepped in to finish changing him.

Later, Linda told Fritzi about it. "I don't think Debby should be around Tommy without supervision," she said told her mother. "She means to harm him. I'm serious."

"Good lord, Linda, don't be ridiculous. Of course, she can be around Tommy. I'm sure it was just an accident. Don't get all Sarah Burn-heart about it. She's only four years old, for heaven's sake."

Still, Linda watched Tommy like a hawk when Fritzi wasn't around. She talked to Rand about it one day when he was in his room, applying decals to that stupid Stratofortress model that still wasn't finished.

"What if she really means to hurt him?" Linda asked him. "I told Fritzi about it, but she just said it must have been an accident. Debby, her little perfect angel." She made a face.

"I don't think she really means it," Rand said, shrugging. "But she's jealous all right. More jealous than we were of her. And at least we had each other. She's got no one."

"Why should she be jealous? She gets everything she wants. Fritzi still braids her hair every morning, and Pop calls her Tinkerbell. She prances around here like she's Princess Grace."

"Now who's jealous? You'd better pipe down, or you'll be the one getting the attention. The wrong kind of attention, if you get what you mean."

"Why, do you think I'm lying?"

"No, but I do think you're exaggerating. Sarah Burn-hearting, as Fritzi would say. Be careful, or they'll all turn against you and Debby will look like the victim. That's just what she wants."

"Well, what are we going to do about it?"

"I'd say, just watch, like you have been. Fritzi's usually around. I'll watch, too, just in case. Let's not let Debby be alone with Tommy, that's all."

"Swear on it?"

They spit in their right hands and shook on it.

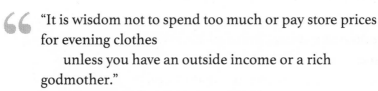 "It is wisdom not to spend too much or pay store prices
for evening clothes
    unless you have an outside income or a rich
godmother."
    —Nancy Shea, *The Air Force Wife*

FAIRBORN, Ohio

"GO AND GET you what you need, honey," Joe insisted. "A few new
things can't cost that much. Since I made Major, we ought to be able
to buy you some clothes."

"Are you out of your mind?" Fritzi handed him a bourbon and
water. "I looked at Rike's, in the Spiegel catalog. Even at the BX,
there's nothing that doesn't cost a fortune and look like something
the cat dragged in. Besides, we've got four children now. There's just
not a lot in the budget for haute couture, if you know what I mean."

"Well, there's no need for a field grade officer's wife to go around

wearing old clothes. We've got a lot of social obligations now. I want
you to look sharp, like I'm used to seeing you."

"Then come up with some major moola, Major, or this field grade
officer's wife is staying home. I wouldn't be caught dead in some of
the outfits hanging in my closet. In fact, I bundled them up and sent
them all off to Goodwill yesterday."

Fritzi sat on the couch next to him and took a sip of her drink.
The children were all in bed, finally; the homework all done, the
dishes loaded into the dishwasher, the TV off. The last diaper
changed. This was their time, a few minutes at the end of a long day
with a drink. A moment to catch their breath.

She watched Joe's temples throb, the way they always did before a
big announcement. "I bought that old Chevy today, the one Ed White
was selling. I figured I could use it to drive to work, so you wouldn't
have to shuttle me back and forth. Give you a little more space in the
day, right? Without having to bundle up the kids and go out to the
base twice a day? It was all for you, Fritzi."

"Great. An old car. Just what we need. You can drive an old car to
work and I can wear old clothes. Won't we be something? Here comes
the Major and his wife, or is it Ma and Pa Kettle?" Fritzi sipped her
drink and glared at him.

"Come on, baby. Gas is cheap, and I paid Ed cash for the car. I was
only thinking of you," Joe said.

Fritzi closed her eyes and took a deep breath. "Joe, I want to do it
all, do everything expected of me, without household help, without
the money for nicer things. Moving every couple of years. All four
children. The yard, the laundry, the Officers' Wives' Club. It's a lot,
Joe. I'm not sure you realize that it's a *helluva* lot."

"That's what you signed up for, Fritzi. You knew it. You wanted out
of Montrose, you wanted away from the small town life. Don't you
see? We are living the life we hoped for, the life we both worked for.
I'm a major now, and I expect to be on the list for lieutenant colonel
in a few years. I'm moving up, and so are you. Believe me, it's all
worth it. You are doing such a great job here. The kids are wonderful
—each different, each unique, but you manage to do it all. If it

weren't for you, this life, this life we've worked so hard for, would all fall apart." He pulled her close and kissed her gently on the lips. "And so would I."

Fritzi bristled. "You can't kiss this away, Joe Stoddard. You may be a hotshot test pilot and a major, but the fact is, it takes more money than we've got to live this life. We've got children to feed and clothe. They come first, of course. You wear uniforms, your clothes are taken care of. Me? I'm boycotting the OWC and the cocktail parties until I get some new clothes. If you can find money for a car, you can find some money to outfit your wife." Fritzi took her drink and stood up, heading for the bedroom.

"Don't be silly!" Joe swatted her playfully on the rear end. "Come back here and talk to me. Don't go storming off."

"You don't know stormy, not by a long shot, Major!" She slapped him across the face. "Sayonara. I'm going to bed."

Joe rubbed his reddened cheek and took a swig of bourbon. "Good night, then."

RAND HUDDLED at the top of the stairs and watched Fritzi get swatted and Pop get slapped. In all of his twelve years, he had never witnessed a fight between his parents. Even in the little duplex at McChord, where he could hear everything—their little kissing sounds, their moans, the honk of his father's nose-blowing, all the toilet sounds— he had not heard them speak harsh words to each other. As he grew older, their open affection for each other was an embarrassment, a mushy sentimentality that offended him. Now, as he watched his mother retreat to the bedroom, he fought the urge to run downstairs to comfort her, and also the urge to beat up his father. Drinking and fighting? Wouldn't Pop say it only happened in enlisted families? Families who had to struggle to make ends meet? When Pop had made major, there was a party at his office, and Colonel Zanger, the base commander, pinned gold oak leaf clusters on Pop's shoulders. They all lined up for a picture with Colonel Zanger. Pop had the picture framed and hung it in his office. Why would they argue about money after Pop's big promotion?

He watched his father below, sitting there, drinking, running his fingers through his thick dark hair. Pop's shoulders began to quiver, and he wiped at his eyes. Perplexed, Rand shifted his weight to get a better view. Pop was crying, not out loud like a girl, but silently, his shoulders shaking with sobs. Once again, Rand witnessed something he felt he could never speak about.

About a week later, Rand was doing his homework at the dining room table when the doorbell rang.

"Get that, Rand?" Fritzi called from Tommy's room. "I'm putting Tommy down for a nap."

Debby ran ahead of him and peered out the sidelight window. "It's a package!" she began jumping up and down, pulling at the doorknob.

"Hold on! You're too young to answer the door. Fritzi told me to get it." Rand pulled the heavy door open.

"Special Delivery for Mrs. Stoddard?" said a man in a brown uniform. "Can you sign for it?"

"Sure," Rand said, feeling manly as he held Debby back. "Mrs. Stoddard is my mother." He signed the clipboard and returned it to the man.

Debby ran into Tommy's room. "Fritzi! You got a present!" she squealed.

Rand looked at the package, wrapped in brown paper. The return address was a fancy sticker from Lois Jeanne's Ladies' Wear in Montrose. He laid it on the coffee table in the living room.

Fritzi, fresh from changing Tommy's diaper, rushed in, wiping her hands on a towel. "What in the world?"

Debby and Rand watched Fritzi rip open the package. "Of course, Mother would go to Lois Jeanne's," she said. He could tell she was trying to sound like she disapproved, but he could see the excitement in her blue eyes.

Inside, wrapped in pale pink tissue paper, were clothes, lots and lots of ladies' clothes. Debby squealed and jumped up and down, clapping her hands. Rand would normally be bored by looking at such things, but the delight in Fritzi's face was something new. His mother looked almost like a young girl, blushing as she pulled skirts, blouses, dresses out of the box—a magician, pulling scarves out of a top hat. The clothes and the tissue just kept coming.

Debby grabbed some of the tissue and wrapped it around her waist so it looked like a ballerina's tutu. Then she began dancing and singing, laughing, clapping.

Rand started to go upstairs and look at comic books when Linda appeared in the hall. "What's all the fuss?" she asked. "I was trying to read my history homework, but the noise..." She spotted the Lois Jeanne's box and picked it up.

"Fritzi! This is the place Grandmamma took me to buy all those dresses last summer. Looks like she sent you some things, too." She surveyed the couch, where Fritzi had draped a black crepe suit, a purple sheath, a fancy bronze cocktail dress with a poufy skirt, and a turquoise pleated skirt with a matching sweater.

"Yes..." Fritzi said, sounding far away. She was holding the purple sheath next to her body, twirling along with Debby.

Rand glanced at Linda, instantly confirming his observation: Fritzi was acting strange, prissy like Debby. It was as though a teenager had just invaded their mother's body.

FRITZI DIDN'T CARE. She knew Joe must have contacted Mother, but she didn't care. She *needed* these clothes. Joe knew she needed them, and they both knew they couldn't afford them. Mother was always looking for a way to insert herself into her life, so let it be. The clothes were beautiful. Lois Jeanne had known her all her life, and she had exquisite taste. She just hoped they fit.

"All right! You all, listen for Tommy. I'm going into my room to try these on."

"I want to come!" Debby whined.

"Nope. Private time for Fritzi only. I'll model them for you if you're good."

She scooped up the outfits and rushed to her bedroom. First, the suit. She needed a good suit. She ran her hand over the fine silk crepe, marveling at the way the light caught the black fabric and made it steely, then silvery, then dark as midnight. She tried on the jacket. From what she saw in the dresser mirror, the shoulders fit perfectly, the sleeves exactly bracelet length, meaning she could dress it up with long white gloves if she needed to. Before she dared try the skirt, she reached into the drawer and pulled on her Maidenform 24-Hour Girdle. Her heart soared with delight when the skirt zipped and conformed to her body. She stood on her dresser stool and looked at the hemline in the mirror. Perfect, just at the knee, showing off her firm calves.

She prissed and preened with each outfit, admiring herself and secretly wondering how Lois Jeanne and her mother might have guessed her measurements after four children. Wait until Joe saw her! The Major would be proud of his clever conspiracy to outfit his wife.

She knew the right thing to do would be to return the clothes, huffily, to Mother, insisting that Joe could afford to buy her nice things. But he couldn't, not with the four kids, and, by God, it was more important to have nice things and look good than to pretend she couldn't accept the favor. It was important to her as a major's wife, and it was important to Joe's career. She couldn't afford to be absent at Wives' Club meetings, or fail to show up on her husband's arm at cocktail parties. Now she could make appearances at all their social events in proper clothing. Not only proper, she thought, but a damn sight better than any other officer's wife she'd met at Wright-Pat.

"I WANT TO SEE!" Linda knocked on Fritzi's bedroom door. "Can I see the new clothes? How they look? Come out and model, Fritzi!"

"Come on in, honey," Fritzi said. There was a note of disappointment in her voice, but Linda didn't care. She couldn't stand to be locked out of the room when her mother was trying on her new things.

Fritzi was wearing the purple sheath.

"Zip me up? Be careful, Linda, not to catch the zipper. And don't bother with the hooks and eyes. I'm just trying it on for size."

Linda caught the glint in Fritzi's eyes and sensed that these clothes had transported her mother to another world. A glamorous, girly world, where she was still Miss Montrose. Linda wasn't sure now, if she wanted to be here, with Fritzi acting so un-motherly. Carefully, she zipped Fritzi's dress and ignored the hooks on the waist and at the top. Her mother turned and looked in the dresser mirror.

"What do you think, Linda? Is the color too much with the hair?"

Suddenly, Linda felt part of Fritzi's inner circle, not just another child like Tommy or Rand or Debby. Fritzi was asking *her* for advice!

"I like it. I think red hair looks good with purple. Like Lucy." They didn't have a color TV, but Linda could imagine Lucille Ball wearing the same color and looking fine.

"Mother always told me not to wear anything but brown, green, and blue," Fritzi said. "Lois Jeanne must have picked this out herself. My mother would certainly never approve!"

"Yes, Grandmamma definitely has her rules." Linda thought of the summer, shopping for what my grandmother called "suitable dresses for an Air Force officer's daughter, and the challenge of "finding something nice in the husky sizes." Until this moment, it was unimaginable to her that Fritzi had undergone the same scrutiny from her own mother. The way Grandmamma talked to Linda, Fritzi was a goddess, the likes of whom Montrose or the rest of the world had never seen. But Grandmamma had given Fritzi strict rules, too—not so much about her weight, but about her hair color. Now, she knew Fritzi understood what she'd been through last summer.

Fritzi ran her hand along the V-neckline of the royal purple dress. "I suppose this does have a lot of blue in it." She turned her back toward the mirror and looked over her shoulder. "Does it cup around the rear end too much? I did put on a girdle, so this is as good as it's going to look. Be honest."

Linda inspected the back. The dress conformed to her mother's shape, narrow at the waist, broad at the shoulders and hips. "It doesn't pull, like things do when they're too tight, if that's what you mean. I think it looks fine."

"Are you sure, Linda?"

"Yes, Fritzi. It looks *nice*." Linda knew too well how clothes looked when they were too tight. Stretched at the seams, pulling at odd angles in all the wrong places. Grandmamma had said Linda looked like a "stuffed sausage" in one fitted dress that was several sizes too small. Fritzi did not resemble a sausage casing in this purple dress.

Linda helped Fritzi out of the dress and watched her, sleek as a seal in her girdle, try on the other clothes. "Now *that* looks really nice!" Linda exclaimed when she tried on the turquoise skirt and sweater.

"You only like it because I look like a school teacher!" Fritzi laughed. "But you're right. It's perfect for PTA meetings. Thank you, sweetheart."

Sweetheart. Linda knew Fritzi loved her, but she wasn't big on endearments, except with Rand and Tommy. Her heart soared.

"My goodness, look at the time!" Fritzi exclaimed, regarding her watch. "I'd better get dinner on. Can you help me get these new things on hangers?"

Linda hustled to be of assistance, a lady-in-waiting, the new confidant of the queen. "Of course. Just get changed and go on. I'll hang these in your closet."

Fritzi pulled on her pedal pushers and buttoned her blouse. "You're a real jewel, Linda. Thanks."

She kissed Linda on the forehead. Linda's heart nearly burst with pride.

THE OFF-BASE HOUSE in Fairborn was paradise. Situated on a corner lot, there was room for a swing set, a sandbox, and plenty of green space to play catch. A hedge of wild honeysuckle grew behind the garage, a great place to hide and watch the bees at work in warm weather. In the two years they lived there, snow came in November and lasted through January. For the first time in his life, Rand could walk to a neighborhood school with Linda. They didn't have to ride a bus that tagged them as "base kids."

School itself was easy. He was in seventh grade now, smarter than most kids, because he'd been in Accelerated Math back at McChord. Math and most of science were a review to him. He was labeled a "brain," and he didn't care. At lunch, he sat ~~with~~ on the edge of a bench, at one of the back tables where younger kids sat. If he sat at the seventh grade table, Harold Potts would throw trash at him and call him an egghead. Potts, a big, ugly guy with a rash of pimples on his forehead, didn't scare him. Rand just didn't want to bother with the hassle. He didn't care if he had no friends. He had everything he wanted at home.

Every place they'd lived felt like home, really. Fritzi made sure of that, because she always put up curtains and arranged the furniture in such a way that gave the family a familiar path to walk from public to private spaces. But here, in the red brick house, he had a room upstairs, overlooking the vast green lawn. At night, he could open the window and look at the stars, or the clouds, or the rain. He loved to sit in bed and fold paper airplanes from pieces of used notebook paper. He could fold them different ways, crisply, so they had plenty of substance and so they formed a certain arc when he sent them sailing out the window. It was best at night, when he shined his flashlight into the darkness, and sent the paper planes into its guiding light. He imagined them on missions, like the ones he knew Pop had flown, and also faraway missions, into space, like John Glenn and Gus Grissom. His planes weren't ordinary jets. They were spacecraft, carrying heroic explorers to another world.

There were special parachutes, too. He fashioned them from Pop's old handkerchiefs. Rand took a needle and thread from his mother's mending basket and made the steering and bridle lines by puncturing each corner and tying them together. Sometimes, he would weight them with a rock and send them sailing through the air. Other times, he would take a plastic Army soldier and let him be the paratrooper dropping to undiscovered territory below. He tried tying some of his plastic dinosaurs to the lines, but they were far too heavy and dropped too quickly, without allowing the parachute to billow and catch the wind.

In the morning, he'd get up early and run outside to gather the fallen aircraft and parachutes. No matter what the weather, he would go bare-footed. The feel of the grass—*their own grass, in this large yard* —under his feet was important. He could gauge the seasons—hot, cold, wet, freezing—and take in the air. In the snow, he would dive outside and retrieve his aircraft as swiftly as he could, imagining a rescue mission in Antarctica. In the rain, he splashed out, a Navy Seal, retrieving survivors from a spacecraft downed in the Pacific. In the heat of summer, he took his time, careful not to step on the clover for fear of a lazy bee finding an easy target on his flesh. That was the best time of day, that early morning, when the air was cool and fragrant and there was dew on everything. Especially the wet handkerchief parachutes.

His sisters loved the swing set, but he just loved the space. A yard without a shared clothesline or a fence to block out the neighbors' view. In summer, room for a large wading pool where he could practice holding his breath under water and fill squirt guns to chase Linda and Debby. The sandbox, where he could take his dinosaurs and create a landscape, photographing them with the Brownie camera to give the prehistoric perspective.

He knew but didn't care that kids in his class went to birthday parties at the skating rink, or flocked to the community pool in Wayne Park. He didn't want to join Scouts either. All the other boys had grown up together, did all the Cub Scout stuff, and were now Boy Scouts. They went to swampy camps and earned badges for doing stupid things like killing small animals and cooking hot dogs over an open fire. Thank God Pop and Fritzi were too busy to coax him to join clubs or participate in sports.

The yard was his territory. He learned to mow with the hand mower, and took pride in the hard work of keeping the grass cut in summer. He swept the sidewalks and weeded the flowerbeds. He climbed the maple tree in the front yard and scared Linda by looking into her upstairs bedroom window. He pulled hoses around and hooked up sprinklers in the dry places. In winter, he shoveled the front walk and the long driveway.

Joe knew he was a good test pilot. He was the guy who'd landed the B-58 out of a spin, the guy who could fly instruments in any weather. But he was just a kid from Louisiana, a hard-working World War II vet who'd gone to Officers' Candidate School and loved to fly. An anomaly among the younger, college-educated men in Flight Test.

Still, Joe had flown the B-52 Stratofortress and the C-130 at record altitudes. He'd done all the zero-G testing and logged more hours than any other pilot in Flight Test. He'd flown the B-58 Hustler on hundreds of takeoffs and landings and recovered from a stall at 16,000 feet. Of course, he'd never told Fritzi about the stall.

But his days in Flight Test were over. They'd chosen Ed White for the Mercury program; Joe hadn't even been a close second. It made sense, White being five years younger and a West Point graduate; plus, the Air Force had sent White to Michigan for a masters' in engineering.

His commanding officer gave Joe a choice: he could join the Strategic Air Command and go to Offutt AFB in Nebraska as an operations officer. Or, he could go to Italy, as a NATO support officer with the Allied Forces Southern Europe in Naples, accompanied by his family, for a three-year assignment flying diplomatic missions.

It didn't take Joe Stoddard long to make his decision. He'd promised Fritzi she'd see the world, and now he could show it to her.

IN MAY, Pop came home excited and full of surprise: he'd been assigned to a NATO base in Italy. The whole family would be moving to a city called Naples once school was out.

Rand turned and ran out the front door. He ran all the way to the Woolworth's in the shopping center, as fast as he could, trying not to think, not to look back, not to imagine leaving this place, the grass in the yard, the snow in winter, the fireplace in the living room. He wanted to run forever.

He went into Woolworth's and ordered a Coke at the counter. He sat on a stool and slurped it down, then crunched on the ice when it was all gone. Then he walked outside and surveyed this American landscape: the Kroger, the Burger Chef, the Western Auto where he'd bought his bike. He would be leaving this, a real town, a place where they lived in a brick house with a fireplace and a lawn, where he could watch the *Twilight Zone* on television. Where people spoke English.

Rand went into the alley and puked up the Coke.

———

LINDA JUMPED up and retrieved the World Atlas from the encyclopedia bookcase.

"That's my girl!" Pop said. "Let's all see where we're going to call home for the next three years!"

Rand got up and walked out the front door.

"Where's he going?" Debby asked.

"Leave him alone. He's sensitive and just needs some time to absorb the news," Fritzi replied. She looked out the picture window in the living room. "He's going for a run. He'll be back in a while."

"I wasn't aware he was going out for the track team," Pop said quizzically.

"I didn't say he was. He's just going for a run," Fritzi replied. She lighted a Chesterfield. "He'll be back soon enough."

"The sooner the better," Pop said, shaking his head. "He's got to face facts. We're an Air Force family, and we will move every two to three years. He knows that. We can't get attached to one place, because there'll always be another!"

"As long as we're together, any place can be home," Fritzi said, stroking the top of Tommy's head. "Don't be so hard on Rand, Joe. We all have to adjust in our own ways."

In the dining room, Fritzi helped Linda open the atlas on the table and find the large map of Italy. She pointed to Naples, in the southern part of the boot, south of Rome.

"Will we be living on base?" Fritzi asked.

"No. We'll be on the economy, probably in an apartment," said Pop. "Or maybe a villa on the beach! We'll have to see when we get there. I put us on the waiting list for approved housing. We'll have a generous allowance, so we can get a nice place. There are American schools Naples, where Rand and Linda will go."

"What about me?" Debby jumped up and down, the prissy little prima donna.

Pop lifted her so she could see the map. "Tinkerbell, you can go to Italian kindergarten! When you're ready for first grade, you'll go to the American school."

Tommy toddled into the living room and looked out the picture window. "Buh? Where Buh?"

"He'll be back soon," Fritzi said.

Tommy's face scrunched and he worked up tears. "Want Buh!"

"Come here, TomTom," Pop said, scooping him into his arms. "Come on and let's see where we're moving! Look at the map."

Tommy shook his big head and launched into a full squall of woe.

"Oh, for pity's sake," Pop said, handing him to Fritzi. "My sons are a couple of sad sacks. The girls are the only ones showing any interest here. Linda, get the Britannica and let's look up Naples."

Linda jumped at the chance to comply, going to the encyclopedia case and retrieving Vol. 18, MY-NAZ. As fast as she could, she thumbed through the pages until she found the entry for Naples, Italy (Napoli).

"Naples is the capitol of the Campania region in Southern Italy. A bustling port, it is home to some 800,000 people, who make their living from fishing, agriculture, and port-related industry..." Linda began reading from the Britannica.

"Right, right," said Pop. "It's home of the Sixth Fleet, too, and the headquarters of Allied Forces Southern Europe. It was the most bombed city during World War II, under Mussolini. And, don't forget..." he made eyes at Fritzi "...the birthplace of Sophia Loren."

"Oh, stop it, Joe!" Fritzi said, reading the Brittanica. "Says something about a volcano . The ruins of Pompeii? Joe, I can't let you take us anywhere that's not safe."

"Relax, honey. Yes, there's Mount Vesuvius, but it's across the bay from most of Naples. It hasn't erupted in hundreds of years. We have the chance to live on the Mediterranean! Travel throughout Europe with our kids! Just think of the opportunities!"

Tommy had taken up vigil again at the living room window, searching for Rand. "Buh? Buh coming?"

Debby must have sensed the drama, so she started her own vigil. "Where's Rand? Did he run away from home? Is he *ever* going to come back?" She puffed her face out into a pout and started to work up tears. Linda ignored her, and, she saw with pleasure, so did Fritzi and Pop.

They were well into a celebratory spaghetti dinner when Rand showed up at at the back door, sweaty and pale. Linda had already wolfed down her plate and asked for extra meatballs.

"Come on in, Horse Fly," Pop called to Rand, "We've saved you some dinner."

"No, thanks, I'm just going to bed," Rand said.

Linda saw Pop's temples begin to throb.

"Say what, son?"

"I said I'm just going to bed. I'm not hungry." Rand stood in the kitchen doorway and locked his blue eyes with Pop's brown ones.

Pop stared him down for a second, but Rand didn't blink. Tommy was already in bed. He sent up a squeal from the bedroom when he heard Rand's voice.

"I'll just go say goodnight to Tommy," Rand said solemnly and started off in the direction of the bedroom.

"No, sirree. You go wash your hands and sit down with your family to eat a proper dinner that your mother has prepared. And you will apologize for running off."

"No. Thank you. I said I wasn't hungry." Rand turned his back.

Fritzi glared at Pop. Debby took a gulp of milk. Pop stood up abruptly, knocking over his chair. He grabbed Rand by the collar and bent his arm behind his back. "You follow commands in this house, son. Understood?"

"Leave me alone! I just want to go to my room!" Rand yelled. They never yelled at their parents.

Pop reached around Rand and kicked his feet out from under him.

"Good Lord, Joe! Stop!!" Fritzi said.

Pop wrestled Rand to the floor and held his hands behind his back. "What'd you say, son? What's that?"

Rand clammed up. Pop put his knee on Rand's back. Linda hadn't witnessed anything like this before. Their parents never spanked them, never had to bully them to behave. This was the first act of defiance Linda had witnessed from Rand, and the first time she'd seen Pop react physically.

"What's that?" Pop said calmly, holding Rand down.

"Don't be ridiculous!" Fritzi got out of her chair and threw down her napkin. "Stop this minute, both of you! I will not have my dinner table disrupted by a couple of thugs!"

"Get up like a man and apologize to your mother!" Pop stood up and pulled Rand to his feet.

Rand, his face blotchy and red, his hair wet and plastered to his head, gave Fritzi a stone cold stare. "I apologize, Fritzi, for being late to dinner."

"Get out of here, both of you!" Fritzi yelled. "Come on, girls, let's clear the table. Tommy's awake. You two boys go take care of the other little boy. Go on!"

Rand and Pop stalked out. Debby began to cry. Linda took one last bite of a meatball. She couldn't look up, couldn't look at her brother, couldn't bear to see the anger in her father's black eyes, the defiance in Rand's. Or the rage in Fritzi's. She did not want to know these people.

"Come on, Linda and Debby!" Fritzi said, gathering plates. "Let's get these dishes loaded up. Dinner is over."

Linda sat on the opposite side of the table, near the wall. Getting up meant scooting out past Debby, who was whimpering. Linda pushed her a little to get her going, and Debby dropped her milk glass, spilling milk all over the carpet.

"Here!" Fritzi threw a dish cloth at Linda. "Help her get it cleaned up. Milk will stain and go sour. The landlord will hold back our security deposit when we move. Blot it, then come in and I'll give you some Spic and Span to wash it."

Linda dutifully washed and scrubbed while Debby whined. Fritzi rinsed and loaded the dishes. Her deliberate clanking and crashing of silverware could be heard throughout the house.

Linda headed up to bed earlier than usual. Debby was now sharing her room, so Linda decided to oversee her sister's teeth-brushing and potty routine to placate Fritzi, who had stormed outside. Looking out into the dusky back yard, Linda saw Fritzi sitting in a lawn chair, the light from her cigarette traveling slowly back and forth to her mouth.

Linda watched her mother for a long time, wondering what she was thinking as she sat there, smoking. She was angry at Pop, of course, for being so harsh to Rand. But Linda wondered if she was also angry at the Air Force, for sending them so far away, to a place with a volcano, a place where they might have to live in an apartment. Fritzi went inside, and Linda heard the screen door slam. She tiptoed out of the bedroom and went across the hall to visit Rand, who was reading comic books and sulking.

"So, you're not happy about the move, huh?" she asked tentatively.

"Shut up. You know I'm not."

"But why? It's not like we have that many friends here."

"That's not the point. The point is, we'll never have a real home. We'll always have to pull up roots and go where the Air Force sends us. Because Pop wants an Air Force career. It just kills me, you know? Why can't he be like other fathers, be a doctor or an accountant, or a judge, like our grandfather?"

Linda had never thought about any of this. She had liked seeing Pop in all his different uniforms. She was proud when he made major, and always thought moving was sort of fun—they got to travel, eat in restaurants, stay in motels, figure out where the furniture would go in their new place.

"I think Pop is a great pilot and I'm proud of him!" Linda said. She didn't like to hear her brother disrespect their dad.

"So he's a great pilot. Maybe it's time for him to grow up and get a real job. Go to bed, Linda." He shooed her out and slammed the door.

10

 "All dependents transported overseas at government expense by surface carrier are required to receive certain immunizations prior to departure from the United States."
—Nancy Shea, *The Air Force Wife*

Wright-Patterson Air Force Base Hospital, Ohio

Tetanus, typhoid, smallpox. Fritzi took all the kids to the base hospital at Wright-Pat one afternoon, and *Bam!* Inject the arms and stamp the yellow vaccination forms. Debby, of course, screamed and cried like a banshee. Rand and Linda took theirs like troupers. (Rand, still in his sullen silence, wouldn't have flinched if he'd been hit by a sniper.) Tommy whimpered. When the shots were over, Fritzi loaded everyone up in the station wagon and headed for Fairborn. Tomorrow the packers would come and dismantle their belongings. After that, they'd be PCSing to Naples.

The June heat hung in the air like leftover sweat in a locker room. Rolling all the windows down and driving fast didn't seem to air out the station wagon. She let Debby sit in front and stopped at the Dairy Queen so everyone could get something cold. She let them all order what they wanted. They took their treats and sat outside on a picnic table, so they didn't drip ice cream all over the car. Rand got a swirl cone, Linda, a peanut buster sundae (the last thing she needed), Debby, an orange popsicle, and Fritzi shared a small dish of vanilla with Tommy.

She spooned a cloud of soft-serve ice cream into Tommy's eager mouth. The toddler smacked his cherry-red lips and grinned. Fritzi took a bite for herself and closed her eyes, relishing the creamy cold relief. Once they got to Italy, the State Department warned them never to eat local ice cream or other dairy products. Americans were at risk for hepatitis, as the Italian dairies did not pasteurize milk. What else was Joe dragging them into?

"Fritzi, something's wrong!" Debby squealed, tugging at her mother's blouse. "Something's wrong with Tommy!"

Rand, startled out of his cone of silence, was on his feet, snapping his fingers in front of his little brother's eyes. "Come on, buddy! Snap to!"

Tommy's cheeks were flushed red to match his mouth. He sat across from Fritzi, staring straight ahead. His pupils were dilated so wide in the summer sun, his eyes appeared to be black. His face had gone slack, void of expression. Fritzi felt his forehead. His skin burned beneath her palm.

"Quick! Just leave everything here! We're going back to the hospital!" She directed Rand to sit in front and hold Tommy on his lap. Linda lapped up the last bit of her sundae and Debby threw her popsicle to the ground, then jumped into the back seat. Fritzi floored the station wagon into traffic and headed back to the base. She glanced at Tommy, and he was chewing his tongue. Rand stuck his index finger in his brother's mouth, and the little one chomped down.

Fritzi didn't look, she just kept driving. The airman at the base gate waved them through, and she kept speeding until they reached the emergency entrance at the hospital. So what if she got a ticket and got reported on Joe's permanent record? Something was wrong, terribly wrong with Tommy.

The stout emergency nurse picked Tommy up out of Rand's lap and carried him behind the reception desk, into a room. "You children, go sit down in the waiting room and be quiet. Mama, come with me," she commanded, and they all obeyed.

Fritzi watched as the nurse lay Tommy down on the exam table and put up rails to keep him from falling. He lay there, stiff, with his black eyes open in an empty stare. For a second, Fritzi thought he might be dead.

She watched the nurse move with swift purpose, taking Tommy's temp and blood pressure. She took a moist towelette from a package and began sponging his face. "Your boy's temp is 102," she said. "They've paged the doc and he's on his way."

"What's wrong?" Fritzi asked fervently.

"Probably just a convulsion, no need to worry," the nurse said, "I can't say. I'm not a doctor."

"Well, goddammit, get the doctor in here!" Fritzi commanded frantically.

"Ma'am, we are working as fast as we can. You will have to leave if you cannot get yourself under control." The nurse's tone was calm but authoritative.

"Don't panic, Mrs. Stoddard, the doctor is here," said a voice behind her. "Stand back, please, while we look at your son."

An anemic looking young man in blue scrubs elbowed past her and washed his hands at the exam room sink. Then he began examining Tommy, looking into his eyes and ears, tapping his knee with a rubber hammer. "He'll come around here in a minute, I think. Nurse, set up an IV. We're giving him phenobarbital, Mrs. Stoddard. He'll be sleepy, but he'll come to..."

Fritzi felt like a spectator, watching these people hover around her son, inject him with an IV port and pump liquid into his veins. She stood against the wall, her mouth wide open.

In a minute that felt like a lifetime, she saw Tommy's eyelids begin to flutter. Finally, he closed his eyes and she saw his chest rise and fall like he was in a deep sleep.

"What the hell?" Fritzi asked.

The doctor turned to her. "Relax, ma'am. I understand your family got your overseas inoculations today. Some little ones react to all those shots, especially the toddlers. He's just had a convulsion, that's all. We'll do an EEG here in a few minutes to measure his brain waves."

"Relax? *You* relax, Doctor! Tell me what an EEG is. Tell me what's wrong with my son."

She felt the nurse's firm hand on her forearm. "Hold on, ma'am. There's no need to get belligerent."

"Belligerent? I'll show you *belligerent* if you don't give me some answers!"

The exam room door burst open and Joe was suddenly beside her, the armpits of his khaki summer uniform stained dark with sweat. "Doctor, we deserve to know. We're PCSing overseas next week, and we want to know—in English—what's wrong with our son!"

"Major Stoddard, sir. The doctor's rank wasn't apparent on his scrubs, but she guessed Joe outranked him. "It appears your son has had what we call a convulsion, an episode where he lost consciousness for a time. I realize your family got their inoculations today, and sometimes the shots—especially the typhoid—can cause convulsions in children under three."

"All right then," Joe's voice was calmer, even. "He looks like he's sleeping right now. What's the prognosis?"

"We expect him to be all right, sir, after he gets rest. His temp is already coming down to normal," said the doctor. "We're going to take an electroencephalogram while he sleeps, to measure his brain waves."

"What for?" Joe asked.

"To see if he has any unusual brain wave patterns that could mean something more serious than a convulsion occurred, sir. We gave him phenobarbital to help him sleep."

Joe put his arm around Fritzi's shoulders. She stiffened.

"It shouldn't take the presence of my husband, Doctor, for you to give me the same information," she said.

Joe nodded in agreement, but shot her a private glance that said "Shut up."

RAND PACED the waiting room like an expectant father. Debby settled down and flipped through the worn pages of an old *Ladies' Home Journal*. Linda picked at her cuticle and gave Rand anxious looks.

It was horrible, everything that was happening. Tomorrow, he'd have to give away his comic book collection, toss out a whole life he'd built for himself in the upstairs bedroom—his open window that brought him fresh air, a view of the stars, the cold magic of the first snowfall, the thrum of the rain, would close forever. Another family would be living in their house; the landlord already rented it. To top it all off, something horrible was wrong with Tommy. In his heart, Rand hoped that the problem with Tommy would prevent them from PCSing to Naples. He didn't want his brother to be sick, but surely the Air Force wouldn't send them so far away if the little guy had something seriously wrong. Some way, somehow, he prayed in his heart, prayed to the God his family addressed only at the Thanksgiving table, don't send us overseas.

Just then, Pop appeared in the waiting room. He looked wrung out, old, in a way that Pop never looked. His usually crisp khaki uniform was wrinkled, with sweat stains in the pits. His black shiny hair was usually slicked to his head, but now it tufted around his ears like bird feathers. There were wrinkles around his face and under his eyes, the whites of which were veined with red. Rand felt his heart quicken. Had Tommy died?

Debby ran to their father, who now stooped to embrace her. Not to be left out, Linda rushed forward and forced him to widen his embrace. Rand stood his ground in the corner, next to the table strewn with worn-out magazines.

Pop stood up. "Tommy's going to be fine. He's had what the doctor called a convulsion, brought on by all the shots. They gave him some medicine and they're running some tests, but the little booger is just fine!"

Debby jumped up and down, and Rand could see Linda's shoulders heave with a sigh of relief. Rand took a deep, strong breath and felt tears sting his eyes. Not now. He wouldn't show tears. He nodded solemnly at his father and stepped forward to join his sisters.

"Where's Fritzi?" Rand asked. No one had even thought to care about what she might be going through.

"She's back with Tommy," Pop said. "She's just sitting with him so he won't be scared."

"That was so scary, Pop, the way Tommy's eyes glowed at us! He looked spooky, like a zombie." Debby shivered and hugged Pop's legs for support.

"Well, are they sure he's all right?" Linda asked skeptically. "I mean, we can still move to Italy, right? And he can come with us?"

"Of course we can! We're going to move as a family, just as we always have," Pop said. He ruffled Rand's hair. "Right, Horse Fly?"

Rand gritted his teeth and nodded. "Sure."

"What's that?" Pop, his voice suddenly stern, asked.

"Yessir," Rand responded. No need to make a scene in the base hospital waiting room. His fate was sealed. He was condemned.

"Phew!" Linda said, obviously trying to lighten the mood. "I can't wait to get on that Pan Am flight and go across the Atlantic. It's going to be a great adventure!"

In that moment, Rand felt the bond with Linda dissolve. She had always been on his side. Now everything in his life was changed forever. He was powerless to change his fate, doomed to live through whatever faced them in Naples.

McGuire Air Force Base, *New Jersey*

Grandmamma had sent another care package from Lois Jeanne's

—a present for Debby and Linda, with a note that wished them a safe journey "abroad," where they should enjoy this little "travel trousseau." Debby and Linda each received mint-colored cotton dresses, sleeveless, with matching Kelly green sweaters. Linda's dress was in a husky size, with a Kelly green waistband. Debby's was hand-smocked across the yoke, and hung loose on her body, like a baby doll nightgown. These were to be their "airplane outfits" for the long flight from New York to Rome. Fritzi laid them out carefully in the temporary quarters they occupied at McGuire Air Force Base in New Jersey. They'd driven there in the station wagon from Ohio two days before.

The family's station wagon would travel by ship and arrive in Naples a few weeks after they did. Pop had sold the old Chevy he'd bought from Ed White. Their everyday life was suspended, with everything familiar gone. Linda felt a thrill of anticipation mixed with fear. She knew the Italy they were entering would not be Venice, and that they would not live on a canal. They would not be anywhere near the Vatican, where the Pope lived, or close to the Leaning Tower of Pisa. She had stared at the Britannica map for a long time, trying to picture Naples. She knew it was a seaport, that it had a volcano, and that it was the headquarters of the Allied Forces Southern Europe, meaning that's why Pop was assigned there. Could she learn to speak Italian? Would anyone speak English?

Pop and Fritzi gave strict orders on how Linda, Debby, and Rand were to act on the Pan Am flight. Debby and Linda were to wear the nice airplane outfits, of course, and Rand would wear a collared shirt, khaki pants, and a sport coat. Tommy wore a sailor suit shorts set. Pop, of course, wore his khaki summer uniform, and Fritzi wore a smart blue-and-white striped shirtdress Grandmamma had sent from Lois Jeanne's.

"We are representing not only our country, but also the U.S. Air Force," Pop said. "Be on your best behavior—no fighting, no whining. Say 'Thank you, ma'am,' to the stewardesses. Eat what you are offered without complaining. Keep your clothes neat and spot-free. Most importantly, keep your seat belts buckled at all times."

After that, he gave Rand and Linda each a package of Doublemint gum. "Save these for the flight. You can share yours, Linda, with your sister. Just give her half a piece, right after takeoff. You two should chew a whole piece, mouths closed. You will need the gum to keep your ears from having trouble due to pressure change."

Linda zipped the gum into the beige leather purse Grandmamma had sent her, along with the note: "Every young lady needs to learn how to carry a purse. Now that you are an international traveler, you should have a good handbag that will serve you well. Godspeed!" The purse was small, not much bigger than a wallet, but it was exquisite, lined in turquoise silk, with small pockets that contained a comb and a coin purse. Linda loved the smell, rich and earthy, and the feel, supple and soft, like a living thing. It closed with a gold zipper with a gold tongue that spelled COACH. Linda was thrilled with the grownup purse and being trusted with a whole pack of chewing gum.

They had spent two nights in the temporary family quarters at McGuire, the whole family in one big room. Fritzi and Pop slept in one bed, Debby and Linda in another double, Tommy in a crib, and Rand on a rollaway bed. They were all nervous, excited about the long journey, except for Rand, who sulked and read *Seven Leagues Under the Sea* without ever speaking to Linda. Linda settled into *The Secret of the Old Clock,* a Nancy Drew she'd bought with her allowance especially for the trip.

Before dawn the next day, they boarded a blue Air Force bus and headed for LaGuardia International Airport in New York. As the sun was peeking over the horizon, they boarded the Pan Am 707 and took their seats. Linda remarked on how everything on the plane was pristine, with freshly starched white cloth covers on every headrest. Much nicer than the smaller TWA plane she and Rand had taken from New Orleans to Seatttle. On this Pan Am flight, they sat three across, just behind Fritzi and Pop with Tommy. Rand claimed the window seat and Linda claimed the aisle, putting Debby between them.

The stewardesses were exquisite, Linda thought. They looked so stylish in their sharp blue uniforms, high heels, and caps perched at a smart angle over their stiff, perfect hairdos. She couldn't take her eyes off them, as they smiled and leaned over each row of seats, ensuring that passengers had fastened seat belts, offering magazines, and, for the children, official-looking pins with the Pan Am emblem. Linda promptly pinned hers to her green sweater, imagining herself as a sharp Pan Am stewardess, perfect and poised.

"Close your mouth, or you'll catch a fly," Rand chided, leafing through a *Boy's Life.*

Linda glared at him, clamped her jaw shut, and felt the heat of embarrassed blush creep up her neck. She had been ogling the stewardesses with her mouth wide open, fascinated by their composure, longing for their grace. Truly, she had never witnessed such beauty. She longed to be one of them as much as she longed to touch each one of them, to feel the smooth back of a hand, or get close enough to sniff their perfume. They awakened something strange within her, so prim and impeccable in their smart suits, yet somehow sensual and inviting, like sylphs flying through time zones, never needing to sleep or eat or refresh their lipstick. Linda was smitten, yet determined not to let her mouth gape or her eyes ogle so that Rand could notice. She popped some Doublemint into her mouth and directed her attention to Nancy Drew.

Somewhere over the Atlantic, the stewardess made a screen come down from the ceiling and directed passengers to "enjoy the latest film from Blake Edwards: *The Pink Panther.*" The smooth timbre of her voice, using "film" instead of "movie," and the way she pronounced "Panther" as "Panterrrre," drawing out the r's like a gentle growl, made Linda's stomach sink with longing. She had to close her eyes to imagine herself, morphed into a stewardess's height and weight, wearing that blue uniform, with her hair still dark, but twisted into a French knot and tiny, pearl earrings on her lobes. What was it like to be such a creature? To fly for a living, to pass out trays of chicken Kiev with the grace of a dancer, as though you never ate anything yourself but celery sticks and olives out of martinis? To have people say to you "What marvelous metabolism you must have" instead of buying you dresses in husky sizes? Linda

ignored the movie and pretended to sleep, making her own movie of
her future self as a perfect stewardess, who pronounced words with
a European accent, who worked for Pan American Airlines and had
her uniforms professionally cleaned and pressed, bagged in plastic
and hanging in the closets of the glamorous hotel rooms where she
stayed in her worldwide adventures. Her future self would have
long ago lost touch with her younger sister Debby, and her old
parents Fritzi and Joe lived somewhere nice, so she didn't worry
about them; a world where she bought Rand and Tommy expensive
gifts, but never had to visit with them or anyone else she didn't want
to spend time with. As her future self, Linda would make her
own world.

Sometime in her reverie, Linda actually dozed off. Debby's
intense sobs woke her.

"My ears! My ears!" cried Debby, putting her hands over them.
The plane was landing, and Linda hadn't given her any gum.

"Here, chew this," Rand said, handing Debby a whole piece. He
gave Linda a look of embarrassed disgust. "Linda should have given
you one a long time ago. Just chew the stuff."

Debby chomped with her mouth open and Fritzi turned around,
placing a hand on Debby's knee. "Hush, honey. We're landing, that's
all. Try and chew with your mouth closed, and you'll be all right."
Fritzi gave Linda the stink eye.

THE AIRPLANE TRIP WAS AN EMBARRASSMENT, sitting next to one
screaming brat sister and one fat, fawning one. Rand slumped in his
seat, trying to pretend he wasn't with them, wasn't part of this spit-
shined, "perfect Air Force Family," with his dad in uniform and his
mother smiling and gritting her teeth, praying, he knew, that they'd
get through the flight without a meltdown from the toddler Tommy
or another scream-fit from devilish Debby. He felt sorry for Linda, all
dressed up with her purse, in awe of it all, staring with her mouth
open at all the chic stewardesses, but at the same time he loathed her,

trying so hard to be grownup, clinging to her ridiculous little purse. He closed his eyes and tried to wipe them all from his mind.

"Ladies and gentlemen, we are descending over the city of Rome, on course for our landing at Fiumicino Airport. Those on the left side of the cabin can see the sunrise over the Tiber River, the bridge, and some of the buildings in the city..."

He was on the left side, and he was already taking it in. Below, it was as if the world he imagined had come to life, a splendid, glittering river, a city with spires and peaked roofs, a graceful bridge, and barges. No shopping malls, Burger Chefs, or motels with flamingo signs. He was arriving in Europe, a timeless place that had seen great wars and great triumphs. A place of beautiful buildings in cities that glittered at sunrise. A world, from this view, as Jules Verne might have imagined, a place of substance, yet a place of dreams.

The chatter of his sisters faded. The drowsy sullenness subsided. Rand felt himself wide awake, eager as a child, longing to experience all that was ahead.

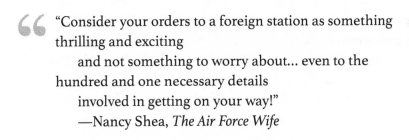

11

"Consider your orders to a foreign station as something thrilling and exciting
  and not something to worry about... even to the hundred and one necessary details
  involved in getting on your way!"
—Nancy Shea, *The Air Force Wife*

NAPLES, Italy

THEY MOVED into the Pink Building, so nicknamed by the Americans in Naples because the eight-story edifice on Via Manzoni was clad in pinkish stucco and orangey-pink glazed tiles. It was a modern palace, with sprawling apartments and views of the Bay of Naples.

Their marble-floored apartment, with three bedrooms, two baths, two balconies, two foyers, and maid's quarters behind the kitchen, was their new home. Outside their front door was a placard above the buzzer, where Joe had inserted his new calling card:

MAJOR JOSEPH R. STODDARD, USAF
ALLIED FORCES SOUTHERN EUROPE

FRITZI STUBBED out a Chesterfield and leaned over her sixth-floor balcony to watch the traffic on the street below. With four kids, they'd chosen the bigger apartment on the street side of the building, the one without the Bay view. The rent was less on the street side, so they were able to come under their housing allowance, which meant they could afford to buy cabinets for the kitchen and wardrobes to hang clothes for each bedroom. Fritzi couldn't figure why, with such beautiful floors and high ceilings, a modern building like this didn't have closets and built-in kitchen cabinets. They also had to buy five portable kerosene heaters, as the building lacked central heat. Marble floors, parquet wood doors, bathrooms clad in hand-glazed tile. Form over function—it was just the Italian way.

Fritzi had never lived anywhere so exciting. Compared to the stuffy base houses, and even the Ohio red brick house with the sprawling corner lot, this apartment was heavenly. A palace full of air and light, and windows they could open without screens, balconies that accommodated their collection of lawn furniture. Six floors up from bustling Via Manzoni, just two blocks from the American schools where Rand and Linda went. The children who lived in the building played in a large courtyard downstairs, gated from the street, with a cement driveway that snaked around the back of the building where they could ride their bikes.

With Rand and Linda at school, Fritzi enjoyed a few minutes to herself as Tommy napped and Debby scribbled in some coloring books. Joe worked outside the city at the Capodichino airport, flying diplomats from NATO all over the southern Mediterranean and into North Africa, Turkey, and Greece. Many of of Joe's passengers were VIPs, further distinguishing her husband as one of the sharpest of the pilots with AFSE. She knew it had been a blow to Joe's ego when he wasn't chosen to step up as an astronaut trainee, but that was life in the modern Air Force. Instead of chasing the life of a perpetual test pilot, her Joe had been true to his word: accepting an assignment that would allow their family to see the world.

It was wonderful, being so far from Montrose. Mother and Daddy would never travel internationally, for fear of catching disease or being robbed. Fritzi was safe here, safe from their intervention, safe from their judgment of the children. Fritzi felt even freer than she had when she and Joe started out in Albuquerque.

Yesterday, she put Tommy in a stroller and walked down Via Manzoni with all four children, to escort Linda and Rand to their classrooms at the American school. Her two oldest were attending classes with American and British teachers, all here to serve the growing number of American families assigned to Naples. There would be children in their classes who'd traveled all over the world with parents in the military or the diplomatic corps. It would be an opportunity for both Rand and Linda to expand their horizons; both of them were bright and curious. She worried a bit about Linda, who had grown plumper over the summer, and who'd insisted on cutting her hair in such a way that she resembled a chubby boy. And Rand— he'd been so sullen and close-mouthed for so long, was finally coming to life. He was the only one of the four who took interest in the museums and the history of Naples—going back to Napoleon and the Bourbons...he was renewed with enthusiasm about history and art. Now, almost in high school, he'd grown taller, more confident, and already was semi-fluent in Italian.

On the way back to the apartment with Tommy and Debby, Fritzi passed a young man who nodded at her. She nodded back, and the next moment she felt a pinch on her backside. Since she was wearing a cotton skirt and no girdle, she thought perhaps she'd been stung by a bee that had flown up the skirt. But when she turned, she saw the young man take off running, grinning over his shoulder at her, owning up to pinching her on her very American behind. Debby held on to the stroller and pointed at him. "Fritzi, that guy is laughing! Why is he laughing at us?"

"I have no idea," Fritzi replied, smiling to herself. She knew that a pinch on the rear end was a lewd compliment from an Italian man. She would keep it to herself, this pinch. Joe need not know; need not take offense at the gesture. She would tuck it away, in her working memory, to pull out whenever she was feeling like a middle-aged frump. She'd say it to herself: *I am a mother of four children, over forty years old. A man half my age admired me enough to lewdly pinch me in broad daylight.*

She held her head up, gazing at the lazy clouds in the bright blue sky overhead. Beneath the olive trees, a small farmhouse stubbornly held onto its turf between the Pink Building and the American school. A crude stucco wall sheltered the house and the yard, where chickens pecked in the dirt, from the constant traffic on Via Manzoni. Naples was a magical place, with no rhyme or reason, no zoning boards or suburbs with shoebox houses. It was at once charming and dangerous, fragrant with sea breezes or stinking from rotting trash.

Ahead, she could see an old man guiding a herd of tiny, horned goats through the traffic. In the stroller, little Tommy pointed and squealed with delight as he saw them approach. Debby ran a few steps ahead, laughing as she moved toward them. The goats ignored her, marching ahead in formation around her as though she did not exist. This caused Debby to cry. Never, ever enough attention for this one. Fritzi hurried ahead to stand beside her daughter, out of the path of the last goat in the herd.

"I wanted to pet them!" Debby cried. "They didn't even stop to let me pet them!"

"Darling, they aren't *pets*. They are going to their pasture somewhere, and they weren't supposed to get out of line, or they could get into trouble," Fritzi replied, brushing Debby's fine blond hair away from her damp face. She was such a pretty child, with honey-colored eyes and a pouty little red mouth. But Debby was never satisfied. Fritzi supposed it came with being the third of four children—wedged behind the intelligent duo of Rand and Linda, just ahead of the impossibly jolly, winning Tommy. Given a choice, anyone would rather play with Tommy or converse with Rand or Linda. Debby was beautiful, but needy and vacant, and, Fritzi admitted to herself, not all that likable.

"Let's go see if Joe has a Coke we can split, all right?" Fritzi said, tugging Debby's hand. "It's gotten awfully warm all of a sudden."

They were less than half a block from their home in the Pink Building, where a friendly Italian-American named Joe ran a small café on the ground floor. A swarthy middle-aged man with kind, dark eyes, Joe looked out for the Americans who lived in the neighborhood, and was always quick to serve up an ice-cold bottle of Coke. Fritzi could feel a full-blown tantrum coming on from Debby, so she told her daughter to stand on the back of the stroller and wheeled it ~~toward~~ toward Joe's, where the owner was just setting tables and umbrellas out on the sunny sidewalk.

"Signora!" he greeted them. When he saw Debby's pout, he pinched her cheek. "*Como si bella, bambina!* What can we do to make you smile?"

"They're both hot and tired. We thought Debby and I could split a Coke, and maybe just some juice for Tommy? If you bring it, I'll just put it in his sippy cup."

"Of course! Have a seat!" Joe pulled out a chair for Fritzi and helped Debby scoot up to the table in a chair of her own.

Joe brought the Coke with two glasses, one large and one tall. He poured the first for Fritzi, and the smaller one for Debby. Debby folded her arms and pouted.

Fritzi thanked Joe, and nodded to Debby to do the same. The girl sat silent, shaking her head. "Debby, you are being impolite," Fritzi cautioned, looking her daughter straight in the eye. "Say *grazie.*"

Debby's face softened as she looked at Joe, and all of a sudden she broke into what Fritzi recognized as a saccharine smile. "*Grazie mille,*" said the girl, batting her lashes.

Tommy sucked gratefully on his plastic sippy cup, which Fritzi had filled from the small bottle of apple juice Joe had set on the table.

Joe threw his head back and laughed heartily. "That little guy was pretty thirsty, eh, Signora?"

"Apparently so," Fritzi answered, relieved that Debby had straightened up. "We'll take the check."

"Oh, no charge, Signora," Joe said, shaking his head. "Consider it a *Benevenuto* to the building."

"Why, thank you, are you sure?"

Joe bowed and walked away. As soon as he'd turned his back, Debby knocked over her glass, sending sticky cola to the warm pavement. She looked defiantly at Fritz, who told her to pick up the glass. After she did, Fritzi grabbed Debby's arm, and pushed Tommy in the stroller into the building and onto the elevator. Debby wailed, crying in the elevator all the way to the sixth floor. By then, Tommy was fussy and had messed his diaper. As Fritzi unlocked their apartment door, Debby burst in and ran to her bedroom. Fritzi got Tommy changed and cleaned up for his nap. She could hear Debby, sobbing intermittently from the bedroom, but she chose to ignore her. In the kitchen, she found the bottle of bourbon and poured herself a drink. It was only ten the morning, but some days were bound to be longer than others.

Today, she'd poured an inch (or two?) of bourbon into a Dixie cup and enjoyed it with her cigarette on the balcony. She imagined that Italian women in the building might be doing the same thing, sipping grappa, a bitter, thick wine, while their maids prepared lunch. People here knew how to live. Even Joe occasionally drank grappa on his coffee break with the Italian officers at the base. Why shouldn't she have a bit of bourbon to top off a morning chasing a toddler and dealing with the demands of Debby?

Below, a man pushed a cart of vegetables and sang out as he came to a stop in front of the building.

"*Signora! Verdure freshche! Pomodori!*" He held up a plump red tomato for her to see... "*Signora—dai capelli rossi—il pomodoro si bello!*"

Below her, other heads appeared from lower balconies, but the man kept his eye on Fritzi. She shook her head and stood back so he couldn't see her. The tomato tempted her. Fresh tomatoes, fresh vegetables of any kind, were hard to come by in the commissary. Besides, there was something so Romeo-ish about his appeal from the street to her balcony. She peered over the balcony again. Downstairs, at least two maids from the building and a couple of other women had converged around the vegetable man, who was busy with them. The tomatoes were going fast.

The State Department had told them that buying fresh vegetables on the local economy was fine, but advised that they be soaked in a solution of water and Clorox before consumption. Italians, it seemed, sometimes used human waste to fertilize their vegetable gardens. She had Clorox; she had running water. The tomatoes were beautiful, and they'd be heavenly, just sliced, with a dash of salt and pepper. She would fry chicken tonight, make a mess of mashed potatoes. The meal would remind Joe of home, the farm, where he'd grown all kinds of vegetables. She needed some tomatoes, now.

Debby was still at the dining room table, coloring a picture of Snow White. "Look what I did, Fritzi!" she said as she saw her mother come in from the balcony.

"I love it! What a pretty picture!" Fritzi exclaimed, crushing the empty Dixie cup. "Listen, honey, I have to run downstairs for a second. Be a sweetheart and just keep coloring. I'll be right back." She grabbed a few *lire* from her purse and headed for the door.

Debby's face clouded and her lips poked out into a pout. "I want to go, too!"

Of course you do. But you're not coming. "I'll just be a minute, downstairs. Stay here and listen for Tommy." Fritzi dashed out the front door and down all six flights of stairs. No time to wait for the elevator.

The vegetable man was handsome. Probably fiftyish, but handsome in a sensual, Neapolitan way. Thick lips, dark eyes, fringed with thick lashes. He wore a starched white apron over an immaculate starched dress shirt, rolled up at the sleeves. Thick, graying hair slicked back from his forehead. A winning smile when he spotted her emerging from the front door of the Pink Building. "*La signora dai capelli rossi!*"

Fritzi felt hot blush creep up her neck as all the women gathered at the vegetable stand turned to look at her. She recognized two American wives from the building, one married to a Navy Ensign, the other to an Army Captain. Their husbands didn't work with Joe, thank God, and Joe outranked them both. Neither of them were likely to gossip about seeing her there; neither would know she left her five-year-old and her two-year-old upstairs. Fritzi put on a prim smile, and nodded.

"*Pomodori per la signora, si?*" He held up two obscenely round tomatoes, both red as lipstick.

"*Si, grazie. Quanto costa?*"

A shrill cry split the air. Startled, Fritzi looked up, expecting to see an exotic bird. Instead, she saw Debby, standing on one of the lawn chairs, leaning far, far over the sixth-floor balcony rail.

"Fritzi!! Come baaack!!" Debby wailed. "Tommy's awake!"

Heart in her throat, Fritzi grabbed the tomatoes and threw a thousand lire bill at the vegetable man. As she ran into the building, she heard the startled cries of the other women. "*No, no, bambina! Vai a l'apartamento!*"

The elevator was, by some miracle, waiting on the first floor. Frantically, Fritzi punched the button for the sixth floor. *Go, go, go. Don't jump. Don't fall, you little hysterical idiot Debby. I'm almost there.*

When she reached the sixth floor, Debby was standing at the elevator door crying. "I was so scared, Fritzi! You left us all alone!" She threw herself at her mother's body, forcing Fritzi to drop one of the tomatoes on the marble floor, where it splattered.

Fritzi's first reaction was to paddle Debby's behind, but she knelt and held the child close to her chest. Peg Cameron, the nervous little Navy wife who lived a half floor up, emerged from her apartment.

"My God, Fritzi, is everything all right?"

"Yes, Peg. Debby is just a little upset, that's all. We're going to go into the apartment now. Somebody needs a nap!"

"All right," Peg said, her hand over her heart, panting. "I just thought...I don't know, it just sounded like an emergency, that's all! Glad you and your little girl are OK."

Peg backed into her apartment and shut the door. Fritzi caught the suspicion in her neighbor's eye.

"I ought to blister you good, little lady!" Fritzi scolded when she'd gotten Debby inside the apartment. "You know you're never to go out on the balcony by yourself! You almost fell, Debby, do you understand that? Do you understand what would have happened if you'd fallen?"

Debby sobbed, stuck out her lower lip, and shook her head.

"You'd be *dead*, that's what. Do you know what *dead* is, Debby? Do you?" Fritzi had the girl by her shoulders, shaking her as if to wake her up.

Debby shook her head.

"It means that you would no longer breathe, walk, or *be*, Debby. It means you'd never grow up. We'd have to bury you in a cemetery, and you'd be *gone forever*. That's what *dead* means." Fritzi clenched her jaw and let go of Debby's shoulders. "It would be the worst thing in the world for your mama and daddy. What the hell were you thinking?"

"I don't like it when you swear."

"Well, I don't like to swear, but, goddammit, sometimes you drive me to it!"

A wail from Tommy's room sent Fritzi skittering down the hall. "Come on, now. Tommy's awake. You stay right by my side where I can see you, young lady. That's an order!"

Debby complied. All day long, she shadowed Fritzi, even following her into the bathroom, Tommy in tow. Every step she took, two little ones underfoot. Fritzi wondered if she should call Joe at the office to tell him what happened, but she hated to alarm him. It was an *almost* event, not a tragedy, after all. She poured herself two more shots of bourbon that afternoon. In a haze, she took Debby and Tommy out into the hallway with her to clean up the splattered tomato. "This could have been your brains, down there, smashed on the sidewalk," she whispered to Debby.

WHEN RAND and Linda returned from school, Fritzi laid down the law. Balconies were off limits unless an adult was present, period. She had Rand help her gather the lawn chairs and table and put them in the foyer. "When your father gets home, you can help him take these to our storage unit downstairs. We don't need to be sitting out on the balcony, anyway. We don't even have a view of the Bay."

"What happened, Fritzi? Why all the fuss?" Rand asked.

"Not a thing, honey. Not a thing. It just occurred to me that we have a hazard here. If you kids want to go outside, you have to do it on the ground floor. Just pretend the balconies aren't here. I can't risk any of you falling, and Tommy and Debby are so little, they just don't understand."

Fritzi saw Rand and Linda exchange glances. She turned to get dinner started. First, she soaked the surviving tomato in a Clorox solution. She fried chicken and boiled rice, heated up a can of peas. She'd have to tell Joe. Confess that she left the little ones alone so she could buy tomatoes. Confess that she left his little "Tinkerbell" screaming and wailing in the apartment, confess that the child climbed on a lawn chair and damn near fell to her death. It was, after all, her fault. She poured herself another shot of bourbon.

By the time Joe got home, she was pretty well sloshed, but dinner was on the table. Her family gobbled up the fried chicken, but she couldn't stomach a bite.

"I'm not well," she said, excusing herself from the table.

"You go on to bed," Joe said sternly. "The kids and I will clean up."

The next morning, Fritzi told Joe everything. The vegetable man, the neighbors, the screaming Mimi that Debby had become. How frightened she'd been to see their daughter leaning so far over the rail. In her panic, she'd wasted a whole *mille* on two tomatoes, one of which she dropped just outside the elevator.

"I don't know, Fritzi," he said, scratching his head. "You grew up with a lot of help. You've held us all together by taking on so much with these four kids. Lots of other families have maids—it's cheap here. Let's have a maid who can come three or four times a week, just to take some of the pressure off. She can cook and clean and watch the kids if you need to go run an errand, or even if you just want to have some time for yourself. Your mama had help, and you should, too. I need you to be involved in the Wives' Club more, make some more social connections on the base. A maid would give you a chance to do all that."

"Are you saying I can't handle our own kids, Joe?" Part of her was angry, defensive. "I know maids are cheap here, but you have to worry about stealing, locking up valuables, all of that. I've heard some stories, you know. And, I'm *not* my mother, in case you haven't noticed. I'm a hell of a lot stronger and more capable that she could ever be. Give me that much credit."

"Grow up, Fritzi," he said, anger in his eyes. "I get that you aren't your mother. But you don't have to martyr yourself and drive us all crazy, because, I'm telling you, these four kids are a lot. I'm going to have to be gone on some overnight trips, too. You need backup, that's all. I don't want to come home to a drunk wife, clearly exhausted by the demands of it all. That's not the woman I married. I'm not going to sacrifice you to the gods of housework and child care. I want you, *you*. Not a frazzled housewife. We're getting a maid, and that's it."

THEY GOT A MAID, a kind, sweet old lady named Assunta, right after Debby tried to jump off the balcony. Assunta came three days a week, did housework, laundry, and sang old songs. She spoke no English. Now that she had a little spare time, Fritzi braided Debby's hair, took extra care, dressing her in fancy clothes and playing Candy Land with her.

Linda understood that Fritzi was scared and must have felt guilty about Debby teetering off the balcony, but she had to admit that she was jealous, deep in her bones, of all the attention her mother gave her sister. She also had to admit that it settled Debby down. She quit being such a pill, throwing her little hissy fits all the time, making everything a desperate grab for attention. Now that Debby had managed to get positive attention from Fritzi, she calmed down like a tamed animal.

Sixth grade was interesting, in a classroom that overlooked the Bay of Naples and Mt. Vesuvius on the other side. Despite the idyllic view, the school was something like a prison camp. No talking during lunch, for example. This skinny third grade teacher, Miss Tomlinson, patrolled the cafeteria with a whistle around her neck. During lunch, you had to eat, period. If she caught you talking, you lost your recess. She didn't bother Linda too much, because she really didn't have anyone to talk to. The girls in her class were all OK, but they all had each other as best friends, and it was clear they didn't want or need anyone else in their little group. So, Linda sat, ate the bologna and cheese sandwiches Fritzi had made—she loved that her mother used German mustard—and tried to ignore Miss Tomlinson.

Her sixth grade teacher, Mrs. Federico, a nice-looking woman with curly gray hair, had the appearance of a kind, artistic grand-mother. She wore cotton smock-like dresses, and was always talking about art and museums the students could visit. Her husband was Italian, an artist, and they lived on the island of Capri. Each day, Mrs. Federico took the hydrofoil from the island into Naples. She liked to talk about this as though her students should be impressed, but Linda wasn't. The teacher had some pet girls in the class who lapped up her B.S. like starved kittens, but Linda and the boys just glazed over and let the woman talk.

It didn't take Linda long to figure out that Mrs. Federico didn't like her. She didn't know why, but she just gave off that vibe that something about Linda was offensive. Linda always scored 100 on the spelling tests, but Mrs. Federico would find some fault with each paper. *Poor erasure here. Make sure you erase neatly. Minus one point for leaving off the date. Skip a line when you number your paper.* Stuff like that, all written in red pencil. Sometimes, Mrs. Federico would forget to mark 100 percent at the top, even though the words were all clearly spelled correctly. Then there were her surprise "desk checks" that she recorded on the Neatness Chart. Federico would walk around the room and inspect each desktop, the book racks under the desks, and the floor around each desk. Her pet girls were all prissy little neat freaks. Linda was neat enough, but never good enough to earn a star on her chart. The other girls all got stars, while the boys (who were downright pigs, compared to Linda) and Linda got "minuses" next to their names.

After the desk checks, Mrs. Federico inspected each student's hands and fingernails for the Health Chart. Pet girls, stars. Boys, minuses. Linda kept her nails so short, no dirt could be found under them or around them, but Federico publicly called her out, more than once. "Now, Linda, your nails are clean, but look at your cuticles!" She marked a minus on the chart.

After Assunta came, Fritzi volunteered to be homeroom mother in Linda's class and in Rand's. Linda told her she didn't have to, that she didn't mind if Fritzi was too busy. Fritzi said it was her duty, because maybe some of the other mothers were enlisted wives who couldn't afford to bring cookies for the Halloween and Christmas and Valentine's parties.

So, on Halloween, Fritzi showed up about two p.m. with decorated cookies and Kool-Aid in the insulated jug they usually took on picnics. She wore the turquoise skirt and sweater from Lois Jeanne's; her hair flamed orange as a pumpkin in contrast. When Mrs. Federico saw her, Linda could see the surprise in her eyes because Fritzi looked more like a movie star than her mother.

"Class, let's all thank Mrs. Stoddard for bringing Halloween treats!" Federico had everyone stand and thank Frizi in unison. Linda felt sheepish and proud at the same time—proud of the way Fritzi looked, but also conscious that the pet girls and some of the boys were eyeing her suspiciously to try and figure out the genetic connection.

The class ate the jack-o-lantern cookies, the sugar ones that Fritzi frosted by hand with orange buttercream icing, and drank Dixie cups of orange Kool-aid during the last 15 minutes of class. After cleaning up around their desks, Mrs. Federico excused the students to go to their lockers. On her way out, Linda grinned and waved at Fritzi. She winked and smiled at Linda—just *Linda*, no Debby or Tommy or Rand within range. She swelled with pride.

Linda went to her locker for her homework books and returned to the classroom to walk home with Fritzi. Her heart began to race when she saw Fritzi looking at the Neatness Chart. Her mother raised one perfectly arched eyebrow in suspicion. Then she moved to the Health Chart. Her index fingernail, polished red, followed the minuses next to Linda's name.

"Mrs. Federico," Fritzi said to the teacher, who was tidying up her desk. "What do these marks next my daughter's name mean?"

Linda shrunk back into the hallway and listened.

"I give the students marks on their neatness and their grooming. How tidy their desks are, how clean their hands appear to be," Mrs. Federico replied. Linda heard her clunky heels walk across the floor to stand next to her mother. "As you can see, Linda needs some improvement in these areas."

"My daughter is a straight A student. She comes from a clean home, and I wouldn't dare allow a child of mine to leave our home without proper grooming," Fritzi said, laying on the Louisiana accent.

Fritzi was about to let Federico have it. Linda held her breath.

"Of course," Federico replied, syrup in her voice.

"Why, then, have you given my daughter deficit marks in these areas? What are your criteria?"

"Oh—just the general appearance of their desks, free of clutter, papers put neatly into binders, pencils sharpened. That's the Neatness Chart. And on Health, I look to see about dirty fingernails, make sure there is no nail biting evident, boys must have shirts tucked in, girls must have neat dresses."

"Are you honestly trying to tell me that Linda has dirty *fingernails*? She keeps them very short, I happen to know. She bathes every evening. I can't imagine she'd have dirt under her nails by the time she gets to school and attends your class every day."

"Linda has cuticles that need attention. She needs to push them back away from her nails."

"I'll see to it, then, that she does that. And what about her desk? I saw where she sits, and it appears to be satisfactory. Is there a reason she has these *minuses, these deficit marks*, next to her name on the Neatness Chart?"

"Linda sometimes fails to sharpen her pencils and keep them handy. Just little things like that."

"Well, Mrs. Federico, I can assure you that I'll speak to her about that. She appears to be the only girl with so many *deficits* next to her name. Is there a particular reason that, perhaps, that something about my daughter offends you?"

"Of course not! She is very bright. I must say, however, that she has failed to make friends with the other girls in class. She sits alone at lunch, plays with the boys at recess. I'm just encouraging her to fit in."

"By giving her *deficits* next to her name? That's a way to better assimilate her to a new classroom? Are you not aware that we are an Air Force family? That my husband's assignments demand that we relocate every few years? That most of these children are also military dependents, and how difficult that life can be?"

"Of course I am, Mrs. Stoddard." Federico sounded tense.

"Then why don't you let me do *my* job—I'll make sure my children are clean and neat—and, by the way—Linda earns good grades on her own, because she is a bright young woman—and you do *your* job. Run a sixth grade classroom, without judging my child on her conformity or her cuticles."

Fritzi packed up the picnic jug of leftover Kool-Aid and met Linda in the hallway. She couldn't look Fritzi in the eyes, afraid she would start crying out of sheer admiration. They walked home to the Pink Building together.

12

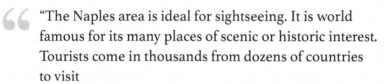 "The Naples area is ideal for sightseeing. It is world
famous for its many places of scenic or historic interest.
Tourists come in thousands from dozens of countries
to visit

Pompeii, Capri, Ischia, Sorrento, Amalfi, Ravello,
and Vesuvius.

These are easily accessible to all personnel
stationed there."

—Nancy Shea, *The Air Force Wife*

Naples, Italy

WITH EASTER VACATION coming up soon, Fritzi announced that she
wanted the family to go to Rome on a three-day tour. It was a bus
tour, organized by the AFSE Officers' Wives Club, with three nights at
a hotel and guided tours of the Vatican, the Coliseum, the Pantheon,
Fontana Trevi, and the Spanish Steps. Basically, a see-it-all, Ugly

American forced march through Rome. Rand would rather swallow razor blades.

"Honey, it sounds fine, but let's be realistic. A toddler, plus three children, on guided tours with a bunch of people from the base?" Pop raised his eyebrows and took a bite of pot roast.

"It's just time that we showed the children some of the culture of Italy," Fritzi said. "All they do is go to school, all you do is go to work. We're here! Why don't we take advantage of some of the sightseeing opportunities?" She put her napkin down and reached for her pack of Chesterfields.

"I want to go to the beach," Debby said. "I don't want to go on tours."

Linda just sat there, eating. She wouldn't let her eyes meet Rand's. Tommy laughed and kicked his high chair.

"Somebody stinks," Linda said, lifting Tommy from the chair. "I'll change him."

"Thank you, honey," Fritzi said, lighting a cigarette. "You're so helpful. See, Joe? We've got a helpful daughter to make traveling easier. We should team up and see Rome as a family. It's only three days, and a great bargain." She blew smoke toward the ceiling.

Rand picked at his food. Cigarette smoke made him lose his appetite.

"What about you, Horse Fly?" Pop asked.

"I don't know. I'd really like to see Rome, but I'm not sure about a bus tour. Seems like we could get there on the train, start walking around, and see what we want to see. I'd like to see the Sistine Chapel, but not the whole Vatican. The Forum. Some of the catacombs. Just not sure this bus tour sounds very interesting, Fritzi."

"That's my boy!" Pop said. "There's nothing I hate more than being marched around and made to look at a bunch of art ... and here's a Bellini... (he affected an Italian accent)...and over there is a Lugosi, the dark period..." He made vampire teeth at Debby, who squealed.

"If you're not interested in art, Joe, I can just go with Rand. *He's* interested. *He* understands that this is a chance of a lifetime." Fritzi tucked one leg under her skirt and flicked cigarette ashes onto the remains of her dinner. "He's tall, almost fourteen but looks older, and even speaks Italian, so he can communicate for me."

"Then what are we supposed to do, if you two go off, galavanting into art galleries? It's Easter Vacation for Linda and Debby, too. And someone will have to take care of Tommy," Pop protested.

Rand excused himself and began to clear the dishes. He brought his mother an ashtray from the living room. He hated it when she flicked ashes onto her dinner plate. He wanted to see everything, drink it all in, at his own pace. If he could go with Fritzi and leave the rest of the family behind, he'd be able to do that. No whiny little Debby, no obstinate Linda, no toddler antics from Tommy. No being called "Horse Fly" if Pop wasn't there. Suddenly, the whole trip sounded like a dream come true.

Rand filled the sink with hot water and added soap. (They sold the dishwasher before they left the States.) "Linda, come on! I cleared, you can wash!" he called down the hallway to Tommy's room. "I know you're back there... come on!"

"You don't have to shout," said Linda. "What's this deal about you and Fritzi going to Rome?"

"Sssh. I think they're working something out. Something that all of us will be happy about," Rand whispered.

"Good, because I don't want to be on a bus with a bunch of people we have to be nice to, and I don't want to go look at any more paintings and sculpture. I was hoping we could go to Luna Park one day next week. Maybe out to Pompeii for another visit," Linda told him.

Rand motioned to her to follow him into the hallway, just outside the dining room. He put his index finger over his mouth and the two of them stood there, listening. Debby and Tommy were in the living room, playing with blocks. Pop and Fritzi were sitting at either end of the dining room table.

"You know, Joe, family togetherness can be overrated," said Fritzi. "When was the last time you took leave? Why don't you take off a couple of days next week and spend them with Debby and Linda? Assunta can watch Tommy if you want to take them somewhere."

"I'll think about it," Pop said. "Lord knows I want you to see Rome, but I just don't have the stomach for the artsy stuff. If our son does, you'll have an escort. I won't have to worry about either of you. And with Rand, you could just take the train over, stay in a hotel for a couple of nights. You wouldn't have to do the tourist thing, on the bus from the base."

"All right. This summer, we can all go together, travel up to Germany. See the Alps. I'd commit to that, as long as I get my art trip."

"I'm due to take some leave. I'll see if I can schedule a couple days off next week. I'll see what Linda and Debby might like to do. There are plenty of things right here in Naples—Luna Park, the beach, maybe take in a soccer game. We'll find something we can all agree on. The weather is great this time of year."

"I'll check the train schedules and get with Rand to book three days in Rome!" Fritzi rushed to Pop and sat on his lap. "You'll see, Major Stoddard. The family that splits up for vacation is a family destined to stay together." She kissed him sensually on the lips.

Rand and Linda turned away, both beaming with delight.

ROME

THROUGH THE BASE TRAVEL AGENCY, Fritzi booked *pensione* in Rome, down the street from the Ponte de Sisto, where she and Rand would have adjoining rooms connected by a common bath. The pensione was an old mansion, bombed during the war, but restored by its owners, who made a living by renting out rooms. Thankfully, the owners spoke pretty good English, and what she couldn't understand, Rand could translate aptly.

Rand. She marveled at her son. Now almost fifteen, he was as tall as she, with bright auburn hair and piercing blue eyes. When they were together, it was evident that they were mother and son—two copperheads in the Easter crowds of dark-haired Italians. People noticed them on the street. According to Rand, one old woman asked him if his mother was the American actress Susan Hayward. Rand had replied no, but said Fritzi was a cousin of Jill St. John. The woman seemed impressed.

The pensione offered continental breakfast and a late supper—a great deal, especially for a three-day visit. Each morning, Fritzi would drink black coffee and nibble at some crusty bread with unsalted butter, while Rand chowed down on chocolate croissants, cannoli, and hot chocolate.

"Aren't you worried you'll break out in acne, honey?" Fritzi asked him on the second morning of their stay.

"Chocolate doesn't cause acne, Fritzi," he replied, "I read about it in *Scientific American*. It's strictly a matter of oily skin, clogged pores, and genetics."

"Well, then you're safe! Neither your father nor I had bad skin as teenagers. And Lord knows, you don't have to worry about being fat! You seem to be able to eat your weight and not gain a pound," she teased, ruffling his hair.

Rand shrugged off the attention. "Yeah, well... I was thinking today, we could take the bus over to the Spanish Steps, then see the Coliseum. I'm interested to see where the gladiators fought, but I don't want to spend the whole day there. How about you?"

"Do you know how nice it is to have someone ask me what *I'd* like to do on vacation?" She tossed her head back and laughed. "But, come to think of it, we never actually take vacations, do we? Just trips when we're transferring to a new base. Or trips down to Montrose to see kinfolk."

"You're right. It's great we could come to Rome without the little kids and Pop. You and I like the same things."

"And you, young man, are a great guide! Can you believe all the attention we're getting because of the hair? It's laughable, but also a lot of fun. I'm not sure Debby or Pop would appreciate it."

"Okay, so I'll take the lead here. How about we spend the afternoon in the Borghese Gallery? I've been wanting to see the collection there for some time. Especially the mysterious Titian's *Sacred and Profane Love*."

"Didn't Titian paint redheads? Sounds like an afternoon tailor-made for us."

THE BORGHESE VILLA ENCHANTED FRITZI, and they took in all of it—the gardens, the sculpture, the splendid beauty of the April afternoon. After walking the gardens in the warm sunshine, Fritzi was breathless—both from exertion and from the springtime beauty that surrounded her. Inside, she drew a deep gulp of air as she stood in the cool darkness of the villa. Before her was *Sacred and Profane Love*, depicting two red-haired women—one naked and one clothed, sitting on a bench that could also be a coffin, in front of a naked child (cherub?), also with red hair, gazing into the depths of the bench/coffin below him. What did the painting mean? Why was it painted? Who was sacred and who was profane? She posed all these questions to Rand, who turned instantly professorial on the spot.

"Meaning? I wouldn't want to guess the meaning. I'm just admiring the depth of color, the perfect composition. People are always ruining everything by looking for 'meaning' instead of just looking at art." Rand's gaze was intense as he regarded the painting. It was as though he could see the brushstrokes.

"I suppose you're right on some level. But don't be too existentialist, my son," she mocked his serious tone. "Sometimes a picture tells a story, whether the artist means it to or not."

Rand sniffed and gave her a cynical half-smile. "I guess. If you must make a story out of it, what story does this tell?"

"The way I see it, being a redhead myself, is that Titian was showing the dual nature of women—especially redheads. One is clothed and perfectly decked out. The other is naked, her hair free, her hand holding a lamp with flame. Not to embarrass you, dear, but it's all about propriety vs. lust. Thankfully, I found both in your father, and that's all I'm going to say about it!"

She saw Rand's face flush red. He was working his temples just like Joe did when he was chewing on her words. "OK. What about the child? What is its significance?"

"I don't know. Innocence? Curiosity? Look how he's dipping his hand in the water. It reminds me of you, the way you'd explore things in your thoughtful, intelligent way."

He shifted his feet back and forth. "All right..." He looked at his watch. "It's almost six. You ready to head back to the pensione?"

"My feet are killing me. Let's see if we can get a taxi, pronto!"

Signor Vitale, the owner of the pensione, stopped them as soon as they entered. *Per favore*, he said, he wanted to inform them that as it was a Wednesday evening, the courtyard at the pensione would be set up for dancing after supper. It was a springtime neighborhood custom, he explained. The Vitales invited neighbors in the residential area to mingle with guests. A local band would play until midnight, and he hoped it would not disturb the Signora. People of all ages were welcome. It would be a joyous neighborhood gathering.

"*Si, si,*" Rand answered for the both of them. "*Sta bene.*"

They went to their rooms to change for supper. Fritzi, acknowledging the dance after dinner, decided to wear a yellow cotton sundress with a full skirt. Of course, she'd throw the white cardigan over her shoulders, but she'd wear the gold sandals with the tiny heels. Packing for the trip, she'd thrown them in at the last minute, not imagining that she'd actually wear them. Tonight, she had a chance, and the opportunity thrilled her in a way she hadn't felt since those warm nights back in Montrose, when she was the belle of the ball at the country club, with suitors filling up her dance card as soon as she arrived.

She looked at herself in the dresser mirror. In the dimly lit room, she looked mature, but sophisticated. Her hair shone as if burnished, and her eyes danced with energy. She applied coral lipstick and blotted it with a tissue before throwing the cardigan over her shoulders. This trip, this wonderful outing with her son, was just what she'd needed. To get away from the clamor of three other children, from the demands of her husband. To travel as a lady, with an escort —and a handsome one at that.

Rand had turned out to be a young man with an old soul. He appreciated art and could speak in esoteric terms about meaning in paintings and the elegance of simple shape and form. This was a side of her quiet, studious son that she'd never had a chance to see in the everyday hubbub of their household. It wasn't as if they could sit at the dinner table and discuss Titian with Joe, Debby, Linda, and Tommy. By taking time to see Rome with Rand, Fritzi discovered that her son had the sensibility of an artist combined with the pragmatic realism of an intellectual. These qualities in a young man were rare. Qualities that, by standards of men like her husband, also indicated homosexuality. In her eyes, they were qualities that, regardless of sexual proclivity, should be nourished, not quashed, by a father who discounted esthetics, or a younger sister who would not stop whining, or a demanding but charming toddler that took all the attention away from Rand, her firstborn and, she had to admit, favorite son.

Supper was served in the dining room. Rand pulled her seat out at a table for two near an open window. The scent of jasmine wafted in from the courtyard outside. Rand wore the navy gabardine sport coat they'd bought him last Easter, and it fit him snugly but well. His shoulders were growing so broad; he looked much older than his fourteen years. She was proud to see his starched shirt, which he must have packed carefully, as Joe had taught him, so as not to wrinkle in transit. His brown loafers were polished, another habit instilled by Joe, and he wore a plaid bow tie she had never seen before.

"What a lovely tie," she remarked, sipping a glass of Chianti.

"*Lovely*? Really, Fritzi, it's not *pink*, last time I looked."

"Oh, you know what I mean. It looks—sharp. I didn't know you had that tie, and I see that it's not a clip-on. I didn't know you knew how to tie a bow tie! See—we're learning a lot about each other on this trip!"

"Oh, I got it from the *mercato* in Naples. Some guys from school and I took the bus down there one Saturday. You can find all kinds of things, real cheap. I bought a handkerchief, too." He took a starched linen handkerchief, embroidered with an elaborate *S* out of his pocket. He'd also bought a switchblade, but didn't think Fritzi needed to know

"Impressive," Fritzi replied. Had she known Rand had friends who combed the mercato ? Didn't some kid from the base get beaten up down there last year? "I hope you're careful when you go. I hear the crowds down there can be kind of rough."

Rand laughed. "I think that's all a bunch of baloney. You're OK as long as you watch your pockets. We didn't have any trouble. My friend Luke bought a Borsalino hat down there and gave it to his grandpa for Christmas. It's all secondhand stuff, but cool."

They were served spring soup, a light broth laced with fragrant herbs and topped with pungent cheese.

"Not exactly Campbell's, right?" Fritzi joked, inhaling the aroma of the soup.

"Really, I can't thank you enough for taking me on this trip," Rand blurted, uncharacteristically. "We couldn't stay in a place like this with the rest of the family. They don't *get* Italian food and art like we do. I'd live here forever if I could."

"Oh, Rand, we'll be back in the States in a couple of years. You'll move on, go to college. You'll see." Her heart ached to think of her son growing up.

Rand's face fell into his more characteristic mask. He ate slowly, with perfect manners—just as he'd been taught.

They talked more about the day, about Titian, about architecture and the aqueducts. Tomorrow they'd explore the catacombs. Rand knew a surprising amount about Rome, and he seemed to enjoy telling her about it. It was as though she'd discovered a whole new person in her son, a person she was surprised to find. He'd simply taken off his mask for her, just her. This young man, she knew, would surpass all expectations. And it was up to her to see that nothing or no one stood in his way.

As they were finishing their espresso (she never knew that Rand enjoyed it), they watched Sr. Vitale set up the courtyard for the dance.

He and his sons had strung lights shaped like lemons and oranges around the trees and across the dance floor. Musicians began to set up their equipment and tune a bass, an old electronic keyboard, saxophone, and accordion.

Soon, a few families arrived. Old mamas in black cloth house dresses, young men with slicked-back hair and sport coats, old men in sweaters, hauling their own jugs of wine. Younger couples with children began to clap as the musicians tuned up with a tarantella. The children—three boys and six girls about Debby's age—teamed up to perform the folk dance.

Fritzi ordered an after-dinner limoncello, and agreed that Rand should have one, too. Here in Italy, people let their children drink small glasses of watered-down wine. Why shouldn't her teenage son enjoy a limoncello with his mama?

"Can we go out there and get a table—in the courtyard, I mean?" Rand asked, taking her by surprise.

"Why—do you want to dance?"

"No, not necessarily, but it's so nice out. It might be fun."

"When in Rome..." Fritzi replied, taking his arm and heading outside.

They sat at a tiny table on the edge of the makeshift dance floor. Some of the older couples were dancing now, ballroom style, to a fox trot rhythm. They were light on their feet, well accustomed to their partners, fun to watch.

"Do you and Pop ever dance?" Rand asked. He'd ordered a Coke.

Fritzi laughed. "I do, but your father just doesn't. He's a perfect man in every respect, but he's definitely not a dancer."

"I thought so," Rand said. "Too bad. Would you like to...dance right now? With me?"

"Really? You mean those Teen Canteen lessons I insisted you take at the base taught you something? I'd love to!"

They took the floor on the next song, which happened to be "Volare." Rand seemed stiff, so Fritzi took the lead, walking him through a modified cha-cha. Surprisingly, Rand caught on and followed her steps, growing more and more relaxed as the song took flight. They were drawing glances from fellow dancers and people sitting at tables. Fritzi noticed that three young women who appeared to be sisters had joined the group. Each of them had her own version of Annette Funicello's flip, and each was dressed in a candy-colored sleeveless dress with a full chiffon skirt. They eyed Rand and whispered to each other. When the song was over, they watched Fritzi and Rand take their seats and giggled.

"I think you have some admirers," Fritzi teased, nodding at the girls. They could have been any age from fourteen to twenty-five. Their makeup and dresses made it hard to tell.

Blush crept up Rand's face. "I doubt it, Fritzi. They're just waiting for some older guys to ask them to dance."

Just then, Sr. Vitale took the microphone. *"Signore e signori, diamo il benvenuto i Fiori Sorelle!"*

Three sisters dressed in pastel chiffon dresses took the stage. The tallest one, dressed in aqua , took the microphone. She looked to be the oldest of the three, with dark, arching eyebrows and thick false eyelashes. In a strong, pop-singer voice, she began to sing "Quando, Quando, Quando." The band backed her up and her sisters harmonized behind her, snapping fingers and keeping time with a step, step dance. The girl in pink kept her eye on Rand as she swayed back and forth to the music. At the end of the song, Fritzi saw her wink at Rand. A little part of her heart thrilled for him to have such bold attention, but the logical part of her mind wanted to protect her son from her attempts at seduction. She saw Rand's Adam's apple rise and fall as his face grew red. He reached for his Coke and took a long sip. But, instead of shrinking away in embarrassment, he grinned and nodded his head in time to the music. Fritzi took a deep breath. Without the rest of the family here, there was no one to tease him and make him feel awkward. With just her, he could be himself. A new, grown-up self.

The Fiori sisters did two more songs, both upbeat, pop numbers that featured the tall one as soloist. The two backup sisters did cute little moves and danced, the one in pink making eyes at Rand. They received standing ovations from the crowd. When they were finished, they sat at a back table and sipped Cokes.

The regular band singer, who resembled Bobby Darren with too much Brylcreem, stepped up to the mike and began to sing Chubby Checker's "Twist," in heavily accented English. "Common, bebby, let's doo da tweest…"

Fritzi was not altogether surprised when Rand got up and made a beeline for the Fiori's table and the girl in pink. An older couple, no doubt the sisters' parents, were also at the table.

"*Vuoi ballare?*" Rand asked, in perfectly accented Italian.

The girl in pink nodded shyly and followed him to the dance floor. Although she wore that new whitish lipstick (it looked like a smear of Crisco), thick eyeliner, and turquoise eye shadow, Fritzi saw that, bold as she was, she probably wasn't a *mostra* girl, the kind of girl that rode on the back of Vespas over in Naples, soliciting sex when the Sixth Fleet was in. She looked to be a teenager, perhaps older than Rand, perhaps his own age, or younger. Her makeup made it hard to tell. Fritzi watched Rand and the girl in pink on the floor, the girl shyly placing her foot in front of her and chastely moving back and forth. Then Rand took off, twisting to the ground and up again, looping his forearms expertly. The kid could dance! She marveled at them, and watched the girl take a cue from his playful "tweest" and begin to move in rhythm. Fritzi watched her closely, to see if she tried to show underwear or shimmy her bosoms. She appeared to be somewhat tasteful, here in this family crowd, as she moved in the modern, detached way in the same way that teens all over the world were dancing. Fritzi's eyes grew moist, watching Rand have fun, watching the girls giggle. When the Twist was over, the band launched into "Moon River," which the vocalist sang in Italian. Rand nodded to the girl, apparently asking her to dance with him this time, and she watched her son take his new handkerchief from his pocket and place it under his hand, so he wouldn't sweat on her dress. Then he took her other hand and they danced, a modified waltz. Her son was leading, and the girl was following. He twirled her, and when she lifted her arm, Fritzi noticed the dark fuzz in her armpit. Not to worry, she told herself, Italian women didn't shave there. When Rand brought her back to him, he left enough space between them so as not to attract the attention of the girl's father, who was sitting at the table with the other sisters.

Fritzi blew her son a kiss and went up to her room. It was time to let Rand have a little fun on his own. Truth be told, it broke her heart to watch him grow up before her eyes.

Upstairs, she tried to read a guidebook she'd bought at the train station, but couldn't focus. She paced in the room, smoking, until about midnight. *Where was he?* She put on her robe and looked downstairs, where Sr. Vitale was stacking up chairs and the band was packing up to go home. The families had gone long ago, and the few dancers who had stuck around were leaving. She couldn't see any of the girls in the bright dresses or Rand. Perhaps they'd taken a walk down to the Tiber together, she reasoned. Or perhaps they'd gone for a late night cappuccino down the street.

What was she worried about? He was a boy, after all, and nearly a man. It wasn't like she'd let one of her daughters out after dark in Rome. Rand could take care of himself—he'd shopped at the mercato in Naples, for creeps' sake. He was smart and fluent in Italian. Would Rand think the girl in the pink dress was sexy, with her curvy little figure and her teased hair? Would her hairy armpits exude some kind of magic pheromone to seduce her son? What if she got pregnant? What if poor Rand had walked into a trap, where the family would extort thousands of dollars from them to support the *bambino* from his one-night stand?

She was about to call Sr. Vitale or the Carbinieri when she heard Rand's key in the adjoining room door. She wrapped her robe tightly around her, lit a cigarette, and met him as he entered his room.

He stood in the hallway, swaying, stinking of beer. His bow tie hung loosely under his collar, and he was carrying the sport jacket . A purplish spot on his neck promised to erupt into a hickey, and it throbbed in the harsh light of the hallway. On his collar, she spotted smears of pinkish-white lipstick.

"Well, well, well, Mr. Irresistible. Did you have a nice evening?"

She took a drag on the Chesterfield and blew a stream of smoke into his face, knowing how much he hated cigarettes.

"I'm sorry," he mumbled. "We were just talking, walking, went for a beer... they let everybody drink here..." he stumbled in and face-planted on the bed.

"Who?"

"Her name is Carlotta. She's nice, funny. She knew a bar where we could by beer, and she paid for it. Honest to God, Fritzi."

"Uh-huh. A girl you just met takes *you* to a bar, and you come home drunker than Cooter Brown, on your first trip to Rome? Wait till your father hears about this!"

He collapsed on his bed, moaning. She slipped off his loafers and made him sit up. "I ought to slap you silly."

"Cut me some slack, Fritzi. It was just a date. You're always nagging me to get a date, for those stupid school dances, for the Cotillion at the Officers' Club. So I got a *date,* for Christ's sake."

She slapped him, not hard. "Don't say for Christ's sake. That's blasphemy."

"It's not like we go to church or anything," he said, rubbing his cheek. "I'm sorry, though. I lost track of time. I had fun, OK? I had fun for once!"

She couldn't stay angry at him. How many times had she nagged him about going to school dances? Gone through his class pictures, pointing out girls, asking about them? He was right. He deserved a little fun, but she sure as hell wasn't going to let him know that.

"Tell you what, Romeo. Sleep it off. Don't throw up in the bed." She went into her room, returned with a bottle of mineral water, and poured him a glass. "Drink this, and we'll talk in the morning. You didn't have *sex* with her, did you?"

"Get real, Fritzi, I wasn't *that* lucky."

They burst into laughter. Rand could do no wrong in her eyes, and he knew it. And tonight, Fritzi went to bed knowing that her son was definitely *not* a homosexual.

Luna Park, Naples

LINDA, Debby, and Pop left Tommy at home with Assunta. In the
early evening, they walked to a pizzeria on Via Manzoni. Then they
took the *funiculare* down to Luna Park in the Mergelina. Fritzi never
took the children on the funiculare; she didn't really speak Italian
and she preferred driving the ancient Ford wagon wherever she
needed to go in Naples. With Pop, and without Tommy, the funiculare was a ride in itself, a train car suspended above the hills, not high
enough to be scary, full of people and their smells and the constant
lilt and passionate vibrato of the Neapolitan dialect.

It was a short walk from the funiculare station to the park. The
night was warm, and, since the park was down near the waterfront,
the air was ripe with the scent of salt and fresh fish. Luna Park was an
old-fashioned amusement park, with funny little rides like you'd find
at a county fair in the States. But here, in Naples, Luna Park was the
main attraction for youngsters, families, and a fair number of seedy-
looking kids who begged for cigarettes and spare change.

Pop bought Debby and Linda cotton candy and a bag of roasted
nuts that smelled slightly burnt. The candy, pure spun sugar, melted
in Linda's mouth, sweet wisps that tasted faintly of bubble gum. In
the bright illumination from lights strung through trees, Linda saw
Pop's face beam like a boy's, his eyes dancing with fun. "Let's ride the
Ferris wheel!" he said, taking their hands and leading them toward
the center of the park.

Debby planted her feet firmly on the ground. "No! It's too scary!"

Pop scooped her up into his arms. "Come on, you just rode the
funiculare down here! If you spend your whole life being scared,
Tinkerbell, you'll never have any fun!" He held Linda's hand and
bounded toward the ride. Linda herself wasn't too keen on the giant
wheel festooned with red, white, and green lights, but she wasn't
about to say anything. She'd been with Pop on lots of Ferris wheels.
He liked to ride them; Linda always made it her business to ride with
him so people wouldn't laugh at a grown man riding by himself.

Debby squealed and cried, even as the seat pulled up and stopped. "Don't be a ninny," Pops scolded. "It's just a ride, sweetheart. Look how calm Linda is. She's ridden with me lots of times."

"That's right," Linda chimed in, "It's a lot of fun. Makes your tummy go wheeeeeee."

Debby scrunched her face at Linda, mad that her sister wasn't her ally.

Linda hopped onto the seat and it swung back and forth with her weight. Pop got in next to her and put the pouting princess Tinkerbell on his lap. Away they went, above the tree line, up up up to the top, until they could look out and see the bay, dotted with lights from boats, the ancient Castel Dell'Ovo, where an ancient Roman writer supposedly buried an egg. Supposedly, if the egg ever broke, there would be a great disaster. High on the Ferris wheel, Linda felt immune from disaster alongside her handsome pilot father, holding tight to her little sister. She inhaled the smells of Naples: burnt peanuts from the park, the salty sea air, the fish from the waterfront, the diesel fuel of trucks servicing the busy port. Linda closed her eyes, reveling in the perfect moment.

Debby looked down and threw up. Pop held her so that her vomit dropped through the spokes of the Ferris wheel, a looping plop of puke that disintegrated as it fell. Linda started laughing, and so did Pop. Debby wiped her face with Pop's handkerchief and grinned.

The next morning, Pop woke Tommy, Debby, and Linda early and made them a breakfast of big, fluffy pancakes. Linda was in charge of butter, which she doled out in large pats to melt between the hot cakes. "Assunta's not coming today," Pop said. "I gave her the day off so we could all go buy a camper!"

"What?" Linda felt her mood brighten as she stopped chewing a mouthful of pancake. "What kind of camper?"

"You'll see. I made a deal with one of the guys at the base. We're going to pick it up today."

"Does Fritzi know?" Linda asked

"No! It's a big surprise!" Pop said playfully.

THEY TOOK what would be their last ride in the old Ford station
wagon down to the Purple Pillars, an apartment building supported
by a series of concrete pillars covered in purple mosaic tile, nicknamed, like the Pink Building, by the Americans who lived there.
Tommy, Debby, and Linda waited in the station wagon while Pop
used the house phone to call Captain Gallagher, his friend from
the base.

Pop motioned for them to get out of the car to meet Captain
Gallagher, a sandy-haired, young-looking guy who came downstairs
with a little boy in overalls and another boy about Debby's age. "Hiya,
kiddos," he said, saluting when Pop introduced them. Captain
Gallagher didn't tell them the name of his boys. The little one had a
string of snot dripping from his nose. The older one just looked at
them up and down, caught Linda's gaze, and glared at her.

Pop and Captain Gallagher walked in front of the station wagon
and began talking. Pop had a folder full of important-looking papers
that he spread out on the hood, and he went over some information.
Pop took the checkbook out of his back pocket, placed it on the hood
of the wagon, wrote out a check and gave it to the Captain. They
shook hands just as the young Gallagher kid's snot dripped all the
way to the ground.

"Ewwwww!" Debby squealed.

Tommy laughed. Linda grabbed the Kleenex box in the back seat
of the station wagon and handed it to the kid. He just stared at Linda
and wiped his nose with the back of his hand. His older brother
grabbed a bunch of tissues and clamped them over the kid's nose,
glaring at Linda.

Linda shrugged, seizing the moment. "Hey, it's not my fault your
brother doesn't know how to wipe his nose."

"Shut up, you ugly pig!" he answered.

"She is *not* a pig, you butthole!" Debby countered, to Linda's
surprise.

Tommy laughed and yelled "Pig! Pig says Oink!"

Linda had been called a pig before, and she usually ignored it, but
not today. Fueled by Debby's loyalty, she went on the offensive. "Yeah,

and a butthole says..." Linda put her arm up to her mouth and blew the loudest fart noise she could manage. Debby and Tommy joined in, laughing. The Gallagher kid turned purple and made a fist like he was about to punch Linda in the face.

"Hey, hey, that's enough!" Pop called. He handed the keys to the wagon to Captain Gallagher. Hop out, kids!"

Debby, Linda and Tommy got out of the car, staring at the Gallagher boy, who hid his fist behind his back.

Captain Gallagher opened the back door of the wagon. "Larry, P. J., get in!" he said. The snotty kid and his angry big brother climbed into the back seat. They drove off into the underground garage.

"What's going on?" Linda asked her father. "How are we going to get home without the car?"

Pop jingled some keys in front of her. "Didn't I say we were buying a camper today? Come on around front."

They walked to the front of the Purple Pillars, and there, parked in the circle drive, was one of those squatty-square Volkswagen buses. Its white top gleamed in the spring sunshine, and its yellow lower body shone like an uncooked egg yolk. Tommy let go of Linda's hand and banged on the side door. "Go for ride?"

"We're gonna do more than that—we're gonna see the world in this thing!" Pop said, sliding the back door open. "Look here, Linda. There's a stove, and this thing—" he unlatched a wooden door —"opens out into a table!"

Linda climbed in and sat on one of the back seats, which looked like a cool couch upholstered in black- and yellow-checked fabric. "If I sit here, I'll feel like I'm riding backward," she said. "It's a lot roomier than the station wagon. Did you sell our car to Capt. Gallagher?"

"We worked out a trade deal! His camper is almost new, but they're PCSing to the states soon and wanted an American car. You kids are growing up so fast, the camper will give us a lot more room. We can travel and camp out—look at this!" Pop took the latch off a door in the roof and it popped up into a tent.

Tommy jumped up and down. "Wanna see, Pop, wanna see!"

Debby climbed in, went to the camp stove and pretended to stir. "I'm making dinner."

Pop lifted Tommy into the tent and let him stick his head out the front panel. "Whee!"

Linda climbed into the front seat. The steering wheel was not angled, as it was in the Ford wagon, but mounted flat, so you would have to turn it with both your hands. She thought of Fritzi, who usually had a cigarette in one hand when she drove, and wondered how she'd manage this. Still, the view out the front windshield was wide, and the height made her feel as though she was on top of the world.

"Move over," Pop said, sliding into the drivers' seat. He started the engine and revved it. The motor whirred and buzzed like a toy. Pop shifted with the stick in the middle of the two front seats, and they moved into traffic.

"Wheeeeee!" squealed Debby and Tommy, bouncing around in the back seat.

Linda stuck her head out the passenger's window and let the spring air fill her lungs and her heart. Pop drove all the way out to the beach. The wind blew sea air into her face and the world was perfect.

13

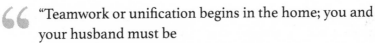 "Teamwork or unification begins in the home; you and
your husband must be
Unified in your thinking. You must be loyal to
each other.
There is an old saying that 'a chain is only as strong
as its weakest link'
so you two should strive to be one of the strong
unified links in the Air Force chain."
—Nancy Shea, *The Air Force Wife*

NAPLES TRAIN STATION

WHEN FRITZI STEPPED off the train, Joe scooped her into his arms and
gave her a long, slow kiss. Fritzi could see Rand turn away, and she
heard Debby, Linda, and Tommy sing out a chorus of "*Ewwwww!*"

The trip to Rome had been a balm, a needed departure from
home life. A way to connect with the world and her oldest child in
ways she never thought possible. Now, in the midst of the rest of the
family, she sighed and resumed her mama/wife role. She smiled and

hugged each of the younger children in her fierce, loving way, grinding her teeth with the love and bitter resentment she felt overtaking her.

They strolled to the parking lot together, exchanging stories, the girls bubbling on about Luna Park, Tommy clinging tightly to his big brother's (Buh's) hand. Fritzi saw that she and Rand had been missed. She could tell by Rand's calm, half-listening face that he hadn't missed his father or his siblings for a moment. In her heart, she was happy to be back with the family, but she wouldn't ever find the words to tell them that she'd had a perfectly delightful time without them all.

Then there was the goddamn yellow van. While she was gone, Joe had traded their sturdy Ford wagon for a German beer can on wheels. She grimaced when she saw it, noting the hope in her husband's face, feeling the giddy expectation of the girls at her reaction. Fritzi gulped down her disgust, and managed to laugh out loud in a sinister, awful cackle. By the look on Joe's face, she could see that he got it.

"I thought I should take some leave in June," Joe said, overly cheerful. "We could drive up the Mediterranean coast, see Pisa, Verona, go into Tuscany—if I can get two weeks, we can even get up to Germany. There are nice camping facilities, with showers and places to barbecue. It'll be a family adventure!" He opened the van to show her the yellow-and-black checked upholstery.

"See, Fritzi, there's even a table!" Debby said, jumping into the back and pulling down the table between the two bench seats.

"And the top pops up, in a tent!" Linda said. By the look on her face, Fritzi knew her older daughter sensed the tension in the air.

"Isn't this great?" was all Fritzi could manage to say. She had to hike up her skirt to get into the front seat. "And it has a truck-driver's steering wheel!" She glared at Joe.

He ignored her and started the engine.

"It sounds like a sewing machine!" Fritzi said, "Oh, and how different—manual transmission, on the floor!" *How in hell would she ever manage to drive this thing?*

Joe guided the bus through the parking lot and turned onto the main thoroughfare for the 20-minute ride home. In the third row seat, Tommy and Rand bounced up and down, laughing. Linda shuffled cards and laid out a solitaire game on the table between her and Debby. Joe switched on the radio to the Armed Forces Network. Fritzi talked herself down, down, down. There was no fussing about seating. There was plenty of room. She and Joe might even be able to have a conversation in the front seat.

"What do you think?" Joe asked, his voice abnormally upbeat.

"You pulled one over on me," she answered. "I'll consent to a few days camping, but I want at least a week at a decent hotel if we go into Germany. I didn't sign on to trek around the countryside like the Joad family. I've got to have my creature comforts." She lit a Chesterfield and crossed her arms, blowing smoke out her open window.

"Yes, ma'am. Duly noted." Joe saluted her sheepishly.

That was two months ago. In the meantime, she'd learned to drive the goddamn thing, with its trucker's steering wheel and its stubborn stick shift that threatened to grind to a halt in Naples traffic. Now, she was preparing to go on "vacation" with four kids, (little Tommy just now using the potty chair) in this breadbox-shaped contraption, cook and wash and sleep in the cussed thing for a whole week.

But, she was a woman of her word. She and Rand had their fun in Rome, and now she had to toe the line, pay up on her promise to vacation with the whole family. The Americans at the base were camping with their kids all over Europe; even the officers' families camped in VW campers just like theirs. Besides, she could read the joy in Joe's face when he showed her all its features—the fold-out tent, the table that came down between the two couch-like seats, the back seat that turned into a double bed. He checked her out on the equipment like he was showing her how to fly a plane—this lever turns on the lights. That's the tachometer, here's the radio. Her husband was a boy in heaven.

So, she'd packed everybody up for two weeks on the road. They planned to spend their first night at a campground in Pisa, make a couple of other stops in Italy, see the sights, head up to Innsbruck,

Austria, and then on to Garmisch-Partenkirken in West Germany. Fritzi went along with it all, but threw in her final bargaining chip: in Garmisch, they'd stay at the General Patton Hotel. It was an old lodge that had belonged to Hitler, but the American Army had turned it into a hotel for veterans, service members, and their families. They would get two rooms there, stay at least four days, eat restaurant food, hike with the kids, and take daily baths before they headed home. Joe agreed, scheduled two weeks of leave in June, and they were off to see Europe with their kids.

"Come on, let's not be burning daylight!" Joe called to Rand, rousting him out of bed before dawn on the morning of their departure. With Tommy underfoot, Fritzi busied herself in the kitchen, brewing a pot of stiff coffee, scrambling eggs, and frying bacon for the whole crew. She had already packed a cooler with bologna sandwiches and snacks. In a second cooler, she packed Tommy's juice, bottles of Coke for the kids, and bottles of Birra Peroni for Joe and herself.

The girls arrived at breakfast in their pajamas, hair disheveled from a fitful night of sleep. Joe, Rand, Tommy, and Linda tucked into the eggs and bacon, while Debby sleepily munched on toast. Fritzi, sipping coffee, watched them eat. What would her mother say if she knew her debutante daughter was about to embark on a *camping* trip? She smiled at the thought. Back in Montrose, only hobos and carpetbaggers camped. No decent person with a fine, comfortable home and more than a nickel to his name would ever try to take a whole family camping. *Who were they, the Joads?* She could picture Mother asking.

"What are you smiling at, Fritzi?" Joe asked, winking at her.

"Oh, nothing. Just thinking about how much fun we're going to have on our adventure!"

"I thought we were going on a trip. A *vacation*," Debby said, eyes wide and near tears. "I don't like adventure."

"Shut up, silly, it'll be fun," Linda chided. "A vacation *is* an adventure."

"Young lady!" Joe stood up and pointed at Linda. "We do *not* say s*hut up* in this family!"

Linda jumped in her seat, startled. She seldom got anything from Joe but approval.

"I'm sorry, Pop. Sorry, Debby. Won't happen again."

Joe sat down and Linda reached for another piece of toast. Rand smirked. Tommy, who now sat at the table, beat his plate with his spoon.

"Go on trip!" he squealed, grinning.

Everyone laughed.

Tommy was a happy little boy, full of energy, and quite a handful, but he was a reminder that Providence had truly blessed her family. Here she was, living in Italy, with four healthy, inquisitive children, a dashing husband she still wanted to jump into bed with, and a life beyond Montrose she never could have imagined.

Fritzi reached over and ruffled Tommy's hair. "That's right, sweetie! Let's get these dishes cleared up so we can hit the road!"

Garmisch-Partenkirchen, West Germany

THEY SAW PISA, each of them posing for pictures like they were holding up the Leaning Tower. They camped at night and ate hot dogs cooked on a cement grill at the campground. They drove to Venice the next day and set up camp outside the city before they ventured to St. Mark's Square and the Grand Canal. Debby cried when she stepped into the gondola, so Fritzi took her and Tommy on the motorboat tour, while he, Pop and Linda rode with the singing gondolier through the canals. In the campsites, they hooked up to water and used the communal flush toilets. Rand got to sleep up top, in the tent, where he pretended none of the people below him existed. Below, Debby and Linda slept on the two seats with the table between them. In the back, Pop and Fritzi folded the long bench seat flat and it made a double bed. Most nights, Tommy slept between them, or in a sleeping bag on the floor. It was tight quarters, but it worked for a while.

A week was about all they could take. Linda's and Debby's hair smelled like sour milk. Tommy scratched mosquito bites till they bled. They had to stop every few miles to drag out the potty seat so everyone could watch *their* little brother do his business and applaud his efforts. On the last night, they camped in Innsbruck, Austria, and Fritzi laid down the law: tomorrow, they were going to a nice hotel in Germany, where they could all get clean and get a little distance from each other.

Now, in this room at the General Patton Hotel, Rand was paying for the trip to Rome. He put his pillow over his head to drown out the sound of his sisters giggling. Tommy lay next to him, his chunky body slightly askew so that it took up an inappropriate amount of the double bed. The kid was breathing heavily through his open mouth, his cheeks sunburned from an afternoon picnic on the mountainside. Pop and Fritzi had a room to themselves, leaving Rand in charge after dark. The rules were simple but strictly enforced: do not disturb Pop and Fritzi before 8 a.m. or after 10 p.m., unless someone was dying.

Rand's role as caretaker to the younger ones made him want to kill one of them, just so he could go next door and let his parents take over. Tommy was a mess; you had to watch him every minute, or he would dart off in search of adventure. At three, the kid was cute and guileless, but he was solid as a little linebacker. His physical energy was matched only by his appetite, and then there would be the inevitable trips to the bathroom with him, or, as had happened last night, the cleanup of his odorous ordure. His two sisters thought Tommy's "B.M. accident" was so funny, they laughed until Debby wet her pants.

Oh, those girls. He'd always figured Linda as an ally, but on this trip, she had defected to Team Debby. Now that she was six, Debby had turned into a bossy girl who commandeered her older sister to do all things girly with her—including whispering, giggling, and playing with those stupid Barbie fashion dolls. In the VW van, Rand got to sleep by himself in the pop-up tent to escape it all. But here in the hotel, he had to spend five whole nights in sibling hell.

"Shut up!" Rand spewed the words across the room in a stage whisper, hoping he wouldn't wake Tommy. "I'm counting to three. If you don't be quiet, your Barbie dolls are going out the window, into that stream down there. They'll be halfway to Timbuktu by morning. One, two..."

"You don't even know where they are, stupid," Linda said, prompting another wave of giggles from Debby.

"That's what you think." Rand got out of bed and went to the dresser across the room. He opened the top drawer, where the girls had put the Barbies to bed. They were covered with a hotel towel and dressed in pink, ridiculously fancy Barbie see-through nightgowns. Rand took a Barbie in each hand and waved them in front of the open window.

More laughter from his sisters.

"I mean it! The stupid Barbs are going down if you don't shut up *now*!"

Debby hopped out of bed and reached for her Barbie, the one with the long blonde ponytail. Linda tackled him, and Rand fell in front of the window, still holding the dolls in a death grip.

Tommy, startled by the commotion, sat up in bed and began to cry.

The girls wrestled with Rand. Linda was able to retrieve her brunette doll, but Rand regained his footing. He leapt to his feet, tossing Debby's doll out the window.

"*Nooooooooo!*" Debby squealed, leaning over the window sill.

Tommy jumped out of bed and ran across the room, curious. He jumped up and down, trying to see out the window. The momentum threw Debby off balance, and Rand grabbed her legs to keep her from falling to the stream below. Linda grabbed Tommy and slammed the window shut.

"*Shut up*, or Pop and Fritzi will hear us!" Linda commanded. "Here," she said, handing her Barbie to Debby. "I'm too old to be playing dolls anyway. You can have her and her Dream House, too. Just shut up!"

"I don't want the brown-haired one! I want mine! I'm gonna tell Pop, and Rand is gonna get it!" Debby darted for the door, but Rand blocked her way.

"Honest, Debby, it was an accident," Rand said. "If you and Linda hadn't attacked me, I never would have thrown that doll down there. Now shut up! I'll go down there and get it. It's right by the creek, not in it. I saw where it landed."

"Yeah, cut him a break—cut us all break! Pop and Fritzi will be furious! It's not worth it," Linda chimed in. "If Rand goes down and finds your Barbie, promise us you won't tell?"

"All right," Debby said, wiping snot on her pajama sleeve. "But you better find her!"

Rand pulled on a pair of jeans and got his flashlight from the bedside table. "Linda, you watch these guys, and I'll be right back. And no telling!"

"Yeah, it's a deal. Just bring the doll back, OK?"

"Buuuuuh!" Tommy clung to his big brother's legs.

"I'll take Tommy with me, just to shut him up," Rand said. "You girls wait here."

The two brothers rode the deserted elevator to the first floor, where they were greeted by a stern night watchman in what Rand recognized as an Army private's uniform. (The U.S. Army staffed the General Patton Hotel.)"What are you boys doing up this late? Do your parents know where you are?" he demanded.

"Yes, sir," Rand said. "One of my sisters was playing with her doll, and it fell out the window," he explained. "I'm just coming down to see if I can get it for her."

"Why did you bring that little guy, then? This looks highly irregular."

"Sir, he's my little brother, and I am charged with taking care of him." Rand lowered his voice. "Our father is Major Joe Stoddard, USAF. He and our mother are in Room 327, and us kids are next door. I'm just trying to calm down my sister, who is very upset about losing her doll. It fell out of our window, out back, by the stream. I assure you I'll go back upstairs promptly after I find it. Please, sir, don't call our parents."

The private relaxed a little, a smile teasing at his lips. "Big trouble, huh? What'd you do, throw your sister's doll out the window?"

"Something like that. Only it was an accident." Rand picked up Tommy so he could look the private in the eye. "We have two boys and two girls in our family. Sometimes, it just seems like the girls outnumber us."

"Come on, I'll show you out back." The private unlocked a back door and led them along a cobblestone walk into the cool darkness.

Rand grasped Tommy's hand. They could hear the stream rushing by, and he knew his little brother would take off toward the water if he didn't hang on to him, tight.

"Here, I'll shine my light," said the private. He aimed his Army-issued flash and flooded the stream bank with light.

There, lying face-down on a rock, was the disheveled blonde Barbie, dressed in the frilly see-through nightgown. The watchman stepped toward it. "That what you're looking for?"

"Yes, sir. It's my little sister's doll." Rand gulped down a lump of hot embarrassment.

"Barbie!" Tommy yelled. Rand had to hold him back.

The watchman shook the doll in their direction, showering them with water from the stream. He handed the doll to Rand.

"Thank you, sir."

"You're welcome. I'm going to walk you up to your room now. Any more commotion, and I'll have to call Major Stoddard. Understood?"

"Yes, sir."

Dachau Prison Camp Memorial

AFTER THEIR STAY at the General Patton, the Stoddards loaded up the bus and headed north to Munich, where they would tour the Dachau Prison Camp Memorial. Fritzi and Pop wanted the children to understand about concentration camps before they headed home. Linda wasn't so keen on the idea; she'd already read *The Diary of Anne Frank* and knew enough about the horrible Nazis.

"I was in the Berlin Airlift, you know," Pop said as they drove out of the General Patton parking lot. "I wasn't a pilot back then, because I enlisted when the war started, but I made sergeant. I didn't go to OCS until after the war, and then I was a cadet. If the U.S. hadn't entered the war, we'd all be speaking German today."

Well, duh, Linda knew that, and so did Rand. They knew American history. And they'd heard all the stories about Pop before he became an officer, about how Judge wouldn't let Fritzi marry an enlisted man, so he worked to qualify for OCS after the war. Linda wasn't sure what OCS stood for, but she guessed it was something about officers. She usually tuned out Pop when he went on and on about his career. It was easy to get lost in all the Air Force acronyms and base names.

"Did you liberate any concentration camps?" Rand asked.

"No, son, the Army marched in on foot for that duty," Pop said. "I saw pictures. Those poor Jews looked like skeletons, so weak, they were half-dead. Little children, women. All had heads too big for their bodies."

"Now, listen, kids," Fritzi interrupted. "You might see some of those pictures at Dachau, in the museum part of the camp. Don't let them upset you. Just be glad you are an American, free to live and visit wherever you like."

Pop parked the car outside the Dachau gates and paid the admission price (family value) to see the memorial camp. The ticket lady looked at Debby and Tommy, then said something in German to Pop. He pretended to understand, then led the way inside, determined to give them all a dose of history.

Linda knew that Anne Frank had died at Auschwitz, the death camp. Dachau, Linda found out, was only a work camp, where the

Germans sent able-bodied men who just happened to oppose their regime. It wouldn't be as bad, *couldn't* be as bad as Auschwitz.

Smart-alec Rand informed Linda that the German government had destroyed the crematoriums and spiffed up the camp so they could let tourists in. At that point, eavesdropping Debby asked if crematoriums were where you could get ice cream. Linda said no, they weren't.

Then Rand had to speak up: "That's where they burned the bodies. Cremated them."

Debby's face went slack, but she said nothing. Tommy ran ahead to an iron gate with the words "*Arbeit mache frei*" spelled out in iron.

"Those words mean 'Work Shall Set You Free,'" Pop said, reading from the tour brochure. "Of course, meaningful work does set the mind and the body free. Not the work created by the Nazi regime, meant to punish people with hard labor. You kids understand that, don't you?"

"What's hard labor?" Debby asked.

"It's when people work like slaves, doing very hard work all day. Like the slaves who built the Pyramids. Like the slaves who worked on the plantations in the South," Rand said.

Debby looked confused. Fritzi rummaged in her purse for a cigarette.

Tommy ran ahead on the trail, toward a chapel named Christ's Mortal Fear.

"Good God," Linda heard Fritzi say under her breath as she stamped out her cigarette.

Inside the chapel, there were photographs of prisoners. When Debby saw them, she started to cry. "I'm scared," she sobbed into Fritzi's skirt.

"Oh, Tinkerbell, don't be afraid," said Pop. He picked up his baby girl. "Look at this picture. These are the U.S. soldiers who rescued these people, see? The Americans came in and saved Germany from the bad old Nazis."

"Wanna see, Buh!" Tommy begged, holding his hands up to Rand.

Rand picked him up and pointed to the photographs. Tommy pointed with his chubby fingers and laughed.

Linda couldn't stand it anymore. "It's not funny!" I said. "Real people died here, don't you see? This isn't an amusement park for the enjoyment of tourists." She turned her face away from the pictures and ran toward the parking lot. She was the only one in the family who had read Anne Frank's diary. Linda always knew that she had a special sensitivity, and it was obvious that she was the only one in the family who did. No one, Linda was convinced, could feel as deeply as she could. She probably had extra-sensory perception. Linda was convinced that if had she lived in Germany, the Nazis would have taken her, a gentile girl, because she was somehow *different*. Her sensitivity was dangerous. She could see things others could not. At any moment, Linda expected to see ghosts of former prisoners shuffling along in her path. She, of course, would be the only one who could see them.

It was Fritzi, however, who stopped Linda's rant. "Who do you think you are, young lady? Sarah Burn-heart? Believe me, your father and I lived through the war. Your father risked his life to fight—*as an enlisted man*! Only nineteen years old! We lost classmates, lifelong friends from Montrose, to the war. We had to ration our *food*. You have the privilege of growing up in a free world, and it's because you are an *American*. Yes, there were tragedies. Yes, people died. That's what we're here to show you; that your freedom as an American citizen is the direct result of the sacrifices your father and men like him made to save the world!"

"You never understand me!" Linda retorted. "I'm upset by this, don't you see? I get that this was a horrible place, in a way that none of you ever will. I'm not just another tourist, Fritzi. I'm a particularly sensitive person. Sensitive in ways you will never know."

"Well, just swallow your sensitivity and get back over here. I don't want you out in the parking lot by yourself, Sarah Burn-heart."

By then, Debby had escaped from Pop and was running toward Fritzi. Of course, she was crying, determined to upstage Linda.

"I want to go home," Debbie whined, crocodile tears running down her little Aryan cheeks. "I don't like this place. Please, Fritzi?"

"Joe, I think we've all seen enough," Fritzi called. "I'm taking the girls back to the van."

Pop waved them on. He and his two sons forged ahead for another half hour or so. Linda could imagine all the gory trivia that Rand was spewing—all he knew about Dachau and Auschwitz and his adolescent fascination with violence. Tommy, she knew, wouldn't care. He just wanted to be outside, where he could run free; where he could be with his Buh and his Pop.

When Debby and Linda got to the van with Fritzi, she reached into the cooler and took out two Cokes for the girls. Normally, she'd have made them split one. "Here," she said. "Good old American Cokes." Then she popped open a bottle of Birra Peroni. "And here's to no more concentration camp tours, right? It's our vacation, too!"

Debby smiled and sucked up. Linda drank her Coke in silence.

14

 "Air Force children are just as much ambassadors of
good will as you are.

    Courteous, well-mannered children can be a
tremendous help in showing

    foreigners a favorable picture of American life."
—Nancy Shea, *The Air Force Wife*

JULY 2, 1963
  Naples, Italy

IT SEEMED to Linda that the whole city had turned out to welcome
President John F. Kennedy on his first visit to Naples. That morning,
Pop drove the van through throngs of Neapolitans waving American
flags—an inconceivable turn of favor. (When the Stoddards had the
old Ford, people sometimes made ugly gestures at them, or spat as
they drove by in an American car. The year before, during the Bay of
Pigs, there had been Marines guarding the American school.) But

today, everybody was waving the Stars and Stripes. President Kennedy was set to ride through the streets of Naples with Secretary of State Dean Rusk, and Italian president Antonio Segni. They would ride in a convertible Lincoln later that afternoon, and excited Neapolitans wanted to welcome the handsome American president with open arms.

A year ago, the First Lady, Caroline, and JohnJohn had spent time in Ravello and on the Amalfi coast. The Italians loved Jackie. *Il Mattino* and even *The Daily American* newspapers had been chock full of pictures of chic Jackie and little Caroline, dressed in bright summer clothes, seeing Capri and being escorted around by Gianni Agnelli, the richest man in Italy and owner of Fiat. Linda had pored over those photos, gazing at Jackie's elegant slenderness, the length of her neck, her sleek dark hair. Jackie was not curvaceous like Fritzi, nor did she have her mother's beauty, but there was a glamour about the president's wife that fascinated Linda. The previous Christmas, when Debby got her blonde ponytailed Barbie, Linda had received the brunette short-haired version. She used to pretend her Barbie was Jackie. On their trip earlier in the summer, Linda had played with her Barbie again out of sheer boredom; it was a way to get along with Debby. They'd managed to have a little fun on vacation, when they could play dolls *Debby's* way. Debby's blonde Barbie was always the movie star, Miss America, or the victim in a dramatic tragedy. Linda didn't care, because she told her sister that her Barbie was an intellectual translator/spy/First Lady. Now that she was about to enter seventh grade, Linda was too old for that stuff.

Because of Pop's position as personal pilot attaché for some generals at the NATO base, the Stoddards were invited to watch President Kennedy arrive at Bagnoli Field. They would sit, Pop explained, several rows behind the dignitaries, to hear the president's speech. The children were to "dress sharp" and be "American ladies and gentlemen" to show respect for their president. Linda was so excited, she forgot to eat breakfast.

It felt very VIP to be all dressed up on a weekday summer morning, heading for Bagnoli in the VW van. Fritzi wore a brown linen suit with a white straw hat and white gloves. Rand had on a navy blazer and striped tie, and Tommy wore navy blue shorts with a little suit coat and plaid bow tie. Linda was a tad too old for matching sister dresses, but she and Debby wore crisp white pique ensembles, Easter gifts from Grandmamma purchased from Lois Jeanne's in Montrose. Linda's outfit was a white pique dirndl skirt with matching bolero jacket, under which she wore Ban Roll-on and a bright blue cotton blouse. Debby wore a full-skirted white pique dress with a bright blue silk sash. Fritzi twined blue ribbon into Debby's long blonde braids and pinned them into a coronet on her head, giving her the appearance of an American Heidi.

Debby and Linda both wore white anklets and white patent Easter shoes. All that white accentuated the dark hair on Linda's tanned, mosquito-bitten legs, and she was careful to drape her skirt over her knees when she sat down, tucking her legs under the chair to downplay their scabby hairiness. Linda had begged Fritzi to let her shave, but she was only twelve, and Fritzi said young ladies shouldn't shave legs before age thirteen. However, Fritzi swabbed Nair on Linda's fuzzy underarms and advised her to shower every morning and to apply Ban roll-on before she got dressed. "I know Italian ladies have hairy armpits, and that's fine for them," Fritzi said, wiping away a glob of Nair, "but you're an American young lady. We don't ruin our nice clothes with armpit hair and sweat stains."

Linda, Debby, Rand, Tommy, and Fritzi took their seats in the sixth row of folding chairs facing the makeshift stage at Bagnoli Field. Flanking the stage were representatives of all the Allied Armed Forces, decked out in dress uniforms. The blinding white U.S. Navy uniforms contrasted with the dark blue of the Italian Navy. It thrilled Linda to behold the different ways the different militaries wore their jackets; some with belts, some double-breasted. There was an assortment of ribbons, gold and silver braid, all sparkling in the midday sunshine. Linda had learned to recognize all branches and ranks, and she ticked them off as she scanned their representatives: U.S. Marines (her personal favorite, with white gloves and swords), Royal Air Force,

Italian Air Force, French Navy, Royal Canadian Air Force, Belgian Army.

Linda's heart swelled as she caught the eye of her own father among the U.S. Air Force contingent. Handsome as Gregory Peck, Major Joe Stoddard stood at attention in the summer sunshine, looking like he hadn't sweated a drop. His face was solemn and strong, but Linda saw him wink at her when she gave him a quick wave. She loved the way he looked in his dress blues, with blue and red ribbons pinned to his broad chest, and his major's gold oak leaves gleaming on his shoulders. Her father took off his hat and held it over his heart as he turned to watch the helicopter land. The NATO band struck up with "Hail to the Chief" as President John Kennedy waved from the helicopter and disembarked. Linda nearly swooned.

Linda watched Pop stand at rapt attention, then salute the commander in chief. As the president returned the salute, she felt alive with pride, proud not only of her heritage, but of her family, her father, and especially and most importantly, of her country's president.

President Kennedy shimmered in the sunlight. His hair, thick and shiny, seemed burnished in bronze. His impeccable blue suit was set off by a crisp white shirt, a white pocket square and a blue silk tie. His big, white teeth dominated his smile, and at that moment, he was bigger and more beautiful than all the Roman statues and busts of ancient rulers Linda had seen in Europe over the last two years. Confident, handsome, friendly, Kennedy spoke in crisp cadence that underscored his words: the United States had a firm commitment to NATO. The United States had united with Allies to end world anarchy, "beyond the Alps and beyond the sea." In his broad Boston clip, he pronounced Italy as "Itt-lee," but somehow it sounded right and proper, Yankee, and quintessentially American. Kennedy personified what America was all about: beauty, passion, energy, resolve. Tears formed in Linda's eyes. Her president spoke of hope, of uniting against evil, of the power when nations converge to save the world. He was speaking about NATO, but all Linda could think about was their recent visit to Dachau, how her histrionics underscored the sheer magnitude of cruelty practiced by the Third Reich. She recalled the photographs in the chapel—not the haunted faces of prisoners, but the ones where there was hope in their eyes as they met the U.S. Army soldiers who liberated the camp. Linda reached over and squeezed Rand's hand.

Her brother gave her a dirty look and withdrew his hand like she was a leper. A few seats down, Fritzi looked excited, but calm; Debby smoothed the skirt of her dress and squinted into the sunlight. Tommy, seated between Rand and Fritzi, squirmed and started to fuss. Fritzi rubbed his shoulder with one gloved hand, and Tommy calmed down. Linda glanced at Pop, but there was no reading his "at attention" face.

Was Linda once again the only truly sensitive person in the crowd? Did no one else feel the electricity generated by President Kennedy's smile? Could they not see the bright promise in his gleaming head of bronze hair?

Then, she felt as I had at Dachau: different. She saw things differently; felt things more deeply. Linda felt special. She couldn't expect her family or anyone else to understand. There was an aura about her president—a glow that perhaps only Linda saw. Others—maybe the Neapolitans with the American flags—anticipated it—but no one, she knew, truly *felt* it like she did.

September 7, 1963
  Naples, Italy

Festa di Piedigrotta. It was a strange Neapolitan holiday that fourth Debby did not quite understand. Not like Christmas, or the 4th of July. This Italian holiday was something about a church being built in front of a cave. A cave that led to hell. The thought scared her, and she wondered if it was something like American Halloween? Only no trick-or-treating; just a parade and lots of fireworks over the bay. It was weird.

All day, she'd kept asking Fritzi: "Is there really a cave? Where is it? Can devils come out? Does the church cover the cave, like seal it off, or what?"

"Darlin', you ask so many questions, I just may seal *you* off!" Fritzi kissed the top of Debby's head. "Wait till Rand gets home. He understands Italian. He knows all about it. Run along now. I've got to give Tommy a bath."

Debby didn't like being dismissed like that. It made her feel stupid and unimportant. Fritzi didn't ever have enough time for her. She was always running after Tommy, or fighting with Linda, or going on trips with Rand. Tonight, they were all invited to General Miroglio's penthouse to watch the fireworks. She wanted Fritzi to fix her hair, help her put on the pink dress she wanted to wear. But as soon as Fritzi got Tommy out of the bath, Fritzi asked Debby to keep an eye on him so she could get ready.

Linda and Rand always made Debby feel like a dumb little fool. They laughed at her; they imitated her. They couldn't see how hard she'd tried to be grown up like them. They kicked her out of their rooms and made her play with Tommy when she didn't want to.

Tommy, he was a spoiled brat. Everyone was always "Oh, look how cute!" "What a little man!" "He caught that football/baseball just like a champ!" No one had ever bothered to play ball with Debby, but Pop and Rand were all excited about throwing balls for Tommy to catch. Why wouldn't they ever give her a chance?

And last summer. Linda finally paid some attention to her on their trip in the van. They'd played with their Barbies, and Linda acted like a real sister for a change, not a moody old troll. Until that night Rand threw her Barbie out the window—after that, Linda buried her nose in a book and acted like she was too old for dolls.

"Come here, Tommy. You can bring your truck." She led her little brother into the room she shared with Linda. "Go over there on Linda's side. You can play with anything of hers."

While Tommy ran his toy truck all over Linda's neat bed, Debby gazed out the window to the street below. It was a warm, humid day; lots of people were out walking because it was a holiday. From her window, she also could see into the back yard of the little farmhouse between the Pink Building and the American school. The old woman who lived there was out back, filling a big pot with water. It could be a cauldron, Debby thought; the woman is probably a witch. A couple of chickens pecked at the ground under her feet. Suddenly, the woman turned and grabbed one of the chickens by the neck. Debby watched as the woman used both hands to choke the chicken until it was limp. She took a hatchet from a tool rack, laid the chicken on a big wooden table, and chopped off its head. Debby watched, mesmerized, as the woman took the chicken's body by the feet and began to pluck it. White feathers drifted everywhere. The woman kept going until the chicken's skin was bare, naked as a baby, and she was standing in a heap of feathers. She rinsed the chicken in the pot; the water went pink with chicken blood. Finally, she dumped the water on the ground to wash the feathers away.

Debby decided she would not wear her pink dress tonight. She'd beg Fritzi to help her choose another and ask her to fix her hair. She closed the curtains and plopped on her bed to keep a close eye on Tommy, who was still making roads on Linda's bedspread with his truck.

Rand didn't want to go to General Miroglio's party tonight, and neither did Linda. Debby listened to them arguing with Pop, and she could tell by her father's voice that he was getting madder and madder.

"But Pop, I promised some of the guys that I'd go down to the Mergelina with them tonight. We're riding the funiculare; we were going to watch the procession," Rand pleaded.

"Negative," she heard Pop say in a stern voice. "No son of mine is going to go down and carouse with that mob! You've been invited, as part of our family, by an *Italian general* to join his family on their holi-day. You will go, you'll be polite, and you will *represent your family and your country because that is what we're here to do.*"

Rand must have given Pop a dirty look, because Debby could hear the scuffle sound that meant Pop took her brother down in a wrestling hold.

"Yes, sir," Rand said, but Debby could tell he didn't mean it.

"And Linda—I know you don't have homework you need to do on a Saturday night. Go take a bath and pull yourself together so you look sharp. We're leaving here in exactly one hour."

"Yes, sir," Linda said, and Debby could tell it was her sarcastic voice. Apparently Pop could not.

They drove down the hill, to a neighborhood that Fritzi said was where the rich Neapolitans lived. The buildings faced the bay, and most of them looked more like palaces than apartment buildings. A doorman at the general's building whistled for someone to come and park the van, and they all got out.

"OK, let's line up for inspection," Fritzi said.

The four children stood in the marble foyer of the building while Fritzi looked all of them over. "Linda, your bra strap is hanging. Here." She pushed the strap under the short sleeve of her dress. Then she licked her finger and smoothed Debby's bangs.

"Rand, get your gig line straight," Pop said.

Rand tucked his button-down shirt into his khaki pants, making sure the buttons on the shirt lined up with his belt buckle.

"All right. Everybody looks sharp!" Pop pressed the button for the elevator. "Except Tommy. Let's get those pants in line." He pulled Tommy's pants up over his round little belly. The elevator had an operator, who knew they were headed for the penthouse. Pop held tightly to Tommy's hand, and Fritzi held Debby's.

The elevator opened on the fifth floor. There was a marble hallway that led to open double doors. A large, handsome man reached for Pop's hand.

"*Benevenuto, Maggiore! Signora!*" He kissed Fritzi's hand. Debby thought this was odd, but Fritzi seemed all right with it.

This was the general. Even little Tommy knew to wait in line to introduce himself to him. Debby, Linda, and Rand all shook the general's hand and wished him "*Buona sera,*" just as Fritzi had instructed them.

The foyer of the apartment was full of people, some familiar, some not. A maid in a black dress with a frilly white apron came with drinks for Pop and Fritzi. They met Signora Miroglio, a beautiful dark-haired woman with a smooth face, penciled eyebrows, and big bosoms that were pushed up like a baby's butt in her low-cut red dress. "Come, the children's party is in here," she said in heavily accented English.

She opened double doors off the foyer to a huge room with books and floor-to-ceiling windows. Some teenagers were gathered around a pool table, aiming their cues. Signora Miroglio closed the doors and retreated to the adults in the foyer. There was a big wooden bar with a marble top. Behind it was a maid opening whole bottles of Coke and orange Fanta. At the other end of the bar, there were slices of pizza, olives, cheese and crackers. Linda and Rand ~~made~~ went for the food, while Debby claimed a whole bottle of Fanta for herself and sipped it through a straw. Tommy disappeared into a corner among some younger kids, who were making something with a bunch of those new plastic blocks called Legos.

Debby spotted Tammy Downs, a girl from her second grade class, and went over to talk to her. Tammy was tagging along with her teenage sister, who was a cheerleader at the American high school. The sister made a beeline for Rand, with the two younger girls giggling at her heels. Rand shot Debby a drop-dead look, but she didn't care. It was fun to see a girl flirt with her brother. Everyone said he was cute, and Debby had to admit he looked pretty good tonight. She liked to think that her brother was "popular" in that way Tammy said her sister was. Tammy's sister and Rand headed for the pool table. Debby and Tammy lost track of them in the crowd of tall teens.

Linda was nowhere to be seen. That was no surprise to Debby, because Linda didn't like parties. She supposed it was because her sister wasn't especially pretty, and Debby could tell Linda was not going to be one of the popular girls in high school. Just then, a cute boy with dark hair and blue eyes tapped Debby on the shoulder.

"Hi, I'm Bino. Bino Miroglio," he said in English. "*Como ti chiari*?"

She knew a little Italian. "Debby," she said, giving him her nicest smile. "This is my friend Tammy. "So this is your house? Pretty cool."

"*Si*, it's nice," he said. "You like soccer?"

"Sure," she said. She really didn't know how to play, but she understood it was something like kickball.

Bino took a small soccer ball out of a toy box in the corner and started bouncing it off his head, grinning. Debby and Tina giggled.

"Ball!" Tommy yelled from the Lego corner. "Wanna play!" He barreled across the room toward Bino.

"Whoa, who is this little guy?" Bino asked.

Debby laughed. "You say 'guy' funny. It's not gah-ee. It's just gu-eye. Like pie. And he's my little *frattello*, Tommy."

"OK, gu-eye. You play good?"

"Yeah, he's quite the sports gah-ee," Debby teased.

Bino opened the door to the terrace.

"Oh it's so big! It's like a real yard!" Debby twirled to impress Bino, her full white pique skirt spinning out around her. The terrace was massive, with potted lemon trees and beautiful furniture grouped in different areas. She wished they had a place like this. They had to go all the way down to the courtyard to play at their apartment.

Debby could see the crowd of adults on the far side of the terrace, sipping their cocktails and smoking.

Bino bounced the ball off his head. "Out here is where I practice kicking," he said, sending the ball her way with a low kick. You can't kick it high, or it will go over the rail."

She returned the low kick.

"Play!" Tommy squealed, running after the ball. He picked it up and tossed it to Bino.

"It's not that kind of ball, silly!" Debby scolded. Bino caught the ball.

"Is OK," Bino said, laughing. "He can play if he wants." Bino bounced the ball off his head toward Tommy, and ran toward the terrace door to retrieve it. Tommy threw the ball to Bino, and the two of them started kicking the ball back and forth.

"It's getting kind of dark. Let's go inside," Tammy said. "I don't want to play soccer, do you?"

Debby followed her friend back to the pool table room. They headed for the snacks. Debby nibbled at what looked like a sugar cookie. It tasted like licorice, so she spat it into a paper napkin and gave it to the maid behind the bar. "*No, grazie*," she said politely.

Just then, Debby heard what sounded like gunshots from outside. Everyone started moving toward the terrace doors.

"The fireworks are starting!" Tammy cried. "Let's go outside!"

The two girls went back out on the terrace. Bino was still kicking the ball back and forth with Tommy, but it was getting harder to see in the fading light. Tommy picked up the ball and ran around with it like he was making a touchdown.

"Tommy, give Bino the ball," Debby said. It's time for the boom boom fireworks!"

Tommy heard the popping fireworks and took off running with the ball, looking over his shoulder at Debby. "Come here!" she cried, but Tommy took off, laughing. She was frightened; it was getting darker, and the fireworks over the Bay of Naples grew louder and louder. Debby scanned the crowd for Rand, because Tommy always did what their big brother told him. He was not in sight, and neither was Linda. Fritzi and Pop were somewhere in the throng of adults on the other side. Debby ran after Tommy.

Tommy ran toward the high terrace railing and looked back at Debby. He ran into the railing and stopped, laughing. Debby closed in on him and grabbed the ball out of his hands. Giggling, Tommy kept leaping at it, trying to reach it.

"*Stop it*, Tommy!" Debby said, eyeing Bino. "Let's go talk to Bino now, OK? Let's go watch the boom boom fireworks.

"*No!*" Tommy was adamant. He'd probably skipped his nap this afternoon and gotten hyped up on sugar at the party. "Gimme ball!" He reached with his chubby hands, swatting at the ball.

Bino had lost interest in playing with Tommy, and was now gathering with the others to see the fireworks over the bay. Meanwhile,

Debby was stuck in the corner of the terrace with a squealing brat who insisted on playing ball.

"Ball's all gone, see?" Debby hid the ball behind her back, then let it drop over the railing and disappear into the darkness below.

"*Want ball!*" Tommy cried. He stepped up on the railing and looked for it.

"Get down, stupid!" Debby reached for his arm, but Tommy was strong and he yanked free. The next second, he toppled over the railing, chasing the ball five stories below.

———————

A WAVE of screams from the opposite side of the terrace carried the news to Joe: his baby son had chased a ball over the edge. Joe bounded down five flights of stairs to the courtyard, where the eerie flashes of fireworks illuminated a small body on the pavement. Tommy had landed face up, his eyes open to the fire-lit sky. Joe slipped off his suit coat and laid it over the little boy's body. He knelt next to Tommy and began to sob deeply, covering his face with his hands as if to erase the reality of what had just happened. In an instant, Joe felt a steady hand on his shoulder and turned to see Colonel Short, his commanding officer, kneeling beside him.

"They'll take him to the Naval Hospital on Manzoni," the colonel said. "My wife is with Fritzi and the kids. I'll ride with you in the ambulance."

COLONEL SHORT SPOKE SOFTLY to Joe as they sat together in the chapel at the hospital. "They're going to ask questions. The Naples police, the Italian Air Force, NATO, AFSE, the American Consul. I've arranged for them all to meet in the morning at my office. We'll nip this in the bud, Joe. It was an accident, that's all. I'll back you up all the way, but it does have international consequences. I'll send a car to pick you up at oh-nine-hundred. Wear your dress blues."

This was no surprise to Joe. He would and should be called on the carpet. The son of an American Air Force officer had fallen to his death from an Italian general's apartment; of course it was an international incident. As a father, a husband, and an officer, it was Joe's duty to take full responsibility for the fact that his child was unsupervised and suffered an accidental death.

The next day, Joe sat ramrod straight at the conference table in Colonel Short's office. A lawyer from the American Consul explained first in English, and then in Italian, that he was passing around an affidavit. The document stated that the death of Thomas Stoddard was accidental, not the result of any negligence or foul play on the part of the assembled parties: the Naples Carbinieri chief, the military police chiefs from NATO and AFSE, and General Miroglio. Each of the officials at the table signed the affidavit. Finally, Joe scrawled his name. Tommy's accidental death was officially on Joe's permanent record.

For Joe, the tragedy of Tommy's death had thrown a shadow on his own career. His record would reflect personal misconduct in the accidental death of his son. He'd forced his family to move to a foreign country, far from all things familiar. He'd promised Fritzi she would see the world, but now her whole world was shattered. What kind of officer was he? What kind of a father was he? Why hadn't he set up some rules for the kids to follow at that party? Why hadn't he thought to put Rand and Linda in charge of the two younger ones?

Joe spent the next two weeks in the Naples apartment, cocooned with his family in a world of sorrowful efficiency. Libby Short, true to her role as the C.O.'s wife, took charge of the Stoddard household. She enlisted Assunta and some of the officers' wives to manage the constant stream of visitors offering condolences. She secured sedatives to help Fritzi rest. She arranged for teachers and classmates to call on Debby, Linda and Rand. She organized the refrigerator and pantry to accommodate the smorgasbord of casseroles and sweets offered up to the grieving family. She kept the doors to the dining room closed, allowing her husband to counsel Joe in private.

"You're my best pilot, so this really hurts," the colonel told Joe.

"Headquarters wants to transfer you Stateside. You'll be grounded for six months, standard procedure due to the accident."

"Yes, sir. I understand." Joe knew his C.O. was only carrying out orders.

"This is the Air Force, Joe. When an accident causes a dependent death, we all look bad. As long as you and your family live in Naples, people will wonder what happened that night at the General's apartment. It's best that you are out of sight and out of mind, as far as AFSE is concerned."

Joe stood up, opened the china cabinet, and took out a bottle of Wild Turkey with two highball glasses. "With all due respect, Colonel, I think we both deserve a drink. Will you do the honors?"

Colonel Short poured two generous glasses. "Look, Joe. For what it's worth, I've got a few Pentagon contacts, I'll see what I can do to get you squared away with a ground squadron. Libby and I will take care of shipping your household goods. The Embassy arranged for a local funeral home to take care of Tommy's body. The Air Force will transport your family back to the States for his burial."

"Thank you, Colonel." Joe managed to choke out the words, but his sprit tumbled into a tailspin. He wondered if that's how Tommy felt, chasing after a ball in a game he was destined to lose.

PART III

Yonder

15

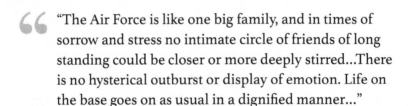 "The Air Force is like one big family, and in times of
sorrow and stress no intimate circle of friends of long
standing could be closer or more deeply stirred...There
is no hysterical outburst or display of emotion. Life on
the base goes on as usual in a dignified manner..."
—Nancy Shea, *The Air Force Wife*

NAPLES, Italy, and Montrose, Louisiana

EVEN IN SUNNY SEPTEMBER, the Stoddard's apartment in Naples was
cold as a tomb without Tommy. Colonel Short, and his wife, Libby,
came over the morning after Tommy died and were a constant presence in those first few days. Libby brought a big coffee urn and kept it
going. There were lots of visitors: every family in the building, both
Italian and American; General and Mrs. Miroglio with their son Bino;
various dignitaries from the Allied Forces Southern Europe, all of
Pop's squadron. Some of the kids from Rand's class dropped by,

mostly girls. Debby's friend Tammy came once with her big sister. Linda's seventh-grade teacher, a kind man named Mr. Deichman, came and brought a bouquet of chrysanthemums.

Pop and Fritzi kept up appearances while all this was going on. They managed to be quietly hospitable, grateful, and kind. The refrigerator was overflowing with casseroles and Jell-O molds. Homemade brownies, cookies, and cakes were stacked on the countertops. Assunta came every day to serve them to guests along with the endless coffee. Linda took *The Daily American* into the kitchen and when the coast was clear, she tucked brownies and cookies between its pages and squirreled them away in the maid's quarters. She'd sneak back there, close the door, and eat her grief, bite by bite.

At night, Linda heard the tinkling of ice in glasses, and knew her parents were drinking their grief. Pop started smoking with Fritzi, and in the morning the Murano glass ashtrays were overflowing with Chesterfield butts. Cigarette smoke and sorrow hovered over the apartment like dense fog.

Every time Linda ventured out of her room, she saw Colonel Short sitting with Pop in the dining room, talking in a low voice, like a minister. Of course, the base chaplain came, and Fritzi told him, kindly, that she didn't want to hear about the "valley of the shadow of death."

"I've lost my baby, you understand. Nothing from the Bible is going to make it better. Thank you for coming. Good-bye."

Tommy's body was embalmed at a Naples funeral home. A week after he died, the Stoddards accompanied his casket on a space available flight to Barksdale AFB in Louisiana. The Ida Rose Funeral Home in Montrose sent a hearse to pick up Tommy and a Cadillac limousine to pick up the rest the family. They all stayed at Fontainebleau.

"Oh, my darlings." Tears streamed down Grandmamma's powdered cheeks when they arrived at Fontainebleu. She hugged Fritzi, Debby and Linda individually, then held Linda at arm's length. "I bought you girls some suitable funeral dresses at Lois Jean's.

Debby's should be fine, but heavens! Linda, you've put on some weight, we'll have to get you a bigger size."

Fritzi's exhausted face ignited with anger. "For God's sake, Mother, just leave Linda alone! We brought our own clothes," Fritzi shouted. It seemed to Linda that Fritzi was angry enough to slap her own mother, but she composed herself with a sigh. "We are all tired. Go on up to bed, girls."

Grandmamma muffled her sobs in a handkerchief. Linda dragged her suitcase up the stairs. On second floor landing, she looked down at her angry mother and her sobbing grandmother. She saw Fritzi put her hand on Grandmamma's shoulder and pull the older woman to her in a short hug. It was a pitiful sight, Fritzi and Grandmamma engulfed in grief.

THE WHOLE TOWN seemed to show up for the funeral. Tommy's body, patched and embalmed and made up with cherry red lips, lay in an open casket. Linda filed by with the rest of the crowd and burst into uncontrollable tears when she looked at Tommy's face.

Debby upstaged Linda with a panic attack, claiming she saw Tommy's chest rise and fall, like he was breathing. Josie, Grandmamma's cook, herded both girls into the ladies' lounge at First Presbyterian for the remainder of the service. Josie sat with them on a sagging old couch and held Debby close, dabbed her forehead with a damp cloth, and sang. Linda didn't remember what she sang, but Josie's low, rich voice wafted over her like a warm blanket. She settled down and just sat there, blowing her nose and listening.

Rand was a pallbearer, along with some of Pop's friends. Linda missed it all, including the long ride to the rural cemetery, because she just wanted to stay on that old couch in the ladies' lounge, listening to Josie. Josie took Linda and Debby back to Fontainebleu, where Grandmamma had a huge reception planned for mourners. Josie had done all of the cooking: fried chicken, ham, deviled eggs, potato salad, caramel sheet cake. As soon as they got there, Josie cut Linda a huge piece and told her to sit down and finish it before her grandmother got back home.

Three days after the funeral, Pop and Fritzi sat down with Rand, Debby, and Linda on Grandmamma's terrace. "We're not going back to Naples," Pop said. "I've been reassigned to Barksdale Air Force Base, heading up a squadron there. Rand, you ought to be excited, because that's where the Stratofortress is based. I'm heading up a maintenance squadron, and I can show you anything and everything you'd like to know about that beast." Linda could tell Pop was trying to inject his voice with some kind of cheer.

Rand's face seemed to fall somewhere below his knees. "What about our stuff? Our apartment? The van?"

"Colonel and Mrs. Short are selling the van and seeing that the rest of our stuff all gets packed and sent to Barksdale. How about that? A move without any work!"

"We'll be buying a new car, of course," Fritzi added. "A Ford Estate wagon."

It occurred to Linda that there was no need for such a big car, as the three surviving children could fit into the back seat of a sedan. "What about Tommy's things?" she asked.

"Assunta has a grandson about his age. She's going to give them away."

"But I wanted his toys!" Debby said, eyes brimming with tears.

"Tinkerbell, just think of that little Italian boy. He'll love having those toys. We don't have...any...use...for..." Pop buried his face in his hands. It was the only time Linda had seen her father cry. Fritzi went to him, sat in his lap and held him close.

BARKSDALE AIR FORCE BASE, *Louisiana*

THEY NOW LIVED in a French Revival home on Barksdale Air Force Base. Architecturally, it wasn't bad for base housing: tall and skinny,

brown brick with mint green shutters and a deep mansard roof. It
had three bedrooms, two baths, two stories. There was a small yard
planted with St. Augustine grass and a big magnolia tree in the front.
A placard attached to the front porch, just beneath the house number
read: MAJ. R. STODDARD.

It became Rand's job to keep the grass trimmed, but Pop
refused to spring for a power mower. The old push mower could
only go a few feet without clogging itself with wet, thick grass.
Rand had to mow once a week even in winter, as Pop could get
written up by the Base Housing Office if the grass wasn't trimmed
below three inches.

Fritzi had lost about ten pounds, and she began to look wan.
Rand worried for his mother; he knew how fiercely she loved, and
now he saw how sharply she felt the loss of her baby. He wanted to
reach out to her, but Fritzi had closed herself off behind a mask of
bitterness. She floated through the days, doing what needed to be
done, but no more. She cooked, showed up at the Officers' Wives'
Club welcome-to-Barksdale coffees for her, hired a cleaning woman
to spiff up around the house. But when she could, Fritzi would sleep
till noon. If she had to get up early, she'd take long afternoon naps, or
go to bed right after dinner. Her body was shrinking; her beautiful
clothes hung off her shoulders and pooled around her hips. Her
shiny copper hair took on the tarnished hue of an old penny. Her face
had gone gaunt. She was constantly smoking, lighting one Chesterfield off another. When she inhaled, there was no exhale of pleasure.
Smoke simply seeped from her nose, leaked from a funeral pyre deep
within.

It pained him to see this deflated, wasted version of his mother.
Rand also felt pain, but as the weeks went by, he realized it was longing, not just for his sweet little brother, but for the life they'd left
behind in Naples. The city. The people. The cacophony of languages
overheard on the hydrofoil to Capri. The crisp crusts of pizza, the
strong steamy smell of dark roasted coffee from the trattorias. The
herds of goats stopping traffic on city streets, the occasional belch
from Vesuvius. Camping in the VW van, sleeping above his intact

family in a tent under the stars. The intact family. A family naïve of tragedy.

Pop soldiered on in his typical way, donning his uniform every day and heading off to work. A maintenance squadron. What a pitiful comedown for a test pilot, a former astronaut candidate, an embassy liaison charged with top secret missions. It seemed to Rand that the Air Force had taken pity on Pop. Colonel Short had connections at the Pentagon who had reassigned him here, to this god-forsaken swamp, where Pop and Fritzi could be closer to the roots they had long ago abandoned when Pop chose an Air Force career.

No one spoke about Tommy. One month had passed since his death. Fritzi spent the day in bed. Pop pretended not to notice the date. Rand and Linda exchanged glances over a breakfast of cold cereal. His sister's grim expression mirrored his; they knew it was the one-month anniversary. Neither of them dared disturb the silence, raise the question, or even offer a prayer. It was confusing as hell, he thought, after the big funeral at the First Presbyterian Church, the organ music, the church choir. Pop and Fritzi acted like that was just something you *did*—you went to church on Easter, said a prayer over Thanksgiving dinner, and when your youngest child died, you held a big church funeral. Period.

Rand had to transfer from the American school in Naples to Bossier High School, home of the Bearkats. It was a fucking hellhole. The only good thing about it was the building, an old fort converted to a school. The people, the students, what a joke. The girls ratted their hair into mega helmets cemented with Final Net. The guys were thugs, big hicks with pimples who chewed tobacco. On his second day at Bossier High, a skinny guy with big glasses and white socks confronted Rand at his locker.

"Are you saved?" he asked.

Rand looked at him and scratched his head. "Saved from what?"

"Do you know Jesus Christ as your savior?" the nerd asked, pushing thick glasses up on his nose.

"I'm not sure what you're talking about." Rand gathered his books and slammed his locker.

"Jesus Christ died for your sins. I'm Dennis Franken. Be happy for you to accompany me to my church on Wednesday evening to hear the Good Word."

"Well, Dennis," Rand said, his voice flat. "I'm afraid that won't work at all. I'm a confirmed agnostic."

"I'll pray for you," Dennis said. "You don't deserve to go to hell."

As far as Rand was concerned, he was already in hell. Bossier High School had no accelerated classes, no advanced foreign languages, and no calculus. Water fountains and bathrooms were designated "colored" or "white." The big-bellied principal wore an obvious toupee, and Rand's French teacher mispronounced everything. The cafeteria served thick cream gravy that looked and smelled like vomit. Even in November, the classrooms were airless and sweltering because they were not air-conditioned. The Bearkat football players were treated like Greek gods; the cheerleaders wore pleated skirts and swished their asses up and down the hallways, calling to each other "Hey, Darla! What's the gooood word?"

Word had gotten around that Rand was not only an agnostic, but also a "base kid" whose father was an officer. As he made his way to the bus stop after school, a couple of thugs blocked his path. One had a toothpick sticking out of his mouth; the other had a crew cut so waxed, he resembled an escapee from Madame Tussaud's.

"So. Do we salute the major's son, or what?" said Crew Cut.

Toothpick sneered. "Carrot Top ain't got no rank. Or does he?" He gave Rand a playful punch in the arm.

In Naples, Rand had learned about confrontation more than once. He and his American friends liked exploring the city, and they always traveled in pairs. Brian Smith had taught him the secret every street-savvy Neapolitan knew: leverage. Especially with big guys. Punch, kick, go for the groin. Then run like hell. If that failed, pull the switchblade he bought in the mercato.

"Just going to the bus stop." Rand shrugged off the punch and stepped around Toothpick.

"Oh, the *bus stop*. Riding the bus to your fancy neighborhood on the *base*. That's where the majors and the colonels live, right?"

Rand gritted his teeth. He didn't have his knife. He braced himself and looked Crew Cut in the eye. Hatred surged within him and lowered his voice to a low growl. "You got a problem with that?"

"What if I do?" Crew Cut spat chewing tobacco at Rand's foot.

Rand kicked the brown wad of mucous onto Crew Cut's ugly work boots. "Get out of my way."

Crew Cut stumbled back, grossed out at his own spittle. Then he narrowed his eyes and lunged at Rand, who ducked a swift punch to his face. Rand grabbed Crew Cut around the waist and spun him, then threw him to the sidewalk and kicked him in the ribs. Toothpick rushed in from behind and punched Rand in the kidneys. Rand doubled over in pain, but slugged Toothpick with a low punch to the stomach. Toothpick punched Rand under the chin; he heard his jaw crack and felt teeth break. By that time, Crew Cut had risen to his feet and began a rapid fire punch assault on Rand's face. Rand retaliated with a knee kick to Crew Cut's crotch. Crew Cut lurched backward and cried out, crossing his hands over his balls. Toothpick kicked Rand's feet out from under him, sending him crashing to the sidewalk.

The fight had drawn a few timid onlookers, including Dennis, the skinny nerd who inquired about Rand's savior. As Toothpick and Crew Cut sauntered off, Dennis ran for help.

RAND WOKE up in the base hospital. Through a pinhole in a red haze, he could make out Fritzi's silhouette over him. He started to speak, but was unable to open his mouth.

"Son. Those goddamn cretins broke your jaw. You won't be able to speak for a couple of days. And you'll need some dental work, but you will be all right," said Fritzi.

He felt her soft hand on an unbandaged patch of his forehead. Her touch, her tone of voice were strong now, much stronger than they'd been since Tommy died. He sank back into a drowsy daze, feeling one thing was right in the world, at least for now, Fritzi seemed better.

On the day Rand was released from the hospital, he propped himself on pillows and turned on the television. They hadn't had a TV in Naples, and Rand was always curious about the different programs and commercials that were on now. He flipped past a boring game show on NBC, a commercial he'd already seen on ABC, and held steady on the CBS channel. There was a melodramatic woman, talking heatedly to a man in a suit about something. A soap opera—that's what they called these things. A curiosity of melodramatic pap, all interrupted by commercials aimed at bored housewives. Was that what Fritzi would become—a housewife—now that they were back in the States?

Fritzi lit a Chesterfield and sat down on the end of the couch. "You need anything, honey?"

He was about to ask for a Coke on ice, when a newscaster interrupted the soap opera. The screen said "CBS NEWS BULLETIN." A man's voice announced: "President Kennedy has been shot in Dallas, Texas. Three shots were fired and reports say the president is seriously wounded."

"What in the goddamn hell?" Fritzi stood up and turned up the volume. The television went back to a commercial for dog chow. Fritzi picked up the phone and called Pop.

"Is it true?" she asked, "Have they shot Kennedy?"

Rand sat in stony silence, unable to speak. Surely there was a mistake. From what he could tell by Fritzi's conversation, Pop didn't know for sure. Fritzi hung up, frustrated.

In a few minutes, the CBS channel went to the newsroom. A man with glasses identified himself as Walter Cronkite and said: "The news, apparently now official. President Kennedy died at one p.m. Central Standard Time, two p.m. Eastern, just forty-eight minutes ago..."

Fritzi was still on the phone. "Joe, I want you to go to school and pick up the girls. Then you must come home. We've got to be together. No, I'm not panicked. Our president has been killed. We all need to be home, now." She hung up and turned toward the TV. "Goddamn Texans. He never should have gone to Dallas."

Tears formed in Rand's eyes. He sat on the couch, still as death, wishing it all was a bad dream caused by pain medication.

NOVEMBER 22, 1963

THAT MORNING, Linda had a strange, queasy feeling as she waited for the bus to Bossier Middle School. Something about the early morning fog was off; something about the sunlight was skewed. The world was a tick off its axis, perhaps, or maybe she wasn't fully awake, or maybe she was still dreaming. Something about this Friday morning got under her skin and clouded her eyes with expectation. Not for something good. It wasn't exactly a premonition, but a disturbance, an uneasiness that lasted through lunch and into the humid afternoon. When her fourth period teacher announced that President Kennedy had been shot, she grasped her three-ring binder and shielded her chest. She could still see his shining hair, his sharp blue suit, his salute to the Naples troops in parade formation. Perhaps she, too, would be shot; maybe they were all doomed. If someone could get to that beautiful president, that confident man who had Secret Service agents, then no one, nowhere was safe.

Linda got a note to go to the office. There was Pop, sweaty and almost breathless. "Come on, honey, we're going to pick up Debby at the elementary school. Rand is home from the hospital, and Fritzi's there, and well, we're just all going to go there. At least for now."

She had never been so glad to see Pop. She hugged him tight, suppressing tears. They went by the elementary school for Debby, who was crying in the nurse's office, and Pop drove them home.

The phone was ringing as soon as they walked in the door. Pop rushed to answer it, while Debby clung to Fritzi and Linda sat down on the couch next to Rand. She stared at her one remaining brother, bandaged and swollen, and wondered if this was the end of everything.

Pop hung up the phone and rushed upstairs. In a few minutes, he came back down with his B-4 bag packed. He was wearing his flight suit and the mask of duty on his face.

"I'm On Alert," he said, stopping to kiss Fritzi's lips. "With luck, I'll see y'all later this evening. If not, I'll see you when I see you. Take care of each other."

Linda watched Pop walk down the front steps and out to an official blue Air Force car that was waiting at the curb. Fritzi locked the front door and turned off the TV.

"Let's have a Coke," she said in a cheerful voice. "Rand, I know you want one. I'll pour it over ice and get you a straw. Come on to the kitchen, girls."

And there they were, all four, huddled together in their base house, each drinking a Coke. With Fritzi trying to soothe them and Pop On Alert, Linda felt safer, but even sadder than she was when Tommy died.

16

"Air Force men dedicated to the Service today are those
airmen who unselfishly
and of their own free will place *duty* first—before
wife, children, parents,
personal desires, ambition, money, or anything
else!"
—Nancy Shea, *The Air Force Wife*

MONTROSE, Louisiana

AS SQUADRON COMMANDER, Pop offered to take Alert over Christmas.
He said his men deserved to be with their families, and he owed it to
them after all the time they put in with the assassination of President
Kennedy and keeping the Gulf Coast safe. Fritzi didn't argue with
him. Debby overheard her say that it was just as well, that this
Christmas would be a hard one, and he may as well spend it working
instead of at home remembering.

Grandmamma and Judge wanted Fritzi and the kids to spend Christmas at Fontainebleu. On Christmas Eve, Fritzi drove the one-hundred miles over to Montrose with Linda and Rand huddled into sullen heaps in the back seats and Debby in front, twirling the radio dial in search of cheerful Christmas music.

Debby liked sitting in front, although she could hardly see over the dash. The front seat meant she was closest to Fritzi, and also had control over the radio. Out here, however, the reception was bad and all she could find were preachers and bad country music. Rand sat hunched in one corner of the middle seat, poring over *Scientific American*. Linda cloistered herself in the way back, reading a new book called *To Kill a Mockingbird*. Debby wondered why her sister would be so engrossed in a book about killing birds when she could be singing Christmas carols, or playing Spot the States on the License Plates. Fritzi was silent, smoking Chesterfields and managing the Cruise Control so they wouldn't get caught in any speed traps.

"Will Santa know that we're at Judge and Grandmamma's?" Debby asked her mother. As a third grader, Debby no longer believed in Santa Claus, but the family needed to think she did. She was the youngest now, and that meant she had to play along with the Santa myth so Fritzi wouldn't miss Tommy so much. No matter how much her mother got involved in the Officers' Wives' Club, or volunteered at her school, or organized the Base Thrift Shop, Debby sensed Fritzi was empty. Her smile was there, but it was no longer magic. Her laugh was hollow. Her eyes were rimmed with red and there were lines on her face where there were none before.

"What, honey?" Fritzi asked, flicking ashes into the tray under the radio.

"I said, will Santa know where we are, or will he go to our base house and leave our presents there?" Debby repeated, miffed that her mother never seemed to hear her these days. Just because Tommy was gone did not mean the rest of them had to stop living, had to pretend that Christmas wasn't happening this year.

"Sure! Santa always knows where you are, because that's his job. He always comes to Fontainebleu for some of Josie's Christmas cookies. Even when there aren't any children there!" Her voice was force-fed with holiday joy.

"What was Christmas like when you were a little girl? Was it special?" Debby loved to hear her mother talk about her childhood, growing up in such a big, beautiful house, with her doting parents. She'd give anything to be an only child, especially now. Tommy's absence cast a pall over everything these days; Debby wished he'd never been born. So much sorrow in the eyes of her parents, so much stillness in the new house, on the stuffy base, with loud plane engines roaring over their roof at all hours of the day and night.

"Oh, honey," Fritzi's voice took on a tone of authentic lightness. "It was *so* special. Leo would cut a big holly tree from the gardens on Christmas Eve, and he and Daddy would stand it up in the drawing room. Later, Josie and I would clip all the little candleholders to its branches with fresh candles—little candles like the ones you put on birthday cakes these days. All white, with silver tin holders. We'd string cranberries and drape them, so red against the shiny dark green. Later, after dinner and the Christmas church service, I'd put on my pajamas. Daddy would light all the candles—dancing, beautiful light—not like electric tree lights at all. I'd hang my stocking, we'd say a prayer, and Mother would read *A Visit from Saint Nicholas* out loud. I'd leave those Christmas cookies that Josie and I had baked, along with a mug of buttermilk and some carrots for the reindeer, on the hearth. Daddy and Mother would tuck me into bed. Even when I was a teenager—it was the same little routine on Christmas Eve." Tears filled Fritzi's eyes, but none tumbled onto her cheek.

"Can we have Christmas Eve like that tonight? It sounds so fun!" Debby's heart rose in her chest like a party balloon. She hadn't felt such hope in such a long time.

"Oh, I don't think so. Judge and Grandmamma switched to electric lights a long time ago, and Leo buys a tree for them at the tree lot. I doubt we'll go to church—it's just too much this year. But we'll have a nice dinner, and I'm sure we'll have a good time." She didn't sound so convinced herself.

"What about the cookies?"

"We'll see. It's been years since I've been home at Christmas. Not sure Josie still bakes them."

Debby's heart fell back into line, back into the place of no expectation, no joy. It wasn't fair, and it wasn't her fault. Tommy ran after that ball. No one forced him to. And no one stopped him. She didn't stop him. She tried, but she didn't stop him. Now, Christmas and everything else was ruined forever.

LINDA'S MOOD was as gray as the Louisiana skies these days. Everything was so humid, so close, even in winter. There was no breeze. On base, there were roaring planes taking off and landing all day. The Christmas at Fontainebleu was clouded by Grandmamma's rules and expectations, her warnings and her predictions of doom—the atomic bomb, the Communists, integration and the end of "colored" schools.

The worst part of the whole holiday experience was Grandmamma's constant reference to Tommy—how sad and awful it was that he had to die on "foreign soil," insisting that they all go visit his grave on Christmas Day. It tore Fritzi up, but she didn't do anything about it. That's the saddest thing. Her mother had lost her fire, that spark that used to fuel her rebellion against Grandmamma's grandiosity. And Pop—he'd chosen to ditch the family and work through the holidays On Alert. Judge was silent, his chin hanging low, smoking a pipe, sitting all day in his library. He didn't even bother to go out fishing with Rand.

Linda chose to stay under the wire at Fontainebleu, where Grandmamma presided over Christmas Eve and Christmas Day. In her red silk dress, Grandmamma summoned everyone to the table. She took Linda aside and warned her to eat "sparingly" and said she held out hopes that she would "blossom into a swan" in high school. Josie had prepared a feast: roasted wild turkey, cornbread dressing, plum pudding. Judge opened a special bottle of claret and served a glass to everyone, even the children. Linda sipped, suppressing tears as she slathered her plate in warm gravy.

Grandmamma invited everyone to sit in the parlor for a "fashion show," featuring Debby modeling a bunch of prissy little dresses that Grandmamma had given her for Christmas. (Rand and Linda had both received Timex watches; they were not asked to model them.) Grandmamma sat regally and applauded Debby's every twirl and swirl, while Fritzi poured herself more claret. Linda watched her sister wallow in the attention like the little whore she was.

Linda didn't know exactly why she started hating Debby in those days. Debby just seemed to ramp up her little cuteness act, while Linda hunkered down and tried to remain invisible. Maybe she blamed Debby for Tommy's death. Her sister was probably trying to process their younger brother's death, too, but she was doing it with cloying prissiness. No doubt Debby was prancing her way through grief, while Linda chose to bury hers in a snarky attitude and antisocial behavior.

Truth was, Linda missed her family. They'd always had Christmas wherever they were—the red brick house in Ohio, the apartment in Naples—they never, ever traveled to be with their grandparents. None of the Air Force families they knew traveled "home" for the holidays; they prided themselves on the fact that *home* was wherever their fathers were assigned.

Before Tommy died, they'd been a shiny, boisterous family, traveling Europe in the VW van, pulling pranks on each other in hotel rooms, laughing and fussing and interacting with each other every day. Now, they were all separate, hiding within themselves: Fritzi, sheathed in uncharacteristic melancholy; Debby, clothed in baby-doll cheer; Rand, sullen and mean beneath dented armor; Pop, cloaked in a facade of rank and duty, and Linda, throbbing in pain and confusion, masked by pubescent moodiness.

BARKSDALE AIR FORCE BASE, *Louisiana*

"WHAT DO YOU MEAN, you can't refill this? It's my prescription medication!" Fritzi looked the young airman in the eye as she showed him her military dependent ID.

"Ma'am, I'm sorry, but the base hospital dispensary no longer stocks Miltown. If you want to fill this, you'll have to go to a civilian pharmacy."

"Well, that's the most ridiculous thing I've heard in my life!" Fritzi took back the ID and the prescription and snapped them into her handbag. She turned on her heel to head out to the car when she bumped into Julia Hinton, wife of a second lieutenant in Joe's squadron, with a feverish looking toddler on her hip.

"I'm sorry, Mrs. Stoddard, I didn't mean to run into you!" Julia said. She had the haunted, sleep-deprived look of a young mother at her wit's end.

Fritzi took a breath and stopped. "Oh, my. Looks like somebody's not feeling well. I remember those nights. What is it, tonsillitis?"

"Ear infection," Julia said, wiping her brow. "Poor little Tony cried for two nights. We finally saw the pediatrician, and we're in line for penicillin." The fussy toddler's eyes were glassy and his nose was snotty. Julia, a petite blonde who couldn't have weighed a hundred pounds, rocked back and forth, shifting her weight to keep from shrinking under her big toddler son.

"Here. Let me hold Tony for a moment, and let's get you to the front of the line," Fritzi said, reaching for the heavy, dark-haired kid. He was hot as fire with fever. "Excuse me, Sergeant," she said to the man at the head of the line, "would you be a gentleman and let this young lady go ahead of you? She's been up all night with this very sick little boy." Fritzi ran her hand over the boy's dark curls, matted with sweat.

The sergeant looked annoyed but stepped aside. "Sure, go ahead, Ma'am."

"Oh, thank you so much, thank you!" Julia pushed her ID and prescription into the dispensary window. "You don't know how much this means to me..."

"Hush now. The Air Force can at least give a break to a mother and child," said Fritzi. She stood tall next to Julia and glared at the young airman in the dispensary. "I'm sure they keep *penicillin* in stock." The airman nodded at her and turned to fill Julia's prescription.

Tony whimpered and started to fuss. Fritzi rocked him back and forth, then reached into her purse for a tissue. "Let's clean up that nose, young man." She wiped, then playfully pinched the kid's nose. He started to grin, and Fritzi just held on to him, heavy as lead, hot as fire, a toddler whose weight somehow grounded her. *Tommy. He would have turned four this month.*

Julia took the boy and showered Fritzi with thanks.

"Don't mention it," Fritzi said. "Get some rest—both of you!"

The weight of that kid in her arms stayed with Fritzi all the way to the car. Once there, she tore up the Miltown prescription and decided to go cold turkey. It had been good to hold a real child. It made her see that Tommy was no longer real. She could no longer hold him, touch him, or soothe his fever. He was gone. Nothing she could do would bring him back, so she might as well stop dosing up with Miltown and pretending the pain didn't exist. It did. But so did her other children.

She stopped by the commissary and picked up a chicken, potatoes, green beans, a gallon of ice cream, and a case of Schlitz. At home, she unloaded the groceries and popped open a beer. There was ironing to do, all piled up on top of the dryer. Joe had given up on her and had begun sending his uniforms to the base cleaners. She looked at the wadded pile of her children's clothing: Rand's plaid shirts, Debby's dresses, two skirts of Linda's. It occurred to her that the children must have been doing their own laundry these past few months. Everything but the ironing. When they left for school, she was often still asleep, so she didn't see what they wore. By the time they got home, she was either in a Miltown haze or running the cash register at the Officers' Wives' Club Thrift Shop. She hadn't been a real mother to them since Tommy. Her own surviving children had become orphans.

Joe was no better. He worked and worked and worked, and on Fridays, he went to Beer Call at the Club. He played golf on Saturdays and read the paper on Sundays. On weekdays, he sunk into a bourbon haze every day after sundown. She couldn't remember the last time they'd made love. He'd long ago given up working with Rand on his Stratofortress, and he all but ignored the girls. They had both abandoned their children.

She plugged in the iron and sprayed the wadded clothes with water. Starting with the full skirt on Debby's polka dotted dress, she pressed the wrinkles away. She put a crease in the short sleeves and a crisp edge on the eyelet collar and hem. She hung the dress, still warm, on a hanger on the ledge above the kitchen cabinets. Then she tackled Rand's shirts, Linda's blouses, skirts. She put a crease in Rand's khaki pants and his Levis. She searched pockets for handkerchiefs and starched them until they were stiff as cardboard. She rummaged through the linen closet and ironed cloth napkins that hadn't seen the light of day since Naples. She did a load of laundry and ironed her husband's boxer shorts. Another beer. She ironed guest towels she'd gotten as wedding presents. Placemats. Tablecloths. She unplugged the iron and took it into the bedroom she shared with Joe. She ran it over the chenille bedspread, chasing puckers and creases until the spread was tight and smooth.

Another beer. She cut the chicken she'd bought into pieces and seasoned it. She made a batter from water and cornstarch and an egg. She heated Crisco in the electric skillet Joe had given her two Christmases ago. (She had detested the gift and hadn't even taken it out of its box until now.) By the time Debby, Rand, and Linda got off the bus from Bossier City schools, they'd be greeted with the sumptuous, salty golden smell of chicken frying.

They ate like the starving orphans they were, wolfing down her crisp chicken pieces, fluffy mashed potatoes oozing with cream gravy. She'd added bacon to the green beans, and the three of them—even picky little Debby—ate every last bite. Fritzi kept the chicken coming from the skillet, and they devoured every piece as soon as it was cool enough to shove into their mouths. Fritzi popped open another beer and sat down with them to watch. Their eyes were half closed as they enjoyed their four o'clock feast, like feral animals feeding on a fresh carcass.

When they'd finished, Fritzi pulled out the gallon of vanilla ice cream, chocolate sauce, and can of Jiffy Whip. "Make your own sundaes!" she said. "And when you're finished, clean up the dishes and do your homework. Your father and I are going out to dinner tonight."

She didn't hang around to listen to them fuss about who was going to clean the greasy skillet or ask her if it was their anniversary or even to thank her for ironing their clothes. She went to her bedroom and dialed the Officer's Club. "This is Mrs. Stoddard. Major Stoddard and I need a table for two for dinner, seven o'clock. A quiet corner in the dining room, please," she said. It was Prime Rib Night. Joe would take the bribe.

She dressed in the purple sheath, which she no longer filled out like Gina Lollabrigida. It hung on her hips and was too big in the shoulders, but it still looked all right. She did her makeup and did what she could to her hair, then dialed Joe's office. "I'll meet you at the Club at seven," she said, her voice giddy after four beers, "The kids have eaten."

Fritzi sat at the bar, sipping a cold martini, watching the door for her husband. It pleased her when a couple of young officers gave her the eye. She still had it, at least in the semi-darkness. At the end of the bar, she spotted Captain Thomas Reynolds, RAF, talking to Rhonda Morgan, a major's wife who was a dead ringer for Jayne Mansfield. So this is what some of the wives gossiped about at OWC. Captain Reynolds's wife, a mousey little woman named Jenny, was six months pregnant and big as a house. The handsome RAF officer liked to grab a few drinks at the club on his way home when he wasn't flying, and word had it that some wives, like Rhonda, joined him when their husbands were out of town. Fritzi smiled into her martini. She didn't like to gossip, but it was so soap-opera ridiculous that this smarmy little drama was playing out in front of her. So ridiculous, so obvious, on a base where all the wives knew each other and all the husbands knew when the men were flying. Did they think they were fooling anyone?

Just then, she felt Joe's lips on her neck.

"Drinking alone?" he asked, signaling the bartender for a bourbon.

"Just waiting for my husband so we can enjoy some prime rib," Fritzi purred. The beers and the martini had awakened her inner kitten. She turned and kissed Joe on the lips.

"Happy New Year," Joe said.

"About a month too late," Fritzi said.

"But it's our first kiss in 1964. First since I can remember," Joe said under his breath. He took the seat next to her and clicked his high-ball with her martini glass. "Cheers."

The hostess showed them their table, a booth upholstered in brown Naugahyde. Cozy, just as Fritzi had asked. They sat next to each other.

They ordered more drinks. Fritzi picked at her prime rib, and Joe ate heartily. He took a break and buried his face in her hair and kissed her.

"Your hair smells like fried chicken. Is that why you're not hungry?" he asked.

"Ha! I cooked for the kids when they got home from school. They couldn't believe it. I even ironed. Everything in the whole house."

"Well, it *is* a new year. Not that I care if you iron. But the kids, they've missed you. It's like you've been gone since we got here."

"Me? What about you? Beer Call? The sudden need to play golf on Saturdays, instead of spending the day with your kids?"

Joe chewed a piece of meat. "We still have three of them, I tell myself. It's just painful—painful to love them so much. I've left the hard work to you, I'm afraid. But, my squadron needs me. You're the kind of wife I know will pick up the slack. That's all."

"Goddamn it, Joe. I've *been* the slack. I've been taking Miltown to help me cope all this time. All it did was deaden the pain. I wasn't there for them, wasn't there for you. You've been AWOL, too. It's time we quit this little pity party."

"We never threw ourselves a pity party, for creep's sake. We lost our baby boy. It takes time. Moving here was the right thing, to get away from where it all happened, to be closer to your folks. I think we're going to be just fine." He chewed, working his temples like he did when he was really thinking about something.

"I don't need to be near my folks, and you know that, Joe. And don't think you can ditch us at Christmas just because it's too hard for you to go through the motions. Don't *ever* think I can't see through that crap. Me—I just went cold turkey. Turned over a new leaf, so to speak. I'm getting off the Miltown—the dispensary wouldn't fill it anymore—and I'm back. And I'm going to stay back. If you want to be with me, you've got to get back to being a father and a husband, just like I'm getting back to being a mother and a wife. So decide now." She downed her second martini and placed the empty glass on the table.

Joe signaled for the check. "Let's take this discussion out of here," he muttered.

The squadron car had dropped Joe at the club, so he escorted Fritzi, now wobbly in her heels, to the station wagon she'd driven from home.

He sat in the driver's seat. She scooted over to his side and grabbed his arms. "I mean it Joe. Pull it together. We've got to take this on. We've got three more kids to get through life."

Joe smothered her in a kiss and stuck his hand up her skirt. "I'm all in," he said.

He drove the station wagon to a remote spot in the parking lot, where they proceeded to make out like rabid teenagers. If anyone had been watching, they would have seen the station wagon rocking gently from side to side.

RAND WAS upstairs reading when he heard them come home.

"Goddammit, kids!" Fritzi yelled from the kitchen. She sounded more than a little tipsy. "Get down here and clean up this mess!"

He shouldn't have left the electric skillet to his sisters. He'd put everything away and loaded the dishwasher without their help, so he assigned them the dirtiest task. Obviously, they hadn't done the job. He went across the hall to their room.

"Get up, you lazy cows! Pop and Fritzi are home and they're none too happy with your cleanup job."

Just then, Rosemary Clooney launched into "Mambo Italiano" from the Telefunken, the fancy German stereo Pop bought while they were in Naples. The bass was turned up so high, it shook the walls.

Debby and Linda jumped out of their twin beds and ran to the top of the stairs with Rand. In the living room, Fritzi was prancing around without her shoes and her bra strap hanging out of her dress. Pop was chasing her around, trying to dance with her. It was two in the morning.

At the end of the song, Fritzi twirled around and collapsed on the couch. Pop covered her with an old quilt his mother had made. They heard water running in the kitchen and the three of them tiptoed downstairs.

Linda, of course, was the brave one. She sneaked past Fritzi on the couch and went into the kitchen with Pop. "I'm sorry. Debby and I were supposed to clean this up, and I guess we just got busy with homework," she said sheepishly.

Rand and Debby followed. Pop was wearing one of Fritzi's aprons over his wrinkled uniform. His hands were immersed in a sink full of suds.

"That's OK, honey," he said to Linda. "I figure it's my turn to help out around here. Can you get me the grease can so I can empty this old Crisco?"

"Sure." Linda glanced at her siblings with a shrug. She tipped back her head and mimed drinking from a cup.

Yeah, Pop must be wasted all right. Rand had never seen him do a dish in his life, much less wear an apron.

The next morning, Fritzi slept in and Pop woke the three of them at nine with the smell of bacon frying and pancakes on the griddle.

Pop stood at the stove and turned a batch out onto a hot plate. "Come on, get some butter on those before they get cold. Chop chop!"

"How come you didn't wake us up for school?" Debby asked.

"I called school and said all of you were sick. I took a day of leave. We're going to play hooky today. That is, unless you *want* to go to school for some reason."

"No, sir!" the three of them said in unison. It had to be a dream. A dream come true—or was Pop still drunk?

"Why?" Rand asked, "Not that I want to go to school, but why all this? Are you guys hungover or something?"

"Shut your mouth, Horse Fly!" Pop was stern, his regular self. "No, we are not 'hungover.' It's just time we did something fun together. Even if it means missing school."

"I'm all for that!" Rand answered, grabbing a bacon strip.

Linda and Debby stuffed their mouths with pancakes. It was the beginning of a strangely wonderful day. After breakfast, Pop had everyone make sandwiches for a picnic to Cypress Lake Black Bayou. They left Fritzi at home and made a day of it, hiking, skipping rocks, and driving along roads paved with shells. It was a chilly day, damp and cloudy. Rand sat up front with Pop and they sang songs—"Be kind to your web-footed friends, for a duck may be somebody's mother... they live in the crick by the swimp, where the weather is always dimp..." and some other dumb songs Pop knew. On the way home, they stopped at an all-you-can-eat catfish house for hushpuppies, catfish, and cole slaw. Pop asked for a to-go bag for Fritzi. When they got home, Fritzi told them go head for the showers because they "stunk like a bunch of swamp people."

The next day, Fritzi got up and bustled everyone out of the house —the kids back to school, Pop back to work. Rand had to admit his mood was better. Somewhere, deep down, he could feel a ray of hope wedge its way into his dark outlook.

On Friday of that week, Pop came home with orders: "We're going to Travis. Reporting for duty this summer."

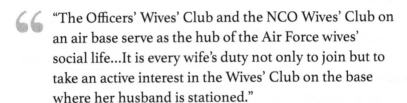

17

"The Officers' Wives' Club and the NCO Wives' Club on an air base serve as the hub of the Air Force wives' social life...It is every wife's duty not only to join but to take an active interest in the Wives' Club on the base where her husband is stationed."
—Nancy Shea, *The Air Force Wife*

Travis Air Force Base, California

RAND WAS SLUMPED in the back seat of the station wagon, absorbed in *The Fountainhead,* when he heard Fritzi and Pop say they were eligible for Capehart housing at Travis. Apparently, this was a big deal because most base houses in California were Wherry houses—small, cramped, and certainly not the quality they'd gotten used to at Barksdale. Now that Pop was to command the 44th Military Air Transport Squadron, home of the new C-141 Starlifter, he was on the short list to make lieutenant colonel. And this all meant they were at the top of the waiting list for a coveted Capehart house in the field officers' housing at Travis.

Rand wasn't sure what all this meant. At first, he assumed Capehart was some kind of genius architect, like Howard Roark or Frank Lloyd Wright. But when they drove up to their new address on Cannon Drive (named after some Air Force general), he figured Capehart wasn't a genius.

The house itself resembled a large wooden crate, set on its side. Six small windows lined up next to each other on the façade, like a child's drawing. The door, set in the middle, was flanked by two strange spiky bushes that Fritzi recognized as yucca. He thought she was saying they were yucky at first, but in fact, she seemed delighted by them. "Don't you remember we had them in Albuquerque, Rand? At the little house on Navajo Drive?"

"Uh, no, Fritzi. Considering I was only three when we left," he said sarcastically, perusing the ugly little house.

"Enough, Horse Fly, of the attitude in your voice," Pop warned.

"I'm sorry, Fritzi. I just meant I don't remember, that's all," he said apologetically.

"That's better," Pop said.

"Uh—is Capehart the architect or something, Pop? I don't get why it's called Capehart housing."

Pop chuckled. "No, son, it's the name of the senator from Indiana who introduced the bill to authorize building these modern homes. Much better than the old Wherry-authorized houses, built just after World War II."

"Oh." Of course, the Air Force would name housing after the big-talking senator who made the appropriation. Amazing how the military-industrialist complex was intertwined. Rand held in a sigh of disgust and opened the car door.

Of course, Debby was running ahead, twirling in the front yard under a big gum ball tree. Trash tree. Piece of shit tree. He glanced at Linda, who seemed content to stand in the tiny front yard. "Just breathe this air! It's so light, and so cool!"

She was right. The heavy, oppressive air of Louisiana was gone.

They now lived in Solano County, north of San Francisco and west of Sacramento. The rolling hills of Northern California, where the ocean breeze met the mountain air. However, the smell of jet fuel wafted over all the houses on Travis Air Force Base. Still, Rand had to admit the place had promise. It felt like a fresh start.

Fritzi unlocked the door with the key they'd picked up at the Base Housing Office. As soon as Rand stepped inside, he sensed the utilitarian cleanliness of the space.

To the left of the front door was a galley kitchen that opened to a laundry room with utility sink and pantry. Off the laundry room was a back door that led to a one-car carport.

Directly ahead of the entry was a living room with a spacious dining room adjoining it. A sliding glass door in the dining room led to a poured concrete patio framed by a redwood fence.

To the right of the front door was a hallway with a bedroom on each side and a master bedroom at the end. One bathroom served the two bedrooms in the hall, and one bathroom, accessible only through the master bedroom, was for his parents.

Despite the plain exterior, which was painted pale yellow with green trim, the Capehart house on Cannon Drive held promise. Things could happen here.

THE BASE HOUSING people came today to install a new nameplate on the front of the house. LT COL J. STODDARD. Yes, Joe had made the L/C list on the first round! In addition to the new nameplate, her husband now wore silver oak leaves on his shoulders and was named Commander of the 44th Military Air Transport Service Squadron. He was in charge of training pilots for the newest strategic cargo plane, the C-141 Starlifter. According to Joe, it was the first cargo airplane with a range of 3,500 miles, and could carry a payload of 60,000 pounds. They were monstrous planes, Fritzi thought, when she was invited to tour one of them with the other officers' wives in the squadron. The wings were mounted high on the fuselage, giving it the appearance of an obese insect. It was almost incomprehensible that the thing could fly. Joe, of course, was happier than a tick on a hound dog, proud not only of his new assignment, but also of the capabilities of the new plane.

Fritzi, meanwhile, busied herself with her new role as wife of the Squadron Commander. Eager to set a good model for leadership, she organized a coffee for the enlisted wives in the squadron, a revolutionary idea that miffed a few of the officers' wives. Some women were just ridiculous snobs. Luckily, she was in a position to ignore them now that Joe was commander. One captain's wife, a fluffy blonde named Mamie Satterfield, was quite vocal.

"It clearly states in *The Air Force Wife* that forging friendships with enlisted personnel and their families could compromise our husbands' chain of command," the hapless idiot stated at one of the organizing meetings that Fritzi held in her home. "I'm just not sure that a coffee where we are expected to socialize with NCO wives is a good idea."

There was an audible gasp from the six other women in attendance. Fritzi managed to give Mamie a kind, condescending smile.

"If you read *The Air Force Wife*, you know that our squadron, our *entire* squadron, is a team. We are the web of families that support our men on the job. The NCO families are essential team members. Under my husband's leadership, it is my responsibility to make sure that all our families know each other. We will have family picnics for the whole squadron. We will organize telephone trees for use in case of emergencies. We will support *all* our children in the base schools. Holding a coffee to meet our NCO wives is part of our responsibility as officers' wives. It is expected that all of you attend the coffee next Thursday. It will be here, in our home."

Mamie raised her hand. "Mrs. Stoddard, are you aware that some of the NCOs are colored?"

Fritzi waited a beat, giving the other women an opportunity to glare in Mamie's direction.

"If you mean they are Negro, yes. The Air Force does not discriminate against men of any race, and neither should we. If there's nothing else, we are adjourned."

Mamie's face turned red. She gathered her white gloves and purse. Fritzi noticed that none of the other wives talked to Mamie or gave her any attention. Fritzi went to the door to say her good-byes, but Mamie stayed until everyone else had left.

"Mrs. Stoddard, I didn't mean to offend you or anyone else," said Mamie. "It's just that I was raised in Georgia, and my upbringing taught me that it wasn't appropriate to socialize with colored folk. My daddy would have my hide if he thought I was participating in a party where Negroes were invited into the home of our Squadron Commander." She looked down at her gloves. "I guess I just wanted to tell you. I meant no harm, but this is all new to me."

Fritzi sat on the sofa—a new one, French provincial style, part of a set she and Joe purchased after they decided to leave their beat-up modern furniture behind at Barksdale—and patted the seat next to her. "Mamie, come on and sit down."

Mamie pursed her lips like a teenager on report, but sat next to Fritzi.

"Now you listen here," Fritzi began, "I know you can tell by my accent that I'm a Southerner. Born and raised in Louisiana, and proud of that. But I left all that behind when Joe joined the Air Force. If you've read *The Air Force Wife*, you know that you are in the service as much as your husband is. Our men are expected to serve side by side with Negroes. That means we are expected to accept our Negro wives and their families, too. The Air Force is a color-blind place. If you want your husband to be successful, you have to retrain yourself. These are not the *colored people* we knew back home. They are not our help. They are Air Force men and their wives, just like we are. Now, you'd better accept that. They are just as much a part of the 44th as you and I are."

"That's a new way of thinking, all right."

Fritzi lit a Chesterfield and offered one to Mamie, who accepted. They sat there, smoking and silent, for a moment. Fritzi seethed inside. She wanted to slap some sense into this air-headed little fool.

But she also felt sorry for her. Although her husband was a captain in the squadron, Mamie still had the look of a slutty small town Southern girl. That bleached hair, her blue eyeshadow. Her ill-fitting, cheap shoes. She had to admit, though, that the girl had brushed up on *The Air Force Wife* enough to know to dress neatly and to take time back-combing her yellow hair. But she hadn't a clue about the real world. She was stuck back in whatever Podunk town she came from in Georgia, trying to please Mama and Daddy and taking an uppity attitude toward "coloreds" as well as the white trash from the wrong side of the tracks. She had a lot to learn, and Fritzi was going to teach her.

"Now," Fritzi continued, "we need help for the coffee. I'm going to put you in charge of food. You organize the other wives, and you can each bring something homemade, like coffee cake, and some fruit, juice, or mints. This will give you a chance to take on a leadership role. If you saw the looks you got this morning, you'll realize you made a really bad impression on the other wives."

FRITZI ENLISTED Linda's help to answer the door for the All-Squadron Wives' Coffee at their house. She had Linda try on three different dresses before she approved one—a beige shift with three-quarter sleeves—to wear for the occasion. She briefed Linda and Debby on what she expected:

"Linda, don't let them ring the doorbell. Leave the door open, stand on the porch, and greet each of our guests as she comes in. Ask her name, introduce yourself, and then hand her the prepared name tag from the table in the front hall. I'll organize them alphabetically."

"OK, Fritzi. Doesn't sound too hard. Think I can handle it."

Linda saw her mother's back stiffen and wished she could have eaten her own sarcastic words. "Now see here, young lady. I'm asking you to be the first person to greet these women. Most of them have never been to a coffee, much less to one in an officer's home. It's an important job, whether you think so or not. Don't give me any of your guff, hear?"

"Yes, ma'am. I'm sorry," Linda answered sheepishly, suppressing an eye roll.

"Now, Debby. You're to stand at the dining room table, where there will be a buffet of sweets and a coffee urn. You are to watch for crumbs and keep everything looking fresh. Remove the picked-over plates and let Mrs. Whitley know when we need fresh coffee cups."

"Who's Mrs. Whitley?"

"A lady I've hired to help out in the kitchen. She will be keeping up with the dishes and tidying up."

"Is she our new maid?" Debby asked in a prissy voice. The kid was so annoying.

"No, she's just helping out for the day. I told you we won't be having a maid here in the States. They're too expensive," Fritzi said. "You girls need to look sharp and remember: you are representing your father's squadron and our family."

"Yes, ma'am," they said in unison. Fritzi was in full press, boss lady mode. This was something new. It was like the sad, droopy Fritzi who was mourning Tommy had receded, and this new, snappy redhead had emerged in her place. A part of Linda rejoiced, even though she disliked her new rigor and take-charge attitude.

THE FORMAT of this coffee was that the officers' wives were the hostesses, and Fritzi was totally in charge. Seven officers' wives showed up a half hour before the coffee was to start, right after a big white-haired lady named Mrs. Whitley put on an apron and took charge of the kitchen. Fritzi ordered all of them around, too, just as she had her daughters. Linda had never seen her mother as nervous as she was that day.

The first guests were a pair of Negro ladies, dressed up in suits, gloves, and hats. Linda greeted them and asked their names, then pinned their name tags onto their jackets. They nodded their thanks and went like conjoined twins into the living room. Fritzi greeted them warmly and took them under her wing to introduce them to the officers' wives in the dining room.

Suddenly, it occurred to Linda why her mother was nervous. She'd grown up in segregated Louisiana, where black people were maids and gardeners who had to ride in the back of the bus. Fritzi hated that segregated society, and always told her children she couldn't wait to get away from it. But now, she was trying too hard, nodding and smiling at these two shy women, coaxing them to fill up their plates, ignoring other guests and chatting them up when they clearly just wanted to make an appearance and go home. Linda wished she could signal Fritzi from across the room, tell her to back off, relax; they weren't in Louisiana any more.

Linda pinned a name tag on a lady with yellow hair named Mamie Satterfield. Mamie seemed younger than the other wives, and her pink lipstick looked a little smeared as she headed into the house. Curious, Linda watched as Fritzi approached Mamie, the two black ladies in tow. Mamie turned on her heel and made her way to the coffee urn, ignoring Fritzi. Turned her back. On *her* mother. Linda abandoned the front door to see what Fritzi would do.

Fritzi strode to the coffee urn and grabbed the skinny arm of the blonde and whirled her around. "Mrs. Mamie Satterfield? I'd like you to meet Mrs. Lorraine Butler and Mrs. Ruthie Bodeen." Fritzi said these introductions through clenched teeth. Her face was ruddy in anger.

Mrs. Satterfield looked at Fritzi with scared rabbit eyes and nodded at the embarrassed Mrs. Butler and Mrs. Bodeen with a faint smile. Meanwhile, Fritzi maintained a firm grip on Mamie's arm. Linda glanced at Debby on duty at the table. Her elf-absorbed sister, along with all the other ladies in the room, locked her eyes on Fritzi. Fritzi took a breath and let go of Mamie's arm.

"Welcome, everyone, to the first annual 44th Squadron Wives' Coffee! Our hostesses today are the officers' wives, headed by Mamie Satterfield here. Let's give them a round of applause for this beautiful spread of food!"

Clapping, muted by gloves, broke out in the room. All the ladies held a collective breath. Mamie broke out in tears and ran into the kitchen.

"I guess she's a little overcome by the day!" Fritzi said. "Please, everyone have a seat. As the wife of our squadron commander, Lieutenant Colonel Joe Stoddard, I want to discuss a few goals for our group."

The ladies obeyed, finding seats on the new French Provincial furniture and on dining room chairs. A few had to stand, as the room was now filled with wives of all shapes and sizes.

"First, let's just say that we are the home team that stands behind our husbands, the officers and the enlisted men of the 44th Military Air Transport Squadron here at Travis. Let's hear it for the 44th!"

Linda held her breath. Why was Fritzi acting like a cheerleader, when she'd barely gotten out of bed a few months ago?

Relaxed applause followed.

"Second, I'd like to thank all of you for your service. It's not easy, uprooting a family every couple of years, pulling your children in and out of school systems all over the world. Here's to us!" She raised her coffee cup out of its saucer.

"Third, I'd like to challenge us to volunteer whenever we can to reach out a hand to one another. We need to support each other as much as we need to support our families. That's what today is all about. Ask Mamie Satterfield. I'm so grateful she stepped in to help today."

As far as Linda could see, Mamie hadn't emerged from the kitchen, but all eyes were glued on the closed swinging door to the kitchen.

Fritzi made her way through the group and pushed open the kitchen door.

Mamie emerged, mascara smudged beneath her eyes. Fritzi escorted her into the room. "Now, y'all help yourself to the coffee and stay to chitchat. Thank you for coming!"

Fritzi abandoned the sheepish Mamie in the group and made her way toward the kitchen. Linda could tell her mother needed a cigarette. The other wives turned their back on poor racist Mamie and treated her like the pariah she was.

Cliques, Linda saw, were not limited to middle school hallways. They existed in her mother's world, and Fritzi was definitely queen bee of the 44th Squadron.

———

THE GRASS on the low hills behind the officers' houses had turned from green to gold at the end of summer. Debbie liked to visit the playground on the hill, above the neat rows of identical one-story houses. If Tommy got on top of their house, for example, he would probably only break an arm or a leg if he were to fall. Even if he fell on his head, he'd be OK, because there were bushes and grass in the yard to cushion him. Unless he broke his neck. Then it would be just like it was in Naples.

Back in Naples, Debby overheard her parents talking with a man who came to the apartment with important papers. The man said Tommy's neck had broken immediately on impact. "He probably never felt a thing." She remembered Fritzi bursting into tears, and her father saying, "That's a comforting thought, but we'll never really know."

How could anyone know, how it felt to die? What did Tommy feel when he leaped into the night of Piedigrotta? Leaped after the soccer ball *she* had dropped over the railing of the penthouse. Debby could remember now. She was angry with Tommy, because he wouldn't settle down enough to let her talk to Bino. She didn't mean to drop the ball off the balcony. Or did she? Even if she did, she thought Tommy was smart enough not to go after it. But he couldn't help himself. He had to chase that ball. She had tried to grab his arm. But Tommy was strong, heavy, determined. How could she be expected to pull him back onto the terrace, when he was so focused on finding the ball? How could she?

At least Fritzi and Pop didn't seem to blame her. They didn't blame Bino for getting the ball out to play with him. Rand, of course, was playing pool, but Linda, come to find out, had curled up in a corner of the general's library with a book. She didn't even come out to watch the fireworks. She didn't even know that her little brother had gone over the railing. Rand had to look for her to tell her.

Rand and Linda, the big brother and sister. They should have watched out for her and little Tommy. Especially Linda. What else did she have to do? She could have been there to make sure Tommy didn't eat too many cookies or guzzle Fanta. Tommy would never listen to Debby. But Linda, she was more like an adult. He would have listened to her. It wasn't Debby's fault about Tommy. No, not at all.

Debby spotted a girl from her third grade class on the swings. Waving, she ran toward her, blonde hair flying in the wind. Debby sat on the swing next to the girl and began to pump, higher and higher and higher.

On the far side of the hill, past the jungle gym, she could see her brother Rand with two other guys about his age. That seemed odd, because Rand came home from school every day complaining about the new high school and how hard it was to make friends. Apparently, he'd made two, and they were huddled together like football players or girls when they are telling secrets. Debby slowed down her swing so she could see better. In a second, she saw the flame from a match. One of the boys lit what looked like a cigar or a brown cigarette, took a puff, and passed it to Rand. Rand puffed and passed it to another guy. This struck Debby as weird because Rand hated Fritzi's smoking, especially on car trips. He said the smoke gave him a headache, and always asked if he could "open a window, just a little, not enough to affect the air-conditioning." Fritzi always said yes, that smoking was a bad habit, one that she couldn't help, so it was OK.

Rand had some new friends, after all, and apparently smoke didn't give him a headache anymore.

THE AIR FORCE had built a new high school for the growing number of teens at Travis and named it Vanden, after a Scandinavian pioneer family. Next to it was a junior high called Golden West. The two campuses were unlike anything Rand had seen. Vanden's classrooms were all on one level, with doors that opened onto a series of sheltered courtyards. The rooms all had wide windows with views of rolling hills and, in this autumn, a cloudless blue sky. Student lockers, color coded by year (freshman, orange; sophomores, blue; juniors, green; and seniors, harvest gold) were inside the courtyards frequented by each level of student. Between classes in this warm autumn, students had to dodge the spray from big, hissing sprinklers that kept the surrounding sod green. Rand wondered how many acres the school grounds occupied, with the new football field and track situated a good quarter mile from the courtyards of classrooms and administrative buildings.

In his junior year, Rand had tested into senior level calculus and physics classes, so he was often among the harvest gold lockers in the senior courtyard. Here, the boys seemed fine-muscled and tan, like cross-country runners. A far cry from the beefy bubbas in his Louisiana high school. Girls, they were another breed altogether. The good-looking ones were lithe as dancers, with short, sleeveless shift dresses that clung to their shapes. He could tell some of them didn't wear bras, much less hose and fakey makeup. A few girls had long, straight hair—a real change from the teased and sprayed flips back in Louisiana.

Moving out here was like moving to a foreign country. Rand wasn't familiar with local customs or ways of dress. Most of his classmates were from Air Force families, but to Rand, they acted like they were born and bred in California cool. Rand figured being military brats made them especially adaptive, but these kids oozed offbeat intellect and effortless style. At least the ones he wanted to hang out with did.

At first, Rand had to admit he was intimidated. The senior guys in his classes were focused, ambitious dudes like none he'd encountered before. However, they weren't at all like their ramrod straight military fathers. These guys at Vanden were inquisitive and questioning of their teachers, just to the edge of being disrespectful.

Rand listened in on their lunchtime discussions as they gathered around the picnic tables in the senior courtyard. They talked about articles in *Scientific American* or books by Jack Kerouac. Rand figured he had to communicate with them very carefully—if he came off as too eager, too awestruck, he'd be rejected as a loser—especially being a redhead. So he toed a fine line between quiet/cool and rebel expatriate, dropping sly references to art in Florence and street fights in Naples. In a few weeks, he fell in with Jon Firestone and Rick Tolbert, two seniors with SAT scores that had earned them scholarships to Stanford and Berkeley, respectively.

Rand fell in as third in line, listening, mostly, to Jon and Rick, but adding his own witticisms and experience like punchlines to their long discussions and manifestos about nuclear fusion and the Cold War. Rand skipped a couple of haircuts at the base barber, and, for the first time, enjoyed parting his hair and shaking his head to flip his long bangs out of his eyes. Pop hadn't noticed yet, being too busy running the squadron and going with instructor pilots on training flights to Air Force bases in Hawaii, Japan, and Viet Nam. Pop called it "flying the line with my pilots," and it was obvious he loved it. Meanwhile, Fritzi was left to run the busy household, as well as the squadron wives. The gradual growth of Rand's hair simply wasn't on his parents' radar.

Linda noticed, and she told Rand she liked his hair. She was having a time of it, Rand knew, adjusting to eighth grade at Golden West Junior High. Girls had it twice as rough. Rand could see how hard it was for his sister every morning, when he waited for the Vanden bus across the street from her bus stop. Linda was a big girl, with short curly hair and a pimply face. She wore dorky horn-rimmed glasses and she didn't shave her legs often enough. She still wore skirts below her knee and white ankle socks with her clunky loafers. Rand pitied his sister when he saw her board the bus to school each morning. He could see the smirks on the faces of the other kids at the bus stop. One morning, he saw one skinny boy elbow another stupid junior high kid when Linda boarded the bus.

They laughed and he could hear them making snorting sounds behind her, like pigs. They thought themselves hilarious.

The next morning, Rand said he'd walk with Linda across the street to the junior high bus stop. "What for?" Linda asked, obviously unaware that she was the brunt of adolescent jokes.

"Because, for your information, there are some punks who catch the bus there. Just so you know, they make fun of you. I don't like it."

"Those idiots?" Linda laughed. "I know. They make pig sounds. Sometimes fart sounds. I just ignore them."

"No, Linda. They have no right to make fun of you. You have to stand up to guys like that. And if you won't, I will."

"Ha! Like my big brother is going to protect me? Come ahead, Rand. Do whatever. I don't care. Those kids are jerks, but they don't bother me. If I let every jerk I meet get under my skin, I'd be infested with jerk leprosy before lunch. There are lots jerky boys and snotty girls who say ugly things, even to my face. Honestly, I don't care."

"Come on, you care! How could you let them humiliate you like that? Where's your sense of pride?"

"They don't humiliate me, Big Brother. They only humiliate themselves when they belittle me. And it's not like I'm the only one they make fun of. Everybody except for a few ultra cool kids is a target. I'm in good company, believe me."

"That sucks. Those bastards can't get away with it. Come on, I'm waiting with you today."

"If you must. Thanks, I guess, for caring about me."

"I'm not doing this because I care. I'm doing this because *you* don't."

Rand strode across the street after Linda arrived at the Golden West bus stop. "Hey, Sis!" he called cheerily.

He was aware that he now oozed with cool, a good-looking high school guy who towered over the squirts next to Linda.

"Good morning, brother dear," she said in a British accent.

The two squirts eyed him warily, their dull eyes narrowed as they looked at him—tall, handsome, confident, with an amazing shock of auburn hair—and sized up his sister—dumpy, ack-faced, with a tangle of dun-colored curls on her round head. Rand heard them snort in unison.

"Who are these runts?" Rand asked his sister.

"I have no idea," she replied, sticking her nose in the air. "Some cretins who happen to take the bus to Golden West. Not sure they have names."

Rand watched one kid bristle under his greasy bangs. The other guy, taller and stockier, smirked.

"What's so funny, dude?" Rand asked. "You got a name?"

"Who wants to know?" the tall one asked.

"I do. I'm Rand Stoddard. This is my sister, Linda. Say hello to her."

The two boys burst out laughing.

Rand went at them both. He shoved the greaseball to the ground and grabbed the stocky guy by the collar. "You listen to me. I see how you act. I know what you do. You two are nothing but shit. A couple of real turds." He put his foot on greaseball's chest and jerked the stocky guy's arm. "Just know that I'm watching you, even when you don't know it. Clean up your act, or you will pay. I will hunt you down with my friends and you will pay for being turds. And you will pay until I say your debt is finished. Grow up. You don't own this bus stop or anything else. Your little turd act is *over*. *Today*. Got it?"

They nodded. "Say it," Rand demanded.

"Got. It." They said in unison.

Rand let go and stood next to them until the bus came. Linda got on in silence. She never looked back.

The next morning, Rand accompanied Linda to the bus stop. The two turds said nothing, did nothing. And they never bothered Linda again.

October 31, 1964

LINDA STAYED HOME, dressed as Morticia Addams, to answer the door for trick-or-treaters. Pop and Fritzi made Rand take Debby, dressed as a black kitten, to "only the officers' housing" with her trick-or-treat bag. Rand didn't take a bag for himself, but dressed as a beatnik, complete with charcoal beard, black beret, and a paperback of Alan Ginsberg poems. (Linda got it, but who else would? And where did her brother get a book of *poetry*?)

Pop and Fritzi sat in the kitchen having cocktails and talking while Linda flipped her long Morticia wig out of her face and answered the door. "Good evening," she said a creepy voice. There were lots of kids, mostly dressed in dime store masks and cheesy costumes, as Snow White, Superman, or the Devil. A few did home-made costumes: old sheets cut with eyeholes became ghosts; boxes with aluminum foil became robots or space men. Around eight o'clock, there was a group of hobos, with ragged shirts and jeans, carrying knapsacks on sticks. She recognized two of them as the turds from the bus stop, but of course didn't let on.

Soon after that, Rand brought Debby home. Her candy bag was overflowing, and she was tired and grumpy. "He made me walk, Pop," she complained, "Walk and walk and walk. He wouldn't give me a piggy back ride when I got tired."

"Ha ha, Tinkerbell, that's what it's all about! Walking your route, like a big girl," Pop said, ice tinkling in his glass. He and Fritzi hadn't eaten dinner yet.

"Run on now, and get ready for bed," Fritzi said to her. "I'll put your candy up here, on top of the fridge. You can save it for tomorrow."

Debby whined about not being able to take her candy to bed. Rand scrubbed the "beard" from his face and appeared in the front hall.

"OK if I go to a friend's house? I'll be home by eleven," he said, halfway out the front door.

"Hold on there, Horse Fly." Pop put down his drink and grabbed Rand by the shoulder. "Negatory."

Linda could see Rand suppress a surge of anger. At that moment, she knew her brother wanted to slug Pop and dash out the front door. Instead, he turned around, his face sullen. "But it's Saturday," he said. "Why can't I stay out until eleven?"

"Because I said so," Pop said, his voice stern. "It's Halloween. I don't want you out there into any mischief."

"Pop, you *know* I don't do mischief." Rand's voice was flat, dripping in sarcasm.

Wish you hadn't said that, Linda thought.

In a second, Pop had him on the kitchen floor in a wrestling hold. "Son. *I said no.*"

Rand let out a long, angry breath of air. "I'm sorry, sir." *The right response. Good.*

Pop let him up. "That's better. Go on to your room now. And Linda, time to close it up for the night. Lock the door and turn off the porch light."

"Yes, sir," Linda said. The Morticia wig had become hot and itchy. She took it off and shook out her hair, afraid to make eye contact with Rand.

"Joe?" Fritzi called from the dining room, "Dinner!"

Linda grabbed a few Tootsie Pops for later, when Debby would be asleep in their room we and she could turn on the flashlight under the covers to finish reading *The Group.* She'd snagged a copy from a girl at school, who said she took it from her mother's nightstand.

LINDA WOKE to yelling from the front yard. The room she shared with Debby was on the back side of the house; Rand's was on the front. According to the Timex alarm clock between their beds, it was two in the morning. Linda leapt out of bed and went across the hall to Rand's room, where the window was wide open. His curtains were blowing in a swift breeze, and her brother's voice came from the front yard.

"Get out of here, you goddamn cocksuckers!" For a moment, Linda envied the way Rand could cuss, and wondered where he'd learned to say *cocksucker.*

She stuck her head out the window. In the darkness, she could see Rand, dressed in jeans and a shirt, run after someone—or something. Her first instinct was to run out the front door after him.

"What's going on?" Pop, in a T-shirt and pajama pants, stood in the hallway. He held a flashlight in one hand and his service pistol, pointed toward the floor, in the other. "Is that you, Linda? Where's your brother?"

Debby emerged from their shared bedroom, screaming, and Fritzi appeared wrapped in her brown chenille robe. "*Ssssshhhhh,*" Fritzi said to Debby and hugged her. "It's all right. Hush, now." She looked angrily at Pop, eyes on the pistol.

"Uh, Rand's outside. He took off after someone... I was wakened by the yelling..."Linda stuttered.

"So was I! It better not be Rand who said those cusswords! Which way did they go?"

Linda just pointed and Pop was out the front door in a heartbeat. He shone a flashlight into the front yard and ran into the street.

Fritzi flipped on the porchlight. "Joe? Should I call the Air Police?"

"Nope." Pop walked toward the house, followed by Rand, who had a scrape on his face. In front of Rand were the two kids. In the dim light, Linda could see one had greasy black hair, and the other was stocky—both much shorter than her brother. *The two punks from the bus stop.*

Rand pointed at the front of the house. "They egged my window! I went after these two idiots."

Pop put the pistol in his pants pocket and shone his flashlight at the window, revealing the gooey ooze of at least six broken eggs. "Looks like you boys have some work to do. Linda? Bring out a bucket of water and Spic and Span. A couple of sponges, too."

Linda complied, thrilled to see the two little turds cowering in the front yard like flushed rabbits.

"Looks like these guys will need a step ladder, too," Pop said. "Rand, you run on out to the carport and get that."

Rand returned with the ladder, and Pop motioned for crew cut to step up. "That's right. Give it a good scrub. Now step down and wring out that sponge. You boys got names?"

They mumbled something.

"Speak up, now, or I'll have to call the APs. Names?" Pop demanded.

"Uh, Steve Randall. And this is Mitch Prather."

"Randall and Prather. Didn't your fathers ever teach you how to answer a question in a proper manner?"

Linda was dying inside, mostly of embarrassment, but also with sweet revenge. Rand stood aside, said nothing. In the dark, they exchanged glances.

"Uh, yes, sir?" Steve said tentatively.

"Better. Your fathers serve on this base? Are you in school with my children?"

"Yes, sir."

"You are aware then, that you have not only disturbed us in the night, but you have done damage to government property. All houses on this base are the property of the U.S. Air Force. That's a pretty serious crime, Randall and Prather. You wouldn't want that to go on your fathers' records, would you?"

"No, sir."

"All right. You will write down your fathers' names and telephone numbers. Finish your cleanup job, I'll go in and make some phone calls, and we can call this a night."

Fritzi, by some miracle of telepathy, produced a spiral notepad and pen. The turds each wrote names and phone numbers. Pop handed his flashlight to Rand. "Thank you. Rand, I'll leave you in charge to see that they finish cleaning. Be right back."

Rand shined the flashlight on the window and inspected it closely when they'd finished scrubbing. "Now pick up these eggshells. All of them," he commanded, shining light on the ground. His voice sounded eerily like Pop's.

In about ten minutes, Pop came out, dressed in his summer uniform. In about 15 minutes, Steve's dad showed up in a Ford Fairlane. He jumped out of the car and saluted Pop. "Colonel Stoddard. Please accept my apology on behalf of my son."

Pop returned the salute. "I think he's learned his lesson, Sergeant Randall. Thank you for coming to pick him up."

In another five minutes, Mitch's father showed up in a Volkswagen bug. He, too, saluted Pop and dragged his son off in shame.

When the turds had gone, Pop turned on Rand. "Those boys did a bad thing, son. But you did something worse. You shouted filthy words out into the night, within earshot of your sisters and your mother, and who knows else. Go to your room. You're grounded for a month."

"Oh, for God's sake, Joe," said Fritzi. "Those punks threw eggs at our house! They're the bad guys, not Rand!"

"That's not the point, Fritzi. Those punks' dads are NCOs. Rand is the son of an officer. What they did is wrong, but what our son did was wrong, too. He set a bad example for himself and our family. He needs to be punished."

Inside, Debby was sitting on the couch, and Linda took a seat beside her. Linda nearly jumped out of her skin when she heard Rand slam his door.

Fritzi lit a Chesterfield. "Now listen here, Joe Stoddard. You are a career officer and we do everything we can to support you. But you have no business grounding your son for 'setting a bad example.' Rand is a great young man, and I'm not going to let you break his spirit."

"A great young man with a filthy mouth! I can't let that go, Fritzi. I'm not about to put another smartass young man out in the world. He's grounded, and that's it."

Fritzi stormed into the bedroom and returned with a pillow and blanket. "Girls, you need to go on to bed so your father can sleep on the couch. Good night."

18

 "One of the most important activities of the Wives' Club
is always the Red Cross.
When you are called, do your bit willingly."
—Nancy Shea, *The Air Force Wife*

Veterans' Day, 1964
Travis Air Force Base, California

FRITZI HAD LAUNCHED an effort to honor veterans with a canned food
drive for the Solano County Red Cross. The wives of the 44th
Squadron had fallen into line to collect canned food, taking time
away from busy households to paint signs, collect donated cans, and,
today, to fill grocery bags with Del Monte and Green Giant and off-
brand cans of fruits and vegetables.

At home, Joe refused to budge on Rand's grounding for a solid
month as punishment for his actions on Halloween. So, every
evening, Fritzi made Joe's bed on the French Provincial couch in the

living room: fitted twin sheet, top sheet, blanket, and pillow. *Good night, darling, pleasant dreams. Don't be so unfair to your son and you can come back to roost with me in our nice, queen-sized bed.* Every night, Rand sulked in his room, brooding and angry, and played hootenanny music on his hi-fi.

Rand worried her. Once, Fritzi tried to talk with Rand, to get on his level, to get into his very beautiful and very intellectual head. Unfortunately, her attempt at communicating with her son just devolved into Rand's questioning everything about Tommy's death. "Why hadn't someone been watching? What exactly did the coroner say? Why did Tommy leap over a railing after a ball? Wasn't he smarter than that?"

Fritzi saw the grief in her son's eyes and heard the desperation in his voice as he kept asking "Why?" For the first time in her life, she had no answers.

Rand would be a college boy. He'd turn 18 in a couple of years, and he'd have to register for the draft. From Joe's accounts, President Johnson was contemplating sending ground troops to a swampy place in Southeast Asia called Vietnam. Eighteen-year-old boys, fresh from the farm or just out of high school or off the assembly line at some factory, would be the ones going. College boys, she knew, got deferments. Rand, she decided, would get a deferment. Her son would not become another pair of boots on the ground—or earn a pair of wings to pilot fighter jets—or set sail aboard an aircraft carrier —not Rand. Not this war, or any other.

———————————

RAND TRIED to picture Tommy's face, the size of his earlobes, his perfect white baby teeth, but he could no longer retrieve those images. Little by little, his little brother was fading from his memory, and he dreaded the day when he could no longer conjure him. He could still hear Tommy's raucous laugh, but not very loudly these days. No one, not even Fritzi, talked about him now that they'd moved to California.

Fritzi hung their family photos in the hallway. In the last one with Tommy, they all looked so happy. They were at the Christmas party at the Allied Officers' Club, all dressed up, all smiling. Pop and Fritzi looked like movie stars. Debby was cute, and even Linda looked pretty in their fancy Christmas dresses. He himself looked like a clean cut, innocent guy, holding the hand of his grinning baby brother as though nothing could ever happen to spoil that moment of holiday bliss. These days, Rand wanted to smash that picture.

He was angry. Angry that the details of Tommy's death were sketchy. Angry at his whiny sister Debby for watching Tommy go over the railing without calling for help. Angry at himself for playing pool when he could have prevented Tommy's death. And more and more, angry that Pop and Fritzi had just gone on, as though burying their youngest child was only a bump in the road, as though it was natural and expected to chalk up a tragedy now and then. It would be different if they ever talked about Tommy, or wondered out loud what happened. If they'd ever questioned Debby about his last moments, or asked Linda why she was alone in the Miroglios' library when it happened. They never even asked him the very question he asked himself every moment of every day: *Why did you let this happen? Why weren't you watching over your baby brother?*

He couldn't bear of the holidays ahead. In 70-degree weather, they'd consumed turkey and cornbread dressing on Thanksgiving without a prayer at the table, without a place set for Tommy. It hardly seemed worth the effort.

The worst was Pop. Something crazy had come over him in California. Rand supposed it was because Pop was now a big shot on base, commander of the gigantic 44th Squadron, leading the way in training pilots on the C-141. Fritzi had appointed herself queen of the squadron, which meant she was always throwing parties or reaching out to a wife or a child who was undergoing some kind of difficulty. Such was the military-industrial complex, he observed. It was a feudal system, and his parents were lord and lady of their little squadron/kingdom.

So what did that make him? The crown prince? That was a joke.

He couldn't do anything right in Pop's eyes. He was only capable of setting a bad example, being a "smartass", using profanity, or disrespecting his mother/sisters/father. Take that incident with those two punks on Halloween. Pop acted like Rand had caused the whole thing. What he didn't know (and wouldn't ask) was that those two idiots had made fun of Linda, and Rand had set them straight. But no, Pop could never assume that Rand had done anything of value. Nope. His Horse Fly was just a big hunk of nothing, a hard-headed guy that needed to be broken just like a raw recruit.

But Rand wasn't a raw recruit. He was an individual, an artist, someone who read widely and was trying hard to pursue the life of the mind. Pop, being a practical man, couldn't see this at all. He couldn't see that Rand was trying his best, raging against mediocrity, seeking to make his way in the world far, far beyond Travis Air Force Base.

Just one more year of high school, and he could take off. His excellent grades had qualified him for the California Scholarship Federation. Pop had said only "That's great, son," in a sort of distracted voice. Didn't he understand that Rand was working hard to get a scholarship to a top school? That his SAT scores were through the roof? No, of course not. Pop had no frame of reference for any of those things. Unless it was the Army Air Corps, the Air Force, airplanes, or the *Air Force Times*, Pop showed little interest. He was just so into being Lieutenant Colonel Joe Stoddard, he didn't have time to be a real person.

At least Fritzi seemed to give a damn. She was always asking Rand about his interests, his thoughts on current events—that is, when Pop wasn't around. Fritzi tried to make time for Rand, but there was never enough, what with the demands of the squadron, not to mention his two sisters. He couldn't get her attention long enough to have a decent conversation about losing Tommy, his perfect score on the Chem 2 exam, or anything else, for that matter.

This existence with his family had become a charade, a sham life. He longed to break free of Fritzi and Pop and Linda and Debby, to banish the sorrow he felt for the loss of his brother. It was high time he made a life for himself, a life that would matter. Somewhere far, far away from this place.

CALIFORNIA WAS a pretty place with nice weather, but the base was unsightly. Debby had never lived in such a stark, ugly home, with such a tiny lawn, a concrete slab for a patio, and plastic closet doors that folded back like squeeze boxes on accordions. Fritzi kept saying how lucky they were to live in a Capehart house, but Debby couldn't see it. She remembered the Barksdale house as fine, two-story, architecturally classic. Like the houses on *Father Knows Best* and *Leave it to Beaver*. This house was like a big shoebox, and her family was crammed into it like five mismatched shoes. She was a ballet slipper, Fritzi was a stylish high-heeled pump, Pop was a polished black uniform oxford. Rand was a big, smelly sneaker with holes, and Linda was a boring brown Weejun.

"Fritzi, when are we going to visit Grandmamma and Judge again? I miss Fontainebleu this time of year. It's so pretty there," Debby said one evening as she was setting the table for dinner.

"Honey, we'll go in the summer, probably. We live too far away to spend holidays with your grandparents," Fritzi answered. Debby detected a false cheeriness in her mother's voice.

"Don't you miss your mama and daddy?"

"Not really. I'm a grown woman. You and Pop and Rand and Linda are my family now," said Fritzi.

Debby pushed on. "But don't you miss ~~the way~~ the way things were when you were growing up? You know, the holly tree and the cookies you left for Santa? All the decorations all over the big, beautiful house?"

"You can't live in the past," Fritzi said. Her tone was darker now. She was not playing along with this conversation at all. "We'll put up our tree on Saturday. We have our own traditions here, now. Wherever we live. We'll make it our own place. That's the life your dad and

I chose. We didn't want to live in Montrose forever. We didn't want to raise our children there."

"But why not? I like Montrose. People there think our family is special. People here don't even know anything about us. And, besides..." her voice trailed off.

"What? Besides what?" Fritzi turned away from the electric frying pan and the pork chops she was getting ready to cook in it. Fritzi's big brown eyes, dark and probing, looked directly at Debby like two lasers. Finally, she had her mother's undivided attention.

"You know," Debby said, blinking back tears. "Tommy's there. I could visit him. Why didn't you ever want to go visit him back when we lived in Louisiana?"

Fritzi put her hands on Debby's shoulders and pulled her close for a small hug. "It's just too hard for me, Debby. Too hard for me to visit my little boy's grave."

"But he was my brother, not just your little boy!" Debby burst into full blown crying mode. Fritzi wiped her tears with her apron.

"Debby, you need to know that when a mother loses a child, it's not a normal thing. Children are meant to outlive their parents. Inside a mother, it causes a special kind of hurt. Bigger than your hurt, bigger than Rand's or Linda's." Fritzi turned and found her pack of Chesterfields next to the sink. She tapped one out and lit it with a match, then exhaled a long plume of smoke.

"What about Pop? Isn't he hurt, too?" Debby let out a little cough and rubbed her eyes.

"Yes. Of course he is. But a mother's hurt is bigger than anyone else's. That's just the way it is. Run along now. Dinner will be ready in half an hour. Have you done your homework?"

"I finished already," Debby said under her breath.

"Good. Go outside and play, get some fresh air. It's all right."

"All right."

Debby went and sat on the front porch step, the concrete cold under her dress. Inside herself, she felt a big, hot bubble of grief and guilt. It burned inside her stomach, her intestines, her heart. Now, it swelled bigger than it ever had before. She'd wanted to talk to Fritzi about how Tommy looked—so happy—in his last moment, running and laughing and leaping. About how she felt so guilty, how maybe she could have stopped him, how her brain buzzed constantly with images of her little brother, of scenarios where she saved him, of scenarios when she herself went over the balcony instead of Tommy, but her mother wouldn't hear it. Her mother would never be able to whisper comforting thoughts to Debby or lull her to dreamless sleep and tell her that Tommy was smiling down from Heaven. Fritzi's own grief surpassed Debby's in importance and magnitude. There would be no comfort from her.

Should she seek out Linda, or Pop? Tell them about the burning bubble inside her, how she wished she could turn back time, how she hated herself every minute of every hour of every day? Pop, no. He was far too busy. Besides, she was his Tinkerbell, his little spark of joy. She couldn't bear to sadden him with her serious thoughts. And Linda? Her older sister was like another species now, pimple-faced and serious. Besides, Linda had enough problems in middle school, with boys laughing and picking on her, and girls shunning her because she was a brainy loner with no style. Debby couldn't expect any sympathy from a sister who was having such a hard time fitting into the world. At least, Debby had friends. And she took ballet at the Base Activities Center. In fact, she had tried out for the part of Clara in their production of *The Nutcracker*.

As for Rand, forget it. He seemed to seethe with hatred for all of them, except maybe Fritzi. He stayed in his room or sneaked off after school to the hills behind the Capehart housing with those older high school boys.

Something like lava burned inside Debby's stomach and up into her esophagus. Normally, she could swallow it back down, but today it was too much. She ducked behind the yucca bush under the kitchen window and let it all spew out. When she was empty, she went inside and washed her face. Pop would be home soon. He'd be proud that she had tried out for the part of Clara. He'd make her believe that she was, for now, a bright spot in someone's world.

IT WAS CHRISTMAS EVE, and Debby was twirling around like a top, surging with pride because she played Clara in her dance teacher's version of *The Nutcracker*. Well, good for her. There were two performances, and Linda had to attend both with Fritzi, since neither Pop nor Rand would dare be seen sitting through a girl's ballet program. At least it gave Linda a little one-on-one with her mother. With all her work in the wives' club, Fritzi was pretty scarce around the house these days. Linda wondered if her mother was as happy as she pretended to be, organizing food drives and attending coffees, during this second Christmas after Tommy's death. Tonight, however, Linda was sick of Debby and her little show. She'd already seen it, over and over again, all her life.

Pop took them to pick out a Christmas tree last week, and it was a disaster. Fritzi insisted on getting a green spruce and having it sprayed with white foam so it would look "flocked." Today, Pop stood it up in the corner of the living room and it was too tall and far too big for the room, with all the new French Provincial furniture. Pop and Rand strung lights on the tree, which was a total fiasco. They fussed at each other the whole time, arguing about extension cords and broken bulbs. To add to the festivities, Fritzi put some Christmas albums on the Telefunken, stupid ones with Bing Crosby and Dean Martin. Nothing sacred, nothing spiritual. All tinselly little tunes that just made everything that much more depressing. This year was even worse than last, somehow. It just didn't seem like Christmas.

Linda missed Tommy. Everyone else was acting like he never existed. True, last year was the first year without him and it was a struggle, with Pop being On Alert and having to travel to Fontainebleau. But this year was even worse, all this bustle about nothing. There wasn't even room for Tommy's ghost. No sign of his stocking. Fritzi must have picked through all the Christmas ornaments to take out his favorites: the rocking horse and the cowboy Santa. They weren't in the box with the others. Linda started to ask about them, but common sense stopped her. The atmosphere in the room sparked with tension. One comment from her might set off a raging drama that she just didn't have the energy to endure.

Fritzi was so chirpy and cheerful, it was like Donna Reed had taken over her body. She had made fruit cake and divinity and fudge to give to all the squadron families, and Linda and Debby had to help her wrap and deliver the goodies like it was manna from heaven. This was surprising, because Fritzi didn't even like sweets. Linda was surprised to see her mother baking and using a candy thermometer; it seemed so out of character.

"I never knew you could make candy," Linda remarked one afternoon after school.

"Oh, yes, Josie taught me," Fritzi replied cheerily. "It was a holiday tradition when I was growing up. I'd help her make all these goodies for her family and the staff at Fontainebleu."

"Can I help?" Linda asked, eager to stir the chocolate in the double boiler.

"No, honey, just run on. I've got a system going, and I don't really need any help."

Fritzi threw herself into making all that stuff, turning up the Telefunken with Christmas music, and banishing everyone from the kitchen so her divinity would set without "little fingers stealing a sample." *Little fingers?* Debby, Rand, and Linda were way past that reference. Did she expect Tommy to materialize and stick his hand into a pan of hot fudge?

The first week in December, Linda watched that new TV show, *Rudolph the Red-Nosed Reindeer*, with the animated puppet characters that all look like stuffed animals. Luckily, Debby was at Nutcracker practice, Rand was in his room, and Fritzi and Pop were at the Club, so no one saw her burst into tears when they got to the part about the Misfit Toys.

Through her tears, Linda reached an epiphany: Heaven for Tommy must be like the Island of Misfit Toys, full of little boys and girls who left their earthly lives for an island, far away from the complicated Heaven where adults went. In his Heaven, no one would tell Tommy to be quiet or make him put his toys away. He could chase a ball as far as he wanted without falling off a fifth-story terrace. He'd never have to take a bath or change clothes or go to bed while everyone else got to stay up. However, unlike the Misfit Toys, Tommy and the other boys and girls wouldn't be waiting for Santa to come and deliver them to a home where they would be loved. They had already been loved, far more than they could imagine, when they departed the earth. In Heaven, they wouldn't remember their moms or dads or sisters and brothers who were grieving for them. They could not experience grief and longing like they did on earth. Best of all, Tommy and the other kids wouldn't have to grow up, learn how cold the world really is, and become mean teenagers or grief-stricken parents. Tommy would always be a kid,. The thought rubbed raw against Linda's nerves. She blew her nose and went to the kitchen for a hunk of fudge.

So here they were on Christmas Eve in California, 70 degrees outside, a foam-flocked spruce in the crowded living room, three stockings hung from a window sill because they had no mantle. Linda felt silly, like a large child in a ~~playhouse~~ too-small playhouse. Her sister was twirling, providing cocktail hour entertainment to their parents, who puffed their cigarettes and poured bourbon over sparkling ice cubes. Her brother sulked in an armchair, his shaggy red hair contrasting against the harvest gold upholstery, brown eyes glazed with boredom. Merry Christmas to all!

19
—————

> " "Air Force teen-agers seem to have come into their own,
> most of the groups being sponsored by the Wives' Clubs
> on the respective bases...Dances, hay rides, wiener
> roasts, candy pulls, golf and tennis tournaments,
> picnics are some of the activities enjoyed."
> —Nancy Shea, *The Air Force Wife*

TRAVIS AIR FORCE BASE, *California*
   September 21, 1965

TODAY, fall arrived. In northern California, that meant the Suisun wind—named for the Native Americans who once inhabited the hills around Travis—was stiff and scorching. The air smelled like onions, due to the onion processing plant in a nearby town called Vacaville. If the odor was this strong a few miles away, Linda wondered what it must smell like in Vacaville.

That year, the Suisun wind brought Linda her first real friend:

Arthur Bodeen. They began meeting after school on the hillside behind the Capehart houses. They'd sit on a flat rock on the far side of the hill, away from the playground that overlooked the yards and patios below. Just a couple of Air Force brats trying to make sense of high school, in this place they were dropped because their fathers chose military careers.

They were both students at the spanking new Vanden High School. Linda was the lone freshman in a sophomore English class, and Arthur was one of the more brilliant students in the class. The son of a decorated Master Sergeant, Arthur was as thin as Linda was stout, as dark as she was white. He wore big bifocal glasses that made him look like an amateur Malcom X. He was smart, funny, and the only person Linda had met in high school with any intellect to speak of. Unlike most other nubile couples who frequented those hills, Arthur and Linda did not meet to make out. They met to discuss things: last summer's political conventions, Barry Goldwater, Lyndon Johnson, the Voting Rights Act, the growing number of American troops in Viet Nam. Whether or not their English teacher, Miss Snapp, was having an affair with their Earth Science teacher, Mr. Whitlock, who had big black nose hairs and was married with two kids. They also talked about themselves in a way Linda had never talked with anyone before.

Arthur knew he was different from other guys. Linda knew she was different from other girls. Arthur was not into the World Series, cars, or the female species. He definitely *was* into guys, which, of course, made him a faggot, and this scared him to death. This was a big secret he had to keep to avoid getting beaten to a pulp, especially because he was a "black faggot." (His words). He divulged this to Linda, only after assuming that she had the same problem identifying with her own gender.

"Linda Stoddard, brilliant student, what do you dream about at night?" Arthur asked, picking at some dried grass. "Like, do you see yourself as a swan, emerging slender at Prom with the quarterback of the football team? In a pink dress, maybe?"

"The quarterback in a pink dress? That would be cool." Linda's sarcastic voice shook with a hint of nerves. Was she totally transparent?

"I'm serious. You. The dress. The guy. All that. I'm not thinking that's what *you* dream about."

"You're right. Maybe just the dress and a girl in it, but that girl is *not* me. Maybe that's my dream."

"Have you heard the word 'lesbian'? Do you know about Virginia Woolf and Vita Sackville West? I believe you have joined their company. Both in intellect and in preference."

Yes, Linda had read all about Virginia and her female lover in a book of Vita's letters she'd found at a used bookstore last summer. She'd read those letters with the same shameful delight she got when she consumed one Hershey's Kiss after another. Arthur's knowledge of Vita and Virginia was just one of the things she loved about him.

"Does intellect determine preference?" Linda countered. "I've noticed that you are quite brilliant yourself. If that follows, then you must dream about Cary Grant in tennis togs. Or maybe Arthur Ashe? Arthur and Arthur?"

"My tastes, dear, are quite eclectic. I do tend to enjoy the pedestrian athlete or actor as well as the pedantic poet or playwright. However, I draw the line at local boys. None of them are mature enough for my taste." Arthur spoke in a British accent and mimed sipping tea with his pinky extended.

They burst into laughter. Wordplay was their foreplay. Linda began to meet Arthur a couple of afternoons after school, and, now, as they faced the autumnal equinox, they also vowed to meet every Saturday afternoon and tell their parents they were at the movies with friends. (Fritzi was delighted that Linda suddenly had "friends" who invited her to the movies.) But today, their usual repartee was more generic than genius.

"My dear, you are aware that the Homecoming Dance is coming up in two weeks? As a freshman girl, you should attend, and you should go with a handsome dark sophomore. Will you be my date?"

Linda's throat went dry and she began to cough. "Are you joking?"

Arthur took her hand and looked her straight in the eye. "No. I'm serious. You should go. I should go. You should wear a chrysan-themum corsage. It's a rite of passage. We should experience it together."

"Uh, yeah! Why should I sit home while all those prissy little freshman cunts go to the dance?"

"Your use of the word 'cunt' is colorful yet crass. Don't use it in mixed company, Miss Stoddard."

"We're mixed company, all right. Pretty *mixed-up* company if you ask me." She laughed nervously. They had grown accustomed to sharing secrets and using raucous swear words in each other's presence. But suddenly his race made Linda uncomfortable. She wondered how Fritzi and Pop would react. She had to muster some words.

"Are you aware that my parents are from Louisiana? I'm not sure how this 'date' will go down with them."

"Yes, you've told me. You forget that my dad is in your dad's squadron. Your mother reached out to mine to unite all the families in the unit. I'm not seeing that this will be a problem, at least not from your mother. My dad says your father is a fair man. Why wouldn't they want their daughter to date a smart, handsome Negro?"

"Why indeed?" The thought made her nervous. Not only because of Arthur, but because her parents would first have to get used to the fact that she, the ugly, awkward Linda, had a date to Homecoming. Then, they'd have to embrace the fact that her date was a Negro. (They were not yet progressive enough to say "black.") "Let me talk to them. I'll let you know."

"Of course. Now, let's talk about what you'll wear. Wrist corsage or shoulder?"

Linda pushed him over, sending him rolling down the hill, laughing. She crouched into a ball and rolled down behind him.

BACK HOME, Fritzi was making Linda's favorite casserole: egg noodles, green peas, and chunks of tuna baked in cream of celery soup. Debby was at ballet class, and Rand was somewhere else. Linda knew she only had a short window of time before Fritzi had to pick up Debby. Then Pop and Rand would be home, and dinner would get underway. There was no other chance to talk about her proposed "date."

Linda took a deep breath. "Fritzi, can I talk to you for a minute?" She made herself speak firmly, with a decidedly upbeat tone.

"Of course, honey. Let me just get this casserole into the oven."

There wasn't enough room for a table in the kitchen, so Fritzi had bought two mod-looking orange plastic chairs for the kitchen corner. She and Pop usually sat there having cocktails before dinner. Linda sat on one of those chairs. Fritzi lit a Chesterfield and sat down next to her. "What's on your mind?"

"It's, um. About the Homecoming Dance in a couple of weeks. I've been asked to go."

"Honey, that's great news! We'll go out Saturday and find you something to wear. Something really flattering. Who's your date?"

"His name is Arthur. Arthur Bodeen. His dad is in the squadron?"

Fritzi's eyes narrowed as she blew smoke. "Master Sergeant Bodeen? Wife's name is Ruthie?"

"I believe so."

"Honey, they're Negroes."

"Duh." Linda got defensive. "Arthur is my friend. It's not like we're going to get married or anything. He's a sophomore and needs a date. I'm a freshman, and I've never been to a dance before. He asked me today, at school. (She dared not tell Fritzi that they met up in the hills several times a week.) He's a real gentleman, very smart."

"Don't 'duh' me, young lady. Do you want to go with Arthur?"

"Of course! I'm in high school! I should do high school things, right?"

"Yes, you should. You'd better thank your lucky stars we don't live in Montrose! The two of you wouldn't even be in the same school." Fritzi flicked ashes into the orange plastic ashtray between the two chairs. "Let me think about this. You haven't told your father, have you?"

"No. Just you." Linda didn't usually confide in Fritzi. She took big issues to Pop and talked about high school issues to Rand. Fritzi was a last resort.

"I know Mrs. Bodeen very well, you see. She is very well respected among the NCO wives. She was instrumental in getting the other Negro women in the group to start coming to our joint Officers'-NCO Wives' meetings. She was a teacher, you know, in a Negro school in Alabama. Very smart woman."

"That's no surprise. Arthur is very smart. He'll earn scholarships for college. Very serious student. Brilliant, even." This was working in Linda's favor. It occurred to her that Fritzi was going to try to make this date happen.

"What attracts you to him?" Fritzi looked Linda in the eye. "His brains or his braun?"

Linda felt a deep blush creep into her face. "We're just friends," she said. "We aren't, like, romantically involved."

"But how do you know you won't be, after this Homecoming dance? Does he have eyes for you? Boys have different urges, you know. Especially Negro boys. I don't want you to go into this situation without knowing that. What seems perfectly friendly now could turn into quite something else after a few dances. Have you thought about that?"

"Of course not! I just want to go to the dance with him because he's nice and he asked me! How many times in my life is *that* going to happen?" Linda was angry and confused. Fritzi was trying to give her the old "facts of life" talk, but she had no real idea why she wanted to go out with Arthur. No idea at all.

"All right. Does he drive? Have a car?"

"No, I don't think so."

"Then you wouldn't mind if your father and I drove you to the dance?"

Linda gulped. "Why should I? We have to get there somehow."

"Of course, we'd have to drive you home, too. Have you thought about other students? How they might react to a Negro boy with a white girl at a dance?"

She sighed. "Fritzi, if I worried about what other kids thought of me, I would have shot myself long ago."

"Stop with the sarcasm. It's disrespectful and dishonest." Fritzi exhaled a plume of smoke. "You never know how people are going to react, even here, on base. What if some white boys decide to beat up Arthur?"

"Believe me, no boy in his right mind cares who I go out with. Arthur is my friend. Why shouldn't we go to the dance together?"

Fritzi stubbed out her cigarette and looked at her wristwatch. "You're right. You have every right to go to that goddamn dance with whomever you like, and so does he. Come with me. We'll talk in the car while I go to pick up Debby."

Righteous indignation had won her mother's heart. As Linda followed her out the door, she wondered what Fritzi would have said if she'd told her she was going to Homecoming with another girl. Linda couldn't picture Fritzi rallying for that cause. But for now, Linda was glad to have Fritzi on her side.

FRITZI PICKED up the olive green phone receiver that hung on the kitchen wall. "Hello, Mrs. Bodeen? It's Mrs. Stoddard," she began. "I wonder if you could come to my house for coffee tomorrow morning around ten? No, it's not about the squadron. I wondered if you'd like to chaperone the Homecoming Dance at Vanden on the first? Great, I look forward to seeing you."

Linda had a Homecoming date! Of her three children, the move to Travis had been hardest on Linda. Fritzi pitied the chubby girl, trudging to school every day with her frizzy hair and pimply face. At least Rand had stepped up, defended her from insults at the bus stop, and seemed to be on her peculiar wavelength. Linda was bright, all right; not as bright as her brother, but why didn't she take an interest in clothes and fashion? Why didn't she bring home friends, like Debby, or care about being popular? Of all the clubs available to her at Vanden, she'd joined some wonky political science group and

Quill and Scroll. What was wrong with Pep Club or some other outlet that would give Linda a social life? Fritzi tried to help Linda, offered to take her shopping, tried to help her count calories as subtle encouragement to lose weight. It was a shame that such a bright girl made no effort to be attractive.

Now, all of a sudden, Linda seemed to have a social life. Granted, she had chosen to go on a date with a Negro boy, but from what Fritzi knew, Arthur was from a good family and was a promising scholar. So, Linda had found someone who was her intellectual equal! Who cared if he happened to be Negro?

At least Sgt. Bodeen was in Joe's squadron. Fritzi knew his mother well. Arthur was their only child, and by all accounts he was a fine young man, raised by two hard-working parents just like herself and Joe—they had all fled the racist, quagmired South by joining the Air Force and raising their children in modern, integrated base schools.

"PLEASE, COME IN," Fritzi said when the doorbell chimed promptly at ten o'clock the next day. She had set her silver coffee service in the living room, brewed a fresh pot of Community Coffee and whipped up a Betty Crocker cinnamon crumb cake for the occasion.

"Thank you," said Mrs. Bodeen. She was a tall, pretty woman with medium dark skin and shining brown eyes. Today, she wore what looked to be a homemade red-and-blue plaid shirtdress accented with a red patent leather belt and matching red pumps. Fritzi instantly approved. This woman had a small clothing budget, but a big sense of style. You could tell she was from the South.

Fritzi offered her a slice of cake. Mrs. Bodeen nodded her thanks and began to take small bites. She lowered her head to take a sip of coffee and gazed up at Fritzi through hooded eyes.

"I understand your son is a sophomore at Vanden," Fritzi said cheerily. "His name is Arthur, right?"

"Yes, Mrs. Stoddard." Mrs. Bodeen put her cup in its saucer and set it on the coffee table. "I'm aware that my son Arthur has asked your daughter Linda to go to the Homecoming Dance. He discussed it with my husband and me first."

"How nice!" Fritzi, taken aback, responded with deprecating humor. "I can't imagine our Rand discussing a girl with Colonel Stoddard and me! You must have bridged the generation gap in your household!" She laughed nervously.

Mrs. Bodeen pursed her lips in a brief smile. "Mrs. Stoddard. Our son is very aware of the boundaries in this world because of his race. We advised him to find a nice Negro girl to ask instead, but there aren't many at Vanden. He said that he and your daughter are in the same English class. It was simply a friendly gesture on his part. He meant no harm, and I can assure you his invitation is made with innocent intentions."

Fritzi took a breath. "Of course, I would assume your son is an honorable young man who simply asked my daughter to go to a school dance. I am thrilled that Linda has an opportunity to go. She isn't the most social girl on the scene." Fritzi reached for her Chesterfield pack.

"What does Colonel Stoddard say? My husband is shocked—and I'll say more than a little embarrassed-- that his son asked the daughter of his commanding officer to a dance. He doesn't want Arthur to go with her."

Fritzi thought for a moment without speaking. If the roles were reversed, Joe would probably forbid Rand from going to the dance and ground him for two weeks because he asked the wrong girl.

"What do you think?" Fritzi asked. "Do you agree with your husband?"

"No."

"Neither do I," Fritzi said triumphantly. "I grew up in a small Southern town where my father was a judge and knew everyone. Every move I made was subject to his approval—or, worse, my mother's. Young people need a chance to make their own mistakes."

"Are you saying that Arthur's invitation is a mistake, ma'am?"

"Oh no! And please, Mrs. Bodeen, don't call me *ma'am*," Fritzi replied, lighting a cigarette. "I'm all for this Homecoming date. But I think, given the circumstances, it's up to us as mothers to make it work. For the sake of the squadron and for the sake of our young teenagers. Do you agree?"

"I suppose it is my duty to agree with you, since you are the wife of our commanding officer. However, I also agree as Arthur's mother. I think he should go to the dance with the girl of his choice. I'd like to make that happen, but given the risks I don't see how."

"Risks?" Fritzi frowned. "What do you mean?"

"Mrs. Stoddard. Like you, I grew up in the South. I taught in a colored school system. I learned where my kind belong and where they don't belong in that world. So did my husband. But this is the Air Force. My husband joined so he could get out of Alabama and build a career in aviation. We needed to raise our son outside of segregation. Still, if my Arthur goes to the dance with your Linda, there have to be consequences. What if Arthur gets beaten up? What if your husband takes out his disapproval on mine and ruins his career?"

"Wait... I never said that Colonel Stoddard disapproved of this date. He doesn't even know about it. But he will, and I will make it my responsibility to see that he approves."

"Can you honestly do that?"

"Yes. My husband is a fair man. Let's just leave it at that. He is not the kind to hold it against Sergeant Bodeen. Your husband's career is not at risk here."

"All right. What about Arthur? He's not the most athletic boy, and as far as I know, he wouldn't know how to defend himself in a fight. What if some boys jump him after the dance, or after school one day?"

"I think we can organize enough chaperones from our Wives' Club to make sure everyone leaves the dance safely."

"And what about your daughter? Have you thought what other students will think of her if she openly dates a Negro boy? How they will taunt her and call her names?"

"They'd be *goddamned fools* if they did." Fritzi swelled in anger, then forced herself to take a breath. "I'm sorry for cursing. Let me assure you that my daughter is quite capable of ignoring stupid opinions. She also has an older brother who attends Vanden and looks out for her. Linda has a mind of her own, and a family to back her up."

Mrs. Bodeen stood up. "I'm grateful that we met today, Mrs. Stoddard. Our young people deserve our support. But it's really up to you and the colonel. I'll be happy to call some of the NCO wives to help at the dance. Thank you for your time."

"Thank you, Mrs. Bodeen!" Fritzi escorted her to the door. "I'll speak to my husband, and gather some officers' wives for support. Thank God our young people don't have to grow up in Louisiana or Alabama!"

THAT EVENING, Fritzi gave Rand a ten-dollar bill and her car keys. "Take your sisters over to the A & W in Fairfield for burgers tonight," she said. "Your father and I are having dinner alone."

"Aw, Fritzi. What if I run into some of the guys from school?" Rand groaned.

"Don't give me any guff, young man. Take your sisters and buy yourselves some dinner!" Fritzi snapped, then handed him an extra five. "Keep the change and just do it. They'll think they've won the lottery, getting to eat out with their big brother on a weeknight. Skedaddle!"

Rand's face brightened a bit at the extra cash. "Yes, ma'am. Thanks."

Joe arrived right after they left. Fritzi met him at the door with a cold martini.

"I thought we should have a night to ourselves," she said, kissing his lips.

"Lord! What did I do to deserve this?" He took off his uniform cap and set it on the kitchen counter. "Where are the kids?"

"Rand borrowed the car and took the girls to A & W. What a nice young man we've raised!"

Joe took his martini and sat in one of the orange kitchen chairs.

Chuckling, he patted his lap and invited Fritzi to take a seat. "What have you whipped up now, darlin'?"

She took a seat on his lap, kissed him firmly, and whispered in his ear. "Linda has a date to Homecoming. With that nice boy, Arthur Bodeen. Sergeant Bodeen's son."

Joe lingered over the kiss. "So I hear. Sergeant Bodeen spoke to me today."

Fritzi pulled away, surprised. "Oh? I spoke to Mrs. Bodeen today, too. Now, Joe, he's a very nice boy from a fine family, and we don't live in Montrose anymore. And, Linda, it's her first dance. She hasn't many friends, and this is a chance for her to..."

"Stop right there. Sergeant Bodeen is an honorable, decorated airman. He didn't want his son to go with Linda, but I asked him why, and of course he made it a matter of honor. 'No son of his was going to try and date his commander's daughter.' I told him I wanted my daughter to go with whomever she wanted to, and if she wanted to go with his son, they should go. *And that's an order.* This the Air Force, not Montrose. Of course, we will need to drive Linda and her date, and we'll need to stay at the dance as chaperones. We don't want any trouble. I'll have an Air Police car stationed outside the Vanden gym. But we drive the kids straight home. No chance for smooching after the dance. And Linda is not to dance to any slow songs with her date. Those are my rules."

Fritzi kissed him again. She should have known Joe would look at Linda's date in terms of his *squadron*. The man had become what the Air Force had molded him to be. He had truly left Montrose behind. "It'll be awhile before the kids are here, and the roast isn't quite done..." she stood up and grabbed his belt buckle. "Let's break some rules, shall we?"

Fritzi led Joe to the bedroom in triumph. Linda was going to have a date!

"You look just like Lesley Gore!" Fritzi said, nearly jumping with joy when she picked Linda up at the base beauty shop, where she'd booked Linda with her hairdresser, Eileen.

"You mean that girl who sings 'Judy's Turn to Cry'?" Linda looked in the mirror and patted her hair. Eileen had gone to town, washing, trimming, teasing and spraying Linda's frizzy head of mousy hair into this bouffant helmet, flipped at the ends. Linda had to admit she did look kind of good. She wondered if Arthur would recognize her.

"Don't crush it, honey!" Eileen said, pushing Linda's hand away from her head and spraying it with a final coat of Aqua Net. "You want it to be perfect for tonight!"

"All you need now is some lipstick and a touch of mascara, and you'll be the belle of the ball!" Fritzi said, sounding a lot like Grandmamma.

"It's not a ball, it's just a Homecoming dance. After a football game. Semi-casual dress, according to the school," Linda reminded Fritzi. "With a wienie roast as a romantic dinner."

Fritzi just smiled and ushered her out to the car. "Come on, we've got to pick up your dress from the alteration lady's house. You have to be ready promptly at six. Then we'll all head over to the wienie roast and the game."

Linda sighed and complied with the errand, while Fritzi did all the talking. Clearly, she was thrilled that Linda was doing something girly and social. Fritzi was also a little giggly-giddy, the way Southern girls get, when they're nervous. No doubt she was worried about the whole interracial date thing, but Linda had to give her credit because she and Pop jumped right on the bandwagon to support it. God only knew how they'd react if they knew that both Arthur and Linda were queer as three-dollar bills.

It would be a long night, orchestrated by Fritzi and Mrs. Bodeen down to the last second. First, the wienie roast in the Vanden parking lot before the football game. Then, the game with Armijo High. Fritzi had made it clear that Arthur and Linda were to sit with their parents in the stands. Finally, they'd all head over to the Vanden gym for the dance, where the Bodeens and the Stoddards were chaperones. No chance for Linda and Arthur to make out (ha!) or to get jumped by some adolescent faction of the KKK. Still, Linda felt cool and iconoclastic to be going on her first "date" with a black sophomore boy who understood her darkest secret. Sort of like being a double agent.

"Are you excited?" Debby asked, her eyes dancing while she watched Fritzi zip Linda's dress. "You actually look pretty, Linda! Wow!"

To Linda's own surprise, she did. With the help of a panty girdle Fritzi had picked up at the BX, Linda's forest green A-line dress slipped over her hips with ease. Her mother had gone shopping for her, and found the dress—small wale corduroy with long bell sleeves and a white Peter Pan collar—on sale in the "husky" section of J.C. Penney's in downtown Fairfield. Fritzi suggested Linda wear black tights and black suede pumps for a casual, fall look.

"Hold still, just one minute," Fritzi said. Carefully, she applied pink frosted lipstick to Linda's mouth and swiped her eyelashes with brown mascara. "There!"

LINDA WAITED in the living room. Promptly at six o'clock, Arthur, flanked by his parents, rang the doorbell and Pop answered.

"Sergeant Bodeen, Mrs. Bodeen, please come in," Pop said, reaching to shake hands with Arthur's dad.

"Colonel Stoddard, this is our son, Arthur," Sergeant Bodeen said formally as they stood in the living room. Linda thought he might salute Pop.

Arthur adjusted his glasses and shook Pop's outstretched hand. "Pleased to meet you, sir."

"Likewise, young man," Pop said.

Arthur, dressed in a button-down shirt and a green-and-gold Vanden letter sweater, nodded to Linda politely. "Hello, Linda." He held a plastic box with a huge gold chrysanthemum corsage.

"Hey, I didn't know you were a letterman!" Linda said, eager to break the formal silence.

"Yes, I earned this last year for Debate," he said. His face broad-ened into a winning grin, all white teeth and pink gums. "I brought you a wrist corsage. Would you like to wear it?"

"Cool! Thank you!"

Fritzi suddenly brandished a camera. "Let's get a picture!"

Arthur stood next to Linda, careful not to touch her. She slipped the elastic on the corsage over her left wrist and held it up for the camera. "Cheese!"

Once they got to the wienie roast, the parents split off into their own group, leaving Arthur and Linda to eat their hot dogs together. There were picnic tables with draped green and gold crepe paper for the students. The usual popular crowd, dressed in their cheer uniforms and football jerseys, had commandeered a table of their own.

"Let's start a new table, shall we?" Arthur said in his British accent.

"Yes, dahling. Let's."

They sat alone at the far end of the parking lot. No one looked their way or made an effort to join them. Despite her Lesley Gore hair, Linda was still invisible to her classmates.

But not to Rand. He and his senior guy friends loaded up their plates and made a beeline for Linda's table. "Hey, sis," he said. "Hey, Arthur." He introduced his friends, some brainiacs who ran the yearbook and newspaper. They nodded at Linda and said "Hey, bro" to Arthur. None of them had asked a date to the dance. They were far too cool for rah-rah high school stuff.

"I see that we are surrounded by progressives," Arthur whispered to ~~me~~ Linda.

"Yeah, Rand has aligned himself with the iconoclasts. We're safe with them."

LINDA'S HAIR withstood the Suisun winds during the game. She kept patting her head to make sure it wasn't flying away. Fritzi, who was seated securely next to her, assured her that it was still intact. Linda had never been to a football game before, but something within her stirred at the spectacle. The bright floodlights on the brownish-green field, the Vanden team with their gold helmets, the bouncy little cheerleaders with the pleated green-and-gold skirts. It was surreal, but at the same time, cozy, sitting there between Fritzi and Arthur. Her best friend and her mom, surrounding Linda with—what? Support and friendship, she guessed, hoping to give her a "normal" high school social experience. Their kindness touched Linda unexpectedly.

Then came halftime, when the Vanden band played and marched, and a parade of convertibles carrying the Homecoming Court circled the field. Linda watched each of those girls, one repre-senting each class, and wondered what their world was like, riding like sacrificial virgins in those sparkling cars, waving at the stands. What did the crowd look like to them? Could they see the individual faces? Did they, as designated royalty for the night, believe in a demo-cratic society? Did they get to keep those rhinestone tiaras? What, exactly, separated those pretty, popular girls who dated popular boys, from Linda and Arthur?

Normally, she would voice those questions directly to Arthur, and they would discuss the question at hand: what makes one queer, and what makes one normal? Arthur always said that being queer went with being intellectually superior to heterosexuals. Of course, Linda knew he didn't *believe* that. He was just as insecure—if not more—than she was. Since Linda had such a girly sister and ultra-femme mother, she wondered if she was the result of some genetic mutation. What were the odds—in a family of four children—that all of them would be little Fritzis and little Joes? Clearly, Fritzi got her girl Debby, and Pop, sadly, had little Tommy. But Rand and Linda—they seemed to defy expectations. Linda, a queer. Rand, an anti-establishment rebel. Parenthood was a gamble.

In the last five seconds of the game, Vanden squeaked by Armijo with a field goal. Victory! The cheerleaders led the way, rushing onto the field when the game was over. Students—even geeky ones who had no stake in this athletic contest—and a few parents followed, eager to join in the sense of collective joy. Arthur looked down at Linda with a smirk. "Team spirit. Rah," he said.

Linda filed out of the stands behind her parents, with Arthur and his parents directly behind. When they reached the parking lot, Pop nodded to Sergeant Bodeen and said, "We'll drive the kids over to the gym. See you there."

Arthur and Linda sat in the back seat of the station wagon.

"Great game, huh, Arthur?" Pop said.

"Yes, sir. Just great."

Pop and Fritzi let them out at the gym doors. Arthur escorted Linda into the dance while they parked the car. "Alone at last," he quipped.

Linda snickered and Arthur smoothed the top of her hair. "There," he said, "It was just a tad too bouffant. Now you look mod."

The assistant principal was on the stage, watching over a junior boy who was spinning records. "Louie Louie" blasted through two huge speakers onto the dance floor below.

"Shall we?" Arthur asked.

"I don't know how. Really, I don't."

"Just watch me and don't worry." He led her over to a discreet back corner of the dance floor and began to shuffle his feet back and forth to the music. "See?"

Linda's new suede pumps were kind of slick on the gym floor. She stumbled. Arthur grabbed her elbow and helped her to her feet.

At that moment, Pop appeared from the dim sidelines. "Everything all right here?"

"Uh, yes, sir," Arthur said, clearly scared to death.

"Fine, then. Carry on. Be careful, Linda."

"OK," she said, and managed to finish the dance.

The whole night went like that: Linda attempting to dance alongside Arthur's lanky, gracefully rhythmic body. Arthur, looking past her head around the dance floor at, no doubt, the guys. Linda, asking to sit down because her feet hurt. Pop, approaching them with cups of punch every time a slow song played. It was so obvious, it was embarrassing.

"Don't worry, Pop. I don't know how to slow dance. We'll sit this one out," Linda finally said.

About ten-thirty, there was more hoopla onstage with the introduction of the Homecoming Queen and her court. The girls all paraded onstage, tiaras intact, while Don Rogers, hunky captain of the football team, crowned Jill Anderson as Queen. Jill was a senior, long-legged, tan, a cheerleader with sea green eyes and hair the color of Coca-Cola. The freshman girl, predictably, was her younger sister Shirley, a rather dull but pretty girl who became popular the instant she showed up at Golden West Junior High last year.

"Hail, holy queen! Hail to the conquering gladiators!" Arthur said, raising a Dixie cup of punch. "What do you think, Linda, of this cultural phenomenon known as a high school dance? Are you glad you partook?"

"Yes, good sir. And thank you for risking your very life to escort me."

"And, you, my lady, for risking your virtuous reputation to accompany this queer Othello!"

They laughed together, so loud, that Fritzi and Mrs. Bodeen came over to check on them. Instantly, they wiped the smiles off our faces.

"Ready to go when you are," Linda said to her mother. "And thank you, Fritzi, for making this possible."

"Good night, Arthur! Thank you for chaperoning, Mrs. Bodeen!" Fritzi said.

They met Pop and headed toward the station wagon. Linda watched Arthur, flanked by his parents, get into their Dodge Dart and waved at him. He grinned, his gorgeous white teeth flashing at her in the dark.

20

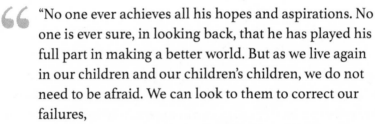 "No one ever achieves all his hopes and aspirations. No one is ever sure, in looking back, that he has played his full part in making a better world. But as we live again in our children and our children's children, we do not need to be afraid. We can look to them to correct our failures,
　　to achieve many of our hopes and aspirations."
　　—Nancy Shea, *The Air Force Wife*

JUNE 3, 1966
　　Travis Air Force Base, California

IT WAS all over the news: Pop's friend Ed White walked in space today. At dinner, Pop talked about Major White, how he'd been such a nice guy back at Wright-Patterson. How he was a West Point grad, an aeronautical engineer, a champion hurdler who'd almost made the U.S.

Olympic team. Pop's voice seemed far too ebullient, a little syrupy on the praise. It irked Rand.

"So, do you ever wish you could have continued in the astronaut program?" Rand asked.

"Son, in the Air Force, you never look back. Never wonder what might have been. You see, as a pilot, you deal with the *now*. The circumstances that prevail, the conditions you must navigate. It's a fine way to live, to look at life, I think."

"Your father is a lieutenant colonel now, after all. He outranks Major White," Fritzi chimed in.

Rand nodded his understanding but refused to let it go. "'The circumstances that prevail,' you say. Do you believe we have no choice in what happens in life? That we have no control over those circumstances?"

"Of course not," Pop said. "That's not what I said at all. You get out of life what you put into it. I put a lot of duty and effort into my Air Force career, and my position as a squadron commander reflects that."

"But wouldn't you rather be famous, like an astronaut?" Debby asked. That was a surprise. She never spoke up at dinner these days.

"Tinkerbell, there's so much more to life than being famous," Pop said, his voice softening toward his younger daughter. "You know that."

"Following that logic, do people who aren't famous lead more fulfilled lives?" Linda asked. "Or do people who become famous also lead fulfilled lives, because they've accomplished something historic?"

Fritzi rolled her eyes. "Always debating."

"Good point," Pop said. "I would argue that those who accomplish something worthwhile—whether or not they become famous—lead fulfilled lives. Why? Because they keep moving forward, navigating the circumstances that prevail. Dealing with the present, rather than resting on their laurels." Pop always favored Linda in debates.

Rand refused to let go. "But back to my question. Do you wish that you could be famous for doing something historic in aviation history, like walking in space for the first time?"

"Son, if you wish in one hand and spit in the other, which gets full first?" Pop said, his temples working in agitation as he chewed his dinner. "I'm not interested in being famous. I'm interested in being the best officer, pilot, husband, and father on earth. That's all. I don't *wish* for anything." He buttered a roll.

Rand picked at his potatoes. Best *officer*, he put that first. Ahead of *husband*. Ahead of *father*.

"I wish all the time," Debby said softly, looking at Pop with her big brown eyes. "I wish that Tommy hadn't died. I wish we were like the way we used to be. Not the way we are now."

"Aww, baby," Pop said, reaching his arms across to table toward Debby. "Come here and let me hug you."

Debby burst into tears and ran to Pop's arms. He hugged her close, his eyes brimming. "We all miss him. But he's in Heaven now. We have to go on, here on earth."

Linda looked at Rand with pursed lips. He knew exactly what she was thinking: *always little Debby. The littlest girl. The one who watched him go over the railing...*

Fritzi pushed away from her plate and lit a cigarette. "Anybody want dessert? There's Neapolitan ice cream."

"No, thank you," said Linda. "I'll clear the table."

"I'll help," said Rand. He felt a sudden sense of solidarity with Linda—and it was a good excuse to leave the table.

"Thank y'all," Fritzi said softly, sounding oddly Southern. "I so appreciate it."

Pop and Fritzi were on his case. It was already the second week of summer, and they were mad because he hadn't gotten a job lifeguarding at the Officers' Club Pool. After all, he'd gotten his Lifesaving Certificate. He could walk to work. He'd be supervising kids and teaching swim lessons. Rand lied to his parents and said the lifeguard position was filled; someone else had beaten him to the punch. Truth was, he hadn't applied because he didn't want to spend a summer lathered in zinc oxide, supervising screaming brats whose parents dropped them off for him to watch all day.

But, he needed a job to earn money if he wanted to use the car, or go out, or indulge in his latest obsession: painting.

He'd discovered his love for painting after taking a mechanical drawing class at Vanden. Although he'd aced the class, the act of drawing objects to scale made him itch to create something that he considered "true." To Rand, that meant something unique, unsuspected, extraordinary. Nothing based on re-creating a tangible object. Paint seemed to be a perfect medium—you could do so much with color, form, composition.

This summer, he would immerse himself in art. Find a job in some art-oriented business so he could learn something and afford to buy paints and canvas. So, he combed the Yellow Pages for art galleries, art stores, art schools, in the nearby town of Fairfield, and came up with one possibility: a place called The Art Shoppe. Last week, he had hitchhiked into town and applied for a job there with the owner, a lady named Mrs. DeSalvo.

Today, he lay in his room, wondering how he could get Fritzi and Pop off his case. Then he heard Fritzi call from the kitchen: "Rand, phone's for you. A Mrs. DeSalvo?"

He flew out of bed and into the kitchen. "Hello?" He couldn't hide the excitement in his voice. "Yes, ma'am. Yes, and thank you! I'll be there as soon as I can!"

Fritzi, finishing the breakfast dishes, gave him a suspicious look. "What was that all about? You seem excited."

"I got a job at The Art Shoppe in Fairfield! I'll be helping out the owner; she's an older lady whose husband is sick. I'll be stocking inventory, running the cash register, cleaning up. Plus, I get painting lessons for free!"

"How on earth did you apply for a job off base? I don't remember lending you the car."

"I got a ride with a friend," Rand said, when in fact he'd hitchhiked with a young airman in a Chevy Biscayne. "Is it OK if I borrow the car today? I said I'd be at work by ten this morning, to help her open up."

"And just what am I supposed to do for a car? Debby's got ballet, and I've got a Wives' Club meeting this afternoon. I'll just drive you and drop you there. What time do you get off work?"

"I think around six. I can get the bus home."

"The bus will drop you outside the main gate, you know. You'll have to show your ID to walk in. You can walk home from there. We'll have to save you some dinner, because you'll get home after seven."

"You sound mad, Fritzi. What's wrong? I thought you'd be proud of me for finding a job—especially a job where I can get a discount on art supplies."

"Don't get me wrong, son. I think it's great, and I know you have artistic talent. It's just that your daddy is going to be so disappointed. He really wanted you to find something on base."

"Well, that didn't work out. The real reason you're upset is you think Pop's going to have a cow because I'm doing something he'd call 'artsy fartsy', right? Pop doesn't get why I'm interested in art. He just doesn't get me, period. Never will."

"That's not true! He just expects you to be more like him. He assumed you'd be interested in flying, in engineering." She lit a Chesterfield.

"Maybe I would have if he'd ever had time to help me finish the Stratofortress, and all those other models. All I know is I'm going to be late if I don't hurry. Thank you, Fritzi, for the ride. From now on, I'll be up in time to catch the early bus in."

THE ART SHOPPE had an old-fashioned sign that hung out over the sidewalk downtown, the kind he used to see in Europe. When Rand opened the door, a bell tinkled. The shop itself was a small space lined with shelves, all neatly labeled. Charcoal pencils, calligraphy pens, sketch pads, canvases, brushes, watercolors, and tubes of oil paints, all neatly displayed next to a color chart. To Rand, it was a candy store.

"Hello, Rand," said Mrs. DeSalvo, who met him at the door. She was a sturdy looking older woman in a long denim skirt and European sandals. She had wire-rimmed glasses and a long, dark braid with streaks of grey that snaked down her back. When she smiled, there were friendly wrinkles around her eyes and mouth. "I've got a new shipment of sketch pads. I'll need you to haul it in from the storeroom and arrange them in the display over there." She nodded to an empty shelf near the back of the store.

Rand took a deep breath and stood up straight. "Yes, ma'am!" he said, and strode toward the storeroom.

"My goodness! You are one eager lad!" She took off the glasses, which hung on a beaded string around her neck, and looked at him with keen brown eyes. "I can't pay you too much, but as I said in the interview, I can offer you a discount on supplies. And, you're welcome to attend any of the classes we offer in our gallery, upstairs."

"I'm really grateful, ma'am," he said

"Let's see. When you're finished unloading, I need you to straighten the oil paint display. A bunch of teenagers were in here over the weekend and messed it up. Then, I'll show you how to run the cash register. And tonight, my niece is teaching a workshop on Abstract Expressionism. I'll need you to set up easels and paints for six students in the gallery."

Rand stopped in his tracks. "Tonight?" he gulped. "Would it, uh, be possible for me to sit in on the class?"

He'd read about the Abstract Expressionists in the *San Francisco Chronicle*. They made true art, not imitative landscapes or boring portraits. It was all about color, composition, form. No sentiment, no emotion. He'd been itching to know more about it.

"I'll ask Lara, to be sure, but I think she would be delighted," she said. "What interests you about this particular class? I'm surprised someone your age understands it. It's a movement that's sort of played out over the last decade, but Lara has some older students who are still eager to give it a try."

"I'd like to try it myself. I messed around with a couple of canvases on my carport at home, but I couldn't quite get the right composition. Or color. I was hoping to learn more about color saturation," Rand said.

He'd started painting last spring, after he used the last of his Christmas money to buy a canvas and some paints. Fritzi made him do it outside in the carport because of the mess. He'd found that paint was a complex medium, a substance with infinite possibilities, depending on how he applied it. He couldn't afford more than one canvas, so he was constantly wiping it with turpentine to start his color experiments.

"Your father will not understand your intense preoccupation with color," Fritzi had said. "And turpentine stinks. I can't have you using it in the house. I think you are a true artist, but you'll have to pay for your own supplies. And you'll have to clean up your mess every day before Pop pulls his car into the garage."

Fritzi had saved him a lot of grief, insisting that he paint only when his father wasn't around. Now he had the job, he had the chance to learn, to create, away from the carport, and, best of all, miles away from the base.

FRITZI COULDN'T FIGURE whether Rand's new job was a good or a bad thing. He seemed to love it, but she could see Joe's eyes glaze over when Rand talked about the shop or how he was learning to paint like an Abstract Expressionist. Rand's job and art were clearly out of Joe's realm, and she could see the gulf between her husband and her son grow larger every day.

At least Rand seemed to be pulling out of the funk he'd been in all school year, and that was a relief. Plus, Joe was on the short list to make colonel, which was causing her husband to alternate between being a puffed-up egotist and an anxious competitor. Debby was immersed in a summer dance program at the Base Rec Center, but she was looking painfully thin. Linda was sullen and withdrawn.

Between her part-time job shelving books at the Base Library and devouring *War and Peace*, she seemed preoccupied; not her usual opinionated self. Fritzi suspected her withdrawal was a reaction to Arthur Bodeen's father being transferred to Offut AFB in Nebraska. When she asked Linda if she wanted to talk about it, her daughter just rolled her eyes shook her head.

Fritzi used to imagine that when her children entered their teens, they would become less needy, more independent. But now, given Tommy's death and the moves to Barksdale and Travis, all three of her children seemed to encounter storm clouds at every turn. Debby complained about her stomach and picked at her food. Linda, on the other hand, ate like a horse, yet complained about gaining weight. Rand, the brilliant hope of the three, had chosen to irritate Joe with his sudden interest in abstract art and hopes of becoming an artist. And then there was Joe, the man she undoubtedly loved without reservation, even though he had become an ambitious pragmatist who put his career and so-called "duty" ahead of her and the children.

She looked back on those days in Naples, before Tommy died, and realized they were the golden times. There was no pressure to be the Squadron Commander's dutiful wife. Linda and Rand were star students who showed academic and social promise. Debby was small, and, although demanding, was just "Tinkerbell" who could be pacified with the simple attention of reading a story or coloring in a coloring book. Joe was an attentive, romantic husband, an adventurous and playful father. Perhaps it was the setting: the ancient beauty of Naples, the easy-going Italian pace of life that was contagious. They lived in an off-base apartment building that had a few other American families, but mostly Italians. They bought food from street vendors and shoes from the marketplace in the Posillipo. Here, living on a base, there were constant expectations, constraints, and, she had to admit, a sheer lack of oxygen.

In her heart, she knew they all missed Tommy. That funny, bouncing toddler had been the glue that held the rest of them together. If he'd lived, Tommy would be five now. In this environment, would he still be that bright, boisterous spirit, or would he be just like his brother and sisters: demanding, stubborn, challenging? His loss had left a hole in her soul that she had to ignore, because paying attention to her own grief would only worsen it. She knew better than to hope for happiness, but she also knew that if she didn't keep going, didn't keep the momentum of her family up to speed, that she would grind to a screeching halt and disintegrate. She simply had to keep going. She had to keep them *all* going.

Dinner. There was always dinner to fix, every single goddamn day. Meat, potatoes, vegetables. The occasional fresh tomato, sliced. When they all finally sat down at the dining room table, the labor that had taken her most of the day was devoured in less than half an hour. Except for Debby's portion. Her food would be scraped and shoved back and forth on her plate so that it became an unappetizing amalgam of protein, starch, and vegetable. Linda and Rand would eat heartily, ask to be excused and then begin to do the dishes. She and Joe would sit and sit with Debby, pleading her to take just one more bite, promising her they'd go to Dairy Queen if she could just finish her potatoes. Lately, Fritzi had simply given up and left the pleading to Joe. ("Please, Tinkerbell! Come on, do it for your Pop! Let's put some meat on your skinny old bones!") *Debby is almost nine years old,* she wanted to scream at Joe, but instead she just left the table and supervised Rand and Linda while they loaded the dishwasher.

Yes, Debby was nearly nine, but she looked like a malnourished six-year-old. Her arms and legs were tiny, making her head look far too large for her body. Her beautiful honey-colored hair was now dry and thin. The girl had bitten her nails to the quicks, and her once shiny brown eyes were dull.

"We have got to do something, Joe," Fritzi said one evening after dinner as they sat on their patio, drinking bourbon. "I've taken her to the doctor, but he says she'll grow out of it. She complains about her stomach, but the doctor says she's just nervous, on account of adjusting to this move and the new school. *Joe!* She's had almost a year to adjust, and she's just getting worse. She's wasting away before our eyes." Fritzi sipped her bourbon and wiped at her eyes.

"Aw, honey, don't cry," Joe said. He leaned close and kissed her forehead. "The doctor's right. Debby's just more sensitive than Rand and Linda. She'll come around, I'm sure. She just needs time and a little encouragement, that's all. Have you tried making her peanut butter sandwiches during the day? Taking her to Dairy Queen for a milkshake in the afternoon, while the other kids are busy? Maybe she's just looking for a little TLC from her mother. You've been awfully busy with the squadron, you know. With summer here, maybe you could slow down and just concentrate on Debby, fix her some good food, give her that extra attention she craves. She's not our smart one, you know, Fritzi. She's going to struggle more than Linda and Rand—boy, is *he* on a tangent, with that artsy job—Debby just needs more of you, that's all. We all do. You are our rock."

"Has it ever occurred to you that I am a human being, and not a goddamned rock, Joe Stoddard? That maybe *you*, as the father of this passel of kids, ought to give a little more of your precious self? When was the last time you took Debby for an ice cream, or tried to talk to Rand about his job, or talked to Linda about how she feels now that Arthur Bodeen is moving to Nebraska? I can't be everyone's 'rock' without weighing myself down, too. And right now, I'm about to go under with the heaviness I'm bearing. It's time you took some of the burden. They're your kids, too. As I recall, you had a lot of fun making them."

"Ssshh—honey, let's take this conversation inside, shall we?" He put a gentle arm around her shoulders and took her empty drink. Come on in, now. I'll put on the attic fan. It's a little warm out here."

"You go on in," Fritzi said, lighting a Chesterfield. "I'm going to sit out here for a while. The kids will hear us if we talk about this inside. I just need some time to myself."

Joe let out a deep sigh and opened the sliding screen door. "All right, Fritzi. I'll leave you to your thoughts." He slid the screen door shut with a bang.

"Debby? Linda?" she heard him call into the girls' room. "Come on, I want to take y'all for a little treat."

It was just like Joe to get his marching orders and go straight to work. No doubt he would load the girls into the station wagon, Linda in the front seat, and Debby in back, and they'd hit the Dairy Queen. Debby would stir a hot fudge sundae until it became chocolate soup and Linda would devour a large dipped cone faster than Joe could finish his Coke. *Check your box, Joe; you think this little trip fulfills your fatherly duties for the rest of the summer.*

Fritzi inhaled her first, deep drag of the cigarette. There was always great pleasure in that first hit of fresh tobacco. She exhaled, and for a moment it was as if the kids, Joe—their demands and problems—dispersed like smoke into the twilight. In this tiny backyard, hemmed by the tall cedar privacy fence, the evening air smelled of jet fuel and the onion plant in Vacaville. Suddenly, she longed for the summer scents of Fontainebleu: lemony magnolia, sweet blooms of honeysuckle, the lawn in the morning dew.

The idea struck like lightning: *take the girls to Montrose.* Debby liked it there, after all. She could use a dose of Josie's cooking, and Mother would fuss over her younger granddaughter so much, she'd stay out of Fritzi's and Linda's hair. Rand and Joe would be left home alone, with no excuse to ignore each other.

She told Joe after the girls and Rand had gone to bed.

"Mother called. She's worried about Daddy's health—he has high blood pressure," Fritzi lied. "Mother simply can't cope—you know how she is. She needs me, and I need to go see about Daddy. I'll take the girls with me. It's too costly to fly—I can drive the station wagon. Can you manage, Joe?"

"Of course, if your folks need you, of course I can. I can get a car from the base motor pool. Rand is already taking the bus back and forth to his job. You be careful, now. Linda is smart, and she can be your navigator. Stay at Holiday Inns, and make advance reservations. Call me collect every night. And take my service pistol. Keep it under the front seat, in case of trouble."

"I promise I'll call every night, just to hear your voice, darling."

She kissed him for a long, long time, and made love with all her might. Tomorrow she would pack her bags and head out for her own "temporary duty"—if Joe could go TDY, so could she.

21

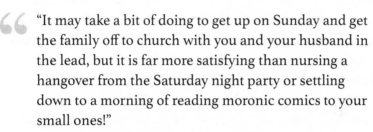

"It may take a bit of doing to get up on Sunday and get the family off to church with you and your husband in the lead, but it is far more satisfying than nursing a hangover from the Saturday night party or settling down to a morning of reading moronic comics to your small ones!"
—Nancy Shea, *The Air Force Wife*

Montrose, *Louisiana*

It was strange to be away from Pop on Father's Day, but Debby loved being at Fontainebleu. Josie had prepared a picnic in the gardens, out by the old rock barbecue. Leo, the resident gardener/handyman/butler, decked out in a white apron smeared with his "secret recipe" barbecue sauce, presided over the barbecue pit, smoking pork ribs over a slow apple wood fire. Debby had helped Josie set the old picnic table with a red checkered cloth and some simple painted pottery. They picked daisies together and put them in an old mason jar for a centerpiece. Fritzi and Linda went to the dime store and bought blue construction paper and glitter to make a "crown" for Judge to wear. He looked silly in the crown, but Debby liked the way her grandfather's eyes lit up when Fritzi put it on his head. She'd never thought about her mother as being Judge's daughter, like she was Pop's. But with the light in her grandfather's eyes, she could see that her mother was the apple of his.

"Have a biscuit, Debby," Grandmamma said. "You remember what we talked about, dear. It's important for your nervous stomach to heal with the proper nutrition."

Debby nodded and daintily reached for one of Josie's homemade biscuits. "Thank you." Leo loaded her plate with ribs and potato salad, and Josie poured her a glass of cold lemonade. Debby took a deep breath and stared at the heaping plate in front of her. Judge, across from her, tied a napkin around his neck and tore into his ribs. Fritzi spooned extra sauce on her ribs. Linda gulped lemonade.

"Slow down, Linda, you sound like a truck driver!" Grandmamma scolded.

"I'm sorry," Linda replied in a flat, insincere tone. "I've been down at the creek fishing, and I'm just hot and thirsty. Excuse me."

Fritzi seemed eager to lighten the conversation. "Daddy, I can't remember when I last spent a Father's Day with you!" She kissed his cheek and sipped at her lemonade. Debby noticed her mother had declined the potato salad and had taken extra slices of fresh tomato.

Debby chimed in with accolades for her grandfather. "Thank you, Judge, for taking me to the cemetery yesterday. I so enjoyed visiting Tommy there."

"Any time, darlin'," Judge replied.

"I didn't realize you'd gone," Fritzi said.

"You could have come along, Fritzi. I wish you would have," Debby said.

"I know, honey, but I just can't. You know that. How nice of Judge to take you."

"I asked Josie, but she said she couldn't go because it was the white cemetery," Debby said. "I couldn't find Linda, and Grand-mamma was busy."

"You could have looked for me," Linda said in that flat sarcastic voice. "I was just out here, helping Leo do some weeding."

Debby fed herself a tiny piece of the fluffy biscuit. "I thought you were down at the creek. I didn't want to bother you."

Linda shrugged. "I might like to visit Tommy's grave, too. Would have meant something to me."

Debby sighed. She hadn't wanted Linda to come along, or anyone else. She just wanted to go with Judge, alone. "I'm sorry," Debby said softly. She meant it for Tommy and not for Linda.

"Now, girls, no need to quibble. I'm sure Judge will take Linda if she wants to go, another time," Fritzi said.

"Might do you some good to go yourself, Fritzi," Judge said. "It's a pretty plot. Your mother and I chose the grave marker, white marble, with a carved lamb. Tommy is buried next to my mama and daddy. He is truly home."

Debby glanced nervously at her mother, who had put down her ribs and was lighting a cigarette.

"Thank you, Daddy, but I'm a grown woman and I will make my own decisions about visiting my little son's grave. And why, may I ask, did you choose to have him laid to rest under the statue of a lamb? He was not my personal sacrifice to the Almighty. He was a just a little boy. A little boy who died. Nothing can bring him back, and no one is going to ply me to visit the cemetery when Josie is not even welcome there."

"Suit yourself," Grandmamma said. "I know you are hurting. We all are. We chose the grave marker because you refused to have anything to do with planning his funeral or his burial. Life has got to go on, Fritzi. You must accept what has happened."

Fritzi blew smoke toward her mother. "You know nothing about what I've had to accept, Mother," she said in a low, slow whisper. "I lost my *baby*. I feel his loss every minute, every second of every single day. I can't see how visiting his grave will make that loss more real to me. If anything, it just might *kill* me." She stubbed out the cigarette on her dinner plate.

Debby felt the biscuit and the rich pork churn in her stomach. Up until now, the visit to Fontainebleu had been pleasant. But now, the depth of Fritzi's pain reached into her own gut. *She had caused this. She did not stop Tommy.*

Judge cleared his throat. "I believe we all need to be quiet now. There's nothing more to be said that won't hurt all of us more deeply than we are already hurt."

Debby struggled to keep the food from coming up. Linda reached for a second biscuit. A blue-black thundercloud obscured the sun.

"I believe I will pack up and it's best that you all head back to the house," Leo said.

In the distance, thunder rumbled. Debby helped gather the plates and ran for the house, praying she could make it to the downstairs toilet.

DEBBY. She and Linda were five years apart, but it might as well be a decade. And wasn't just their age difference. It was Debby. She still acted like she was some sort of pet, needing attention and constant grooming. Picking at her food and looking like a stick figure. Linda had tried to talk with her sister--at night, when they were in their twin beds at home--about Tommy, how she herself felt bad because she had sneaked into the Miroglio's library when she could have been looking out for him, and for *her*. Here at Fontainebleu, Grandmamma had fixed Debby a bed in the sunroom off the master bedroom, so she could be close to her and Judge at night. They had adopted Debby like she was a hurt little kitten.

Linda, they hardly noticed, and that was just fine. At least Grand-mamma wasn't on her case about dressing up and going on diets. Their grandmother was totally focused on Debby, who seemed to be thriving. Debby had put some flesh back on her bones in the week

they'd been here. Well, good for her. Linda was grateful that Grandmamma wasn't on her case about counting calories.

When Fritzi announced that they were driving out for this visit,
Linda had pitched a fit. *"Why would I want to spend a summer in that
swampy place? Grandmamma doesn't even like me..."* and so on. When
she finally shut up, she saw something in Fritzi's face. Instead of
laying down the law or punishing Linda for talking back, Fritzi just
looked at her with sad, pleading eyes. Linda could see, just for a
moment, her mother's great pain. Suddenly, she realized: this trip was
necessary.

"Linda, I need you to go. I'm driving the station wagon. It will be
just us girls, and you'll need to navigate. It won't be like the time you
spent out there with Rand, I promise."

It was unlike Fritzi to tell anyone—much less Linda—that she 1)
promised something and 2) needed help. Linda was filled with pride
when she heard this, and her attitude suddenly changed. She saw
that her mother was sad, somehow broken. Why? Linda wanted to
ask Fritzi if she was worried about Grandmamma and Judge. Where
they ill? Or did something happen to make her want a divorce from
Pop? (God forbid). Or was Fritzi just worried about how thin Debby
was getting?

But Linda didn't ask, because Fritzi wouldn't have answered
honestly. Linda could see it all in her eyes: they were going, and Fritzi
needed her.

The drive out was fun. Fritzi let Linda choose all the radio
stations, and they listened to cool music all the way: "Satisfaction,"
"Mrs. Brown, You've Got a Lovely Daughter," even "Eve of Destruc-
tion." Fritzi seemed to like rock 'n' roll. Sometimes, they'd be so far
away from a good station, all they could get was scratchy old country
music—"Your Cheatin' Heart," or some gospel tunes interrupted by a
hellfire and damnation preacher. When this happened, Fritzi sang
along, in an exaggerated twang that made Debby and Linda nearly
hysterical with laughter. They had spent three nights in Holiday Inns
—all of them with swimming pools. Fritzi had packed her bathing

suit and gotten in the water with them. They ate late dinners and took all the little soaps with them when they packed up the next day. Without Pop and Rand, they acted like three girlfriends out on a lark.

Of course, all this changed once they got to Fontainebleu, where Grandmamma's rules and schedules prevailed. Grandmamma and Josie took charge of Debby, coaxing her to eat special things, taking her to the beauty parlor for a trim and style, and, of course, outfitting her at Lois Jeanne's. Judge seemed to love having Fritzi at home, and he embraced Linda along with her. He taught Linda to bait her own hook down at the creek, where she caught a few crappie and learned to clean them under his tutelage. He took Fritzi and Linda to the Montrose Family Drive-In Movie Theater to see *Shenandoah* and *Sons of Katie Elder*. (Grandmamma and Debby chose to stay home.)

During the day, Fritzi and Linda took walks ~~around~~ around the wild places at Fontainebleu. Fritzi showed Linda where she'd once had a treehouse, and where she and her friends used to skinny dip in the creek. Fritzi wore shorts and Keds, like Linda, and they inspected each other for ticks outside the back door before they went in for baths. Once, they were sitting on a warm rock in the sun, looking over the pasture where Fritzi's horses used to graze. She reached into her shorts pocket for her Chesterfield pack and matches.

"Would you like to try a smoke, Linda? Just once, so you don't have to sneak behind my back?"

Linda had never thought smoking was glamorous, and she'd heard all the warnings about cancer. But this offer from Fritzi was a bonding moment. "I guess I could try it," she said, like Fritzi was a popular girl who'd just issued a dare.

Fritzi handed Linda a cigarette and told her to put it in her mouth. She struck a match, and, using her hand to shield the flame from the wind, lit the end. "Now, breathe in," Fritzi instructed, "to get it going."

Linda did, and coughed violently. Fritzi patted her back and then lit her own Chesterfield. "Like this," she said, inhaling slowly as she lit the end, then exhaling an elegant plume of smoke. "It's like you take in all the bad feelings you have, then blow them all out and get rid of them!"

Linda laughed and tried again, choking and coughing. "Sorry, I just don't think it's for me," she said.

"Good! I'm glad. Anyway, you can say you've already tried it if anyone asks, and just say 'no thanks.' Although, I've got to admit, it does curb your appetite."

"Well, don't tell Debby! She'll start smoking just so she won't have to eat!"

Fritzi laughed. "Put that out, Linda. You know, there's something seriously wrong with your sister. She has a psychological problem of some sort. I honestly don't know how to deal with it. That's why I brought us all out here. Ran home to my mama with my girls, because, I'll tell you something, honey, it's a lot. I'm just thankful that you and Rand are healthy and smart. You two are the shining stars Pop and I can always count on." She put her arm around Linda's shoulders for a quick squeeze, then looked at her watch. "Nearly time to get our baths before supper. Let's head back." "Linda," Fritzi said, standing up. "I didn't mean to worry you just now. Debby will be fine. She just needed the TLC that my mother and Josie can give her. We'll head back home in a couple of weeks and things will be better."

Fritzi and Linda walked to the square the next morning. She showed Linda the courthouse where Judge worked, and told stories about all the shops that used to line the square. Some of them had gone out of business since she was a girl. There was a new Rexall Drug on the corner, where Fritzi said there used to be a soda shop. A funeral home where there used to be a ladies' tea room. And, of course, Lois Jeanne's Dress Shoppe. A few blocks south of the square, she pointed out the hospital, a large square brick building, where Linda was born. "I swelled way up with preeclampsia, so I had to be in there the last month before you came," Fritzi explained. "Your daddy was in Korea, and I was here living with Mother and Judge. It was not an easy time."

Linda half expected her to end the story with "but I'm so glad you were born," or something to that effect. But not today. Fritzi was not feeling sentimental, Linda could tell. She was simply giving her a tour of Montrose, nothing more. Linda was happy to have that time with her, just the two of them.

FRITZI SAID they could stay an extra week, and Debby was so excited, she asked Josie if she could have an extra macaroon after lunch.

"Of course, child, you can have one," Josie said, reaching for the cut glass jar where she stored her fresh-baked goodies. "Take two, put some meat on your skinny bones."

"I wish everyone would stop calling me skinny. Sometimes I just don't feel like eating, that's all."

"Why is that? Everybody likes to eat good food. You like my food, don't you?"

"Of course, Josie! You make the best biscuits and fried chicken and pie... everything is just delicious here. Food seems to taste better here than at home."

Debby sat down at the kitchen table and looked at the big gas stove, the cast-iron pots and pans, the knives that Leo kept sharp. "How did you learn to cook, Josie?"

Josie poured herself a cup of coffee from the big percolator on the stove and sat across from Debby. "My mama was a cook for Mrs. Fontaine's mother-in-law, here at Fontainebleu. I grew up coming to work with Mama. It was my job to help her in the kitchen and stay out of the way when she got really busy. She had me taking out the garbage, scrubbing pots and pans, picking vegetables out there in the kitchen garden, before I was six years old. When Mama got old and sick, she stayed out at the farm, and I came on in to do her job. The old Mrs. Fontaine still paid Mama, and she paid me, too."

"How old were you then?"

"I imagine I was about fifteen."

"Didn't you go to school? Wasn't it hard doing all this work?"

"Honey, nigra girls who lived in the country didn't have a school to go to. We all just went to work."

"What do you mean? Fritzi went to Montrose High. Why didn't you go there?"

"Living out there in California, I expect you don't know how it was here in the South. Negro children and white children went to separate schools. Still do in some parts. Montrose High wasn't integrated until a couple of years ago. By then, I was long past being a teenager, and besides, I had a job here."

"But did you ever want to be anything other than a cook?"

Jose threw her head back and laughed out loud. "Sure did. I wanted to be a lot of things. A queen. A nurse. A blues singer... but I knew this'd be my job. And I was lucky to have it. The Fontaines are the finest family in Montrose. They treat their help good. My mama worked here for nearly forty years and never wanted for anything. Raised three of us children out there on the farm."

"Did you ever get married?"

"Sure did. Found me a good man. He went to war and didn't come back."

"Did he die?"

"Child, what do you think? That's not a polite question to ask, by the way. Yes, he died, on a beach in Normandy. During the invasion."

"Excuse me for being impolite. Were you sad for a long time?"

"Yes, but I was young then. Thought my life might be over, too. I loved that man. Name was Raymond. Raymond Collier."

"What did you do about being sad? Did you want to die?"

"Of course I did. I loved Raymond. But I just went to church and got on my knees and prayed to the Lord Jesus to deliver me from my grief. And I just kept working. Every day, came to work, cooked for your grandmother and Mr. Judge and your mother, too. Pretty soon, the sadness faded. But it was still there. Is there to this day, but Jesus has given me strength to keep going. And the sad keeps fading. All that's left is the love."

"I'm *still* sad. About my little brother Tommy. It's been almost three years, and the sadness just gets worse. It never fades. It hurts inside me, like my stomach is rotting." Debby's brown eyes welled with tears. "But everyone tells me not to cry, not to be sad anymore. Tommy is gone, and he's in Heaven. But I'm still sad, and sometimes I don't want to live anymore either. I want to be in Heaven. Let other people be sad about *me*."

"Hold on there, little missy, that's no way to talk!" Josie reached across the table and grabbed Debby's shoulders. "Jesus will take you when your time comes! It's a sin to wish away your life. Think of your mother and daddy!"

"I can't think of anything but Tommy."

"Why do you suppose that is? I'll tell you why. It's because you don't know Jesus. You don't know how to trust your savior to take away the pain in your heart."

Debby blinked, shedding tears. She let out a big sob.

"Come here, child. Just sit in old Josie's lap." Josie hugged her and swayed gently, as though comforting a baby. She gave Debby a napkin.

"Here. You wipe your eyes and I'll get you a cold lemonade. Anyone ever talk to you about Jesus, honey?"

"Not too much. Fritzi doesn't like church, so we don't go. There was a chaplain who tried to read the Bible to us when Tommy died, but Fritzi asked him to leave. She didn't like the "valley of the shadow of death," and all that stuff. I didn't understand any of it."

Josie opened the big refrigerator, which seemed to take up one whole wall in the sunny, white kitchen, took out a frosty pitcher, and poured Debby a tall glass of lemonade. "Use a coaster," she warned, and Debby dutifully reached for a hand-crocheted coaster in the basket in the middle of the table.

"Well, it's not my place to preach to you, but I think you ought to ask Miss Fritzi to take you down to First Presbyterian with Mr. Judge and your grandmother on Sunday. You might find some answers there."

"I've already been with Judge and Grandmamma. Fritzi won't go. Couldn't I just go with you? Where is your church?"

"I expect that's something you might want to take up with your mother. And your grandparents. They might not approve of you going to my Negro church."

"Why, because I'm white?"

"Just ask them, child. You'll be welcome if they say it's all right."

OF COURSE, Fritzi didn't care if she went to church with Josie. "If she has invited you, then, of course, go ahead. I'll be happy to drop you off. Just don't tell Grandmamma. She may not approve. Promise?" Fritzi crossed her heart and Debby did the same. "Don't be surprised if you're the only white person there. That won't bother you, will it?"

Debby shook her head. "No, not at all."

"Good. Go on, pick out a nice dress to wear so Josie will be proud."

ON SUNDAY, Debby wore the outfit she'd laid out the night before: a short-sleeved cotton pique shift the color of butter, along with white anklet socks and white patent leather shoes. She insisted that Fritzi get up early enough to braid her hair with the yellow and white polka dotted ribbon that matched the dress. When she was ready, Debby looked in the mirror. The dress was cut slim, and it used to hang pitifully on her bony frame. Today, it was still loose but her arms had fleshed out, and her knees had ceased to look like two Tinkertoy knobs with sticks attached. She applied some Chapstick. Her braids were perfectly even and tight to her scalp, with the ribbons laced evenly throughout the hair. Her pale skin had taken on a little rosiness, now that she took daily walks in the fresh air. Surely, Josie would be proud.

Fritzi, dressed in her bathrobe, drove her from Fontainebleu, past the stately old houses with magnolias and river oaks, through the downtown, past the low-slung brick houses with neat lawns, and across the railroad tracks, and out into the country. Houses were small and far apart, set away from the road with dirt driveways and chain link fences. They passed a trailer park with a barking dog

chained in the yard. Finally, Fritzi turned off the main road. Pine trees
shaded the road as Debby heard the *ping ping ping* of gravel on the
station wagon's underside. In a small clearing, lit by bright morning
sun, was a white clapboard church with wooden steps, and Josie was
waiting out front.

"My, aren't you a picture!" Josie remarked. She was dressed up,
too, in a bright purple dress, stockings and a straw hat with a purple
hatband. Josie waved to Fritzi as she drove away, took Debby's hand,
and they walked together into the church.

Debby had never seen so many women in bright dresses and hats.
Josie led her in. They sat right in front of the altar, where there was a
big wooden cross, a podium, and a woman playing a piano. Some
men and women dressed in white cotton robes paraded down the
aisle and began to sing and clap. "Praise Jesus, come Holy Spirit!"
over and over again. The piano grew louder, and soon the people
stood and began to sing, including Josie. Although she didn't know
the words, Debby sang, too. She felt a strange lightness enter her
chest, as though her heart had sprouted wings.

The singing was followed by a man, robed in white, who took the
podium. "Who is that?" Debby whispered to Josie.

"Pastor James," she answered. "He's going to preach the
sermon now."

Debby recalled the First Presbyterian services she'd attended
with her grandparents, and settled into the pew to listen politely.
But as the pastor spoke, people rose and shouted "*Amen!*" and
"*Praise Jesus!*" Pastor James kept talking, as though it was OK for
people to shout, and soon he was sweating. His voice became a roar
as he spoke about the "Holy Spirit." He spoke the names of people
who had received healing through the Holy Spirit. One of the
names he said was "Josephine Collier." Josie stood and shouted
something that sounded like a foreign language. Debby was startled
to hear Josie, who was so polite and reserved at Fontainebleu, shout
at the top of her lungs, in a language she hadn't heard before. Josie's
eyes were closed, her hands outstretched, and she began to speak
louder than the pastor, in strange words that flowed from her as

though she was singing. Soon, people around her rose to their feet and shouted "Praise, Jesus!" "The spirit among us!" and some of them began to utter strange words as well. Debby felt her heart pound against her ribcage as though it longed to escape. But instead of panic, Debby felt peace. She stood next to Josie and raised her hands, and began to shout odd words; words she had never said, words she had never known. She closed her eyes, and when she did she saw light instead of darkness, and she felt her heart slow down and began to beat in a new cadence. She heard buzzing, as though every cell in her body hummed at a high pitch. The light behind her closed eyes took the shape of rays around a sun. It grew brighter and brighter, like high beams on a car as she grew closer and closer.

And then it was dark. Debby opened her eyes; she was lying on the pew. Josie was fanning her with a palm fan, as were other ladies, all gathered around her in their bright hats. "Don't be afraid, child," Josie said softly. "You just met the Holy Spirit. You were baptized in the Word of the Lord."

Debby sat up. Pastor James was still speaking, but his voice had grown soft. A few other people were shouting, but most of them were now seated, fanning themselves with the palm fan like the one Josie was using. She blinked at Josie, who hugged her close. "Your mama isn't going to understand," she whispered to Debby. "Best keep this between us until you understand the gift you have received."

When Fritzi drove down the road to pick her up, Debby looked at the world with new eyes.

"How did you like Josie's church?" Fritzi asked, stubbing out a Chesterfield in the front seat ashtray. She was dressed in her brown linen suit.

"I loved it so much! I want to go again next week! I met the Holy Spirit!"

"Well, hallelujah!" Fritzi said. "Come on now, Judge is holding a table for us at the Country Club. He and grandmamma have invited us to brunch. Now, don't you tell them about Josie's church. I told them you were still asleep this morning and needed your rest."

Debby didn't tell. She was too busy eating a big plate of grits, red-eye gravy and ham steak. All of a sudden, she was famished.

"I never knew you had such an appetite, Debby!" Grandmamma exclaimed. "It's about time!"

It wasn't just her appetite. All of a sudden, Debby felt insatiable for the Holy Spirit to enter her again.

22

> "The word 'morale,' borrowed from the French, denotes a quality prevalent in every successful military organization. It is a spirit built up in the affections, mind, and heart of the individual who is an active leading member in a favored Service."
> —Nancy Shea, *The Air Force Wife*

TRAVIS AIR FORCE BASE, *California*

WITHOUT FRITZI and the girls at home, Rand and Pop had fallen into the routine of bachelors: sandwiches eaten over the kitchen sink, monosyllabic utterances of hello and good-bye, and weekly "KP" of the kitchen, house, and laundry to clear the debris of daily living. Pop spent long hours at the squadron, and on weekends he played golf. He'd grown to accept Rand's "arty" job, but clearly didn't want to talk too much about it, which suited Rand fine. Rand took the early bus into Fairfield to open The Art Shoppe, and took the latest one back to the base at night, after he'd cleaned the painting studio.

One Sunday after Fritzi and the girls had gone to Montrose, Rand heard an engine vroom in the carport. He ran from the kitchen to see Pop behind the wheel of a dark green Jaguar roadster.

"What do you think, Horse Fly?" Pop's face was plastered in a shit-eating grin.

"Can I drive it?" Rand opened the passenger door and lowered himself into the saddle-colored leather seat.

"Sure. Let's take it out where we can really run the engine."

Pop drove to a place on base far beyond the flight line, where new blacktop service roads were surrounded by barbed wire fence. Pop obeyed the twenty-five miles per hour speed limit the whole way out there, but once they were out of sight of the main terminal, Pop floored the accelerator. The dials on the dashboard spun to life as Pop gathered speed. He shifted into high gear; Rand watched the MPH hit 112 and the tachometer go crazy. Gripping the handle on the passenger side, Rand yelled with delight. Pop pulled up short at the end of the blacktop and shifted to neutral.

"Now you can drive," Pop said.

"Really?" Rand couldn't believe it. His father had barely spoken to him in the last few months. "Where did you get this? Is it yours?"

"Bought it off a captain in the squadron. His wife is pregnant, and there's no room in this thing for a baby seat! It's a 1959 model, low miles, original British racing green. It's in great condition."

Rand recalled the time Pop bought the VW camper while he and Fritzi were in Rome. "Does Fritzi know?"

"Nope. Thought I'd surprise her. It's about time we had another car, anyway. You and I are batching it, but we still need transportation, right? Or, at least I do. Here, let's see how you manage this beast. Are you ready?"

Rand took a deep breath, thrilled but afraid of making a fool of himself. The only car he'd ever driven was Fritzi's lumbering station wagon.

Rand sat in the driver's seat. Pop cleared his throat and spoke in his no-nonsense instructor pilot voice. "The clutch, on your left, the brake in the middle, the accelerator on your right. Ease in on the clutch, that's right... then shift into first, straight ahead."

"All right. Good. Now, ease out on the clutch and give it some gas."

Rand did as he was told, but the car only lurched forward and stalled. Pop was patient. "Too fast on the clutch and not enough gas, Horse Fly. Now let's try it again."

Lurch, stall, just a couple more times, and Rand finally got the rhythm of the car. He felt a surge of power as he accelerated to third, fourth, and finally fifth gear as he reached seventy miles an hour. The wind in his face, the hum of the engine. The power of the gearshift, the dials on the dashboard, the smell of the leather seats.

"Take it easy, Horse Fly," Pop said. "Let's turn around now and head for the Club. Remember the speed limit on base. Feel like a burger?"

"Yes, sir!"

They ordered cheeseburgers and fries at the bar in the Men's Grill, and Pop ordered two Budweisers, on tap. "Here's to the men in the family!" Pop said, clinking mugs with Rand.

MRS. DE SALVO's niece Lara taught evening classes at The Art Shoppe. She was a graduate student at Berkeley, a long-stemmed beauty with raven hair and eyes as blue as the Bay of Naples. Lara was taking the summer to work on her thesis, earning a little cash with the painting classes in the studio upstairs. Her field of study was Abstract Expressionism, and Rand was her most promising pupil.

Lara took an interest in Rand's painting, and schooled him on color saturation technique as well as gestational brush strokes. She also had a stash of pot that she shared freely with Rand when he was cleaning the studio after night classes. Rand had smoked with his high school friends, but the quality of the experience was greatly enhanced in the presence of a gorgeous woman who advised him to inhale, hold the smoke in his lungs, close his eyes, and exhale ever so slowly.

"Damn. You are beautiful," Rand told her one night when they were sharing a joint. "I know I'm a kid, a stupid kid, but you are the most beautiful woman in the world, and I just had to tell you."

She touched his hair and kissed him on the cheek. "I see it in your eyes. You don't have to tell me." She didn't laugh. She smiled and stroked his forehead.

"I'm an idiot, I know," he said, mesmerized by her eyes.

"No. You're an artist. You're brilliant. You're beautiful. But you *are* a kid."

Rand swallowed hard and reached for the joint. How could he be so cheesily stupid? He normally held in all his emotions. He didn't even tell his own mother that he loved her. Why did Lara make him so weak? Why was he being such a dweeb?

"Will you kiss me, just once?" he asked, "I promise I won't bug you..."

Lara pulled him close and kissed him on the mouth, hard. He drew back, stunned. "Am I dreaming here? What was that all about?"

"Come on into my room. Stay the night. I'll do a lot more than kiss you, and in the morning you won't be a kid anymore."

Conveniently, Pop was gone for two days at a conference on a base in Texas. With Fritzi and his sisters away for the summer, there was no one home to care. He'd hit pay dirt and Nirvana all at once. Rand followed Lara down the hall to her tiny apartment, which consisted of a bedroom and adjoining bath.

Lara unbuttoned his shirt, slowly, kissing his chest along the way. She unbuckled his belt and unzipped his chinos, then slipped underwear off over his erection.

"Now, undo my jeans," she instructed. Rand did, and they dropped to the floor. She was wearing no panties. She took off her T-shirt. "Unhook my bra now," she said, and he did, after he'd taken a long look at the bra itself, a concoction of beige lace and chiffon. Nothing like the white cotton bras he'd unhooked on high school girls.

Lara reached into her bedside table and handed Rand a foil

packet. "No offense, I'd love it if we could be skin to skin, but I don't want to get pregnant. I make all my men wear them."

Dutifully, he unwrapped the condom. She showed him how to put it on, which was no problem, because he was hard as a rock. She pulled down the bedspread and reclined on the white percale sheets. "Come here," she said. She patted the space next to her. He lay down, and she pulled him on top of her with a strong kiss.

"That's it! That's it."

Rand writhed on top of her, and she arched up to meet him, guiding his cock with her hand so he could enter her. She let out a loud moan and began to quiver. For a moment, Rand wondered if she was hurt, and then he felt himself burst into flames. "Jesus!" he cried. He had made himself come many, many times, but being inside Lara was a holy experience—even with a layer of latex between them.

Rand woke sometime before dawn, startled that he wasn't in his own room, then remembering the bliss he'd experienced. He watched Lara sleep, her lips parted slightly, the steady thrum of her breath making her chest rise and fall.

As the morning light filtered through her window shade, he shook her awake. "I'd better go home and shower so I can open the shop." He got up, found his clothes, and looked at his watch. He could make the early bus to the base if he hurried.

She nodded at him sleepily. "I'm teaching class again tonight," she said sleepily. "I'll need you to stay and clean up, OK?" she blew him a kiss.

Hesitantly, he leaned down and kissed her cheek. "You got it."

He ran down the stairs, out the back door, and all the way to the bus stop.

RAND CONTINUED his liaisons with Lara, but he had to catch the last bus to the base instead of stay with her in her bed. He couldn't count the times he'd stumbled, stoned and dreamy, onto the bus with its bluish florescent lights, and collapsed in a seat midway back. Most nights, there were only a few late riders, but on Fridays, the bus was filled with young airmen going back to their barracks on base. On these nights, Rand was careful to sit behind the driver and keep to himself, lest he make eye contact with a half-drunk airman first class intent on a fight. Despite his haze, Rand kept his wits about him, his wallet and ID card listing his father's rank at the ready. He was too smart and too stoned on love to fight anyone.

The first week of August, Rand got to work early, hoping to encounter Lara before she left for the day. He went upstairs to her apartment, only to find the bed stripped and the closet empty.

"She got some horrible news," Mrs. DeSalvo said when Rand inquired about Lara. "Her fiancé has been killed in Viet Nam. He was a Naval officer. Poor Lara—she just packed up and headed for San Diego to arrange his funeral. We're sure going to miss her. We had to cancel the night classes—by the way, could you call the students on this list and tell them not to come this evening? We'll be issuing refunds for the remaining two weeks. Such a shame. They were a beautiful young couple, just starting out, each of them so brilliant."

Rand swallowed hard and forced himself to stand up straight. "I'm so sorry to hear this. Of course, I'll call the night students."

"Thank you, Rand," said Mrs. DeSalvo. She handed him a list of phone numbers. "I don't know what we would have done without you this summer."

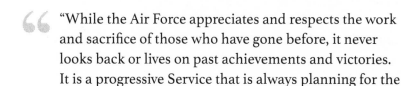

23

"While the Air Force appreciates and respects the work
and sacrifice of those who have gone before, it never
looks back or lives on past achievements and victories.
It is a progressive Service that is always planning for the
future safety and defense of the American nation..."
—Nancy Shea, *The Air Force Wife*

LABOR DAY 1966
Travis Air Force Base, California

LINDA KNEW her sister had finally gone crazy, speaking in gibberish
and claiming she'd found Jesus in Montrose. Debby said she didn't
want to go back to Travis to the base school. Grandmamma was so
taken with Debby's drama that she persuaded Fritzi to let her stay at
Fontainebleu and attend the small elementary school there. For two
weeks at the end of July, conversations in Grandmamma's house
sounded like this:

Debby, eyes brimming with tears: "Fritzi, please, pleeease let me stay here with Josie and Grandmamma. I've prayed night and day that I might go to fourth grade here."

Grandmamma: "Honestly, Francine, our little Debby is thriving here—can't you see? She's eating well, and she likes living here with us, where we can properly care for her. She's a sensitive young lady, and I know how busy you are back on the base. Debby needs special care and attention—attention *I* can give her. Please, use our phone to call Joe long distance. I'm sure he will agree that Debby will thrive in our care."

Fritzi, annoyed, lighting a cigarette: "It's too much to think about, Mother. Debby will miss us, and God knows we'll have to come and get her."

Debby: "No, Fritzi, honest! I love it here and I've already met some of the kids who'll be in fourth grade next year. I just can't bear that old base school and those mean kids at Travis. I want to stay here. It feels like *home*."

Grandmamma, matter-of-fact bossy tone: "Just take a look at this beautiful girl. She's finally eating well. Her hair is shiny again. Her pretty brown eyes are clear and bright. Being at Fontainebleu has certainly brought her around. Let her stay, Francine. Think of it like boarding school."

Fritzi, blowing smoke: "Mother, I'm perfectly capable of raising my own children. Our little family has been through enough; we need to stay together more than ever."

One day, Judge broke up the conversation, taking an emotional but rational approach: "Fritzi, you have experienced a great loss. Little Tommy was your baby, and Debby told me she was the last one to see him alive. Surely your little daughter needs some special care.

The kind of care we can give her, now. We're your family, too, you know. You and Joe can rely on us to help Debby get through this fragile time. No doubt, honey, it would be a great help to you."

It stunned Linda to see Fritzi take in Judge's words. Fritzi melted, tears running down her cheeks. She let her father hug her and comfort her. In that moment, Linda could see that losing Tommy and coping with Debby—not to mention, raising two older teenagers and all the stuff that went with being the squadron commander's wife, had worn her mother down. Despite her tough façade, Fritzi *was* fragile.

This all had to do with Debby coming home from church with Josie one Sunday. At dinner the next day, Debby insisted that she offer the blessing before the meal. When she did, she held out her hands, palms up, and began to speak in a strange, rhythmic, singsong language. Linda almost laughed, but Debby continued for some time, until Fritzi tapped her on the arm.

"That's enough, honey."

"She is speaking in tongues!" Grandmamma exclaimed. "The child is speaking in tongues! Leave her alone!"

"Hush, now," said Judge. "She's just praying, that's all…"

"No, she is speaking in tongues. A gift from the Holy Spirit. I know we Presbyterians don't do it, but Josie's Pentecostal church does. This child is blessed. She has a gift!"

Linda wanted to puke. If Debby wasn't dancing, whining, crying, or showing off, she had to find some other way to get attention. This sudden religious "gift" was sickening.

"May I be excused?" Linda asked.

"Yes," Fritzi said, glaring at Debby, "You may."

Linda went upstairs to her room, but the conversation below was loud enough for her to hear.

Josie was called in, and she confirmed that Debby did have the gift. "She prayed in tongues the first time she went to church with me. Brother David says she truly has the Holy Spirit speaking through her."

So, that's how Debby became the little miracle girl. She went to live at Fontainebleu with Grandmamma and Judge until she went to high school. The whole time, Debby was a tongue-speaking, Bible-thumping, hymn-singing darling of Josie's Pentecostal congregation, as well as the sweetheart of the Youth Group at Grandmamma's First Presbyterian. Linda would finally have a room to herself back at Travis.

On the way back to California, Fritzi let Linda drive on long stretches of Interstate without much traffic. Linda would set the Cruise Control to seventy-five miles per hour and her mother would lie down in the back seat and sleep. Linda had never seen her sleep so much. Fritzi didn't rouse or complain, no matter what music was on the radio. Linda felt the need to check the rear view mirror every few miles to make sure her mother was still breathing.

Linda had harbored hopes of connecting with her mother in a special way on the trip back to California, but it was not to be. They spent three nights at Holiday Inns with pools, but Fritzi didn't don her bathing suit and get in with Linda. She just ordered room service and bought herself a bottle of Jack Daniel's from a package store along the way. At night, Fritzi sipped and smoked while Linda dried her hair and watched whatever was on TV.

When they got back to Travis, the whole world had changed. Pop got word that he'd been promoted to "full-bird colonel." He'd bought a green Jaguar. He and Rand had cleaned the house and seemed to be best friends. Also, Rand was walking with a certain swagger Linda had never seen before.

"I guess that job at The Art Shoppe worked out pretty well after all," Linda said to Rand one day as he ate his Wheaties. "You look like you had a good summer. How's it feel to be going into your senior year?"

Rand looked up from reading the *San Francisco Chronicle* and shrugged. "The job—yeah. It was great. I actually sold a couple of my own paintings when they had an art show last week. I hung one in my room. I saved one out for you if you want it."

"I'd have to see it first," Linda said, "but I'm actually ready for something more sophisticated than puppy calendars and butterflies on the wall. One of your abstracts might be just the thing."

"Yeah, I guess you can decorate the room your way, with Debby gone and all. What's all this about Debby becoming really religious or something? What happened when you were back there? Is she really doing better?"

Linda sighed wearily, miffed that the conversation had, like most other ones, turned toward Debby. "She went to a Pentecostal church with Josie, and she started praying in a weird voice that sounded like another language. Crazy, if you ask me, but Josie and Grandmamma seemed to believe she was touched by the Holy Spirit. Frankly, I'm glad she stayed out there. It was obnoxious as hell."

Rand smirked and shook his head. "Sounds like a desperate grab for attention, but don't ask me. I feel for the kid. She was the last one who saw Tommy alive, you know."

"Yeah, I know. Must be rough on her. She is sort of obsessive about things, so I imagine it makes her crazy. Makes me crazy, too, but I seem to be handling it better, right?"

"No, you've always been crazy!" Rand jabbed Linda with his elbow. "But seriously, I know what you mean. We all miss Tommy. We all feel horrible. Not just Fritzi and Debby. You, me, Pop. That's why I can't wait to get out of here. The memories, the thought of Tommy; I feel so bad, but there's nothing I can do. Fritzi and Pop never talk about it, do they? They just keep going, one step in front of the other, like zombies. I don't know how they do it."

"I think Debby being away will be good for everyone. It'll be kind of like before she and Tommy were born—when it was just you and me, remember?"

"*Those* days are long gone, but yeah, I think it's a good thing for Debby and for all of us. And Pop—what about that sports car? He bought it two days after you left, before he even knew if he made colonel. He taught me how to drive it. Even let me borrow it a couple of times. He's been in a good mood, too."

"Pop wouldn't dare have a woman on the side, would he?"

Rand burst out laughing, spewing milk out his nose. "Are you kidding? Fritzi would kill him!"

Linda laughed along with her brother. "Get this," she said, "Fritzi let me drive almost all the way back. I don't even have my *permit* yet, but she didn't care. Without Debby along, I think she just kind of relaxed. She slept in the back seat the whole way home."

Linda and Rand went on, talking like that, for another half hour. It seemed to Linda that a great cloud had lifted from the horizon, and they could finally see ahead instead of looking behind.

OCTOBER *1966*

JOE HAD FINALLY MADE the grade. He was now a full colonel. He wore the eagles proudly on his shoulders, and Fritzi had pinned them there herself on Friday. Tonight, the officers in the 44th were throwing a cocktail party at the Club to celebrate Joe's promotion.

Joe had worked so hard at every assignment, gone above and beyond in the line of duty. Even when Fritzi knew his heart was breaking; even when he was tired and angry and disappointed, Joe had not failed. Not when Tommy died, not when she had a breakdown, not when Debby needed to stay at Fontainebleu to get better. Joe did what he always did: soldier on.

But tonight, she saw wistfulness in her husband's eyes. Joe chatted and shook hands in the receiving line, careful to thank everyone in the squadron who had given the party. However, they both knew that a full colonel could not expect to stay as squadron commander. In a few months, a transfer would be inevitable. Joe had spoken about the possibilities: perhaps a base commander position in Oklahoma or in Delaware. There were some openings for senior officers in the Pentagon and in the War College. Joe and Colonel Short had worked their network of cronies for a hint at what might be ahead, but they both knew that another overseas assignment was inevitable.

"Let's go home, Fritzi," Joe said after he'd made the rounds. He finished the last of his martini.

Fritzi knew the protocol all too well: no one would leave the party until Joe, who was now the ranking officer, departed. "That's nice of you, honey. I'm sure lots of these young officers have babysitters to pay." She kissed his cheek.

"Right. But I want to go home with *you*. I want you all to myself. It's been a long, long summer."

"It has. Besides, I want to ride in that sexy car of yours, Colonel."

They headed home in the autumn twilight, the Suisun wind wafting over the convertible. Fritzi shivered. Joe downshifted as they reached their driveway, then turned in and stopped. "Fritzi, I've got my orders. I've been assigned as Wing Commander of a Tactical Fighting unit, the 333rd."

"But I thought you were a lover, not a fighter," she said, ribbing him. "Where are we moving now?"

"We aren't. I am. The unit is at Da Nang Air Force Base. Viet Nam."

24

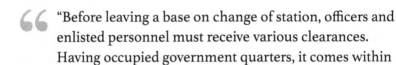 "Before leaving a base on change of station, officers and
enlisted personnel must receive various clearances.
Having occupied government quarters, it comes within
the housewife's realm
    to see that they are left clean and in good
condition."
    —Nancy Shea, *The Air Force Wife*

DECEMBER 1966
  Fairfield, California

WITH JOE LEAVING on an unaccompanied tour to Da Nang, Fritzi had
to move off base. Just before Christmas, she found a two-bedroom
bungalow in an old neighborhood on the outskirts of Fairfield. They
put most of their household goods in storage, and Fritzi moved into
the off-base cottage, chosen because it would allow Rand and Linda
to continue at Vanden High School.

With Debby safely in Montrose, Fritzi settled with her two oldest children into the tiny rent house, much smaller than their field grade officers' quarters on Travis. There was no name and rank sign on the front porch, no rules about how long the grass had to be, where your garbage cans had to be stored, how your car should be parked. No "Reveille" played on the base loudspeaker at seven a.m.; no "Taps" at five p.m. No Wives' Club meetings (although the Travis Officers' Wives made her an honorary lifetime member), no mandatory events to attend. And no jet fuel fumes—only the smell of the onion plant in Vacaville.

Judge brought Debby for a visit in early December so she could say good-bye to Joe before he left for Da Nang. It was wonderful to see how radiant and healthy Debby looked—she was clearly thriving in Montrose. She was talkative about spiritual things—good for her —but she drove them all nuts with her insistence that they stop to listen to her long prayers before meals.

As a beloved squadron commander, Joe's promotion and deployment to head up a fighter wing in Da Nang were big news. On the morning Joe left, a photographer from the base newspaper showed up at the terminal. There was a moment when Debby stood over her father and laid her hands on his shoulders. She prayed aloud for his safety and for "God's mightiest archangels" to watch over him. Fritzi saw Linda and Rand, who were both close to tears, back away from their sister and give her the stink eye. Fritzi wanted a photo of the whole family, but with Debby's prayer antics, the photo that made the Travis biweekly newspaper was one of Joe, dressed in his flight suit, seated on a bench, bowing his head as his beautiful nine-year-old daughter stood with her hands on his shoulders, praying.

To Fritzi's chagrin, the *Air Force Times* picked up the picture and ran it on the front page in the January issue. By that time, Debby had gone back to Montrose, leaving Linda and Rand to ridicule their sister, talking about how she ruined their private good-byes to their father. Fritzi didn't blame them a bit. She loved Debby with a mother's love, but she had to admit that the child seemed to suck up all the oxygen in any room she entered. This new prayer/spirituality habit was one Debby had learned in Montrose, and she clearly belonged there. Outside of the Bible Belt, Debby's evangelism seemed odd and a little disturbing. Fritzi was glad to be in California, and secretly happy that she didn't have Debby to deal with every day. She was happy to see Debby and Daddy go back to Montrose for Christmas.

Linda and Rand surprised Fritzi on Christmas Eve with a tabletop tree they'd made from spray-painted pinecones. "I used my discount at The Art Shoppe for the paint and glue," Rand said, grinning.

"We didn't think we'd have room for a big white-flocked tree in our cottage," Linda said, laughing along with her brother.

Fritzi began to cry. "Thank you," she said, "I love you so much."

MARCH 1967

AS A SOPHOMORE WORLD HISTORY STUDENT, Linda had found her calling. She read everything about political history she could get her hands on, and aced every test. She wrote long, scholarly papers with perfect bibliographies. The other kids in her class resented Linda; she set the curve on all the tests (which were admittedly difficult). She raised her hand to comment on every point their teacher, Mr. Holbrook, made when he lectured. Linda was chosen to represent Vanden at a regional debate, a forum on world politics. She won that competition, and was elected to serve as a head delegate in the statewide Model United Nations.

Subconsciously, Linda channeled all her focus and energy away from the danger that Pop faced in Viet Nam—the news was worse every night—and dedicated herself to changing the world. She became a history buff and a policy wonk.

Right before Easter Break, Mr. Holbrook pulled Linda aside. "You should apply for this." He handed her a brochure about the American Field Service Exchange Program. "I recommend that you apply to go to The Hague in the Netherlands," said her teacher. "They have a program in concert with the United Nations. It could open doors for you later on."

Linda talked it over with Fritzi, and she agreed. "Take on the world," Fritzi said, a tear running down her cheek. "You ought to fly, Linda, just like your father does."

FRITZI AND LINDA corresponded separately with Joe every day. About once a week, a bundle of letters from Joe would arrive—half of them for Linda, and the other half for Fritzi. Joe was so proud of Linda for going as an exchange student to The Hague, he wrote time and time again in letters to both of them.

It was a sad that Joe never wrote to Rand, but Fritzi knew Joe had his son in his heart and a plan to secure his future. Fritzi had a file of letters that Joe had written on Rand's behalf, and soon, her son would see results from his father's effort.

Rand was finishing up what had been a stellar senior year at Vanden. His grades and high test scores had earned him acceptance to U.C. Berkeley, Cal State Polytechnic Institute, and Louisiana State University. He'd earned partial scholarships at all three, but ruled out LSU, was lukewarm about Cal State, and had his heart set on that hippie haven, Berkeley. Rand was a hard-headed little S.O.B., but Fritzi knew that Joe had sealed Rand's fate long before he left for Da Nang.

One day in April, Rand got a letter from the University of British Columbia in Vancouver.

> Dear Mr. Stoddard,
> We are pleased to congratulate you on receiving our Outstanding International Student Award, based on your excellent academic record at Vanden High School and your exceptionally high scores on the Scholastic Aptitude Test.

This coveted award allows us to offer you two years of
full tuition at the University of British Columbia.
We are also able to offer you housing in the Honors
Dormitory on campus, and up to $1,000 in
vouchers to cover your academic books.
You will find UBC to be among the top universities in
the world, offering not only excellent academics,
but also the opportunity to live in and explore the
beauty of Canada's Pacific Coast...

"This has to be some kind of mistake," Rand said, "I never applied to
British Columbia."

"Well, perhaps your high school counselor sent your transcript
and test scores?" Fritzi suggested, but she knew better.

Before Joe left for Da Nang, he had secretly sent letters to U.B.C.,
McGill, and the University of Calgary, all good engineering schools.
He left Fritzi a thick file of all the applications he'd made on his son's
behalf, with the following instructions:

Dearest love,
I won't be able to write this from Da Nang, so I will
write it and leave it for you to read after I have gone
to my new assignment.
Our only living son will turn in 18 this spring, while I
am away. If I were home, it would be a tradition for
me, as an Air Force officer, to accompany him to
the Draft Board to register.
Since I will be away on his birthday, I ask that you
ignore his obligation to register. Do NOT let him go
to the Draft Board, understand, my darling? I know
this will be your wish, too. We have already lost
one son; we don't need to lose another to this

insane (yes, I use that word, although I am serving) war.

You read the papers and see the news stories on TV. But I have overseen the squadron whose men fly troops to Da Nang and Que Sang, those hopeful young draftees with buzz haircuts and heartbreaking grins. I didn't talk about this at home, but for the past two years, the squadron under my command has also flown back the body bags, filled with the remains of those young men. The odds are not good. One in 10 of our boys will be killed or injured if they are sent to Viet Nam. The way the war is going, more and more will be sent. Mark my words, the exemption for college students will go away. At some point in time, our firstborn will be called up.

But they can't call him if he's not registered. And they can't make him register if he isn't in country.

You will find enclosed a file of letters I have sent to universities in Canada on behalf of Rand. I have been working with the counselor at Vanden to meet the deadlines for Fall application. It is my prediction and my wish that our son attend college outside the U.S. He may receive acceptance letters from these places; when he does, make sure he goes. But under no circumstances are you to reveal that I have gone behind his back to alter his fate. I will fulfill my duty as an Air Force officer. But first, I will fulfill my duty as a father.

I am confident that I will return in one piece. God is too afraid of your wrath to let me expire on foreign soil.

I love you beyond words. I love our family.

You may not like being our "rock," but you are the force of nature who keeps us from flying apart.

Your loving
Joe

JOE HAD PLANNED IT ALL. Rand would go to college in Canada.

September 1967

Fritzi sat on the front steps of the cottage, watching the Suisun wind blow leaves from the eucalyptus tree around the tiny front yard. She struck a match, sheltering it with her hand, until it lit her Chesterfield. She inhaled deeply, closed her eyes, and exhaled into the wind. Her husband and three of her living children were out in the world, doing what they needed to do. She was, at last, alone.

A normal wife and mother would worry. A normal woman with a husband at war, a little girl being raised by her grandparents, a sixteen-year-old daughter in Europe, and a son starting college in Canada, would start knitting or crocheting or drinking or popping Miltowns to offset the worry.

But Fritzi had never been a normal woman. And, sitting in the autumn wind, she did not worry. She loved Joe, Debby, Linda and Rand fiercely. She had loved Tommy fiercely, too. Worry had no power over love. Worry could not prevent bad things from happening. Worry caused wrinkles and ulcers and sleepless nights. She loved too many people to worry about them. They were all launched in the right direction.

There was no dinner to prepare. No one to pick up or drive anywhere. No Officers' Wives Club, no jet fuel fumes, no roar of planes taking off or landing. There was, now, just the sound of the Suisun wind, the rustle of eucalyptus leaves, and her own heart, beating a steady rhythm of peace.

PART IV

Taps

25

> "A morbid preoccupation with one's own tragedy is as distressing to others as callous flippancy. Dignified, honest sorrow is no discredit to any person, man or woman, and is never out of place."
> —Nancy Shea, *The Air Force Wife*

AUGUST *17, 2008*
Georgetown, Washington, D.C.

POP WAS DEAD. He suffered a massive heart attack on the sixteenth hole at Apple Valley Country Club. Linda couldn't manage to cry; her father had lived for eighty-three years, a full and rigorous life. One of his golf partners, an old guy named Jack, called Rand up in Vancouver to let him know. Rand called Linda; Linda called Debby. It was their pecking order, and then little Tommy. But Tommy was gone, and so was Fritzi, buried next to each other in the family plot in Montrose.

Linda knew, however, that Pop didn't want to be buried in Montrose. Pop had told Linda that he wanted to be buried in Arlington National Cemetery. Linda figured her siblings didn't remember this. Debby and Rand were so self-absorbed, Linda couldn't expect either of them to remember anything that didn't concern them.

Since Linda lived and worked in D.C., she promptly secured a place for Pop at Arlington and put herself in charge of the funeral. All she had to do was clear her schedule at the State Department, which was complicated—much more complicated than Rand and Debby would ever understand. All they had to do was get themselves to D.C. As for accommodations, Linda and her wife Tina had plenty of room, so Rand and his wife Sandy could stay with them. Debby and her family, with their contempt of Linda's "lifestyle," should stay at the Key Bridge Marriott in Rosslyn across the Potomac from Georgetown, but still close enough. Linda could get them a discount.

She guessed that Debby would haul along her three big boys, and, of course, her husband, Nick. Linda had nothing against Nick— he was an honest, hard-working cattle rancher with a natural gas well on his ranch. Nick wasn't bright enough to equate earthquakes in Oklahoma with the fracking he allowed on his land. Debby's boys, however, were all fine young men. Handsome, too. The twins were in college at Oklahoma State. The youngest boy, Charlie, was home-schooled because he was bullied his freshman year at Enid High School. *Hello?* He was gay, and Linda had seen from his behavior at an early age that Charlie also had gender identity problems.

Linda had tried to broach the subject with Debby, back when Charlie was just six years old. She'd taken him to Toys R Us in Tulsa and Charlie made a beeline for the Barbie aisle. When Linda told Debby about it, Debby just cried and told her not to spread her "poisonous lifestyle" all over Charlie.

Three years ago, Linda had invited Debby to her wedding to Tina; it was a family-only ceremony held on Martha's Vineyard. Debby sent the invitation back to Linda with her regrets and a quote from Scripture about Sodom and Gomorrah and perversion, begging Linda not to go through with it. Linda sent it back to her with the words GO TO HELL scrawled in red across the Scripture. Looking back, she should have just bought Charlie a Barbie instead.

Rand, on the other hand, had married Sandy, a real Canadian sweetheart. Linda hoped Sandy would come to Pop's funeral. Sandy really loved Pop, and was always so sweet to him, especially after Fritzi died. Rand and Linda had been close as children but grew apart after Rand left for college in Canada to avoid the draft. Linda went to Brussels as a high school exchange student, and they never seemed to reconnect. She'd barely seen Rand since he delivered the flawless eulogy at Fritzi's funeral, more than twenty years ago.

Fritzi and Pop. They had managed to stay in love and march together through a difficult and demanding life with four children. In their own way, they were great parents, defining family life as a series of "assignments" where they'd live for a few years and move on. What was most important, they always said, was that they took care of each other. No matter how snotty the kids in the new school were, or how many times Rand got beaten up for being the redheaded officer's son, when they gathered around the table for dinner, they'd at least made it to home base.

Even though Pop chose to live in California, he and Linda had remained close. He would call her just to shoot the breeze, and they'd talk about his golf game and surprisingly moderate politics. Politics—that's where Linda connected with Pop. They could talk for hours about gridlock and the government shutdown and E.J. Dionne's latest column in the *Washington Post*. Pop always subscribed, because he was interested in Washington. He'd have been a great senator, but instead he was just a great man. A full bull colonel for ten years before he retired at the age of fifty-five. Linda was fifty-seven now, and she planned to work until she was at least seventy. Tina had made it clear that she wouldn't tolerate her political animal energy at home all the time.

Rand was flying out with Pop's body, and Linda had to admit she was jealous. But it was fitting, Rand being the oldest and only surviving son, for him to bring the Colonel to his final resting place.

Rand agreed with Linda that Pop ought to be buried in Arlington, and he told Linda outright that moving Fritzi's and Tommy 's remains there didn't make any sense. A lot of work, a lot of emotion, a lot of expense. Besides, Rand acknowledged, Pop ought to be buried where Linda lived. After all, she was probably his favorite.

Favorite! In a family with four kids—two boys and two girls— you'd think Pop and Fritzi would have had a balanced sense of equality. But their parents had showed their favoritism all the time. Pop was proud of Linda for being the valedictorian, champion debater, and National Merit Scholar. He liked to hold up Linda's standings to the other kids and ask them why they "couldn't take a tip or two from Linda. She knows what hard work means. It means success. Right, Linda?" Linda would shrug, blushing, feeling hate lasers shoot from Debby and Rand. Little Tommy never got old enough to get compared to her. Fate spared him that.

When it came to Fritzi, Rand was her boy. He was a redhead like her, no freckles, and cornflower blue eyes. Together, Fritzi and Rand shone like two new copper pennies. They radiated beauty and poise and strength. People said the two of them should have posed for a Breck ad. Rand was three years older than Linda. Tall and broad-shouldered, Rand could have lettered in football, basketball—the sports that were so important to everyone else. But Rand was a loner, an iconoclast with loads of testosterone who also loved *art*. He was smart, too, although more spatially smart than book smart like Linda. When they lived in Italy, Fritzi took him everywhere because Rand was the only one interested in looking at museums and sculpture and all the cultural stuff. He and Fritzi were a doyenne and her young consort, traveling to Venice, Florence, Rome, seeing it all, while Pop and the rest of the family stayed in the apartment in Naples or went sightseeing on their own. Pop, he wasn't much for museums unless they showcased aviation. He and Linda would rather wander around in Pompeii and marvel at the mummified corpses, imagining the lava that overtook the people, than look at the frescoes.

Often, Pop and Linda would go their own way and leave Debby and Tommy in Naples with their maid, Assunta. She was a big, kind lady who spoke only Neapolitan dialect but who loved little children. Rand and Linda were too old for her cheek pinching and sloppy kisses, but Debby and Tommy, they put up with it all. So the little ones were Assunta's favorites for those four years in Naples. Rand and Linda had already laid claim to Fritzi and Pop.

Looking back, Rand and Linda were the lucky ones. Fritzi and Pop showered them with pride and individual attention in their own ways—Pop for Linda, Fritzi for Rand. Linda wondered why we weren't *enough*; why their parents felt the need to have two more. When she turned eleven, Linda had sprouted dark hair under her arms and between her legs. Her thighs began to rub together and her breasts grew until they sagged against her midsection. Fritzi urged her to curb her hearty appetite so she wouldn't grow into a "fat teenager." Meanwhile, slight, petite Debby, with her Bambi eyes and honey blonde hair, was entering grade school. Linda could see Fritzi's joy in dressing Debby in the femme stuff Linda would never wear. Debby would leave her hair in pigtails with ribbons from early morning until bedtime. This visibly delighted Fritzi, and Linda began to suspect that her parents had Debby so Fritzi could have a *real* girl.

And if Fritzi had her real girl, then Pop deserved his real boy. So, when Fritzi was just shy of her fortieth birthday, she gave birth to Thomas Fontaine Stoddard, a whopping nine-pounder delivered by C-section. Tommy was, as Pop used to say, "a real pistol." When he walked at eleven months, he took off running. He'd climb out of his crib, hoist himself up onto tables, fall down, and bounce back up again as though invincible to pain. The kid had dark hair like Linda's, big brown eyes like Debby's, and Pop's big feet. Tommy was delightful, a puppy boy who never tired of play. Even when he pooped his diapers and Linda changed him, Tommy made her laugh instead of gag at the mess and the smell. Pop would throw a little football to Tommy, and Tommy would fall all over himself to try and catch it. He'd manage to pitch it back to Pop, giggling with delight when Pop caught it and threw it back. Rand would hoist Tommy on his shoulders and parade him around like a prince. "Tommy, what does a horse say?" Rand would ask, and Tommy would neigh. He could do a cow, a moose, a cat and a dog, too. Linda didn't remember Tommy's first words or even recall a full sentence he ever put together, but he was always the best playmate, fueling Pop's great hope for a quarterback in the family.

But hope is just hope and children are just children. For a few short years, they were a healthy, boisterous American Air Force family, living wherever Pop's career took them. Each of them finally took root in a spot where they landed and had to bloom. Now that they were all rooted—Linda in D.C. with Tina, Rand in Vancouver with Sandy, Debby on a ranch in Oklahoma with Nick, and Tommy in the family plot next to Fritzi—they didn't seem to need each other any more.

Linda came to terms with herself and her sexuality in 1986, right after Fritzi died. When she told Pop she was gay, he just shrugged and said he didn't want to know the biological details, but warned her to not to settle down with "some crazy lesbian." (Tina, Linda was proud to say, was *not* crazy, and Pop really liked her.) Rand said he'd known all along, congratulated Linda, and said he hoped she wouldn't dress like Charlie Chaplin in combat boots. Debby—that was another story.

August 18, 2008
Vancouver, British Columbia, to LAX, Los Angeles, California

IN HIS LONG career as an architect, Rand Stoddard had traveled all over the world. When he flew commercial, he only traveled in first class; coach simply couldn't accommodate his long legs. He liked the service in first class, the highballs served in heavy glasses that felt right in a man's hand. The warmed cashews in a little white dish, the younger, attractive flight attendants who worked the cabin. First class was worth every penny, even when he couldn't upgrade on miles or charge travel costs to a client.

This was one of those times. He was flying Air Canada Flight 1429

from Vancouver into LAX, even though there was a regional airport
much closer to Apple Valley. He'd have to drive more than a hundred
miles to the funeral home to claim his father's body. Rand would
need that hundred miles to wrap his head around the fact that Pop
was finally dead.

Finally. That was harsh, Rand thought, but his father had been
more than eighty years old. The old man had to know that his time
would be up any minute. Fitting that he died on the golf course. The
image of his father, a little stooped and wizened with age, lining up
the ball on the tee—that was Pop, all right. At least the Pop he
remembered. He raised his Scotch and toasted the memory.

"Would you like the beef or the chicken?" asked the blonde flight
attendant, handing him a warm towel.

"I special ordered a vegetarian plate," said Rand. "The name's
Stoddard."

"Oh, yes, sir, I see," she said, pursing her lips and nodding. "May I
refill your cocktail?"

"Yes, that would be great," Rand said. He'd been a vegetarian
since 1970, and people, even health-conscious Canadians, always
looked surprised when he eschewed meat to feast on vegetables.
People just expected big, tall men to be carnivores.

He was glad Sandy hadn't come with him. She'd fly out to D.C. for
the funeral, of course, but she was sad and devastated by Pop's death.
His wife was a beautiful, small-boned woman, full of spirit and
spunk, but she was hopelessly and almost cheesily emotional. Not
tough, like him. His sister Linda was tough like him. She'd already
taken charge—being the bossy diplomat she was—and said she'd
handle the funeral. That was fine with him, because if Sandy got
involved, she'd probably want to sing a bunch of hymns, plus "Up We
Go Into the Wild Blue Yonder." Sandy was from a big farm family in
British Columbia. She loved Pop like he was her own father, and she
firmly believed in going all out for every occasion—especially funerals. She'd probably make a scrapbook out of the whole experience.

His sister Linda had always been bossy, just like Fritzi. A take-
charge woman who couldn't stand people who pussy-footed around,

Fritzi could organize the Officers' Wives Club on every base into a formidable machine. She knew that rank had its privileges, but it also had its obligations. So, she'd organize a Thrift Shop to benefit enlisted families who couldn't make ends meet. She commanded a room without rank on her shoulders because she had a *presence*. "Always enter a room with presence," she'd tell Rand. "You are *somebody*. Hold your shoulders back and stride in like you own the place. If you act confident, they will treat you with respect."

They, of course, were always the kids they'd have to encounter in every new assignment. Rand felt for his sisters—Linda, so big and awkward—and Debby, such a sensitive, fragile wimp. Fritzi was always on them. She put Linda on countless diets and made her walk around with an encyclopedia on her head. When Debby showed signs of anorexia, Fritzi let her stay with her grandparents in Louisiana until she was healthy again. "Own the world, or it will own you," Fritzi would tell his sisters. "We'll be moving on in a year or two, so make them remember that you were here."

Pop outranked most of their classmates' fathers. That was convenient in all the schools that served only base kids. But sometimes, they moved to small towns where they were thrust into a school with kids who had known each other all their lives. To Rand, this lifelong knowledge was strangely enviable. That continuity, that connection throughout life in a small town seemed idyllic but also surreal—like a *Twilight Zone* episode where everyone was frozen in time.

Rand dozed for awhile, awakened only when the flight attendant set his vegetarian plate before him and asked about his choice of accompanying wine.

"Red," he said, "followed by lots of black coffee."

26

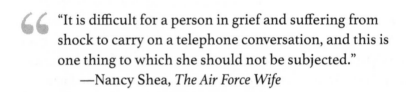 "It is difficult for a person in grief and suffering from shock to carry on a telephone conversation, and this is one thing to which she should not be subjected."
—Nancy Shea, *The Air Force Wife*

AUGUST 17, 2008
  Twin Stars Ranch, outside Enid, Oklahoma

THE NEWS HIT Debby squarely between the eyes like a rifle shot. "We're orphans now," she managed to whisper on the phone to Linda. Her heart broke open and the tears wouldn't stop.

Linda had all but ridiculed Debby's tears. "For heaven's sake," Linda said, "You're a grown woman, not the baby of the family anymore. You ought to be glad Pop lived for as long as he did, and he didn't end up in one of those warehouses they call nursing homes. Think about someone other than yourself."

"I was thinking about us all," Debby sobbed. "Tommy, especially.

Pop can be buried with him and Fritzi now in Montrose. They're together in Heaven."

Then Linda broke the news that Pop would not, in fact, be laid to rest next to Fritzi and little Tommy. Debby couldn't believe her ears.

"Pop told me years ago he wanted to be buried in Arlington, with full military honors," Linda said in that same boastful voice she used whenever she talked about her important job in Washington.

"Well, couldn't Fritzi and Tommy be moved there, too? Then they could all be together..."

"For God's sake, it's a burial, not a family reunion! It would cost thousands to relocate those graves from Montrose to Arlington! That's not what Pop would want. Get a grip, Debby."

It was no use for Debby to protest the decisions already made by Linda. It never had been.

Pop had lasted so many years after Fritzi died, it just seemed to Debby that he'd be around forever. She hadn't been out to see him enough, not nearly enough. Just once a year at the most, she and Nick would drive out to Apple Valley. But it was almost a three-day drive, so they only stayed a couple of days before they had to head back. Pop seemed to like living alone. Debby always felt guilty when they'd leave, like there was something she was supposed to do if she just had time enough to do it.

She couldn't expect her sister, Linda, or her brother, Rand, to understand what it was like for her. She and Nick had raised three sons while eking out a living raising cattle. Raising boys was hard enough—the first two were twins, followed by little Charlie—but they also had the daily challenge of feeding, herding, vaccinating, and selling the cattle. Rand and Sandy just had one daughter, Celina. And Linda, with her partner, Tina, had, thank the Lord, not adopted, because they were both too busy with careers to bring children into their sinful lives.

Still, Debby thanked God that she and Nick had chosen the righteous path. They'd married young, pledged their lives to each other; a living covenant to God's plan. They'd waited a long time to have children, and when they tried, she'd had two miscarriages. Debby attended the women's Bible Study Fellowship regularly. Living just outside Enid, she and Nick were proud to be part of a conservative community, where everyone was expected to pull their own weight, where personal responsibility still meant something.

Jared and Daniel, their twins, had both qualified as Eagle Scouts and played football for Enid High. Now they were roommates at Oklahoma State, where Jared was studying business and Daniel was an honors student in agriculture. They'd both earned scholarships to OSU, but she and Nick made it clear they needed to come home every weekend to help on the ranch. They were good boys, both of them. Nick was sure to keep them busy with ranch work so they wouldn't be tempted to hang around with frat boys and party the weekends away in Stillwater.

Charlie—he was a completely different story. Like Debby, he was small and slight. While the twins never argued about pre-dawn wakeup times, Charlie had to be rousted out of bed to do his chores. He'd rather sit and read than throw a football with his brothers. And when it came to cattle, Charlie still puked when they castrated the spring calves, and cried when the mature animals were shipped to the slaughterhouse. Two years ago, he'd announced he was a vegetarian. The boy subsisted on baked potatoes, apples, and carrots. Pig slop food, Nick called it, trying to get a rise out of Charlie. Charlie shrugged it off and went to his room.

Last fall, after the twins were in college, Charlie started coming home with bruises on his face. Once, he had a black eye, and twice, his lips had been split open by classmates who'd slammed him against the lockers or ambushed him on the way to the bus stop. Without his popular big brothers to protect him, Charlie was a moving target at Enid High School.

Black eyeliner. Long black bangs swooped to one side, girly. She and Nick wouldn't have let him out of the house like that, but somehow that boy fixed himself up to look like some kind of freak. It was like he was asking for it. So now, Debby homeschooled him. It just made life easier.

Back when Charlie was little, Linda had come for a visit. Jared and Daniel were busy with football practice, so Aunt Linda offered to take Charlie on an errand she had in Tulsa. She promised to take him to Toys R Us because his birthday was coming up. When they came back, Linda asked Debby to sit down at the kitchen table while Charlie helped Nick with chores.

"He wanted a Barbie, Deb," Linda said in an accusatory tone. "I wanted to buy him one, but I didn't think you and Nick would want me to."

"What am I supposed to do with *that* information?" Debby remembered saying. Then she mumbled something about GI Joe and action figures.

"No." Linda shook her head. "That's not what I'm talking about. He wanted to spend the whole time in the girls' section. I wish there weren't such a thing as a girl and a boy section in a freaking toy store, but I'm telling you, heads up. Your son Charlie was born a boy, but he has the mind of a girl. He wants girl things, Debby."

"What are you trying to say? You don't know my son! He's been raised out *here*, here with *us*, on this ranch. He's all boy! He's just more sensitive, that's all. Don't read so much into it. Don't go looking for something that's not there."

Here it came. Linda being Linda. "What? Just because I'm gay means that I think everyone else is secretly gay? Is that what you think?"

"I didn't say that." She could see Nick and Charlie heading for the back porch. "Don't say anything to Nick or the other boys. And stop worrying about Charlie!" She eyed the Toys R Us bag at Linda's feet. "By the way, what did you get him?"

Linda reached inside the shopping bag. "Polly Pocket's farm," she said, holding up a plastic barn with plastic animals and a tiny plastic girl in a pink dress. "I told him the Barbie was too expensive. This is what he finally picked out."

"Give me that!" Debby swiped it and threw it in the trash.

IT WAS HARD, this life Debby had chosen with Nick. Physically hard

work every single day of the year, raising boys and cattle. At night she
was too exhausted to worry any more. Charlie would be fine, just *fine*.
She would help him find his path. She would protect him from the
gay-sayers and the bullies. For all she knew, Jesus was just like her
son: sensitive, kind, a scholar cut from a different cloth. It was up to
her, just as it had been up to Mary, to guide her son on a righteous
path.

Nick clearly favored the twins. "Go on out there and help them
load the cattle truck, Charlie. Stop sitting around with your finger up
your nose. Get to work like your brothers!" He'd swat Charlie on the
butt and shoo him out of the house. "Get on out, you little twerp!"

But after the twins left home, Nick went from the swatting Charlie's butt to slapping him across the face. Or drawing Charlie up to his
staggering height with a fistful of the boy's shirt. To regularly saying
"Chuckie boy, you are gonna man up if I have to beat the living tar
out of you!"

Charlie would react with a sullen glare at first. Lately, that sullen
glare had turned to raw hate for his father. She could see it in his
black-eyed gaze. She didn't dare step in to override her husband's
sovereignty, but she customarily filled two tumblers with water and
handed one to her husband, one to her son. Nick would gulp like a
man dying of thirst, and she could see Charlie pause just short of
throwing the glass at his father. This seemed to cool Nick's rage, for
he was still a God-loving man who rarely raised a hand to his wife.
His son, this Charlie, however, needed to be trained up to respect
himself and his father, no matter what it took.

So, Linda's takeover of Pop's burial was, in some ways, a relief to
Debby. That was one reason for her tears. She had come a long way
from being the spoiled "baby of the family," but Linda would never
see that. Debby was a dam ready to break, and the news of her
father's death was just one chink in many holes of her façade. In
some ways, she envied Linda, who had no children, no husband, no
constant worry. Her smart, bossy sister had always managed life on
her own terms: a compatible woman for a partner, a job that made
her feel important, and two spoiled Yorkies that yapped and licked

her face when she came home after a long day solving world problems at the State Department.

Linda thought she was worldly, but she was, in fact, naïve. She wasn't pretty or popular growing up, but she didn't care because she was just focused on being the best, scoring the highest, and bulldozing anything in her way. She was free of caring if she had pleased a boy enough to be asked on a second date because she didn't care about boys. She didn't fret about clothes or makeup because no one expected her to look good. Even Fritzi gave up on her when she reached eighteen. No more forced charm lessons or weight-loss regimes. Linda, as captain of the school debate team, had bigger agendas, and Fritzi finally left her alone.

Debby, however, was Fritzi's protégé. Fritzi liked her to wear her silky hair long, embellished with ribbons in braids, or simply tucked behind her tiny pierced ears. This was all fine with Debby, as she enjoyed the grooming and attention. She envied, however, the accolades Linda earned from her schools, her Rhodes scholarship, her fellowship to Harvard. She didn't understand most of the hoopla, but Pop clearly shone with pride at Linda's accomplishments. And Rand —he was out of the picture by the time Debby hit puberty—she hardly knew her older brother. Then there was Tommy—the little prince. The *real* baby of the family.

It had been Debby's job to be the bright, sweet light to Pop and Fritzi, while Rand and Linda went on to carve out lives far beyond the base houses where they grew up. Well, it was hard, being that light. For a few years, Debby went to stay with Fritzi's parents in Montrose. After Pop returned from Vietnam, when Rand and Debby were both in college, Debby went back to her parents on Altus Air Force Base in Oklahoma. Hard, being the only child left at home with two parents still grieving. Linda and Rand didn't have to be there, day in and day out, when Fritzi dulled herself with bourbon, and Pop stared at the TV all night. They didn't have to be that girl in ninth grade, the one with the perfect clothes, the Marcia Brady hair, who was taunted as the "snotty prissy prince-ass." They didn't have to live in that sprawling brick house on Command Circle, where Fritzi built a veritable shrine to Tommy in the spare bedroom. A cabinet full of his matchbox cars, his limp little brown Teddy bear, a faded red fire engine. Pictures of Tommy at birth, on Rand's shoulders at the beach near Naples; sitting on Linda's lap as she read him a Babar book.

The only picture of Debby with Tommy showed them playing with a Tonka truck, but at the time, Debby was trying to take it away from Tommy. The photo was framed and hung on the wall with all the others. The smaller photos were satellites to a large color portrait of the whole family at the Officers' Club Family Christmas Dinner in Naples. Fritzi, decked out in a purple cocktail dress, her copper hair framing her smiling face; Pop, wearing his major's dress blue uniform, his thick dark hair parted and combed above his smooth brow. Next to Pop was Rand, tall and handsome as an Everly Brother in a sports coat and tie. Linda, a chubby pre-teen in a red velvet dress, grinned eagerly beneath her thick brows and bobbed dark hair. She held the hand of Debby, slender and doe-eyed, with gossamer hair that spilled over her shoulders, all the way to the waist of her red velvet dress. Finally, the ruddy-cheeked, dark-haired Tommy, dressed in a miniature suit with a red sweater vest, stood holding Rand's hand, his little mouth open mid-laugh. They were the perfect Air Force Family, scrubbed and shining in the light of Pop's dedication and pride. Always ready for the next assignment, they were a team willing to live and work and go to school anywhere that advanced Pop's promising career.

Debby understood that Fritzi cherished those memories, those heady days when the family was young and bustling, achieving and arguing, full of energy and hope and promise. And adventure. Camping in the VW minibus all over Europe; traveling "space available" on an Air Force transport to the Greek Islands, taking the hydrofoil across the bay to Capri or Ischia. Fritzi had never stopped remembering, never stopped talking about "all the fun we had, and the wonders we saw!" She embellished those years and told endless stories at cocktail parties, making their life sound like one big Doris Day movie.

What she never talked about was Tommy. What happened or

how she felt about it. They all longed to talk about it, but no, Fritzi and Pop kept things "upbeat." They had to keep moving forward, to the next assignment, or they would drown in the bay of sorrow that surrounded those memories of that beautiful family. The unspeakable tragedy was, when it was all said and done, unspeakable. Fritzi and Pop made sure of that.

Perhaps that was the reason Debby had found her voice in the "tongues" of Josie's Pentecostal church, and why she lived at Fontainebleu for those few years. Perhaps the attention from Judge and Grandmamma sustained her through the pain, sheltered her from having to face Fritzi and Pop every day, knowing she'd been the last to see Tommy alive.

Debby had been there, with Tommy when it happened, and all those years afterward with Fritzi and Pop—after Rand and Linda had flown the coop. It was she, Debby, who saw her parents' silent pain all those years; it was she who lived like the only child in a home that longed for everything to be the way it was in that old Christmas photo. And yes, she was "spoiled," because it gave Fritzi and Pop pleasure to give her things and fuss over her. It wasn't Debby's fault.

When she'd met Nick in college, his love offered a way out. His faith offered her structure and community and righteous living that contradicted the "upbeat" secular façade her parents had artfully crafted.

Now, so many years later, she actually had a *real* life. A stable family, a life grounded in work and seasons and prayer. She and Nick would sort things out with Charlie, without Linda's imposition of lifestyle and assumptions of depravity.

Debby would show up to the funeral, to the burial at Arlington, to whatever else Linda wanted to arrange. Debby would stay out of the way, and let Linda run *that* show—as long as she kept her nose out of Debby's family business.

She would pray for Pop. And Fritzi and Tommy, and all of them. Someday, she knew, they would all join in Heaven—except for Linda.

AUGUST 18, 2008

FEELING fuzzy from the red wine, Rand stepped off the plane at LAX, into the air-conditioned terminal. He made a beeline for the Admirals' Club, away from the madding crowd, where he could clear his head before he picked up his rental car. He showed his card to the polite receptionist and entered through the sliding glass doors. At last, a restroom where there was enough room for a man his size to relieve himself, wash up, and get a grip on the job he had to do.

Rand took extra time washing his hands, rubbing them together in a semi-compulsive pattern. Then he took a long look at himself in the mirror. His eyes were rimmed in red; red veins snaked around his blue iris. A squirt or two of Visine, a quick blink, and they looked instantly better—still tired, but not as bloody bloodshot. He straightened his shirt collar and retucked his shirt into his pants, then ran a quick hand through his sparse, once-red hair. Better. He could feel Pop's eyes on him, inspecting his gig line (straight), his haircut (decent), and his posture (fine). Now he was ready for the trip to the Apple Valley funeral home where his father's embalmed body awaited him.

He thought about ordering a shot of Glenfiddich at the bar, but gulped down a club soda instead, then made his way to the Avis counter, and sped away in a beige Prius.

"Come on, Rand, be a man about this. You have to be a pallbearer. You are his big brother. Stop acting like a goddamn baby."

Rand could hear his father's stern voice on that horrible September day in Montrose. At age fifteen, Rand had burst into tears when he saw two-year-old Tommy laid out in his small dark coffin. The kid had on the new Easter suit he'd worn to church in Naples that spring. His dark hair was parted and neatly combed, giving him the look of a spit-polished airman. It was so out of place, so fake, he thought, to make his scruffy, roly-poly little brother look like this. They'd flown his body from Naples to Montrose, where the travel-wearied family gathered for the little boy's funeral.

The family viewed Tommy's body at the Ida Rose Funeral Home, a humid old Victorian house in Montrose. His mother's parents, Judge and Grandmamma, both sobbed out loud when they saw their little grandson laid out in a coffin. His father just stood behind Tommy's coffin in his winter uniform, his rank (major) and service medals bright against the blue serge suit.

God, what about a uniform? Rand hadn't seen his father alive in more than two years. He was a skinny, stooped old man then. His old uniforms would hang pitifully on his body. Was he supposed to make that decision? What to dress the body in? Did he have to wear a uniform for a military burial at Arlington?

He pulled into the circle drive in front of the Peterson Funeral Home in Apple Valley about seven p.m. Typical Apple Valley landscaping: white rocks, succulents, an occasional evergreen. Outside the Prius, he breathed in the hot, dry air. It seared his lungs, but it felt like the first real air he'd breathed since he left Vancouver that morning. Inside, a blast of air-conditioning and the subtle strains of piped-in classical music reminded him that this was a place for the dead. He blinked to adjust his eyes to the dimmed lights.

"Mr. Stoddard?" A slight young woman with long dark hair greeted him. She looked even younger than his daughter, Celina. "I'm Mrs. Peterson."

"So nice to meet you." Rand held out his hand to shake hers.

"We have your father, Colonel Stoddard, in one of the viewing rooms. Just follow me," she said. "I hope you had a pleasant trip here?" She had on a navy jacket over a matching skirt. She looked like an American Air Lines ticket agent.

"Uh, yes, thanks," he said.

She opened a pair of dark paneled sliding doors. The room beyond had dark patterned wallpaper and a landscape painting illumined by a brass light fixture attached to its frame. The casket, in the center of the room, looked to be dark blue and shiny, illumined by a muted spotlight above. "Your sister, Linda? She ordered the casket and told us to embalm the body," said Mrs. Peterson. "Would you like to see your father?"

"Yes." Rand set his jaw as she lifted the top panel to reveal Pop's face. The first thing he saw were his father's closed eyes, fringed by thick, gray lashes. His bushy unibrow had been nicely combed, and his bald head shone as though waxed. His scrawny neck protruded from beneath a white sheet. "So he's not dressed?"

"We didn't have any clothes, no," she said. "The emergency people brought him here in his golf clothes—we set those aside if you would like them. Would you like us to dress the body? Your sister said there would be an open casket at the Colonel's service."

"Yes, go ahead," Rand said, taking a deep breath. Tears welled in his eyes. *Stop acting like a goddamn baby.*

"I know you have a flight out with him tomorrow. If you can bring us the clothes, we can dress him tonight," Mrs. Peterson said, nearly whispering.

Rand nodded and headed for the Prius.

POP'S HOUSE was just as he'd left it: tidy except for stacks of newspapers and *Air Force Times* and *Afterburner* magazines by Pop's chair in the living room. It was your basic three-bedroom ranch backing up to the Apple Valley Country Club, 2,100 square feet, with a kitschy Hawaiian-style lanai room overlooking the seventh hole. Pop and Fritzi had retired there in the late 1970s, and most of the place still had the beige shag carpet Fritzi had picked out when they built the place. Of course, the tropical plants that Fritzi was so proud of in the lanai had long since died, leaving the tile floor stained with brownish rings left by the big terra-cotta pots. The master bedroom had newer, chocolate brown Berber. Rand figured Pop had it put in to cover the worn places to and from the bathroom and the incontinence stains of old age. It smelled of urine but looked tidy enough, except for a few strewn towels in the peach-colored bathroom. He opened the walk-in closet and saw most of Fritzi's clothes still hanging there, even though she'd died in 1986. On Pop's side, he saw his neatly hanging golf shorts, a few pairs of pants, four golf shirts from the Apple Valley Club, and a few Ralph Lauren polos his sisters must have sent as gifts.

Three pairs of golf shoes, nicely cleaned, a pair of tennis shoes, some brown Florshiem brogues that still shone with polish. No uniforms.

Rand had only visited a few times. The layout, however, was familiar to his architectural sense: three bedrooms. A closet in each. A hall closet for coats. Pop wasn't one to save sentimental stuff, but surely he had his colonel's dress uniform, mess dress, and flying suit stored somewhere.

The second bedroom had a double bed, neatly made with a flowered bedspread and matching drapes that Fritzi picked out in 1980. The Closet in that room had only an assortment of wire hangers from different dry cleaning places and Fritzi's set of blue Samsonite.

In the third and smallest bedroom, Pop had put a big metal desk (base surplus, Rand guessed) and made it into his office. The walls were covered with photos of all the aircraft Pop had flown: the B-52, Superfortress, C-141 Starlifter, C-5 Galaxy. Some fighter jets he'd flown in air shows in his test pilot days. A Cessna Pop had owned for about 10 years after he'd retired. Plaques from every base, commemorating commanding assignments at Wright-Patterson, Naples, Travis, and Da Nang, and Altus. From flight crew, to base operations, to squadron commander, to wing commander. Plaques neatly arranged, showing all the places they'd lived, without the stinging memories of housing difficulties, new schools, toys "lost in the shuffle" every time they moved, friendships abandoned, and, of course, Tommy. Rand shifted his focus to the closet. When he smelled the mothballs, he knew he'd hit pay dirt.

There, neatly zipped into plastic covers, were Pop's uniforms. Rand couldn't bear to unzip them, to see the broad-shouldered jackets that the shrunken old man couldn't hope to fill out. He did, however, open each of the three hatboxes. Two held blue dress uniform hats, one with a plain patent leather bill. One had a bill adorned with silver clouds and lightning bolts—Pop called them "farts and darts"—he acquired the insignia when he became a field grade officer, a major. (After almost 50 years as an expatriate, Rand still recalled the military lingo he'd heard at home.) The third held Pop's formal dress hat—to go with the "mess dress" his father hated.

It was white, with farts and darts on the black patent bill. Rand recalled that most New Years' Days, his parents had gotten dressed in formal attire, heads still pounding from martinis consumed at parties the night before, to attend a mandatory afternoon open house at the Officers' Club. No wonder Pop had hated that uniform. He had to get up early, shower, shave, and shove himself into the equivalent of white tie and tails when the civilian world was hunkered down in Lay-Z-Boys, watching bowl games.

Rand turned back to the zippered bags, now lying across the desk. Unlike his father, he had always found the mess dress elegant. When they dressed for formal occasions, his parents looked like British royals—his father tall, his broad shoulders accentuated by the cut of the coat (which had been custom made in Hong Kong when Pop was in Vietnam), the rows of medals on his chest, his slender waist with the black cummerbund, the patent leather shoes. Fritzi always got her hair done up like Zsa Zsa Gabor and wore something chiffon, with bugle beads or sparkly sequins, nipped at the waist, floor length. And opera gloves, white kid. His mother was queen, his father a handsome consort.

It wouldn't do to dress Pop as a consort now. In his final appearance, Rand knew exactly what Pop should wear. He unzipped the plastic cover on Pop's olive green flight suit. His sisters might not like it, but too bad. Pop wouldn't want to be buried in an ill-fitting tux or the blue serge suit that would swallow his shrunken body. The flight suit, with its zippered pockets, squadron insignia patches, and colonel's rank would be perfect for the old man. Like a comfy but cool onesie for an eternal rest in that blue metal coffin his sister had chosen. He grabbed the flight suit, turned out the lights, and locked the front door before his father's ghost could chase him into the twilight.

Pop would wear a flight suit on his last trip into the wild blue yonder.

"WE CAN LET your brother and his wife stay upstairs in the guest suite," Tina said, pouring two glasses of Pinot Noir. "Your nephews can stay together on the second floor, in the small bedroom, and your sister and husband can stay in the office, on the pull-out bed. They can share the hall bath with their kids..."

"No, honey. You're kind, but my sister Debby is not welcome here. I've booked her and Nick into the Key Bridge Marriott." Linda sipped her wine. Willie, Tina's gassy old Yorkie, jumped into her lap.

"It just seems weird, that's all," said Tina. "Family ought to be together when the patriarch dies. You need to stay up all night and drink and eat and cry in your pajamas. You all don't even act like a family."

Linda knew Tina was right, but she couldn't let it go. "Yeah, well, we aren't a touchy-feely-talky bunch like your kin. You and your sisters can go on forever, all night, all day, hardly taking a breath, yakking and laughing and crying. I'll never forget when your mother died, you all stayed up for like, seventy-two hours straight, crying, laughing, acting like a bunch of fools."

"Come on, we included you, babe!" Tina said, reaching for Linda's hand. "We didn't mean to leave you out, if that's what you're thinking."

"Hell, no! I didn't feel left out! I was glad you had your sisters! They brought you a lot of comfort when I couldn't. My family just doesn't have that kind of energy, to talk and laugh together. We didn't grow up that way."

"You've told me that many times. But you had that sassy Southern mother, that prince of a dad. I can't believe you didn't sit at the dinner table and act out scenes from *Father Knows Best*," Tina teased. "I thought all white families acted like that, you know, or like June and Ward on *Leave it to Beaver*. You were definitely the Beaver in your family..."

"Father Knows Best and Beaver never lived in base housing; they inhabited some suburban town with stone houses and chimneys. We lived in squat little boxes or dank, historic colonial French houses, on bases where they played 'Taps' in the evening over the loudspeakers. Where the sound of jet engines taking off lulled you to sleep because we knew Pop and his mighty Air Force where protecting us from the Russians."

Tina sipped her wine. "Yeah, like you had it so bad! Try sharing a room with your three sisters!"

Linda laughed. "It must have been hell when the four of you got going on the same cycle! What are you all, like a year apart?"

"Something like that. We were stair-steps, Momma said. Like the four Little Women, only black. I, of course, was Jo. There was plenty of drama."

Linda figured that whatever drama there was in Tina's household was superseded by just getting by. Still, Tina was close to each of her sisters. She was also a woman of faith who had been raised in the Methodist church.

"There's one thing about your nice, church-going, close-knit family I'll never understand. Why do all your sisters—and Talia a *Republican*—accept you and *us*, when they're all married with children of their own? "

"I told you! I didn't ever have to *come out* to any of them. Momma told me when I was fifteen that she knew I was different. She didn't push boys on me, or judge me when I got crushes on my sisters' girl-friends. I tried to hide it, but she knew. Two of my sisters are older; they started catching on. And my little sister Sheila just figured I was a tomboy. Hate to rub it in, Linda, but in our household we didn't have much. All we had was each other, and Momma said that was all we needed."

"I get it, I know. I thought it was all bullshit until your sisters gathered here for your mother's funeral. You all have something. A bond that I never developed with any of my siblings."

"It's a sista thing. You white people lack souls." Tina refilled her wine glass. "Nita comes tomorrow to clean. I'll leave her a note to check the guest room and make sure there are sheets on the bed. And what are we gonna feed all these people? Have you thought about that?"

"I thought maybe I'd just starve them out. No, seriously, I did get by the store on the way home. I bought a bunch of bagels, cereal. Deli meats and bread for sandwiches. We can walk down to the Pizza Paradiso for dinner. Honest to God, I don't even know what any of my family eats. Last time I checked, Rand was a vegetarian. Those big nephews probably forage like livestock, and, as I said, I don't care about my sister. She's the only one who doesn't drink, so I'll stock up at the liquor store. My brother can really put away the Scotch."

"All right, then. Guess we're ready as we can be. Now let's you and me head out to that new Indian place in Penn Quarter, for some tandoori chicken. They have an incredible crispy spinach appetizer. It will get your mind off everything."

LINDA WOKE AT 3:20 A.M. The tandoori churned in her stomach as the logistics of Pop's funeral spun in her head. She needed some bubbly water and some Advil. Careful not to wake Tina, she padded into the kitchen for some relief.

Linda opened the Sub Zero and reached for a cold Perrier. In the blue light of the open fridge, she gazed at the kitchen—the smooth marble island, the stainless steel gas range, the matching convection oven with digital readout. She loved this place. She and Tina had gutted all three floors of their townhouse, spent a fortune shoring up floors, rewiring, replumbing, decorating. The place reflected their sensibilities, their character, their love of eclectic furnishings and folk art, Linda's collection of Stieglitz prints, Tina's knack for balancing bright colors with neutral spaces. It was not a place Linda had ever expected her siblings to visit or stay as houseguests. Now, without Pop, there were just three Stoddard kids, and in less than twenty-four hours, they would all meet again. The last time they were together under one roof was Fritzi's funeral in 1986, down in Montrose.

That was something. It was February, wet and cold for Louisiana.

They gathered at the Ida Rose Funeral Home, a Victorian house straight out of an Anne Rice novel. Pop had flown from Apple Valley into Shreveport with Fritzi's body on a commercial flight. Linda had flown in from Boston, where she was an adjunct professor of political science at the Harvard School of Government. Rand and Sandy, with baby Celina, flew in from Vancouver. Nick and Debby, newly pregnant, had driven in their Suburban from Oklahoma. They didn't say much to each other, but Linda envied her married siblings for their intimacy with partners outside the immediate family.

Since she'd always been closest to Pop, Linda appointed herself his aide-de-camp, hoping Pop would open up and tell her about Fritzi's last moments; how he felt at her loss. But he didn't. Back then, Linda was still speaking to Debby. Linda had been pretty harsh, telling Debby and Rand about her visit with their parents at Christmas, admonishing them for not paying more attention to Fritzi and Pop. Back then, Linda loved the self-righteous satisfaction of knowing she was the last of the siblings to see their mother alive.

Fritzi's death wasn't sudden. She had been sick for years with lung cancer that spread to her bones, and finally, to her brain and liver. Linda had managed to get out to California to see Fritzi and Pop at Christmas, 1985. Linda knew her mother had lost her hair to chemo, but Fritzi refused to let anyone see her bald. On Christmas morning, Fritzi sat in a wheelchair with an oxygen tube in her nose, dressed in a green velvet housecoat and wearing a shiny red wig too bright for her pale skin. She'd powdered her face and slicked on some red lipstick. Linda wished her mother hadn't gone to such trouble, because the makeup made her look like a ghoul. Fritzi sat in her wheelchair, with Linda and Pop on the sofa, drinking coffee and opening gifts like they'd always done, as though nothing had changed since the days when there four stockings hung on the fireplace mantle in that rental house just off Wright-Patterson AFB.

On her last Christmas, Fritzi had wrapped the gifts to match the tree—a silver Pom Pom sparkler—adorned with bright red balls. It was, Fritzi said, their "California tree," suitable to a couple of "modern desert dwellers like your dad and me." She acted like she was too busy to fuss with conventional decorations, like she was out playing golf with Pop every afternoon or going over to the country club for duplicate bridge. She never talked about being sick, never called Linda or the others to give them dire news. Fritzi left all of that to Pop. Without going into great detail, he gave his children the prognosis: Fritzi wasn't ever going to get better.

Linda offered to fix breakfast, but Pop said no, Linda was their guest, and he would make pancakes. Fritzi wheeled up to the dining room table, chattering about the Christmas 1962, when Linda had gotten a Barbie doll, and did she remember that? And Rand's SLR Canon camera, and little Debby's Chatty Cathy. Tommy had been just a baby—what did Santa bring him? Fritzi couldn't remember.

Pop's pancakes were always light and delicious, but the lump in Linda's throat manifested the sad reality of the situation, the loss that was palpable in the air. Linda felt a sudden longing for her childhood self, to have Rand and Debby and Tommy here with Fritzi and Pop. She wanted one of their childhood Christmases, before things fell apart, when they had real green trees strung with bubble lights and silver aluminum icicles.

After breakfast, Fritzi insisted on getting cleaned up so she could help Pops prepare the turkey. "Come on, Linda, let's get dolled up together. Just bring your makeup and stuff into my bathroom," Fritzi said, wheeling herself down the hall.

"I don't have a makeup bag, you know," Linda reminded her.

"Well, hell, then use some of mine! My friend Dorothy sells Mary Kay. She's always giving me samples. It's a holiday! Come on, you can help me with a sponge bath. And I need you to pencil in my eyebrows. I might be bald, but damned if I'm gonna look like a spook on Christmas Day. You could use some fixing up, too."

Linda followed her mother into the master suite. In the bright morning light, she saw the dark spots on the beige shag carpet. Although Pop had probably worked hard to scrub them clean, their shadowy presence made Linda anxious to know what blood, shit, or vomit had caused them. The signs of illness were everywhere— prescription bottles lined up like soldiers next to Fritzi's vanity sink, the clean bedpan on the floor near the rented hospital bed. Fritzi wheeled up to the sink and began rummaging through her makeup drawer. She handed Linda a tiny tube of red lipstick and compact of blush. "Try it, sweetie. You need some color!"

Normally, Linda would protest and give her spiel (oh, how many times had she turned her back on her mother as a teen, decrying animal testing of cosmetics, declaring how women were pawns of the beauty industry—how many egregious fights with slammed doors and Fritzi yelling, "*Well, I'm only trying to help!*)—but Linda dutifully swiped on the lipstick and brushed the blush on her cheeks. "There! You look positively eighteen! You really are an attractive woman, Linda. Just give yourself a chance!"

Linda smiled, pretending to like her image. "OK, let's get you cleaned up and fill in those eyebrows," she said, running warm water into the sink. Gently, she dabbed at Fritzi's fragile skin with a washcloth. First, her face, following up with Oil of Olay for moisture. Fritzi closed her eyes, a faint childlike smile on her face. Linda couldn't remember Fritzi ever looking so relaxed, and actually pleased to be in her company. Linda nearly burst into tears as she sponged Fritzi's tiny arms, now covered in bruises and pocked where she'd been stuck for IVs. Her mother's skin was soft, fragile as parchment, and her bones so prominent, Linda feared she would shatter a wrist, a collarbone, with the slightest pressure from the washcloth. She took the softest towel she could find and patted her mother's skin.

Linda did her best on Fritzi's eyebrows, but the result gave her mother a crazed expression à la Gloria Swanson in *Sunset Boulevard*. "Thanks, honey, that's fine," Fritzi finally said, signaling that Linda could put down the eyebrow pencil. "You can start on the eye shadow now. How about that subtle green?"

Linda chose a shade that complemented Fritzi's dark green velvet housecoat and brushed the tiniest bit on her crepey lids. She touched Fritzi's sunken cheeks with some blush, and then finally moved to the lips. Her mother liked her lips red, and she didn't give a "flying flip" about people thinking it clashed with her red hair. Fritzi nodded her approval in the mirror. "Now, we look like we're going to a Christmas party!"

Fritzi was sixty-one years old, and despite the makeup job and the oxygen tube in her nose, she looked beautiful. Her eyes, like deep sapphires, sparkled, and she exuded that familiar Fritzi-ness—pure energy—that had fueled them all through the best and the worst parts nomadic family life. She smiled, tilting her chin sassily and looking up at Linda, the same expression she wore in the pictures when she was crowned Miss Montrose of 1946.

Linda's heart swelled, and she longed to tell Fritzi how much she loved her. But she didn't, because words would have spoiled the moment. One sentimental confession might lead to another and another—and soon Linda might have poured out her heart —letting go of all her secrets. Her inner censor stopped her from spoiling Fritzi's last Christmas.

Fritzi died two months later. Pop took charge of all the arrangements, choosing to have a short service in at the Ida Rose chapel in Montrose, followed by a graveside blessing from the pastor at First Presbyterian. They all rode in a stretch limo and stood under the tent, on the Astroturf laid over the chilled ground. After a prayer Linda couldn't recall, Rand stood in front of of the family.

"I've written a few words," Rand said, to Linda's surprise. Her brother had never been one for public sentimentality. He reached into his jacket pocket. "If you'll indulge me."

Pop squinted, looking confused, but nodded his head.

Rand began: "We called her Fritzi because she would not be called 'Mother.' Her spirit, her energy, sustained me, and, I think all of us, through the hardest moves, the worst schools, the loss of our brother. I could go on and on, spouting Fritzi-isms, telling anecdotes, but I wanted to just say what she was to me. Without her, I would not be an architect. I would not live in Canada, nor have my wife, Sandy. Without her, I would have been a reluctant soldier in a war against my beliefs, a lost soul among young men who didn't know that they, too, were lost. Fritzi knew I loved art; she understood me. When we lived in Italy, she took the opportunity to show me everything I

longed to see and more. With her help, I attended college in British
Columbia and studied architecture, when my peers were all going to
state schools or into the armed services. I owe her my career, my life,
in every sense of the word. Her personality was larger than life, far
larger than any of us, and she loomed bigger and more fierce than
any force of nature. For me, her force was gentle, understanding,
encouraging. I never had a coach or a teacher or a mentor who
matched my mother's gift of knowing and believing in my art, in my
science, in my need to create. Perhaps I took too much of her,
demanded more time than my siblings. I stand here today knowing
that she gave the best of her effort on my part. I am forever grateful,
more than I ever expressed to her, for her advocacy and the privilege
of being her favored son. And I acknowledge to each of you that I
appreciate that status. A status I never earned or never asked for. But
it was Fritzi's gift, and I am forever grateful. Thank you."

Pop, standing next to Linda, reached into his jacket pocket for his
handkerchief and dabbed his face. Linda took Pop's hand, and he
squeezed hers in understanding. Rand had said what they all knew.

Silently, they watched Fritzi's polished oak casket as it was
lowered into the family plot. Next to her was Tommy, a son she could
favor in the ghost world they now inhabited together.

Linda finished the Perrier and felt her stomach settle down.
Through the front window overlooking the street, she saw the newspaper delivery truck stop and throw the *Washington Post* on the front
stoop. Today was the day. She padded back to bed and curled up next
to Tina.

27

> "Your principal job, besides making a home, rearing a
> family, and strengthening
>   Your husband's morale, is to help him to make
> friendly contacts
>   with the people among whom you are stationed."
>   —Nancy Shea, *The Air Force Wife*

AUGUST 19, 2008
  Arlington, Virginia

"I TOLD you to take Exit 8A. You'll have to turn around because you missed it," Debby said.

"Shut your trap! I know I missed the exit," Nick said, irritated. "Just give me a chance. This traffic is nuts."

"Mom's only trying to help. Give her a break," Charlie said, smart assness in his voice.

"Enough from the peanut gallery," Nick said, eyeing Charlie in the rearview mirror.

Debby wished the twins were with them, but they needed to stay home and tend the ranch. At least they would buffer the tension between Charlie and Nick. No one could buffer the tension between her and Nick.

Tension. She took a deep breath and rolled her head to release the tightness in her neck. It had been a long drive in the old Suburban. Two full, ten-hour days with an overnight stop at a Motel 6 in Indianapolis. Finally, they were at the Marriott in Rosslyn. She could get a shower and call Linda in the morning. She couldn't face her tonight.

Linda and Tina. She didn't know if she could pretend that two women living together and having sex was normal, pretend that her sister hadn't blasphemed the Lord by "marrying" a woman. She'd have to get it out of her mind, that was all. It would take a good meal and a long night of sleep before she could see her sister.

Sister. How'd she'd longed for a real sister, a sister she could talk to. Someone who would stay up all night, telling secrets. Someone who would cut out paper dolls with you, pass down her Nancy Drew collection, take her to the Merle Norman Studio at the mall for a makeover. Instead, she got Linda. Linda who was large and in charge. Linda who looked down on her from the day she was born. Linda who got all the attention from Pop. "Why don't you join the debate team like Linda did? Why don't you study more? You could make good grades like your sister if you tried... a little hard work never hurt anyone." She could hear Pop's voice as if he were sitting next to her in the Suburban.

Linda always set the bar in Pop's eyes. Why couldn't he love his "Tinkerbell" as much? Pop was so proud of Linda, he couldn't see the beauty of his second daughter that was right in front of his eyes. If there was a "middle child" in the family, it was Debby. A small, lost soul that had to follow Rand and Linda, only to be upstaged by the jolly joy of baby Tommy.

People—especially Linda—always thought Debby had it easy.

"You're just Fritzi's little precious dolly, aren't you?" Linda would tease. Rand, who only communicated with Linda and Fritzi, didn't seem to notice Debby. Tommy liked Debby just fine, but then, he liked everyone.

Debby had gone to Montrose to live with her grandparents and with Josie, who understood her connection to the Holy Spirit. They didn't compare her to anyone else, they just loved her and nourished her. She had thrived there, away from the bases they lived on and the constant comparison to her older sister. Once, Debby had overheard Fritzi and Pop talking, and Pop said, "Debby may have lots of potential, but no one can see past her prettiness. Someday, she'll wake up and wish she'd worked harder in school and not relied just on her looks to get attention. Someday, she might actually make something of herself."

Something of herself? Pop, being who he was, marked success by awards, medals, promotions. Why couldn't he just love her without all that? Why was she expected to try so hard? Judge and Grandmamma understood. They loved her, they fed her, they sheltered her. They let her pray in tongues, although they didn't understand it. They tried to understand the horror that constantly haunted Debby: she was the last person to see Tommy alive.

"ALL RIGHT. Guess we can start unloading," Nick said. He'd already checked them into the Marriott and walked out to the car with two card keys in one envelope. "Two double beds, third floor. There's an indoor pool and somehow we got free breakfasts as a perk."

They headed up to the room, where Charlie changed and headed for the pool. She and Nick took off their shoes and flopped on their bed, exhausted. In a minute, she heard Nick's deep snorting breaths become a series of regular snores. She knew he was tired, but it was his own fault. He'd insisted on driving the whole way, even though she and Charlie had offered to take their turns at the wheel. She closed her eyes and dozed into a half-sleep, and all she could think about were the miles clicking on the odometer of the 15-year-old Suburban.

She couldn't remember the day Tommy died. She had tried again and again over the years, but she just didn't have it stored anywhere in her mind. Yes, she had been there, on the terrace at the Miroglio's penthouse. Yes, she had seen Bino play soccer with Tommy. Then Bino had left, and suddenly the ball was in play. Had she thrown it, knowing Tommy would chase it over the edge? Surely not. But she had seen him chase the ball. And she saw him jump over the railing to go after it. She told him to stop, she knew she told him to stop; *surely she had told him to stop.* Had she?

Then, he was gone. Gone over the edge, into the back driveway behind the building. She remembered screaming, screaming so loud her throat hurt. Then people rushing, the Miroglio's maid, the grownups with their cocktails, who had been watching the fireworks on the other side of the terrace. Where was Linda? Where was Rand? No one had ever asked that.

She shook the image from her mind, focusing on the hum of the air-conditioning in the hotel room. She developed a way to focus on something else during the worst memories. She'd close her eyes and listen, just listen, until she could detect some repetitive sound—a hum from a fan, traffic whizzing, a train in the distance. Usually, she could hear something, hone her focus, and erase the image.

You simply had to focus on something else, she learned. Don't talk about it. Don't dwell on it. In the days after the tragedy, the other Americans in the Pink Building and the officers' wives from Pop's squadron were constantly present in the Stoddard apartment. They brought tuna casseroles, chocolate cakes, brownies, Jell-O molds, as if stuffing the Stoddards was going to relieve their grief. She seemed to recall Captain Swinson, the Navy chaplain from the NATO base, coming by to offer a prayer. Pop and Fritzi had no church affiliation, so they thanked him and showed him out. There were no grief counselors, no psychiatrists covered by her father's Air Force medical plan. The only counseling she got was from an admiral's wife, who stopped by to drop off a casserole: "Stop crying, don't you see your parents have lost their son?" *Buck up.* That was the message.

She did her best. So did Pop and Fritzi. Rand and Linda, though, took to their beds and read books for days. Thankfully, they had no TV in their Italian apartment, no way to hear news reports of the little American boy who fell to his death from the General Miroglio's penthouse during Piedigrotta.

Debby hadn't seen Rand or Linda for a few years, and the prospect of facing them was like walking straight into hell. Now that Pop was dead, the three orphaned Stoddards were all that was left of that once-perfect, shining example of an American Air Force family.

August 19, 2008
Arlington, Virginia

RAND ARRIVED at Dulles with Pop's casket and went with the hearse to the Murphy's Funeral Home in Arlington, where Linda was waiting.

"So great to see you," Linda said, holding her arms out for a brief embrace.

Although Linda was shorter and wider than he'd remembered, she wore a beautifully tailored gray silk suit. Her neat crop of curly dark hair showed a few gray strands, but was styled fashionably. She wore sensible, low-heeled black leather shoes, shined to a military finish that would make Pop proud.

Rand gave his sister a quick hug. "They took the casket around back. They embalmed him back in Apple Valley."

"Good," Linda said. "The staff here will prepare Pop for a viewing, which can begin tomorrow. I've reserved Room 3, off the front hall here. I haven't heard from Debby yet, but they were supposed to be driving in today."

"Really? You and Debby are speaking again?"

"Don't be ridiculous. She's our sister. I can't help it if she's a pompous bitch who despises my lifestyle."

Rand burst out laughing. "I've missed your humor. Where has the time gone?"

"Where time always goes: to our jobs, our friends, our houses, our yards. Our wives. Don't worry. I never made time to visit you either," Linda said. "How's Sandy? Celina?"

"Both great. Sandy is devastated about Pop, of course. She'll be here tomorrow. Celina and Jean-Paul are in Montreal; they've just informed us that we're going to be grandparents."

"You! A grandfather!" Linda's face lit up with a grin. "Wouldn't that be wonderful! You lucky bastard."

"Lucky, yes. Bastard, no. We always teased *you* about being the adopted one, remember?"

"Etched in my memory, those years. You looked exactly like Fritzi and I looked like no one. You were always prettier than I was."

A man in a dark suit, striped tie, and an American flag lapel pin greeted them. "I'm Robert Lyon, your funeral concierge," he said. "A pleasure to serve you and your family."

Odd moniker, "funeral concierge." Rand wished for a Scotch.

"We met over the phone," Linda said, shaking hands. "This is my brother, Rand. Our sister will be in for the viewing tomorrow."

"Wonderful. Let's go over the plans, shall we?" said the concierge.

There would be a viewing in the morning from ten to noon After that, there would be a short prayer service in the funeral home chapel.

Then came the big stuff. Really big stuff.

"I arranged for a full honors service," Linda said. "It's what Pop would have wanted."

"OK. What's that?" Rand asked.

"It's a very formal procession to the gravesite," said Robert, the "concierge." "The Air Force will provide a horse-drawn caisson, a four-piece band, and a color guard. I'll march in front of the caisson. The family will follow in a limousine. The band will play until we reach the gravesite, which will be tented in case of rain. The band will play as the body bearer detail—there will be six in Air Force men in uniforms—unload the flag-draped casket and take it to the gravesite. The chaplain will offer a prayer. Then, a firing party will be called to attention and fire in a three-rifle volley. Finally, there will be a bugler who plays 'Taps.' The detail will fold the flag. The only question is: to whom should they present the flag?"

"God, we haven't thought about that part," Linda said, glancing at Rand.

"Wait a second," Rand said, "What if one of us wanted to say a few words? Where would that come in?"

"I don't think Pop would want that," Linda said. "You know how he hated sentimentality."

She was right, Rand knew. "Well, I gave the eulogy at Fritzi's. Don't you want a turn this time, for Pop?"

"As I said, I don't think Pop would want anyone to give a eulogy."

"What about Debby? What if she wants to say something?"

"So what? Pop wouldn't want the sentimentality. If you don't believe me, I've got his wishes in writing. By the way, he made me executor of his will. I've got a whole file back at the house. I'll show you later. He left a big envelope addressed to you."

"Looks like you've got this all figured out, Linda. I know you were closest to Pop. No hard feelings on my part, but it seems like Debby ought to be in on this. After all, she was his Tinkerbell."

"Then Tinkerbell should have gotten here sooner," Linda said firmly. "We'll see her tomorrow."

"Is she staying at your place, too?" Rand asked.

"No. She, Nick, and Charlie are at the Key Bridge Marriott in Rosslyn. Not far. Tina and I have room, but they don't approve of our 'lifestyle.'"

"What about the twins?"

"Debby said they had to stay in Oklahoma to take care of the ranch. They send their condolences."

Rand nodded.

"If there's nothing else, then, I will see you in the morning?" the concierge interjected.

"Thank you," Linda said, "No, nothing else. We'll let you know about the flag in the morning, all right?"

"Fine, see you then." Robert rose and shook their hands, then turned to leave, closing the door behind him. Softly, as only a funeral concierge knew how.

LINDA'S TOWNHOUSE in Georgetown was, even to Rand's architect's eye, a treasure box full of art, quiet warm spaces, and, this evening, candlelight. Linda's wife, Tina, was the perfect complement to Linda. Where Linda was driven, purposeful, and direct, Tina was laid back, warm, nuanced. The yin to his sister's yang. A match of two opposites.

With a backdrop of soft Nina Simone music, Tina poured Rand a Glenlivet, neat, just the way he liked it. Her calm, easygoing demeanor was a salve for his frazzled head after learning about the hoopla of Pop's funeral. He couldn't help but worry a little about the moment when Debby and Linda would have to be in the same room.

Linda emerged from the study with a thick manila envelope addressed to him, in Pop's handwriting. The flap was sealed, oddly, with old Easter Seals.

"I'll show you the will, tomorrow, when Debby is here," Linda said, settling on the sofa next to him with a glass of merlot. "Pop left strict instructions that I was to deliver this to you personally. So, here you are." She sipped her wine.

"What on earth? Could this be the missing directions to that model Stratofortress we tried to build together? Some back issues of *Scientific American*?"

"Hey, that's for you to find out," Linda said. "You don't have to open it in front of us if you don't want to."

"Are you kidding? I can't wait to see what the Colonel sent me!" Carefully, Rand slid his index finger under the Easter Seals.

On top of the pile of papers was a handwritten letter. "Looks like he wrote this to Fritzi, when he went to Da Nang," Rand said. He scanned his father's angular script. He took a long sip of his drink and looked Linda straight in the eye.

"Pop told Fritzi to make sure I didn't register for the draft," he said, handing the letter to Linda. "Am I right? Is that what this says?"

Linda read the letter out loud. *".... Do not, by any circumstance, let him go to the Draft Board, understand, my darling? I know this will be your wish, too. We have already lost one son; we don't need to lose another to this insane (yes, I use that word, although I am serving) war...* Well, Pop always said he was a lover, not a fighter, but geez...*"*

"I always thought it was Fritzi's doing, when I got that sudden scholarship to UBC. She hustled me off to campus before I turned eighteen, and told me not to come home for the holidays. She told me she wasn't going to support my going to Berkeley with the hippies, and she wasn't sending her son *and* her husband to Viet Nam. So I had to go to Canada."

"This is mind boggling," Linda said, "So unlike Pop."

"I always thought he was, you know, the ultimate Air Force officer. Thought he always resented me because I didn't want that life." Rand shook his head in disbelief. "I don't know what to say." Tears welled in his eyes.

Tina reached for Rand's glass. "Another?" she said gently.

"No, thanks," Rand said. He took the envelope. Behind the letter to Fritzi were letters Pop had written to UBC, MacGill, the University of Calgary. Beautiful letters, describing *"my son's aptitude for mathematics and engineering... his outstanding SAT scores, and enclosed recommendations from his high school counselors and teachers..."*

"I think I'll just go up to bed," Rand said.

The guest room's palette was soft gray and white, soothing to his overworked mind. In the bathroom, he squirted Visine into his tired eyes and brushed his teeth. Then, above the toilet, he saw the black-and-red abstract painting he'd given Linda back at Travis, that summer when he'd worked at The Art Shoppe. Back then, Linda had hung it in her room on base, and in the rental house once Pop was in Da Nang. It stunned him, in this house full of Stieglitz prints and precious folk art, to see his high school painting in the guest room bath. He smiled, called Sandy, and went to bed.

AUGUST 20, 2008

HELP ME GET THROUGH THIS, Debby prayed as she entered Viewing Room 3 at Murphy's Funeral Home. In front of Pop's steely blue casket was a row of white folding chairs. From the rear, she recognized Rand's lank, towering frame, dapper in a charcoal gray, Armani-looking suit, his auburn hair gone nearly white. Next to him, she spotted Linda, her choppy dark hair laced with gray. She was wearing a tailored black dress with matching jacket. They did not turn to the back as she entered, so she announced herself in a soft voice: "Hello. I'm here!" It was a familiar theme from growing up with these two larger-than-life achievers.

Rand turned around first, stood and strode to meet her at the door. Awkwardly, he extended his arm in a half handshake, half hug. "So glad you made it, Debby."

Debby pulled her brother close for a moment. Her heart pumped a rhythm of fear as she fixed her gaze on Linda's back.

Linda turned slowly and locked her dark eyes on Debby, who froze in place. Linda made her way to the back of the room and drew Debby close in a strong embrace. "How was the trip?"

"Oh, fine. Long. It's just me this morning. Nick and Charlie will be here for the funeral. I thought it best, to, you know, have a little private time? Just us?" A voice in her head chastised her for being so tentative with her siblings.

"Do you want to see Pop? He looks pretty good, except I was expecting he'd be in his blue uniform. Our brother, however, chose the flight suit Pop wore when he went to Da Nang. Remember that picture in the *Air Force Times*?" Linda's voice registered part sarcasm, part accusation.

"Oh." Debby looked at her siblings for the next cue. Rand took her elbow and escorted her to the casket.

Debby took a deep breath and gazed at her father's embalmed body. Pop looked like himself: nearly bald head, handsome oval face tanned and wrinkled from days on the golf course. His mouth was slightly upturned, a natural expression for Pop, as he was always optimistic. Even in the casket, they'd managed to jut his chin slightly forward, the way he would look when he was driving, flying a plane, leading the family or the squadron or the wing on whatever mission was at hand. His long gray eyelashes broke her heart, but it was the flight suit with his colonel's eagle patches that made her weep.

Rand, standing on her right, put an arm around Debby's shoulders. Glancing up, she could see his Adam's apple rise and fall as he swallowed his own tears. Linda, standing on her left, looked Debby in the eye and said, "He's at peace."

Her sister's words hit Debby like a slap. Linda, always in charge, trying to staunch Debby's natural flow of tears. Debby fumbled in her purse for a tissue and wiped her face. She blew her nose and began to cry with deep, heartfelt sobs. Linda turned away and sat in one of the front row chairs. Rand followed her.

"If you don't mind, Debby, I'd like to go over the plan for the day," Linda said, "Come and have a seat."

Debby sat down and Linda handed her a printed program with a black-and-white official photo of Pop, taken when he'd made colonel, and the words:

Joseph Randolph Stoddard
Colonel, United States Air Force, Retired
1925–2008
"I have slipped the surly bonds of earth"

THE PROGRAM LISTED the events to take place today, including a procession to the Arlington Cemetery with a band and a horse-drawn caisson carrying Pop's casket.

"This is very nice," Debby managed to say, "but it doesn't mention anywhere that Pop was a good Christian, a loving father and husband."

"Well, we all *know* that," Linda said. "That's why we're here. And frankly, I didn't want Pop's last wishes to be highjacked by the practices of any church. He left me written instructions about his funeral wishes. I'm just carrying out orders."

"But funerals are to comfort the living," Debby said, "We know that Pop knew Jesus and accepted Him as his savior. He is in Heaven. The rest of us have to go on. We need comfort, and comfort comes from prayer."

"Wait just a minute," Rand interjected, "I don't recall that Pop and Fritzi belonged to any particular religious congregation. I'm with Linda on this. Funerals may be for the living, but it's our duty to conduct this one according to Pop's wishes."

"Debby, the facts are that I live here and I have Pop's last written will and funeral requests. It's too late to change anything now," Linda said in her best diplomatic voice.

They always ganged up on her. The little sister who didn't matter. The little sister who went off to live with Judge and Grandmamma because she was too "sensitive" for base life. The little fool who let Tommy fall to his death.

"I can see that some things never change," Debby said wistfully. "You all have figured out everything, and Linda put herself in charge. The three of us are orphans now, don't you get that? We are the only three Stoddards left. Pop's not even going to be buried next to Fritzi and Tommy and our grandparents. I get that he wants an Arlington grave, but in his honor, it seems to me that we ought to treat each other as equals now. That means I'm equal to you, Linda, and to you, Rand."

Rand's phone blurted the three-tone signal of an incoming text. "Excuse me," he said, stepping out with his phone.

Linda took a deep breath and looked her sister in the eye. "That means my marriage is equal to yours, Debby, and to Rand's. Pop knew it. It would make things a hell of a lot easier if you would acknowledge it, too."

If Linda only knew. Debby's marriage was imploding; she and Nick were like two oxen yoked together in a burning barn.

"Linda, I acknowledge your love and your civil marriage," she said softly. "But the church will never see it as holy."

"Good enough for me," Linda said. "Now let's get this party started."

AUGUST 20, 2008

THE DAY BELONGED TO POP. And to Rand. And to Linda. And to Debby. Tina, Nick, Charlie, Sandy, Celina and her husband, John Paul all showed up to back them up.

Rand stood and spoke at the prayer service at the funeral home. He credited Pop with "working behind the scenes to fulfill his duty as a father first, and as an Air Force officer, second. I now realize that my father not only gave me the freedom to pursue my vocation as an artist and architect, he also worked without my knowledge to ensure that I would have the opportunity and the education to do so. He defied his government to keep me out of Vietnam, while at the same time serving as a wing commander at Da Nang Air Base. My father was a man who loved and lived with strategic purpose, never faltering in his dual missions to sustain his family and to serve his country."

The family rode together in funeral home cars to the cemetery, to a building where the procession would begin. Low thunderclouds gathered in the suffocating heat. Rand, Debby, and Linda got out of the car and positioned themselves to march behind the casket, mounted on a horse-drawn caisson. A four-piece brass band played "The Air Force Song" at a slow tempo to mark the journey. When they arrived at the gravesite, six airmen carried Pop's casket to the

grave, and sheets of rain began to pour. The family sat under the
graveside canopy, grateful for cover, and grateful that storm hadn't hit
while they were processing over. The four horses drawing the caisson
whinnied in the booming thunder. Linda sighed with relief when
soldiers led them out of the storm and back toward their stable.

When Robert, the funeral concierge, stood to offer a final prayer,
Debby stood up. "Please, let me," she said, and Robert stepped aside.

Debby, thin as a rail, her pretty skin weathered from ranch work,
her hair unfashionably long, stood in a polyester black dress, her
dark eyes intent with purpose. She looked a little shaky. Rand gave
Linda a strange look, and she just shrugged. Their prissy little sister
was now a tired-looking woman who had lived a life of hard work
and hard choices. Linda's eyes filled with tears.

Debby spread her arms, as though to take flight, and began to
sing "Amazing Grace" in a haunting, frail soprano. Tina was the first
to join in, her strong alto complementing and shoring up Debby's
thin voice; then Nick and Charlie, Sandy and Celina, John Paul, then
Rand. And finally, Linda. There were tears and rain and a final cool
breeze that blew the rain up under the canopy.

Lightning flashed as the bugler blew "Taps," but the brave airman
stood in the storm nonplussed. The honor guard fired the final volley
of shots in the three rounds of seven, competing with the thunder
and lightning of the storm.

With rain dripping from their caps, the honor guard took the flag
from Pop's casket and folded it into a neat triangle. Linda motioned to
Debby and Rand. The three Stoddards stood with their hands
outstretched, ready to receive Pop's flag together.

—The End—

ACKNOWLEDGMENTS

First, I must thank Nancy Shea for her 1956 guide, *The Air Force Wife* (Harper & Brothers, revised, New York). This was always on my mother's bookshelf, and I cherish her copy. Passages from *The Air Force Wife* introduce the chapters in *Beneath the Wild Blue.*

Writing is a lonely undertaking with no guarantee of compensation or affirmation.

I could never pursue my dream of being a novelist without the love and courage my husband, Jim McCarthy, has given me over the years. My daughters, Madeleine and Caitlin, have put up with my rigid insistence that I be "left alone," when all along I could not have accomplished anything without their love and without the opportunity of living in the present, as only motherhood demands that you do.

My dear sister, Susan Milner Lind, was one of my first readers. I'm thankful that she did not take offense at any resemblance this manuscript may have to the life we led as Air Force Brats. Susan gave the book to her book club, who became my beta readers, for whom I am immensely grateful.

My fellow writer, Cheryl Forrest, agreed to read my first drafts and gave me the fierce encouragement and self-imposed deadlines necessary to complete this story. My other writing friend Mary Bundren gave constant encouragement on the walking trail.

My friends the Gypsies have been my sisters in crime and a source of constant friendship: Janet Pagano, Kathy McKeown, Kim Sherrod, Leigh Farrar, Anne Jones, and our dear Susan Fesperman.

For my critique group of talented writers, Mary Jane Morgan, Cathy Morgan, Emrys Moreau, Ada Harrington: thank you for listening and helping me hone the rough edges of this manuscript. For the encouragement from Rilla Askew, Billie Barnett, and Ken Busby. For the last-minute edit, thank you to my friend and fellow author, Joanne Fox Phillips.

For Mary Edwards Wertsch, author of *Military Brats: Legacies of Childhood Inside the Fortress*, thank you for the research and observations that affirmed the Baby Boom "Brat" experience. For Pat Conroy, whose Marine fighter pilot, Bull Meacham (aka the Great Santini), inspired me to tell the story of an Air Force pilot and a very different family.

And, for that childhood friend, Lise Swinson Sajewski, from the Pink Building, who grew up to edit for National Geographic, and who donated her time to edit this entire manuscript for me. For Mike Brown, author, film producer, and Air Force Brat, for reading excerpts. For Lydia Haferland Hawkins, my best friend and fellow Base Kid, who helped me decide to seize the day.

Finally, to all Military Brats everywhere, thank you for your service. Your parents couldn't do it without you.

ABOUT THE AUTHOR

Marian Milner McCarthy is a writer with a long career as a free-lancer, corporate communications consultant, technical copywriter, columnist, ghostwriter, editor and writing teacher.

In 2014, she turned her focus to fiction. The result is BENEATH THE WILD BLUE, a mainstream novel about a military family in the middle of the twentieth century. Is it a memoir? No. Is it based on her experience as a Baby Boomer military brat? Yes.

Like most military brats, Marian has always hungered for stories that reflect her own peculiar childhood--moving frequently, making and losing friends, giving complicated answers when someone asks about a "hometown." She was in awe of Pat Conroy's THE GREAT SANTINI, not only for the writing, but for its honest portrayal of one military family.

But plenty of military families, including her own, did not have an abusive father who bullied the family into submission. Marian's own father, a decorated Air Force pilot who served in three wars, was always a lover, not a fighter, at home. As in most military families, her strong mother was the one who martialed the troops at home, made sure the kids passed muster, and held them all together each and every time they moved.

Please visit Marian's website at
www.marianmccarthy.com
and follow her on Facebook at Marian McCarthy, Author

Made in the USA
San Bernardino, CA
09 September 2018